Zoë Barnes was born and brought up on Merseyside, but now lives in Gloucestershire. She had a variety of jobs, from hearing–aid technician to French translator, before becoming a full-time writer. Zoë and her partner Dmytro share their cottage near Cheltenham with their four cats, Grizzle, Griselda, Juno and Jupiter.

Zoë is the bestselling author of BUMPS and HITCHED, also published by Piatkus.

KT-556-600

Also by Zoë Barnes

Bumps
Hitched

Hot Property

Zoë Barnes

PIATKUS

First published in Great Britain in 1999 by
Judy Piatkus (Publishers) Ltd of
5 Windmill Street, London W1

This edition published in 1999

The moral right of the author has been asserted

A catalogue record for this book is available from the British Library

ISBN 0 7499 3111 6

Set in Bembo by
Action Publishing Technology, Gloucester

Printed and bound in Great Britain by
Mackays of Chatham, plc

To Dmytro
and everyone at Piatkus
for their unique contribution

Prologue

Once Upon A Time . . .

'Teletubbies to the main stage please, Teletubbies . . .'

The public address system boomed across the lawns of Brockbourne Hall, so deafeningly that all the sheep in the next field started bleating in protest. Not that anyone could hear them; not above the din of several hundred children pursuing a man in a rubber brontosaurus costume into the tea tent.

'My God,' panted Lorna Walsh, staggering up the last few steps to the second-floor landing. 'Is it always like this?'

Claire wedged a cardboard box of books between knee and chin, and used her left hand to nudge open the front door of the flat. 'Don't ask me,' she replied cheerily. 'I don't officially start work here until tomorrow.'

She staggered into the flat and Lorna followed, dragging an immense suitcase behind her, two-handed.

'I can't imagine why you'd *want* to work here,' Lorna went on. 'In fact I can't imagine why anybody would.'

'Why not? The money's good – and it's a change of scene.'

'Change of scene? It's a madhouse. I'd advise you to leg it while you've still got the chance, only I can't face lugging all your stuff back down those stairs.'

Claire stood in the middle of the flat and surveyed her surroundings. Her new home. Two nice big rooms, her own bathroom and kitchenette, pretty casement windows straight out of a Rossetti painting and carpet so thick you could lose your toes in it. Living over the shop had never seemed so good.

'Come on Lorna, of course it's not like this all the time. Mostly it's conferences and seminars and stuff like that. This is a Children's Fun Festival, the punters are bound to be a bit . . . lively.'

'Steer well clear of animals and children, darling,' warned Lorna. 'Take it from me, they're bad news every time. I should know, I was the back end of Esmeralda the cow in Skegness.'

'It's hardly the same as being operations manager at a prestige conference venue, is it?' scoffed Claire.

'Prestige?' laughed Lorna. 'Obviously you've never had your tail ripped off by a gang of six-year-old hooligans.' She dragged the overladen suitcase another half a yard, abandoned it in the middle of the carpet and collapsed down on to its bulging lid. 'What have you got in here – bricks?'

'Nothing that exotic.'

'Oh, I get it. Just the decaying corpses of a few ex-lovers, huh?'

'Yeah, and the loot from my last bank job.'

'That's all right then.' Reaching to her left and rolling on to her side, Lorna dived into one of the many cardboard boxes strewn around the living room. A second later she emerged triumphantly with a bright yellow electric kettle. 'Tea, Miss Snow. Now. Or I shall expire on the Axminster.'

'Be my guest.'

Lorna flopped on to her back in a flourish of shoulder-length black curls. 'I am dead, Horatio.'

'Yeah.' Claire snatched the kettle from her best friend's hand and headed for the kitchen. 'Dead hammy. If that's the best you can manage, it's no wonder you haven't made it to the Old Vic yet.'

Lorna sat up. 'You won't mock when I'm Dame Lorna and you have to stock my dressing room with fresh orchids and pink champagne.'

A voice floated through the open door from the next room. 'Lorna.'

'What?'

'There's no milk for the tea.'

'So we'll have it black.'

'There's no tea either.'

'Gawd, Claire. For a professional organiser you're pretty darned useless.' Lorna kicked off her desert boots and padded into the kitchen in her purple socks. 'So what are we having? A nice reviving cup of hot water?'

Claire presented Lorna with a dusty bottle, wiping her hands on the seat of her Levi's. 'There you go.'

Lorna wrinkled her nose. 'What's this?'

'Vimto cordial. I found it under the sink.'

Lorna blew the dust off the bottle. 'Urgh, I'm not drinking that, it's gone all brown!'

'Well, it's that or drain cleaner.'

Lorna shrugged. 'Fair enough. But I want a choccy biscuit to take the taste away.'

The tannoy blared again, the sound so loud it was distorted. 'Ms Vance to the worm farm please, Ms Vance . . . '

Lorna cocked an ear. 'Worm farm? I could have sworn he just said "worm farm".'

'He did. It's one of those eco-friendly things – you know, like that ant farm we made in Biology. Educational. The kids love it, apparently.'

'Give me candyfloss and roundabouts any day.'

Claire gazed out of the kitchen window as she waited for the kettle to boil. Two storeys below, the grounds of Brockbourne Hall sloped verdantly away to the distant river. Green hills clustered round on three sides, dotted here and there with flocks of sheep which had learned not to be surprised by anything. They had seen it all: sales conferences, survival weekends, family fun days, management training courses, even Bryan Adams in concert. Now that *was* a frightening thought.

She looked down at the milling crowds, trying to make out exactly what was going on. Stilt-walkers, scary clowns with orange hair, people in unidentifiable fun-fur costumes, fire-eaters, fairground rides, kiddies' entertainers – they were all

3

here, for one day only. Monster trucks, monster burgers, monster kids. God, but it was chaotic down there.

Not that chaos had ever bothered Claire; in fact she thrived upon it. Problem-solving, trouble-shooting, organising things and people: it was what she did best, without ever really trying. Somewhere at the back of her mind she secretly hoped that one day she might come across something she couldn't cope with. It would almost be a relief.

They stood by the window together, drinking their Vimto, looking like two people who could not be more different if they tried. Lorna was tall and dark and bosomy, Claire petite and pretty in a Goldie Hawn kind of way, with short, naturally blonde hair that she had given up dyeing because it invariably ended up green. It wasn't just that the two friends looked different; they hardly ever agreed about anything, either. Funny that they had been such good mates for so long.

'First aider to the funhouse please, first aider to the funhouse.'

Lorna opened the kitchen window and stuck her head out. 'What's he doing down there?'

Claire joined her. 'Who?'

'That kid in the red parka. Is he doing what I think he's doing?'

Claire stifled a giggle. 'No, I don't believe it! If his mum catches him . . .'

They were so busy laughing that they didn't hear the knock on the outer door. In fact, the first Claire knew that she had a visitor was when an apologetic head stuck itself into the kitchen.

'Er, hi. Mattie Sykes. We met at the interview, remember?'

Claire smiled and stuck out her hand. 'Hi.' Something on Mattie's harassed face told her that this was not just a social call. 'Is there a problem?'

Mattie achieved the impossible and looked even more embarrassed. 'Hey, I'm really sorry about this, and I know you don't officially start work until tomorrow . . .'

'But?' interjected Lorna.

'But could you get over to the funhouse right away? The Smurfs are kicking hell out of Mr Blobby.'

Chapter 1

'So *then*, he starts screaming.'

Claire poked her plastic fork around her paper plate, hunting for edible bits in her carbonised burrito. It took concentration. 'Screaming?' she said vaguely. 'Who?'

'Roderick Usher,' repeated Lorna, with a despairing sweep of her large, dark eyes. 'My mate Worm.'

'Oh, *Worm*. Why didn't you say so?'

'I did!' Lorna's gaze was accusing. 'You've not been listening, have you?'

'Of course I have,' protested Claire. 'I always listen. But you lost me after that bit where the assistant stage manager put his foot through the diorama.'

Claire pushed her plate away with a queasy burp, and asked herself for the umpteenth time why a night out with Lorna invariably meant supper at the Cotswold Cantina. It had been suggested many times that Les, the owner, should diversify into indigestion remedies. He'd be sure to make a fortune.

It was well after midnight, and Claire and Lorna were the only two people left in the café. They'd probably have gone home half an hour ago, only a savage March wind was howling down Albion Street, whipping up flurries of wet crisp packets and sticking them to the shop windows. It wasn't a nice night out there. And at least it was always warm in Les's Cantina.

Lorna looked wounded. 'If you don't want to hear about my play, why don't you just say so?'

'Of course I want to hear about it.'

'Oh yeah.'

'I do!'

'Hrrmph.'

'Stop being a prima donna and get on with it!'

It was a pact they'd shared since schooldays. Lorna would make supportive noises while Claire went on about how unchallenging her latest job was, and in return Claire listened sympathetically to Lorna's never-ending fund of theatrical mishaps.

Despite all the evidence to the contrary, Lorna was going to be a big, big star. It was a long, hard road though. Ten years she'd been in the business, and she was still at Cheltenham Rep, understudying people you'd never heard of, with the occasional starring role as a victim on *Crimewatch UK*. Yet her dedication never wavered.

Claire was a different kettle of fish entirely. The longest she'd ever stuck a job was fifteen months in her current one, and sometimes that felt like fourteen too many. It wasn't that she was no good at her work, or that she wasn't quite fond of it, just that she got terribly restless. In the six years since she'd left school, she'd never found anything that felt like a proper challenge.

She stifled a yawn, and tried to ignore Les's meaningful stares at the fly-specked clock. It was way past her bedtime and she had a conference of German beer salesmen to organise tomorrow, but like the bride of Dracula, Lorna didn't really come to life until after dark.

'So,' Claire coaxed, 'Worm was screaming, was he?'

'Of course he was screaming!' Lorna waved an arm and sixteen Indian bracelets chimed in unison. 'Look, it was Saturday night, OK, and the leading lady's locked in the loo with explosive diarrhoea. Well, I'm over the moon, aren't I? At last, I've got my chance to play Madeleine. It's going great, I've

6

got the audience eating out of my hand, and then Worm, that *idiot* . . . ' She snorted. 'You just won't believe it.'

'Try me.'

'You know how method he is, darling. If the script says shoot someone, he wants real bullets. So what does he do? He only goes and accidentally nails himself to the door of the crypt, doesn't he?'

'No!'

'As I live and breathe. Screamed the place down, blood everywhere, fleets of ambulances . . . '

'Oh Lorna . . . '

'Naturally the whole performance had to be cancelled, and – hey, stop laughing, it's not funny!'

'I'm not laughing.' Claire tried so hard not to that half a cup of hot chocolate shot up her nose. 'And you actually share a house with this lunatic?' She grabbed a paper napkin and blew a stream of chocolate-brown snot into it. 'I hope you keep all the sharp knives locked away.'

Lorna harrumphed. 'Just wait till you have a major life trauma and you want *my* shoulder to cry on.'

'Ah, but I don't have traumas,' Claire reminded her. 'They're a complete waste of time.'

'You've got Kieran,' retorted Lorna.

Claire laughed. She'd only been seeing Lorna's house-mate for a few weeks. In fact it was so casual between them, she had difficulty thinking of him as her boyfriend – particularly after this evening's stupid row. 'Kieran? He's not a trauma, he's just a . . . a . . . '

'Another waste of time?' enquired Lorna archly.

Claire considered. 'Just a bloke. And you know what it's like with me and blokes. Sooner or later they always end up annoying or boring or both.'

'So which one's Kieran?'

'I'll keep you posted.' Claire cradled what was left of her hot chocolate. 'The thing is, I like my life the way it is. Men are fun, but . . . '

Lorna winked filthily. 'But why have one Mars bar when you can gobble the whole sweetshop?'

'Lorna Walsh, you're disgusting.'

'And you're a jammy little devil. You've got it made. Lots of money, a free flat in a country mansion, all those hunky rock stars you get to meet.'

'True,' Claire agreed. 'But don't forget the lardy sales reps and the spotty management trainees who grab your bum. It's not all open-air rock concerts you know – besides, you'd hate all that pandering to people's egos.' She chuckled. 'Mind you, you'd love it whenever things went horribly wrong.'

'What's that supposed to mean?'

'It means, you're only happy when you're having a crisis.'

Lorna flicked her silk scarf over her shoulder. 'That's a vicious lie!'

'Ahem,' grunted a low-pitched voice from behind the counter. Claire screwed her head round. Les Lynch was lugubriously flicking his teatowel at a fly that had somehow escaped the Insect-o-cutor. 'You two going home tonight, or shall I get you a couple of pillows and a duvet?'

The clock on the wall said twenty-five past midnight. 'Uh-oh.' Claire fished in her pocket for a tenner. 'I think we're about to be thrown out.'

'It's my turn to pay,' Lorna promptly announced, and started rummaging in her fun-fur duffel bag.

'You said you'd only got five pounds to last you till next Thursday.'

'Yes, well, there's probably some change in here somewhere.'

'It's all right, you can owe me.' They had this argument every week, mused Claire; she could have repeated it word for word. By now, Lorna probably owed her about three million quid, but that was actors for you. She went across to the counter and slapped down the note.

'Enjoy your meal, ladies?'

'Nope,' replied Claire cheerfully. 'Was that washing-up liquid I could taste in the chimichangas?'

8

'Could be,' admitted Les. 'That or the authentic blend of exotic Mexican herbs and spices.'

'Washing-up liquid,' decided Lorna, scooping up Claire's change and pocketing it. She followed Claire out into the street. Huge raindrops were bouncing off the pavements like jumping beans and the two friends sheltered under the awning for several minutes, loath to move. 'You coming back to mine for a bit?' enquired Lorna. 'Or are you still mad at Kieran?'

Claire considered. It was such an effort being mad at Kieran, particularly since he hardly seemed to notice. But that was the problem with blokes; if they were bright enough to understand why they'd pissed you off, they generally thought they had a perfect right to take over your life and arse it up for you – so you wouldn't want to go out with them anyway.

'OK,' she said. 'I'll give you a lift back. But I'm not sitting in that armchair with the spring sticking out of the seat.'

'You drive a hard bargain, Claire Snow.'

'And your landlord's got a perverted sense of humour.'

Claire parked as close as she could to the house on Jardine Crescent, but she and Lorna were still wet through by the time they'd negotiated the broken gate, the tricky paving stone and the brambles that poked sneakily across the path between the overgrown shrubs.

Number sixteen skulked apologetically near one end of the crescent. Architecturally identical to all the other square-cut Victorian villas, it nonetheless managed to draw instant attention, like a crooked tooth in an otherwise perfect smile.

At least the darkness camouflaged the worst of its peculiarities: like the cracked exterior paintwork (in three different shades of mauve); and the so-called conservatory, tacked on to one side like a 3D jigsaw of orange-boxes and corrugated PVC. Then there were the gardens: a random tangle of unchecked greenery for the most part, in stark contrast to one long cultivated strip, lovingly dedicated to the owner's obsession with exotic vegetables.

To cap it all, number sixteen Jardine Crescent *knew* it wasn't like all the other, smarter houses in the road. It suffered from the worst affliction possible for a house with social pretensions.

It had *tenants*. Lots of them.

Rainwater trickled down the back of Claire's neck as she shifted from one foot to the other on the doorstep, waiting for Lorna to find the front door key.

'So what's all this about Facade?' demanded Lorna, lifting up her bag and angling it so that it caught the faint glimmer from a street light, twenty yards away.

'I told you, they've gone all New-Age-pagan. They're re-forming to play a Millennium solstice gig at the Hall.'

Lorna's eyebrows lifted. 'Bit of a leap from New Romantic isn't it?'

'Oh, anything to make a bit of cash I expect. Do you remember when they split up, back in the mid-Eighties?'

'All because Brent Lovelace went all Sisters of Mercy on them?' A slow grin spread over Lorna's face. 'I was only thirteen you know, but boy did I fancy him. Oooh, the sight of his bum in all that tight black leather . . .'

Claire snapped her fingers. 'Oh *yes*. You wanted to get a death's head tattoo and black lipstick, so you could be just like him.'

'And Mum said if I dared come home looking like a warmed-up corpse, she'd make me sleep in the cemetery.' Lorna turned the key in the lock, opened the front door and stepped inside, shaking herself all over the hall carpet like a wet Airedale. 'Not that I cared, I would have done it anyway.'

'Oh, I know you would. Only you got a crush on Adam Ant and painted a stripe across your nose instead.'

Lorna chuckled. 'Poor old Mum.'

They crossed the hall, past a line of wet nylon underpants gently steaming on the radiator. From somewhere deep in the bowels of the earth, Claire could make out the sounds of 'Arrivederci Roma' being played, very badly, on a B-flat cornet.

'How on earth does anybody ever get any sleep in this place?'

10

she marvelled. 'No matter what time I turn up here, there's always somebody making a racket.'

Lorna didn't bat an eyelid. 'Oh, that's just Mr Veidt in the basement. It's all right, he'll stop practicing at quarter to, he always does.' She pushed open the kitchen door. 'Coffee?'

Claire glanced at her watch. 'All right, but make it a quick one, I've got an early start in the morning.'

The kitchen light clicked on, revealing the kind of beige Formica wall units that had never been the height of fashion, not even in 1972, a bolognese-spattered microwave and a beaten-up fridge-freezer adorned with a single, upside-down magnet in the shape of an ice-cream sundae.

In the middle of the kitchen a young man was snoring serenely, slumped on a kitchen chair. He wasn't bad-looking, if you like them big and craggy, though the he-man effect was somewhat diluted by the single red rose sticking out of his shirt pocket and the cushion tightly cuddled to his manly chest. On the table in front of him sat the remains of a makeshift supper: half a jar of pickled gherkins, a packet of dry-roasted peanuts, and a McDonald's strawberry milkshake.

'Aah,' smirked Lorna. 'Sweet. Now how could anybody be angry with that?'

'Easy.' Claire pursed her lips and tried not to laugh. She was, after all, still annoyed with Kieran. He had stepped out of line tonight, and she didn't see why she should forgive him just like that. All right, so it had been a silly argument about a pair of shoes she didn't even like that much, but being compared unfavourably with your new boyfriend's fifty-year-old mother wasn't exactly flattering.

On the other hand, she knew perfectly well that Kieran hadn't *meant* to be a tactless oaf; it just came naturally. Hopeless, hapless and brainless, that's what he is, she thought to herself. Pity he's cute as well.

'Kieran.' She first prodded then shook him, but all he did was mumble incoherently and roll over in his chair.

'I shouldn't bother,' counselled Lorna. 'That boy could sleep through an earthquake. White or black?'

'White please.'

Lorna opened the fridge and selected a carton of milk from the row of six or seven on the shelf. The label on it read 'Kieran's milk, hands off'. Opening it, she gave it a cautious sniff. 'Ugh, God!' She checked the sell-by date. 'It's a fortnight old!'

'In that case, black's fine.' Claire jumped up and perched on the end of the kitchen table. She helped herself to a peanut. 'Don't suppose you've ever thought of buying your own milk?'

'Lord no. And Worm does a lovely line in contraband loo rolls. He steals them from the—'

'Don't tell me, I don't think I want to know.' Claire contemplated the sleeping colossus on the chair. 'What do you reckon, should I chuck Kieran?'

Lorna looked horrified. 'After all the trouble I went to to pair you two off? No way!' She poured hot water into two mugs. 'I bet he bought that rose for you, to say sorry.'

'Pity he couldn't stay awake long enough to give it to me.'

'At least it's a nice thought. Go on, forgive him. Just this once.'

Kieran's nose twitched in his sleep. He didn't look like a great big hairy hydraulic engineer who'd just spent five years in Saudi; he looked like a little boy cuddling his teddy.

Claire smiled. 'Oh all right then, maybe I will. But not until I've made him sweat a bit.'

It was laughably late by the time Claire got back to her flat at Brockbourne Hall. So late, she really ought to have gone straight to bed without even bothering to take her makeup off.

But thanks to Lorna she was wide awake now; and not in the least bit tired. So she put on her comfiest pyjamas, made herself a milky drink and stood at the window, watching the rain lash down into the fountains two storeys below. It wasn't everybody who could say they lived in an ex-stately home, even if they were only the hired help.

12

In this little self-made world she felt cosy, warm, and secure. This two-room flat might be tiny, but it was a perfect fit. Since she had come to work at the Hall she had made it that way, packing it with gifts and mementoes, pictures of friends, a favourite photograph of her brother, Pete. Perhaps some people had noticed that there were no pictures of her parents on the mantelpiece, no netball cups or swimming certificates on the walls, no threadbare old teddies on the pillow – in fact, nothing at all that related to her childhood. Perhaps they noticed. But if they did, they were far too polite to ask why.

The sound of the rain hammering against stone and glass was pleasantly hypnotic. Claire wondered idly what the next day's work would bring. Nothing she couldn't cope with, she was sure of that. Perhaps it was time to move on, find something different to do with her life.

She settled into her comfy armchair and sipped the last of her hot milk. No, she decided as she drifted off to sleep. It wasn't time to move on. Not just yet.

Chapter 2

'Which one's Johannsen? I can't remember,' flustered Naomi Vance, sweeping her arm across the desk and knocking the calculator into the wastepaper bin. Claire stooped to fish it out.

'Johannsen's the tall blond one,' she said patiently. 'You met him before, don't you remember? At Kidderminster.'

Claire willed her boss to tap into some inner reserve of resilience, but Naomi was never the most clear-thinking of people under stress, PhD or no PhD. And she was finding the cut-and-thrust of the commercial world a real shock after five years organising academic symposia on plankton.

'Kidderminster? Did I? Oh God, I don't remember.' As Naomi rifled through the papers on the desk, Claire couldn't help noticing that she had forgotten to varnish three of the fingernails on her right hand. 'Where are the notes for my speech? I know I left them here somewhere. You know what I'm like, if I don't have my notes I'll never be able to—'

'Here they are.' Claire whisked them out from underneath a plate of stale ham sandwiches. She'd already taken the precaution of copying her boss's notes and locking the copy in her own desk, just in case they had a repetition of the time Naomi accidentally threw out her own personnel file and it turned up three weeks later on a landfill site. 'And here's the complete guest list for this morning.'

Naomi scanned the guest list for the grand opening of

Brockbourne Hall's new management training wing. Michael Tang, Claire's Singaporean colleague, mimed something derogatory from across the office, but Claire didn't respond. She wasn't best pleased with that young man.

After all, it was Michael who'd got Naomi into this state in the first place, winding her up about how important the new wing was going to be to the company, and how many national newspapers had promised to turn up to cover the event. Michael seemed to derive a perverse delight from showing people up at every possible opportunity, especially his boss. Claire had a shrewd suspicion he rather fancied being the boss himself.

'Tell me again,' said Naomi, passing a hand over her brow. 'Which one's the one who doesn't like the other one's wife?'

Outside, watery March sunlight crept timorously across the lawns of Brockbourne Hall, slowly illuminating a large blue and white marquee and, beyond it, lush green hillsides dotted with the obligatory huddles of sheep. Some days, thought Claire, it would be rather relaxing to be a sheep. Nothing to do all day but eat, bleat and wander about looking woolly. Rather like Naomi in fact. She chased the unkind thought from her mind.

'Don't worry about any of that,' she reassured her boss. 'We'll take care of the political stuff, won't we Michael? You just concentrate on your speech.'

Michael forced a smile as he shrugged on his sharp new jacket. 'Certainly we will, Naomi. Just leave it all to us.' Everything about Michael Tang was sharp, thought Claire. Sharp suit, sharp tongue, sharp wits. One of these days he was going to cut himself.

Naomi took a deep breath and stood up. 'How do I look?'

'Great.' Claire gave her boss's chiffon scarf a discreet pat so that the ends lay flat on the smart black dress, subtly flattering to Naomi's slightly lumpy figure. 'But I'll just brush these few hairs off before you go, shall I?'

'Hairs?' Naomi swivelled her head round to see the back of her dress, and let out a gasp of horror. A thick white circle of Persian cat hair had adhered to her bottom like a portable seat-cushion. 'Oh no!' she moaned. 'I must have sat on Snowball's special blanket.'

'It's fine, no problem.' The clothes brush was already in Claire's hand. Her tone of voice was the sort she would generally have deployed on a tearful two-year-old, but it seemed to work on Naomi too. 'Just hold still, all be gone in a minute. There, all lovely and smart again.'

The whole room seemed to let out a relieved sigh as the door closed behind Naomi, only one minute thirty seconds behind schedule. Michael picked up his walkie-talkie from the desk and threw one to Claire. 'Why do you always cover up for her like that?'

'Because I like her. And she's my boss.'

That produced something between a pitying smile and a sneer. 'Oh come on Claire, we both know she should never have got the job in the first place.'

'And you should, I suppose?' she countered.

'At least I know how to do my job properly.'

'Yes, well, that's a matter of opinion. Teamwork's supposed to be part of this job, remember?'

He laughed. 'You don't honestly believe all that personnel-speak, do you? Get real, Claire. Or do you want to be running around after no-hopers for the rest of your life?'

By eleven thirty, the gracefully landscaped slope that led down from the Hall to the river was an untidy mosaic of Mazdas and BMWs. Good turnout, thought Claire. Pity nobody thought to organise the parking properly.

She switched on her walkie-talkie. 'Mel?'

It crackled into aggressive life. 'Wot?'

Claire winced and distanced the radio from her ear. Mel had the loudest, most distinctive voice of anyone Claire knew, and the dress sense to go with it. A Brixton girl and proud of it, Mel took the attitude that if Cheltenham didn't like her the way she was, it could sod off.

'Can you get the marshals to clear the area down by the

16

Bourton Road entrance? The caterers can't get their truck out.'

'Come on Claire, that's not my fault, it's Julian's. I told you he couldn't hack it, didn't I?'

'Mel.'

'Can't you get Michael to do it? He's good at smarming up to people.'

Too right he is, thought Claire. Out of the corner of her eye, she could see Michael Tang ruthlessly networking with the head of the Stuttgart delegation. That boy never wasted an opportunity to further his career. Sometimes his sheer relentlessness exhausted her.

'*Mel*,' she repeated.

'Wot?'

'Save my life and just do it.'

Claire walked back up the slope past the marquee, already assembled for Saturday's big wedding. This job was all about planning ahead. Of course, Mel was one hundred per cent right about Julian, but then every company she'd ever worked for had had its Julian – a boss's son, a complete embarrassment, hopeless at everything except getting in the way. Managerial progeny were an occupational hazard; you just had to live with them and put them to work somewhere where they couldn't bugger up anything too important. Especially on a day like today, when there were so many things for him to bugger up.

The bulk of the crowd was bunched in front of the house, some listening to the inaugural address, most taking the opportunity to gape at the brand-new wing. Its 'innovative' design had sparked a long-running row in the local paper, since the only concessions to blending in with the original house were a couple of concrete gargoyles cemented on either side of the electric sliding doors. It had cost a fortune and was, quite simply, hideous.

In fairness, Brockbourne Hall could not really be described as an architectural gem. Insufficiently winsome to feature in a BBC costume drama and insufficiently old to have been slept in by Elizabeth I, it was consequently forced to earn itself a proper living. It did look rather fine today, though. The Hall was always at its most photogenic with a bit of sun on it. Sunlight flattered the yellow-grey stone, turning it a buttery colour which lent the illusion that the ex-stately pile was built entirely of shortbread.

It had been a long morning, and Claire's empty stomach grumbled. She tried not to think about food as she tagged on to the edge of the crowd. Professor Jup Johannsen, Denmark's most eminent management theorist, was standing at the lectern in front of the new block, mumbling unintelligibly into his microphone as the sheep on the other side of the electric fence did their best to drown him out.

As Claire stood and listened Mattie Sykes arrived on the scene, shaking her wise, mother-of-three head. Claire had a lot of time for Mattie; she'd learned all her PR skills at the university of single parenthood, and could have licked the UN Security Council into shape in five minutes flat.

'Naomi should've gone for that American,' sighed Mattie.

Claire stopped trying to work out whether Professor Johannsen was speaking in English or Danish. 'Which American?'

'That woman professor who teaches crisis management by dumping you in Las Vegas with fifty dollars and no trousers. At least she'd have got this lot going.'

Claire laughed. 'Johannsen's a professor of management information sciences, Mattie. Not Robbie Williams.'

'True. But it wouldn't do him any harm to have a bit of charisma.'

As entertainment, the opening ceremony might leave something to be desired, but at least the media had turned out in force – that was one thing Naomi Vance had been spot-on about. There were quite a few familiar local faces in the crowd: Chelt FM of course, and the *Cheltenham Courant*, not to mention a dozen assorted trade magazines. Publicity, that was what really counted at the end of the day. Because publicity meant cash. What did it matter if most of the journos were only here because word had got out about the free booze?

'What I'm saying is,' reasoned Mattie, 'if the press don't get a good story we won't get the publicity, will we? What this thing needs is livening up a bit.'

Claire shrugged. 'It's no good saying all this stuff to me, Mat. I'm just the operations manager. As long as the toilets don't flood, I'm happy.'

Polite applause rippled through the audience as Naomi stepped back up to the microphone. 'Ladies and gentlemen, I'd now like to ask Professor . . .' She glanced down at the biroed name on her hand. '. . . Jup Johannsen, from . . .' Glance. '. . . Copenhagen, to cut the ribbon and declare the new wing officially open.'

Applause rang out, more enthusiastically this time. Taking the professor's arm, Naomi steered him across to the front entrance of the new building. He was so startled that he went without a murmur. 'Now, Professor,' she prompted him in a stage whisper as she thrust a pair of silver-plated tailoring shears into his hands.

'Pardon?'

'Cut it now, professor.' Naomi mimed scissors with her fingers. '*Now.*'

'Ah, yes, very good.' The professor snipped at the red ribbon, managed to cut it at the second attempt, and mumbled something that might have been a shopping list for all Claire could tell. It didn't really matter. Everybody clapped anyway, and the crowd shuffled forward a few paces, eager to get first go at the finger buffet. Naomi beamed triumphantly at the sea of faces as the electric doors swished open behind her, revealing cool white marble pillars, an expensively carpeted foyer, and . . . no, it couldn't be. Necks craned. Eyes bulged. But it was, definitely . . .

A sheep.

Standing just inside the foyer was a very large, thoroughly evil-looking sheep with half a baguette dangling from the side of its mouth. As the doors opened, it strolled nonchalantly out into the spring sunshine like Lee van Cleef swaggering down Main Street to a noonday showdown.

Nobody moved. For a couple of seconds there was complete, stunned silence.

'Oh my God,' hissed Claire, eyes fixed on the trailing baguette. 'The finger buffet!'

Mattie groaned. 'The *carpet*!'

Somebody laughed. Then that one laugh sparked off another and rippled right across the crowd.

'Ow!' squeaked Naomi. 'Get off, get *off*!'

And at that precise moment two dozen press cameras flashed in unison, capturing forever the image of Naomi Vance being butted in the backside by a sheep.

'No, no, no, no *no*!' shrieked Petronella, crashing her hands down on to the keys with such force that her music fell off the piano.

The five figures on stage at the Jasper Kendall Theatre froze into drooping poses like wilting foliage.

'Oh for God's sake!' sniffed the male lead, stumping to the front of the stage and peering down into the orchestra pit. 'What was wrong with it *this* time?'

'Too straight, darling, *obscenely* straight.' Bending down, the musical director snatched her score off the floor and jammed it back on to the stand. She rapped out a chord of A major, fortissimo. 'Positions, everybody.' The actors on the stage trailed back to their original places. 'From the top. And this time, Glyn darling, remember to *flounce*!'

Lorna sat with Worm in the front stalls, watching the principals rehearse. The bit-part players had been here two hours already and hadn't been on stage once yet. Still, that was always the way with rehearsals. Five hours of hanging around being bored out of your skull, then they'd all be stuck here till two in the morning, trying to get some stupid fan-dance right.

'He's completely wrong for it, you know,' she commented.

Worm turned to look at her. 'Glyn, you mean?'

She waved her pack of Polo mints at the distant stage. 'You should be playing that part, not him.'

'Me? Oh I don't know about that.' He scratched his nose, rather cautiously, with his bandaged hand. 'People have seen the film too many times, they've got preconceptions.'

'So?'

'So they don't expect the compère in *Cabaret* to be six foot four, do they?'

Martyn 'Worm' Bennett stretched out his immensely long legs and tried to get comfortable in the dilapidated bucket seat. Every joint in his spine crackled in protest. The Jasper had been built over a hundred years ago, when people were shorter, and Worm was gangly by anybody's standards. The fact that he was also painfully thin and pale, with a pile of frizzy, light-ginger hair, only added to the overall impression of an anorexic piece of string.

Lorna dismissed his doubts. 'I'm telling you, you're perfect for it. Nobody does camp like you.'

'Oh ta very much, duckie!' he retorted with an exaggerated toss of the head.

'Shut up, you know what I mean. You're good.' She wrigged down in her seat and rested her Timberlands on the back of the one in front. 'God, I think I'm going to *die* of boredom.'

'Don't exaggerate.'

'I'm not! That or starvation. I could murder one of Les's chillis.'

'Don't you mean the other way round?' asked Worm archly.

'Oh very droll, I'm sure. The Cantina's not that bad, it's just a bit . . .'

'Vile?' suggested Worm.

'Basic. Like this place.' Lorna cast a critical eye round the interior of the old theatre; the RSC it was not. It had seating for two hundred if you didn't mind sitting on somebody's lap, dressing rooms modelled on the Black Hole of Calcutta, and a plasterwork ceiling which regularly shed lumps of itself on to the audience below. 'Come on, let's go and get a takeaway, it'll be ages before they get round to our scenes.'

'In a bit. I just want to see how Glyn plays this sequence.'

'Like he plays every other one. Badly.'

In fact, Glyn and Petronella were now playing out their very own scene across the footlights; the MD looking increasingly peevish, Glyn glowering down at her, hands on hips, menacing her with his full five foot five.

'If I can play "Corrie", dear, I can play this,' he glared. 'And I'm playing it the way *I* see it.'

'But that's just it, Glyn darling,' replied Petronella with venomous sweetness. 'You're only doing this because you're *not* doing "Corrie" any more, are you?'

'Touché,' muttered Worm.

Glyn took another step closer to the edge of the stage. 'What are you implying?' he snapped.

'Implying?' Petronella mimed '*moi?*'

'Are you trying to make out I'm washed-up or something?'

'Darling,' replied Petronella, all wounded innocence now. 'Do you really think I'd do a thing like that?'

'Lisen, I'm not standing here and letting you victimise me, just because I'm a well-known television artiste, and . . . and this lot . . .' He flicked the hair out of his eyes with a gesture of disdain. 'This lot couldn't even play a village bloody panto.'

Lorna tugged at Worm's sleeve. 'Oh hell, he's going into one, we'll be stuck here all day. Come on. You're buying.'

The Cotswold Cantina was just across the street from the Jasper; in fact it owed most of its trade to the theatre, mainly because it was open all hours and the food was dirt cheap – suspiciously so, some might say. Many a struggling actor had eked out his Equity minimum on a diet of Les's economy chilli, but no one had ever dared ask him what he put in it.

'The usual?' enquired Les, sniffing his right armpit as though he had only just discovered its existence.

'Oh, go on then.' Worm counted out a handful of five-pence pieces from a plastic bag in his pocket. 'But easy on the garlic,

22

Lorna's got a hot love scene this afternoon.'

Lorna wrinkled her nose. 'You call that a love scene? With *him*? It's OK Les love, you can put in double if you want.'

They took their lunch over to the window and perched on high, circular plastic stools that wobbled and fell over if you spun round on them too fast. 'It's not right, you know,' said Lorna through a mouthful of tepid rice.

'What isn't?'

'Bringing in all these B-list celebs to take the best parts, so we have to make do with whatever's left. I mean, we're the regular rep company aren't we? What about showing a bit of loyalty to us?'

'Ah, but people like Glyn Marchant are *famous*, aren't they? They've been on the telly.'

'So? We'll be famous one day, too. A damn sight more famous than him.'

'Hmm,' said Worm non-committally. 'The fact is, the Jasper's not making any money. We need star names to get people to come to the theatre. Otherwise . . .' He drew a finger across his throat.

'Stars? Like him?' scoffed Lorna. 'He's nobody.' She chewed furiously on a lump of gristle. 'You know what you should do, don't you?'

'Am I going to like this?'

'Of course you are. You should get Petronella to let you understudy all the male principals.'

'Why'd I want to do that?'

'Well, it'd be a few extra quid a week, wouldn't it?'

'Yeah, it would. For a lot more work. And by the time I'd paid tax on it I'd be about five p better off. It's not worth the hassle.'

'Ah, but then I could lure Glyn here for a romantic supper *à deux* and poison him with one of Les's deluxe Mexiburgers, and you could get to be the star of the show!'

Les loomed over them with two pint mugs of tea. 'What's all this about me poisoning people?'

Lorna smiled sweetly up at him. 'Just my little joke.'

'Oh yeah?' Les banged a mug down in front of her. 'There you go. Two sugars, extra strychnine.'

'Ta.'

'And a pickled egg.'

'What?' She contemplated the cold, white wobbly thing on the counter in front of her. 'Why?'

'Special offer.'

Lorna smiled as he went off to refry yesterday's chips. Les Lynch amused her; intrigued her, too. It suited him to behave like a complete slob but Lorna knew an act when she saw one. She had a hunch he might not be bad-looking if he had a shave and put on a clean shirt once in a while. Rumour had it he'd been a journalist before he opened the Cantina, but he never talked about it, or what on earth had possessed him to open up this dive – in select Cheltenham of all places. Lorna loved mysteries. Maybe one day she'd charm the truth out of him.

Worm let out a groan. 'Oh no.'

Lorna spun her stool round and the seat almost fell off. 'What?' Worm had his nose bured in one of the local free papers. 'Reading your horoscope again, are you? Don't tell me, you're going to meet a short actor with no talent.'

'Worse. Look.' Worm slid the paper towards her, jabbing at the headline on page two. 'Read it and weep.'

'REDEVELOPMENT LATEST,' it said. 'LAME-DUCK THEATRE NEXT TO GO?'

Kenton Mayberry, chairman of the board of Brockbourne Hall, was not so much a businessman as a force of nature. The day after the launch, he descended on Naomi's office like a tropical storm.

'What in hell's name do you call this?' he demanded, bursting in and hurling an armful of newspapers onto Naomi's desk.

Naomi shrivelled visibly. 'Mr Mayberry . . . Kenton . . . I . . .'

Claire stood up, events folder in hand. 'Perhaps I should leave you two to . . . ?'

Mayberry ignored her. Seizing a copy of the *Courant*, he brandished it in Naomi's face. '"EWE-NIVERSITY CHALLENGE" — I suppose you think that's funny, do you?'

Naomi swallowed. 'With respect . . .'

'Or do you prefer this one?' The *Daily Argus* carried a huge photograph right in the middle of page one, surmounted by the jaunty strapline, 'THE SHEEP OF THINGS TO COME'. 'Well?'

Claire normally kept a pretty tight rein on her temper, but she was tempted to make an exception for Kenton Mayberry. He really was the typical playground bully: the kind who got his kicks from pushing the littler kids around, the kind Claire had always loathed. And he wasn't even giving Naomi a chance to get a word in edgeways.

When Mayberry paused for breath, Claire looked meaningfully at Naomi, willing her to defend herself; but Naomi had gone very white-faced and silent.

'Mr Mayberry,' Claire began in a firm, clear voice. 'Perhaps *I* can explain about yesterday?'

The chairman's bulldog head snapped round. 'Who are you?'

'Claire Snow. I'm Naomi's deputy.'

'Oh you are, are you?' The small, red-rimmed eyes looked her up and down. 'Well make yourself useful and get me a coffee.'

Claire opened her mouth to tell him that making coffee was not part of her job, but Naomi got in first. 'That's a good idea,' she said, a little too eagerly. 'Go and make Mr Mayberry a coffee, Claire.' Shut up and go, her eyes beseeched. Let me sort this one out my way.

'Right,' said Claire, tight-lipped with anger. 'Coffee.' She didn't bother to ask how Mr Mayberry liked his coffee. He was getting instant with coffee creamer in an unwashed mug, and if he didn't like it that way, he could stuff it.

It took a real effort not to bang the door as she emerged into the outer, open-plan office she shared with most of Brockbourne's dozen or so administrative staff. Several pairs of eyes focused on her.

'Trouble?' enquired Michael Tang.

'Oh you'd love that, wouldn't you?' she said tartly.

He looked taken aback. 'Pardon?'

'Never mind, it's not important.' She pushed past him and went into the kitchen, telling herself that this was crazy. It wasn't like her to get so involved, this was only a job, for goodness' sake; and it wasn't her problem if Naomi Vance was too much of a wet lettuce to stand up for herself.

She filled the kettle and allowed herself to imagine Kenton Mayberry accidentally sitting down on a very big metal spike. It made her feel quite a lot better. Then she remembered that there were some really ancient digestive biscuits in a tin under the sink, so she fished them out and arranged them prettily on a plate; with any luck they'd taste disgusting and might even be mildly toxic.

Mattie put her head round the kitchen door just as the kettle was coming to the boil. 'Claire.'

She looked back over her shoulder. 'Hmm?'

'There's a call for you on line five.'

'Couldn't you take a message?'

'He says it's important.'

Claire tailed her back to the nearest phone and picked it up. Mayberry would just have to wait a bit longer for his coffee. 'Claire Snow, can I help you?'

'Good morning Miss Snow. My name's Owen Pendle, you won't know me.'

'Oh?' This was starting to sound suspiciously like a hard sell for double glazing. 'Do I want to?'

He laughed. 'I hope so.' His was quite a young voice, but not a salesman's somehow. 'I work for Doorman, Glossop and Pendle.' He answered her next question before she'd asked it. 'A firm of solicitors in Cheltenham. We're handling the estate of the late Miss Mary Willenhall.'

Claire frowned. 'Willenhall? That was my mother's maiden name.'

'So I believe. As far as I can establish, Mary Willenhall was

26

your great aunt – your maternal grandmother's sister. Would that be correct?'

'I really wouldn't know.'

'You never met her then?'

She searched her memory. 'I don't know. I may have done. It's a big family but we've never been that close.' She didn't add that she hadn't so much as heard from her own mother for over three years. Cradling the phone between chin and chest, she rummaged for a pen under the piles of paper on the desk. 'So this lady ... she's died, you say?'

'I'm afraid so. A couple of months ago. I know it must be a shock for you, but if it's any consolation, she was very old.'

'I see.' It felt odd, being told that one of your relatives had died and not feeling anything. But how could you feel something for somebody you didn't even remember? 'Can you tell me anything about her? Where did she live? What part of the country?'

'She was quite local. Lived at Lilcombe Magna, it's just the other side of Cirencester.'

The name of the village rang no bells, yet something small and distant stirred in her mind; no more than half a reminiscence, a blurred image. How old had she been? Six, seven? No older. She was in a cottage garden with her little brother Peter and lots of butterflies, and a nice, rather whiskery lady was bending down, offering them fresh strawberries from a china bowl ... And then it was all gone.

'I don't remember, I'm afraid. Not really.'

'Well, it seems your great-aunt remembered you. As I said, she died a few months back, and we've been trying to locate you ever since.'

Claire blinked. 'Me? Why? You're not actually saying she left me something?'

'Quite a large something, actually,' replied the solicitor. 'She's left you her house.'

27

Chapter 3

The back door of Paradise Cottage opened all of three inches, stretching the security chain to its limit. A single eye appeared in the darkness beyond.

'Bugger orf.'

The man on the doorstep insinuated his nose into the gap. 'Come on Ted, you daft old sod,' he wheedled. 'Open the door.'

'Why should I?' retorted the unseen voice.

'I only want a look round.' He turned up the collar of his waxed jacket against the keen March wind. 'Come on, it's bitter out here. Look,' he reasoned, 'why not let me in? This cottage'll be mine soon anyhow.'

'Yes, well, that's where you're wrong,' came back the reply. ''Cause that there solicitor reckons he's found the rightful heir to this place. So you might as well bugger orf out of it an' leave me be.'

The man on the doorstep did not seem unduly perturbed. 'Fine. So I'll buy it off the heir. One way or another, Paradise Cottage'll still be mine in the end.'

Owen Pendle sprang forward to meet Claire as she entered his office, his hand already outstretched in greeting.

'Miss Snow, hi, I'm Owen. Do take a seat.'

'Thanks.' She unbuttoned her coat and sat down.

Pendle was one of those people who look nothing like their voices: he was at least a foot shorter than he sounded on the telephone, several years younger, and considerably more fluffy. This initial impression was reinforced by coffee-stained cords and a chunky beige sweater, and the kind of peculiarly choreographed woolly blond hair that nature had inflicted on Art Garfunkel. Altogether rather a disappointment, thought Claire: more Shaun the sheep than Perry Mason.

'It's good of you to fit me in so late in the evening,' she said, by way of breaking the ice.

'Not at all, not at all. I'm only sorry you had to wait two days for an appointment. I know all this must have come as something of a shock.'

That, at least, Claire could agree with. 'Yes, it has rather. Mr Pendle . . .'

'Owen, please.'

'About this will. Are you absolutely certain I'm the beneficiary?'

The young solicitor selected a buff-coloured folder from the heap on his desk, untied its red ribbon and flicked through until he found the page he wanted. 'Well, let's get the formalities over with. You can confirm that your name is Claire Joanna Snow? Currently residing at Brockbourne Hall, near Cheltenham?'

'That's me.' She took out the birth certificate and bank book she'd brought with her and laid them on the desk in front of him.

'Your father is Terence Arthur Snow, recently remarried and living in Kettering?' She nodded. 'Any brothers and sisters?'

'Just my brother Peter. He's four years younger than me.'

'Good, good. And what about your mother? Can you give me her full name?'

Claire passed the tip of her tongue over her lips. Suddenly her mouth was very dry. 'Veronica. Veronica Jane Snow.'

'Well, that all seems to be in perfect order.' Pendle looked up. 'I must say Miss Snow, it's no wonder it took us so long to track you down.'

29

'Oh? Why?'

'Miss Willenhall's papers are in a dreadful jumble. There seem to be six or seven different addresses for you in this file, and we don't seem to have an address for your mother at all. Have you moved around a lot since you were a child?'

Her childhood. She wished they could move on to something else. Claire didn't talk about the past, or at least not willingly. No matter what people said, some hurts didn't get better with time.

'My parents split up when I was quite small; when I was eight I went to live with my father.'

'Ah, ah yes,' said Owen Pendle, looking uncomfortable. 'I did hear something to that effect. I'm sorry we have to look into people's private lives in such detail, only . . . '

'Only it's your job. I know.'

'So what about Mary Willenhall? Have you remembered anything about her?'

Claire shrugged. 'Not really. After my mother left, we didn't see any of the Willenhalls any more. And then we started moving around because of my father losing his job – I guess we just lost touch with that side of the family.'

He reached into the file and took out an old black and white photograph. 'This might jog your memory.'

Claire took it. It showed a lady of sixty or so, standing under an apple tree with a big willow basket of fruit. There was something very, very familiar about that face; she was convinced she had seen it somewhere before. But where and when, that was the question. Then again, maybe she was mistaken. It was the sort of face that cropped up all the time in advertisements for stairlifts and tartan slippers.

'I *think* I recognise her,' she said. 'It's hard to say. But if I did meet her, it must have been a long time ago.' She leaned foward, embarrassed by her own impatience to know more. 'I was wondering. About my great-aunt's . . . er . . . will.'

'Of course, of course. I do apologise, I've kept you in suspense quite long enough.' Pendle produced a sheaf of yellowed papers. 'Here it is, the last will and testament of Miss Mary Willenhall, Paradise Cottage, Lilcombe Magna.' He shuffled the pages until he found the one he wanted, and cleared his throat. 'There's just one paragraph which pertains to you. It's very short and to the point. Shall I read it?'

She nodded. 'Yes please.'

'To my great-niece Claire Joanna Snow, I bequeath my house, Paradise Cottage, Lilcombe Magna, in the county of Gloucestershire, its gardens and all its contents.' She swallowed hard. This was starting to feel real, and she couldn't decide if it was creepy or exciting. 'May I see?'

'Of course.' He handed her the relevant page.

There it was in black and white: 'To my great-niece, Claire Joanna Snow.' 'This is really me? You're absolutely sure?'

'Absolutely, Miss Snow. The house is yours. And there's a small bequest to your brother too. A car, I believe. I don't know the exact details.'

She flopped back in her chair, shaking her head. 'I don't believe this. Her house! Why leave it to me?'

'Mary Willenhall had no children of her own.'

'But she must have had closer relatives, surely? Or friends? I didn't even know her.'

Owen Pendle threw up his hands. 'I'm sorry, Miss Snow. There are some answers I just don't have. But it's obvious she really wanted you to have her cottage.'

'Yes. Yes, I suppose so.' Claire looked down at her hands, half expecting them to be shaking. 'I've never been in this kind of situation before. What do I do next?'

'There are a few legal formalities of course, but I can guide you through those. The main thing is for you to decide what you want to do with Paradise Cottage. Oh yes,' he snapped his fingers. 'I was completely forgetting. There's the sitting tenant to think about as well.'

Claire blinked. 'What tenant?'

'I'm sorry, I should have mentioned him before.' Pendle rifled through the papers. 'There's an old chap been living there

31

for years, keeping an eye on the place, doing odd jobs, that sort of thing. Real old character I seem to recall, I met him once, ooh, years ago. What was his name? Ah, here it is. Merriman. Theodore Merriman.'

'Good grief,' said Claire, her head in a whirl. 'Suddenly I'm a landlady as well!' She could just imagine all the rude comments Lorna would have to make about that one.

Pendle smiled sympathetically. 'It's nothing at all to worry about, I assure you. It happens all the time. But perhaps I should accompany you when you go to view the cottage? Then I can introduce you properly.'

'Thanks, I'd appreciate that.' Claire didn't make a habit of relying on other people, but she knew when to play the helpless little woman; being blonde wasn't *always* a disadvantage.

He flicked through his desk diary. 'How about Saturday afternoon? About three? I could meet you at the Cirencester office and drive you over.'

'Saturday would be fine.'

'Right then. Till Saturday.' He stood up and offered his hand. 'Oh, just one more thing. There's a bequest to your mother too. I don't suppose you have any idea where I could contact her?'

'I'm sorry, no.' Something twisted inside her; a little dark, distant nugget of pain that she had spent many years trying to forget existed, without ever quite succeeding.

'You don't have a forwarding address for her?'

She took a deep breath. 'Mr Pendle, my mother walked out on us when I was seven years old. I have no idea where she is, I haven't seen her in years, and frankly I don't care. The last I time heard from her was three years ago, on my twenty-first birthday. And even then all I got was a postcard from Portugal.

'I'm sorry Mr Pendle. But if it's my mother you're looking for, I really can't help you.'

It was eleven o'clock on Tuesday morning, the absolute nadir of the working week, with last weekend a distant memory and the next one impossibly far away. Just to make Claire's day complete, everything that could go wrong was doing precisely that. There was woodworm in the orangery, the society bar mitzvah of the year had just been cancelled and the gift shop had run out of novelty keyrings. What next, she wondered as she passed the ornamental rose garden on her way to the new training wing.

Claire stepped into the foyer just as Naomi burst through the doors from the Mayberry Suite, wrenched off her glasses and burst into tears. 'Why, Claire?' she sobbed. 'Why are they doing this?'

'Who? Doing what?' Claire turned to Michael for an explanation, but Michael was too busy pacing up and down, jabbing at buttons on his mobile phone. 'I said, get me MicroNet UK. What do you mean they're engaged? Just get them, OK?'

'It's the computers,' sniffed Naomi. 'They've all gone mad.'

'Naomi,' reasoned Claire, 'computers can't go mad. They just break down. Tell me what happened.'

'I did the introductory talk, and Mattie booted up the chocolate factory simulation, and it was all going according to plan, and then suddenly everything went crazy.'

Claire steered Naomi towards a chair, sat her down and thrust a box of tissues at her. 'What do you mean, crazy?'

'It's that study group we had last week from MicroNet,' seethed Michael, 'I'm sure it was them. They've tampered with the whole computer system. When I get my hands on their MD . . .'

'The Russians are bound to lodge an official complaint.' Naomi's expression was panic-stricken. 'Knowing my luck, there'll probably be a diplomatic incident.'

'No there won't,' said Claire firmly. 'Because we're going to sort this out.'

Giving up hope of getting any sense out of Naomi, she walked through the door into the training suite. There she found five middle managers from a recently-privatised Russian chocolate factory, sitting in a row, looking completely bemused. Which was not that surprising, as their computers were all blaring out the Soviet national anthem in pristine Dolby surround-sound. To add insult to injury, smack in the centre of all five bright-red screens a cartoon Lenin was merrily thwacking a cartoon Trotsky on the head with an ice pick, in perfect time to the music.

Hmm, thought Claire. Somebody's idea of a joke, huh? She glanced across the room, clocked Mel, and made a beeline for the central control unit. 'Mel!' She intercepted her hand as it reached to snatch out the plug. 'Mel, don't do that, you'll only make things worse.'

Mel directed a kick at the control panel. It beeped merrily back at her. 'Bloody thing. Effing bloody bastard.'

Claire grabbed her by the arm. 'Leave it.'

'But I've got to—'

'I said leave it, Mel. How much do you know about computers?'

Mel looked sullen. 'Naff all.'

'And what's Mr Mayberry going to do to you if you break his new toys? Hmm?'

That at least shut Mel up. Even Mad Mel would think twice about getting up Kenton Mayberry's substantial nose. Thank God it's Gold Cup week, thought Claire. I just hope his horse doesn't come last.

She managed to locate the right switches and shut down the system; at last the glaring red screens flickered into merciful darkness. 'Come on,' she beckoned to Mel. 'Council of war. Now.'

In the foyer outside, Naomi was pacing up and down fretting about Kenton Mayberry, Mattie had turned up with a Russian dictionary, and Michael was managing to whisper and yell into his phone at the same time. 'I *told* you, will you just *listen* to me? Your managers, yes, *your* managers . . .'

Claire tapped him on the shoulder as he rang off. 'Michael, give me a hundred quid.'

'What!'

'A hundred quid. Actually, two hundred would be better.'

'Oh it would, would it?'

'Naomi's in no fit state to think straight, and I know you've got that much on you. You'll get it back.'

He stared at her. 'Why the hell should I give you two hundred pounds?'

She smiled sweetly at him. 'Because I'm going to use it to get those five lovely Russians off your back for the rest of the day, and save your unworthy hide. Deal?'

Tang let out a bad tempered grunt and extracted a black calf-skin wallet from his inside pocket. 'Deal. But I want a receipt.'

She pocketed the money. 'Dream on.'

'So what did you do with all those Russians then?'

'Took them to Bristol Zoo. We had a great time.'

'On Michael Tang's money?'

'Too right.' Claire rummaged in her bag and took out a pencil sharpener in the shape of a polar bear. 'Here – Michael bought you a souvenir.'

Lorna caught it, inspected it and stuck it on the mantelpiece. 'Mmm, very nice. I never knew he cared.'

'Neither did he.'

Crossing to the other side of the room, Lorna dusted off the top of a giant papier-mâché dragon's head, lit an aromatherapy candle and carefully balanced it on top.

'I don't know,' said Claire with an amused shake of the head. 'You and your clutter.'

'It's not clutter!' protested Lorna. 'It's theatrical memorabilia.'

'Whatever it is, one of these days you're going to set the whole house on fire.'

'No chance of that,' laughed Lorna, arranging herself in a decorative pose. She was the only person Claire had ever met who could look good sitting on a Man United official club beanbag. 'It still hasn't dried out since we had that flood. I bet you could grow watercress on the TV room carpet.'

Claire shuddered. 'Well don't tell that weird boy in the top flat, he'll probably give it a go.'

Compared to Claire's tidy little flat, Lorna's room was like a set from *Steptoe and Son*. At first glance it looked as though a small tornado had just passed through and turned the room upside down, pausing only to replace a quarter-inch of dust on top of every item. Claire knew Lorna well enough to understand that it only *looked* like chaos: every discarded jumper, half-drunk glass of wine and prosthetic nose had its allotted place in the grand scheme of things; even Dog, the scraggy old mongrel, knew better than to move from his designated floor cushion. In short, the whole dusty vista was supposed to make some kind of artistic statement. Or on the other hand, thought Claire, maybe she just hates housework.

'Kieran's been gone ages,' commented Lorna, offering Claire a Venetian carnival mask filled with dry-roasted peanuts. 'You don't suppose he's got lost on the way to the chippy?'

'Probably. He needs a map to find his own nose.'

'Well I hope he hurries up, I'm starving.'

'I thought you were dieting, so you could look gorgeous in fishnet tights for *Cabaret*.'

'Oh sod that. Besides, I'm gorgeous already.' Another handful of peanuts made their way into Lorna's mouth. 'Aren't you hungry?'

Claire shook her head. 'I've lost my appetite. It's this cottage business.'

Lorna looked baffled. 'Why? What's the problem? Suddenly you're a woman of property!'

'I know. That's what's bothering me.' She groaned. 'I've got responsibilities, Lorna.'

Lorna choked on a peanut. 'Claire darling, you've got responsibilities every day of the week, with that bloody awful job of yours. You *adore* responsibilities!'

'Yes, but this is different. Those are other people's responsibilities.' Several thousand butterflies took flight in Claire's stomach. She wasn't used to feeling apprehensive, and she didn't much like it. 'Lorna, I've got a *tenant*!'

This provoked a gale of laughter, as Lorna rocked back on her beanbag. 'And you think that turns you into some kind of pillar of respectability? My God Claire, you've led a sheltered life. Look at my Mr Papajian.'

'He's hardly the typical landlord, surely,' protested Claire.

'Don't you believe it. There's thousands of Mr Papajians out there, my girl. Relax! After all, Mr Papajian's relaxed about *everything* . . .'

'Yeah,' grunted Claire. 'Remember that business with the boiler? He was very relaxed about that. You could all have been gassed in your beds for all he cared.'

'There you are then. QED. And God alone knows what he's got locked in that cellar.'

'You don't honestly think I want to be like Mr Papajian!'

'No, of course not,' conceded Lorna. 'But you can hardly do a worse job can you? I mean, if there was black mould growing all over your ceiling you wouldn't just slap on two coats of brilliant white, now would you?'

'I don't suppose I would, but—'

'Mr Papajian did. And two weeks later the kitchen ceiling fell in. Relax, take my advice.'

The door opened. 'For God's sake don't take Lorna's advice on anything!' Kieran appeared, preceded by an aroma of warm salt and vinegar. 'She advised me to buy this sweatshirt!'

He dumped a large plastic carrier bag on the little drop-leaf table. 'Three large haddock, six large portions of chips . . . '

'Six!' squeaked Lorna.

'I'm a growing boy.'

'You'll be a porky boy if you eat that lot.' Claire pinched his midriff affectionately, but it was all solid rugby-playing muscle.

He pulled her towards him and whispered romantically, '. . . and a big bucket of mushy peas.'

Lorna raised an eyebrow in Claire's direction. 'Lovely. Well I shouldn't go near him for a couple of days if I were you. And then only with a gas mask on.'

Claire watched Kieran ladling fish and chips on to three of Lorna's mismatched dinner plates. It wasn't that she couldn't

37

afford matching ones, though she wasn't exactly loaded; but according to Lorna it was more 'spiritual' for each person to eat from a plate that matched his or her personality. Lorna's was bright orange with blue flowers. Kieran's was red with blue stripes. Claire's was an unattractive shade of grey with a crack up the middle. Hmm.

Dog was watching too, peering longingly at the haddock from underneath a single huge overhanging eyebrow that made him look like the missing Gallagher brother.

'Don't even think about it,' warned Lorna, tossing him a chip. 'One false move and it's the glue factory for you.'

'What's this Lorna's advising you about?' asked Kieran, pushing smooth brown curls back from his forehead with the back of a vinegary hand. He was rather appealing, Claire had to admit; handsome even, in a healthy, hunky, firefighter kind of way. You could forgive a man an awful lot if he looked like a fireman, even if he didn't have the uniform to go with it.

'About this cottage my great-aunt's left me.'

Kieran paused, a chunk of greasy batter halfway to his mouth. 'You never told me she'd left you a cottage.' His face cracked into a big grin. 'Bloody brilliant, when are you moving in?'

'I'm not, at least not yet. The solicitor's taking me to see it on Saturday. Lorna said she'd come with me for moral support.'

'Moral support?' The batter met its doom between Kieran's perfect incisors. 'Tell you what, I haven't got a game this Saturday. Why don't I come too?'

It was raining again. Great big stair-rods of the stuff were blasting down out of a sky the colour of molten lead as Owen Pendle's 4×4 swished its way through the Gloucestershire countryside.

Sitting in the front with Owen, Claire listened to Kieran trying to explain the rules of water polo to Lorna. Judging by the size of some of the puddles she could see through the rain-streaked windscreen, they should have brought a beachball and some swimming cozzies with them.

'This is it,' announced the solicitor. 'Lilcombe Magna.'

'Where?' Kieran leaned forward between the seats. 'I can't see anything.'

'Just up ahead. See – where those houses are?'

Elegant wrought-iron gates glided towards them, backed by a large expanse of gravel drive. Kieran's eyes widened. 'What – those two big houses over there? You've not been left one of those, have you Claire? My God, they're twice the size of my dad's farmhouse!'

Claire gaped. Lorna looked impressed. 'I thought you said it was a cottage!'

'It is.' Owen Pendle swung the steering wheel and the 4×4 veered left, up a narrow street lined with identical stone-built cottages. 'Sorry folks, that's the squire's old house.' He chuckled. 'Paradise Cottage isn't quite in that league. It's out on the other side of the village.'

They drove through Lilcombe Magna in about ten seconds flat. It was, thought Claire, the sort of place you didn't even realise you were in until you'd gone right through it, and even then you weren't sure if you had or not. She counted one pub, one telephone box, one weathervane in the shape of a cow, and a shop that seemed to sell nothing but Calor gas and wellingtons. And that was closed.

As they travelled further and further from the stumpy little market cross, the cottages got smaller and smaller and less and less impressive.

'At this rate,' commented Lorna, 'It'll be the size of a corn-flake box.'

'Ah,' said Kieran, 'but that doesn't matter does it? Just call it bijou. People'll pay through the noses for a cottage out here.'

Claire peered out at the rain-soaked village, apparently empty of all life save one elderly lady in a Pacamac, relentlessly dragging a fat Jack Russell behind her on an extendable leash. Bourton-on-the-Water it was not. 'They will?'

'Oh absolutely,' nodded Owen Pendle, steering round a hairpin bend so tight that everything in the car slid sideways.

'Easy commuting distance from Cirencester, lovely countryside, plenty of traditionally-built English properties . . . '

'You mean it's a weekend ghetto for chartered accountants?' sniffed Lorna.

'Heavens no, not at all. Lilcombe Magna has a lovely village atmosphere. At least it did the last time I was here.'

'When was that?' demanded Claire.

He considered for a moment. 'Oh, about ten years ago, but I don't suppose things have changed much. By the way, I wasn't able to contact Mr Merriman to tell him we were coming.'

'Why not?' asked Lorna.

'It's odd really. There seems to be something wrong with his telephone. Still, I'm sure he'll be pleased to see us. Ah.' He braked and the 4×4 slid to a muddy halt. 'Here we are at last. Paradise Cottage.' He squinted through the windscreen and looked perplexed. 'Hmm, that's odd.'

'What is?'

'It doesn't look quite the way I remember it . '

'Oh my godfathers,' gasped Lorna, clasping both hands to her face as the four of them stood staring at the heap of stonework that dared to call itself Paradise Cottage.

Claire felt her stomach descend to her boots, faster than a runaway lift full of bricks. 'Are you sure this is it?'

"Fraid so.' Owen Pendle pointed to the sign dangling by one rusty nail from the five-barred gate. It read: PARADISE COTTAGE. KEEP OUT. He scratched his head. 'I can't understand it, the last time I was here it was so . . . '

'It's not that bad,' said Kieran gamely. Bless him for trying, thought Claire, unconvinced. 'I bet it's really nice inside.'

That might be possible, but it didn't strike Claire as even remotely likely. Whereas other country properties might inspire such words as 'rustic' and 'charm', the ones which sprang to mind when you first set eyes on Paradise Cottage were 'rotting', 'clapped-out' and 'eyesore'.

At first sight, the cottage was a tiny, narrow-fronted thing built of oddly-sized stones that looked as if they had been looted from an assortment of Roman villas and medieval monasteries; and it didn't so much stand as cower, its roof sagging beneath the weight of the elements. On one side a murky-looking stream gushed merrily past on its way to drown village children; on the other, a nasty-looking barbed-wire fence poked aggressive spikes at anyone who might think of trespassing.

'I'm going home,' said Claire.

'Oh no you're not,' declared Lorna, grabbing her by the arm and hauling her back. 'You're going in there and you're going to say hello to nice Mr Merriman.'

'But he doesn't know we're coming. He probably isn't even in.'

'He must be,' said Kieran. 'Look, the front door's open.'

The moment she set foot on the front path, Claire knew that this was a very, very bad idea. Maybe it was some sixth sense, maybe it was the fact that the other three seemed in no hurry to take the initiative.

'Mr Merriman?' she called. There was no reply. She took another couple of steps up the muddy path. Lorna, Kieran and Owen Pendle dawdled by the front gate. So much for moral support. 'Mr Merriman, my name's Cla—'

Claire never got the rest of the words out, because at that moment something pink and hairy and truly enormous came hurtling round the side of the cottage. As it aimed itself at her chest, she went down like a poleaxed elephant, landing on her back in a pool of something so black and so foul-smelling that she could only pray it was mud.

The next thing she knew, the big pink thing was standing on her chest and a man with a red face and wild white hair was shouting down at her: 'Who the bloody hell are you? And what do you think you're doin', traumatisin' my pig?'

Chapter 4

What did it matter if the March rain was turning most of Lilcombe Magna into a swamp? In the lounge bar of the Saxon Cross, you could toast your toes in front of a roaring hearth and forget all about the weather.

True, the open log fire was in reality a log-effect gas burner set into a reproduction fireplace; and an attack of rampant death-watch beetle in the Sixties had put paid to most of the original oak beams; but the Cross was still quirky enough to be called authentic.

It was more of a growth than a building. A hundred years ago the Cross had been a smithy, two hundred before that, some kind of watermill; but over the centuries so many bits had been added and subtracted that its precise origins were lost in the mists of time. The pub took its name from the stumpy little market cross that stood just outside its front door. Through the centuries it had gazed uneasily across the tiny triangular village green to St Ogmore's, a constipated little church so unattractive that Pevsner's *Buildings of England* had relegated it to a terse footnote: 'Not worth a diversion, but west door formerly used for crucifying warlocks.'

Aidan Ross was not terribly interested in warlocks. He much preferred counting the profits from his upmarket building business; or propping up the bar in the Cross, drinking his mate Neville's real ale and offering pithy advice. Oh, then there were women of course. Aidan quite liked women. On the whole. And in small doses.

'You've got to sort them out, Nev,' he declared, holding his glass up to the light and admiring the clarity of Vanbrugh's Old Irregular.

'I know, I know. But the thing is,' confided the landlord in his distinctive, white-Trinidadian drawl, 'I can't decide which one of them I like best. I mean, Rosa's a lovely woman, but so is Jane. And then I think, if I tell Jennifer we should stop seeing each other, and she takes it bad . . . '

Aidan sighed and passed tanned fingers over his swept-back black hair. Nobody's idea of a typical builder, he was tall, athletic, good-looking and intelligent enough not to be self-conscious about it. Which was more than you could say for Neville. Mind you, being called Neville Shute was enough to get anybody down after a while, even if you were a distin-guished ex-cricketer and a bit of a local hero.

'Listen to me, Nev,' he said, taking another sip of his pint. He raised a hand to acknowledge a grunt from a table on the other side of the bar. Everybody in Lilcombe Magna knew Aidan Ross, and some of them liked him, although not nearly as much as he thought they did. 'You've got to stop letting women run rings round you.'

Neville wiped a damp cloth across the sticky bar-top. 'I don't!' he protested.

Aidan responded with a sceptical frown. 'Oh come on, you had six on the go at once last year, and five of them you didn't even fancy!'

'Yes I did. I just . . . '

'You just didn't want to tell any of them they were chucked. Well, did you?' Neville didn't reply. 'You're too nice for your own good, that's your trouble. And they don't thank you for it in the end, you know.'

Neville sighed, served a couple of pints and then helped himself to a small brandy. 'You can't fool me, Aidan.'

'I'm not trying to fool anybody. What you see is what you get.'

'Don't give me that. You're always trying to make out you don't really get on with women. That's why you never have a girlfriend.'

'What!'

'I don't mean going out with a different bimbo every week, I mean a proper girlfriend.'

'If you mean tying myself down to some woman for a fifty-year stretch, then no thanks. I had enough of that with Adrienne.'

Neville wasn't that easily put off. 'Look, just because you had your fingers burned once . . .'

'It was a bit more than that, Nev.'

'I know. But that was five years ago. And you've turned thirty now, Aidan.'

Aidan looked faintly discomfited. 'So?'

'So you can't go through the rest of your life never getting close to anybody in case it happens again.' Nev smirked. 'Besides, you're going to need a nice respectable lady-friend on your arm, aren't you?'

'Am I?' Aidan eyed him suspiciously over the rim of his empty glass. 'Why?'

'Well you're always going on about putting yourself up for the parish council, and you know what a conservative lot they are round here. Got to think about your image, haven't you?'

Aidan snorted. 'Thank you Max bloody Clifford. For your information, I haven't made my mind up yet.'

'No? I thought you called in at the office for a nomination form.'

'Yes, well, maybe I did,' admitted Aidan. 'And I may still decide to stand.' He laughed. 'After all, I've already rebuilt half the village. Perhaps I should start running it as well.'

Back at Paradise Cottage, things were not going well.

It was chucking it down, a large pig had just walked over Claire's chest, and Theodore Merriman was about as pleasant as a dose of shingles. After the initial shock, Claire started to feel very, very angry.

44

'Get that bloody animal away from me!' she shrieked. 'Now!'

The pig leapt away with a squeal and ran to hide behind the old man in the greasy overcoat. Kieran and Lorna hauled Claire to her feet, with a terrific squelch of black mud, but she swatted them away. 'Thanks for nothing, I'm sure!'

'How was I to know you were going to be run over by a pig?' pointed out Kieran. She hated him instantly for being absolutely right.

'And what were we supposed to do anyway?' enquired Lorna. 'Mud-wrestle it?'

'Just not standing there and pissing yourselves laughing would have been a start.'

'Are you all right?' asked Kieran hopefully.

'Do I *look* all right?' She glared at the pig. It blinked back at her with innocent pink eyes. 'Bloody animal.'

'You keep your 'ands off my pig,' warned Ted Merriman, laying a protective hand on its snout.

'Don't worry, I wouldn't touch it with a bargepole.'

Owen Pendle shifted from one foot to the other. 'I think this may be partly my fault. Miss Snow, Mr Merriman, please.'

Ted Merriman glared from beneath bushy white eyebrows so massive that they looked capable of leading independent lives. ''Oo the bloody hell do you think you are?' he repeated. The pig peeked timorously round the side of his gumboots. 'Comin' in here like you own the place!'

'Actually,' said Pendle, 'she does. Miss Snow is Mary Willenhall's great-niece.'

The look on Ted Merriman's face spoke volumes, none of them suitable for inclusion in a respectable library. 'I don't care who she is, she's on my bloody land.'

'As a matter of fact,' snapped Claire with a sudden flash of temper, 'You're on mine.'

'I tell you what,' said Owen Pendle with the weakest of weak smiles. 'Why don't we all go inside out of the rain, and have a nice cup of tea?'

★

45

Lorna sat on the toilet and squinted down between her feet. 'Hey, guess what I've discovered? You're going to love this.'

Claire stood at the sink, trying desperately to coax a thin stream of rust-brown water out of the taps. She was muddy, she was cold, she was pissed off, and right now it was going to take something really amazing to impress her. 'I wouldn't bet on it.'

'Something's eaten right through this floor. If you sit here and look down, you can see into the kitchen.'

Faintly alarmed, Claire peered through the hole. She could see the top of Ted Merriman's head, instantly recognisable by the sort of coiffure that comes from sticking your fingers in a plug socket. If she angled her head to the left, she could just make out Owen Pendle and Kieran, sitting round the kitchen table making painfully polite conversation about the price of sprouts.

'Fascinating,' she admitted grudgingly, picking her way back to the cracked white sink across a floor that boinged ominously, like an under-sprung trampoline. She felt very slightly guilty about abandoning Kieran to Ted Merriman's mercies, but not nearly guilty enough to go downstairs and rescue him.

'Of course,' reflected Lorna. 'If you were sitting on the loo and there were people in the kitchen, they could look up and see your knickers. But then I guess certain people might quite like that.' She looked up. 'What do you reckon?'

'If you really want to know ...' Claire flicked mud-caked hair out of her eyes and recommenced battle with the taps. 'I reckon this whole place is a very bad joke. Somebody's set me up up for a TV docu-soap and any minute now a camera crew's going to burst out of that airing cupboard.'

Lorna brightened visibly. 'You really think so?'

'Oh yeah, and old Merriman's pig is really a two-headed alien from the fifth dimension. Of course I don't! Now, are you going to just sit there, or help me wash this filth off?'

'Well, all right. But don't get it all over my jacket, it won't wash out.'

Frankly, Paradise Cottage was worse than a bad joke. It was a disaster. You'd go a long way to find such a perfect specimen of decrepitude, and there couldn't be many houses with such a unique . . . ambience.

'He gives that pig the run of the house you know,' commented Lorna as they waited for the sink to fill. 'Says it's house-trained.'

'Yes,' retorted Claire. 'Trained to leave its trotter-prints all up the living room walls.'

'And what about the smell? Don't forget the smell.'

If only I could, thought Claire. Nice, twee little country cottages might smell of pot-pourri, freshly-brewed coffee or homemade bread. Paradise Cottage stank of Brucie the pig: an aroma so powerful that it seemed to follow you around on its own four legs.

'God, this water's taking ages,' commented Lorna. 'Have you tried the other tap?'

'I can't shift it.'

'Here, let me try. I'm brilliant with pickle jars.'

Lorna took a grubby towel, wrapped it round the tap and gave it an almighty wrench. Possibly she didn't know her own strength; or possibly it was just one wrench too many for the ancient plumbing. One minute there was a sort of juddering, glugging sound; the next, a funny grating noise as the entire tap snapped off its stem.

'Oh hell, Claire, I'm really sorry!'

It was one thing being stood on by a pig, covered in stinking mud and insulted by a man with no teeth. But being hit in the face by a vertical jet of freezing cold water was the absolute final straw.

All of a sudden Claire felt curiously detached from the disaster working itself out around her. Why the hell was she getting so worked up about all of this? As far as she was concerned, it had absolutely nothing to do with her.

She grabbed the towel and swabbed her dripping face. 'Right. That's it, I've had enough.' With a kind of Zen inevitability, the brass door knob came off in her hand as she

47

dragged the door open and stalked out on to the landing.

'Where are you going?' panted Lorna, bounding after her as she ran down the stairs, narrowly avoiding the cavernous hole between the fifth and sixth treads.

'I don't bloody care. Anywhere but this place,' replied Claire, making for the front door. 'And you can tell Ted Merriman he's welcome to it.'

In the warm, dry public bar of the Saxon Cross, with a large brandy and two packets of crisps, it was a lot easier to get things into perspective.

'Do you reckon Pendle'll sort everything out?' ventured Kieran, tongue-tip between his teeth as he engineered a tower of beer mats on the pub table.

'He'd better,' replied Claire. 'Because I'm not setting foot in that hovel again. Not without safety gear and an armed escort.' She yawned and leaned back against the windowsill. 'God, what a day.'

'What a *house*,' echoed Lorna, working steadily through her third gin and tonic. 'Look, I'm really sorry. About the tap and you getting soaked . . .'

'Oh, I've almost forgiven you.' Claire managed a wry giggle. 'But only almost. If you buy another round I might even forget about it.'

'Don't encourage her,' said Kieran. 'She's half cut already.'

'Cheek!' Lorna gave him a shove and the beer mats came tumbling down.

'So what are you going to do with the cottage then?' enquired Kieran, retrieving mats from under the table. 'Do it up and flog it, I suppose?'

'What with? I'm not made of money, and you saw the state of it.' She mused for a moment. 'I guess I'll just have to get a loan, tart it up as best I can and hope there's some lunatic out there looking for an investment.'

'A lunatic who doesn't mind a sitting tenant,' Lorna reminded her.

Claire groaned. 'Go on, tell me. I'm going to be stuck with that blasted heap for the next twenty years. I'll plough every penny I've got into it until I'm bankrupt, and Ted Merriman'll live till he's a hundred and forty-five.'

'That's right,' nodded Kieran. 'Look on the bright side.'

'And in the end I'll have to come and live in the damn thing because nobody wants to buy it.'

'Mmm,' grinned Lorna, draining her glass. 'What a lovely thought. You and Ted and Brucie, the perfect *ménage à trois*.'

'Oh puh-leeze.' Claire's gaze drifted to two men standing at the bar. Neither of them looked exactly local, or at least neither of them looked remotely like Ted Merriman. In fact the tall, dark-haired one in the designer casuals looked like he ought to have more sense than to bury himself away in a place like this. People were weird on the whole, she decided. Definitely weird.

She poked Lorna in the arm. 'Where's my drink then?'

'What drink?'

Kieran finished the first storey of his beer mat pagoda, and sat back to admire his handiwork. 'The round of drinks you just offered to buy.'

'I never did!' Two empty glasses slid themselves across the table-top. 'Oh all right, what are you having?'

'Same again,' said Claire. 'With ice and lemon.'

'And another bag of crisps, I suppose?'

'Nope.' A malicious smile spread over Claire's face. 'This time I think I'll have a very, very big packet of pork scratchings.'

Chapter 5

I must be stark, staring mad, thought Claire as she trudged along the Regent Arcade for the umpteenth time. Why else would I be wasting my precious Sunday morning traipsing round Cheltenham, trying to buy a present for Ted Merriman?

She knew the answer, of course. It was just that she didn't want to admit it. It was Lorna who had brought the truth home to her. 'Face it, Claire, even if you're going to drop Paradise Cottage like a hot brick, you're going to have to get that man on your side. Else how are you ever going to sell it?' Claire groaned inwardly. Lorna was annoyingly right, she *would* have to make her peace with Ted. She just wished it didn't mean eating such a big slice of humble pie.

Present-buying for Ted Merriman was a tough assignment, but the saleslady in Waterstone's went out of her way to be helpful.

'Pigs, madam?'

'Pigs, yes. Do you have any books about pigs?'

'Why yes, of course.' Thank heavens for that, thought Claire. My feet are killing me. The assistant bent down and produced something large and colourful from a dumpbin by the door. '*The Eeny-Weeny Cuddly-Wuddly Fluffy Pink Pig Book*, it's one of our bestsellers for the under-fives.' She lowered her voice. 'And of course it's wipe-clean too, for those little accidents.'

'Ah,' said Claire. 'I don't suppose you've got anything for

someone a bit more . . . well, older?'

'The over-sevens, you mean? There's *Mr Oink's Marvellous Magical Hat* – that was nominated for the Smarties Prize.'

'Well, actually I was thinking more of the over-seventies.'

'Sorry?'

And that was the end of that conversation. By half past twelve Claire calculated that she must have visited every shop in the High Street at least twice, even the hardware shop and the rather peculiar place that sold red nylon underwear. She was getting desperate. What *did* you buy for a man whose only interest seemed to be the fifteen-stone porker in his front room?

Then she thought of trying Past Times. They had presents for everybody, surely. But as soon as she set eyes on the silver-plated faux-medieval pig-shaped candle-snuffer, she knew it was definitely not Ted Merriman. She might as well give up, go home and forget all about Paradise Cottage.

Just as she was getting into her car, she remembered something Kieran had said. 'Bloody horrible things, pigs, can't stand 'em. Bright though. Mate of mine once trained one to sit up and beg.' Aha, thought Claire. So pigs are just like dogs. Now dogs she knew something about. She and Peter had shared a daft spaniel called Ajax when they were kids, and you never forgot the fun you had with your first dog.

Within twenty minutes she was queueing at the checkout in the pet superstore, buying a big bag of doggie chocs and a medium-sized rubber ball. If they didn't do the job, nothing would.

When she reached Lilcombe Magna, just before two, it had stopped raining completely. There was even a hint of mellow spring sunshine glinting off the heap of rusting tractor parts outside Paradise Cottage.

To say that the cottage looked better in the sunshine was fair comment; to say that it looked positively picturesque would be stretching a point too far. Even if you had surrounded it with pink fairylights and a choir of angels, it would still have been a

51

heap. Still, mused Claire, it was a start. And it was, after all, *her* heap.

She parked up and walked across the road to the front gate. Brucie the pig was squatting on his haunches under the sole surviving apple tree, scratching his ear with his back leg. He looked bloody enormous. When she caught the gleam in those little pink piggy eyes, Claire could have sworn he was laughing at her.

He caught sight of her and let out a grunt. She backed off a step. He lumbered to his feet. She gulped. He trotted over with little squeals of recognition. She fantasised about running away. He inspected her knees with his snout, through the bars of the gate. Remembering Kieran's advice about dogs, she forced herself to smile, leaned over the gate and waggled the rubber ball in his face.

'Who's a lovely piggy then?'

Grunt.

'Lovely piggy want to play, does he?'

Interested grunt.

She waggled the ball again, and the pig looked up at her with expectant eyes, its mouth hanging open and spit drooling out. There were an awful lot of teeth in that mouth. She tried not to think about them. Drawing her arm back, she flung the ball as far as her strength would carry it, and Brucie sped off across the mud-wallow of a garden with little oinks of ecstasy.

Bless you Kieran, thought Claire. Bless you for being agricultural. Before Brucie had even caught up with the ball, she was through the gate, up the path, into the porch and hammering on the front door. 'Mr Merriman? Mr Merriman, are you in there?'

After what seemed like about ten years, Ted Merriman appeared round the side of the house, braces dangling down over his saggy old corduroys. They were the kind of trousers you couldn't buy in any normal shop. Special old men's trousers: the kind that started just under the armpits and hung down in vast, grease-encrusted swathes. They might originally have been green or maybe even brown, but frankly it was anybody's guess.

'Urr,' said Ted, not a trace of expression showing on his unshaven face.

'Hello,' said Claire.

'What you doin' there?'

'I . . . er . . .' Come on Claire, she scolded herself. You can do it. You *have* to do it. 'I came to apologise. For yesterday.'

The expression – or lack of it – did not alter one iota. 'I don't use the front door,' he said. ''Cept to get the wheelbarrow through when I'm carting muck.'

'Oh,", she said. She tried to chase away the mental image of a barrowload of manure trundling its way through the cottage. 'I didn't realise.'

Ted snapped his fingers. 'Brucie? You come here now, you 'ear?' For the first time, a trace of warmth appeared on the craggy features. 'What you got there then?'

'Who? Me?' Claire turned round, following Ted's gaze. The pig was standing expectantly behind her, the ball clamped in its jaws, its ludicrous little tail wiggling furiously.

'Oh, the ball? I gave it to him,' she admitted, suddenly feeling rather foolish.

'Why?' demanded Ted suspiciously.

'As a present.' She produced the bag of doggie treats from her anorak pocket. 'And I got him these too.'

Ted took the bag and examined it minutely, suspended between a tobacco-stained thumb and forefinger. 'You can't give a pig these!'

'Can't you?'

'Lord no, probably poison the poor animal.' Opening the bag, Ted extracted a doggie choc, popped it into his toothless mouth and started sucking. Claire stared in horrified fascination, her stomach heaving. After a few moments he noticed her looking at him and held out the bag. 'Want one, do you?'

She took a step back, parrying with her hands. 'No thanks, I've just had lunch.'

Ted sucked on his doggie choc a while longer. His rheumy eyes looked her up and down with what looked like genuine fascination. 'Well I'll be darned. Mary's sister's girl.'

'No, that would be my mother. I'm Mary Willenhall's great-niece.'

'Are you now? Well I'll be . . . ' He sniffed and wiped his nose with the back of an arthritic hand. 'Not much to you is there?' He thrust the rest of the packet into his pocket.

'I was wondering,' said Claire. 'Could I come in for a few minutes?'

'Don't know what you're asking me for,' replied Ted, turning his back and trudging away towards the cottage. 'This whole place belongs to you now, don't it?'

Although she had already seen it once in daylight, the full horror of Paradise Cottage had not struck Claire until now.

As she followed Ted through the random straggle of rooms to the kitchen, she began to realise how many things there were that she'd been too shell-shocked to take in the first time. Like the two-inch gap between the staircase and the wall; the strange vegetation growing out of the hall floor; and the fact that half the electrical wiring seemed to be hanging out of the ceiling.

Claire felt suddenly sad as she sat down on one of Ted's wonky Windsor chairs. It wasn't just the awful ramshackleness of the place that shocked her, it was the terrible aura of neglect. A frail old man living alone in a broken-down old house he couldn't cope with. But to judge from the state of him, it was all he had in the world. And here she was, trying to take it all away from him.

'Mr Merriman,' she began.

'You'll take your tea strong? With two sugars?'

She sensed that it wasn't a question. 'Thank you,' she said, trying not to notice that something brown and wriggly was crawling up the wall behind Ted's head. Yeurgh, it was two inches long and it had legs. Lots of them. 'About yesterday . . . '

He went on spooning tea into what might once have been Great-Aunt Mary's best china teapot. 'You look like her,' he said abruptly, without turning round.

54

'I beg your pardon?'

'You look just like her. Mary. When she were young.'

'Do I?'

'Same nose see.' His tone was gruff, but there was emotion in it. He made a fourth attempt to light the gas, and Claire noticed that his knobbly red hands were so shaky that the match was nowhere near the gas jet.

'Can I help?' She was half out of her seat, imagining the whole house exploding, and Paradise Cottage becoming the first house in orbit. 'Shall I do that for you?'

'I can manage fine on my own.' He didn't look as if he was managing, but at the seventh attempt the gas spluttered into life and he hauled the kettle on to the ring.

She watched as two cups emerged from a cupboard over the stove; one was white with no handle, the other had flowers on but was cracked from top to bottom. Ted gave the floral one a rub on his trousers and put it in front of her. With a shock, Claire realised it was probably his best china.

'I suppose you'll be sellin' up now,' he said gruffly.

She squirmed under Ted's accusing gaze. 'I haven't made my mind up yet,' she lied.

Just as she was cursing herself for bottling out, the peace and quiet of Lilcombe Magna was shattered by the roar of furiously-revving engines, followed by a car horn blaring out the first few bars of 'Dixie'. Half a second later came the unmistakeable sound of a pig squealing at the top of its voice.

Ted froze and dropped the tea-caddy on the floor. 'Brucie!'

Claire got to her feet. 'What's wrong?'

But Ted didn't answer. He just grabbed a garden rake from behind the door and rushed out into the garden.

When Claire reached the front of the house, Brucie was cowering behind the old henhouse and three youths in a car were hanging out of the windows of a battered red Capri, hurling insults and anything else that came to hand.

'Oi, piggy piggy piggy!'

'Squeal little piggy!'

'Want a crisp, piggy? They're smokey bacon flavour.'

Ted advanced towards them, the garden rake menacing them with its three remaining prongs. 'You get off my property, you 'ear?'

'We ain't on your property, grandad.'

'Yeah. We're on the Queen's highway, ain't we? No law against a nice little Sunday drive, is there?'

'I said, get out of here an' don't come back.'

'You threatening me, grandad? Ooh, I'm really scared.'

Claire laid a hand on Ted's arm. 'Leave it, Mr Merriman, they're not worth it.'

The oldest of the three youths turned his gaze on Claire. 'Fancy a bit do you darlin'? Hop in, I'll take you for a ride.'

She returned his leer with a glacial smile. 'Sorry boys, I only date my own species.'

'Wot? You takin' the piss or somethin?'

'Come on Wayne, I'm bored. Let's go an' do over them allotments.'

The car roared away in a spray of brackish mud. Brucie's snout emerged from behind one of the outbuildings, sniffing the air to make sure that it was safe to come out.

'Bloody hooligans,' snarled Ted, shaking the rake at the retreating car.

'Who are they?'

'Townie yobs. Eric's mates.'

'Who's Eric?'

Ted looked at her, flummoxed. 'Eric,' he repeated. 'Eric what lives next door.' He glanced across the barbed wire that separated Paradise Cottage from a weed-fringed field. 'Your cousin Eric.'

Veronica Snow knew very few words of Portuguese, and the ones she did mostly amounted to 'hello sailor'. It was at moments like these that she wished she'd persevered with the language course.

'Duarte,' she called after the succulent naked body just disappearing over the bedroom balcony. 'Duarte, don't go, it can't be him – he's not due back till Thursday.'

As it happened, she was wrong and Duarte was right; it *was* him. Him being her second husband, Ronnie Callaghan, one-time Army middleweight champion and now owner of Callaghan's Golf Resort on the Algarve. He burst into the bedroom like Tyson coming out for round one, fists up, all guns blazing.

'Where is he, Veronica?'

She clutched the pure Egyptian cotton sheet to her modesty and tried to look coolly innocent. 'Where's who, darling?'

'That dago bastard you've been shagging. Where is he, I'll have his nuts for cufflinks.'

'I really don't know what you're on about darling, I was just having a lie-down, I think I've got one of my heads coming on.'

But she must have glanced towards the window and given the game away, because Ronnie lunged across to the French windows and reached the balcony just in time to see Duarte's naked buttocks vanishing into the driver's seat of a purple Mazda convertible.

Enraged as only a portly old has-been could be, Ronnie swung round and turned the full force of his displeasure on his wife. 'You slag! You disgusting, two-faced little . . .'

She winced. There was no denying it, the game was up. And he might be rich, but in the full force of the afternoon sunlight Ronnie wasn't much to look at. She remembered all the times she'd put up with his tedious jokes and his halitosis, and a mad impulse overtook her.

'Ronnie darling.'

'What?'

'Your toupee's on back to front.'

For a split second his face froze in horror, then he drew himself up with all the dignity he could still command, and pointed a quivering finger at the door.

'Out.'

She began to regret her quick tongue. 'Oh Ronnie, I'm sorry, I never meant . . . I mean, it won't happen again.'

'Too bloody right it won't,' he replied, wrenching open the bedroom door. 'This is the last time you make a monkey out of me, Veronica. Get out and don't bother coming back.'

Chapter 6

Maybe it was the general messiness of the place, or perhaps it was just the faint stench of well-rotted manure, but there was something about Low Common Farm that put Claire right off.

Mind you, she had never been mad keen on the country; not like her brother Pete. Never one for trudging through cowpats in a Puffa jacket and gumboots. And she'd certainly never seen herself owning a cottage in the middle of nowhere. Come to think of it, she'd never really thought about the future at all.

The farmhouse clung with squat determination to the side of a steep, stony slope. As a building it was practical rather than pretty, with small, deep-set windows and a low tiled roof that looked for all the world like a pair of scowling eyebrows. A line of wet washing flapped in Claire's face as she rounded the end of a row of outbuildings, and as she ducked her head to walk underneath it a piebald chicken fluttered out of the way. A new-looking tractor was purring in the yard but there was no sign of a driver. In fact the only signs of life were the chickens and a solitary brown cow, peering impassively at her over a stable door.

She negotiated the slippery cobblestones and made it to the front door. The lion's head knocker hammered against its mounting with a clatter that echoed all the way down the hill to the village, but nobody came to see who was at the door. She knocked again, then noticed a small, yellowed note sellotaped to the bootscraper.

TRADESMEN USE OTHER DOOR.

Other door? She looked around. What other door? Well, she wasn't a tradesman, but she could either stand here until she took root or go off in search of it. She picked her way round the side of the house, through the thin mulch of chicken-droppings, and walked full tilt into a dumpy middle-aged man in blue overalls.

'. . . and you can tell him forty a ton's my best offer . . . ' The two bodies collided. 'What the . . . ?'

'Excuse me,' said Claire, picking her handbag out of the mire. 'Are you Eric Willenhall?'

Thick fingers rubbed at a stubbly black beard, peppered here and there with silver hairs. 'Who wants to know?'

'Claire Snow.' She extended a hand but he didn't take it. 'I'm your new neighbour.'

A flicker of interest registered in the small, sly eyes. 'Oh yes?'

'My great-aunt was Mary Willenhall. I've just inherited Paradise Cottage.'

'Have you now? Well, well, well.' As if by magic, the last trace of surliness vanished, to be replaced by a mouthful of crooked teeth. He wiped a paw on his overalls and thrust it in her face. 'Geoffrey Willenhall, Eric's my son. So you're Veronica's girl are you?' He patted her on the shoulder like a favourite poodle. 'I should have known, pretty little thing like you.'

Ugh, thought Claire, stepping away. I think I preferred you surly. 'I felt I had to come and have a word with you,' she said, remembering why she had come. 'It's about Mr Merriman.'

'Ah,' said Geoffrey, nodding knowingly. 'Been having problems with old Ted have you? Can't say I'm surprised.'

'Actually it's more the problems he's been having with your son.'

Geoffrey slid an arm round her shoulders. 'Tell you what, why don't we go inside where we can be nice and comfy?'

Claire wasn't at all sure she wanted to be comfy with Cousin Geoffrey, or indeed have him anywhere near her, but if she was going to sort this out she didn't have much option. Reluctantly she allowed herself to be steered through a heavy oak door into a vast kitchen, where a short, spherical woman in a green striped pinny was standing at the sink, ill-temperedly scrubbing at a roasting tin.

'If that's Eric's new case-worker—'

Geoffrey cut her short. 'This is Claire Snow, dear.' The woman looked unimpressed and went on scrubbing. '*Cousin* Claire, Veronica's girl.'

'Oh yes?' The woman put down her Brillo pad and looked the stranger up and down.

'Claire's just inherited Paradise Cottage, isn't that interesting? Claire, this is my wife, Emmy.'

They shook hands. 'We're going in the front room, bring us a pot of tea,' said Geoffrey imperiously. 'And some of those bourbon creams.'

'You had the last of them yesterday.'

'Then send our Paula down the shop.'

'I don't want to put you to any trouble,' interjected Claire. But Geoffrey wasn't taking no for an answer.

'Nice pot of tea, Emmy. And the best china, mind.'

Emmy's parting glare could have turned a troll to stone.

'Well, well, this is nice,' said Geoffrey, rubbing his squat red hands together as he ushered Claire into the sitting room. 'Have a seat, make yourself at home.'

Nice? No, nice was not the word for the Willenhalls' front room, decided Claire. Loud, that was the word; with tacky and nauseating in hot contention for the runner-up spot. On the brown and orange swirled carpet were arranged four immense pink Dralon armchairs, squidgy as strawberry marshmallows. These clashed interestingly with the red flock wallpaper, straight from a curryhouse; the overmantel groaning with gilded plaster cherubs and limited edition plates of Princess Diana; and a Fifties-style corner bar, complete with highball glasses, naked lady cocktail stirrers and authentic black PVC quilting.

'Sweet sherry?' offered Geoffrey, pouring himself a large tumbler of Bristol Cream.

'No thanks.' Claire perched on the edge of her chair, terrified to sit back for fear of disappearing into its voluminous pink folds, never to be seen again. 'About your son Eric . . . '

'Go on,' said Geoffrey. 'What's he been up to now?'

She explained at length about the red Capri, and the gang of youths; about Brucie quivering behind the henhouse and poor old Ted Merriman, defending his pig's honour with a rusty garden rake. 'It won't do, Mr Willenhall,' she said sternly.

'Now, now,' he smarmed. 'Call me Geoffrey.'

'It really won't do . . . Geoffrey. Ted's an old man, that sort of harassment could give him a heart attack or something.'

Geoffrey strode across to the door, opened it and bellowed up the stairs. 'Eric!'

A faint reply floated down, just audible over the strains of 'Bring your Daughter to the Slaughter'. 'Wot is it?'

'Get your useless arse down here. This minute.' The farmer turned back to Claire with an apologetic smile. 'Pardon my French.'

A couple of minutes later a young man slouched into the room, hands thrust in the pockets of his tracksuit bottoms. He was short, squat, bullet-headed and the image of his mother.

'Wot you want now?'

Without warning, a meaty paw sliced through the air and fetched Eric a terrific smack on the head. He staggered sideways, clutching an ear. 'Ow! What's that for?'

'That's for threatenin' old Mr Merriman.'

'I never!'

'No, but your mates did.'

A look of puzzlement wandered across the broad, speckly face. 'But Dad, you said—'

'Never you mind what I said,' Geoffrey cut in hastily. 'Now get out and finish mendin' that fence, or you can wave goodbye to that new pair of trainers.'

The door crashed shut behind Eric with such a bang that a shelf of Staffordshire-style shepherdesses tinkled together like cowbells. Strange boy, thought Claire; he must be at least her own age if not older, and here he was, still living at home and begging his dad for a new pair of trainers.

'Easily led,' confided Geoffrey. 'But he's a good boy really. I don't care what that magistrate said.'

'I'll have to take your word for it.'

He settled himself in an armchair, dragging it nearer so that his knees were almost touching Claire's. 'So. Paradise Cottage, eh? Terrible state they've let it get into. Must be practically derelict by now.'

'Pretty bad,' admitted Claire, feeling stupidly disloyal to the old wreck of a house.

'I bet you can't wait to get shot of it,' mused Geoffrey, sipping his sherry. 'Mind you, it won't be easy, not with a sittin' tenant.' He chuckled. 'And old Ted's not exactly big on the social graces, is he?'

'Well, no.' Now she was feeling disloyal to Ted, too, and she didn't even like the old grouch. 'Actually I haven't decided what to do about the cottage yet, I'm going to think about it for a while.'

The door opened and a reedy-looking girl with straggly black hair and hunched shoulders came in with a tray. She didn't look at all comfortable with being the only tall, thin person in a family of garden gnomes. 'Mam says there's no more biscuits and you're to go easy on the milk.'

'Don't talk like that, Paula, we've got a guest. Say hello to your cousin Claire.'

Paula sniffed.

'Hello,' said Claire.

'Yeah, right.' Paula plonked a plate of buttered teabread on the arm of Claire's chair. 'The dog had the end off it but I cut off all the chewed bits.'

'Oh. Thanks.' Claire peered down at the brown speckly thing. 'Actually I'm not that hungry.'

'Run along, Paula,' said her father. 'Your cousin an' I have got important things to discuss.' He waited till the door closed, then leaned forward and gave Claire's knee a squeeze. 'Daft as a

63

brush is our Paula. Knows her way round a difficult calvin' though.'

'Excuse *me*.' Fuming, Claire twitched her leg out of Cousin Geoffrey's meandering hand.

'What for?' He looked genuinely puzzled.

'Oh, nothing. It doesn't matter.'

Emptying his sherry glass, Geoffrey set it down on the tray and poured out two extra-strong cups of tea. More tea, groaned Claire, wondering if she could get out of here alive before her bladder exploded. Handing her a cup, he sat back and crossed his legs. 'I won't beat about the bush, I want that cottage.'

She concealed her surprise with a mouthful of tea. 'Oh yes?'

'Plain fact is, I've been wantin' that bit of land for years, only your great-aunt was that stubborn she wouldn't hear of sellin' up.' He shook his head. 'I ask you, an old woman alone in a place like that, it made no sense at all.'

'She had Mr Merriman,' pointed out Claire.

Geoffrey laughed sarcastically. 'And how much use was he to her? I'm tellin' you Claire, she'd have been far better off sellin' to me and goin' into a nice home.' He offered a winning smile. 'But I can see you're not like her, you're a sensible girl. And seeing as you're family, I'll make you a generous offer. A *very* generous offer.'

She tried to keep things as pleasant as possible. 'Well, like I said, I haven't decided yet if I'm going to sell at all.'

'You won't get a better offer, I promise you that.' He patted her hand. 'Come on, what do you say?'

'I'll think about it,' she promised, forcing herself to nibble at the teabread. But inwardly she was thinking, sell to you, Geoffrey Willenhall? I'd rather stick a scorpion up my nose.

Early on Monday morning, just as Claire was stepping out of the shower, the telephone rang. She picked it up with a soapy hand.

'Claire Snow.'

'Geoffrey here. Cousin Geoffrey.' The voice was smarmy. 'I was wondering about Paradise Cottage.'

'Sorry,' she said, 'I haven't really had time to think about it yet.'

Then she put the phone down on him.

Lorna knew her latest script was good. The scripts she wrote were always good. It was just that other people couldn't spot talent if it jumped up and bit them.

Richard Craddock, manager of and major investor in the Jasper Kendall Theatre, sat behind his desk, listening with his usual good-mannered patience; but she could see he wasn't convinced. Reluctant to give up without a fight, she went for one last big push.

'I see it being like . . . like a cross between *Boogie Nights* and *The Rocky Horror Show*,' she enthused, miming the dance moves round Richard's filing cabinet. 'Only more Eighties, of course.'

'Of course.' One sandy eyebrow rose, hovered, and fell again.

'It's a good idea, Richard. In fact it's a great idea. You know it is. And there's a huge Eighties' revival right now.'

'I'm not saying it's a bad idea.' The manager fiddled doubt-fully with his fountain pen. 'You wrote the lead role for Worm, yes?'

She nodded emphatically. 'He'd be wonderful in it. Can't you see it, Richard? Shocking-pink Lycra and *lashings* of eye makeup?'

In spite of himself, Richard Craddock chuckled. 'Oh, I can see it all right, Lorna. I wish I couldn't. But what I'm asking myself is, is your show right for this theatre?'

She hopped up on to the corner of his desk. 'I don't know why you're even *asking* that question. It's going to be a huge hit! All you have to do is get behind it, give people a chance to see it.'

Craddock drew a doodle on his jotter. 'Have you actually discussed this with Worm?'

'Well, not exactly, but—'

'Then I think you should, I really do.' He stood up and walked across to the stationery cupboard, opened it and took out a box of paper clips. 'Do some more work on it, polish it up.'

'It *is* polished! I'm a good writer.' She followed him with despairing eyes. 'Richard, what's wrong?'

He dropped the paper clips on the desk and stood staring down at them, as though lost in thought. 'Nothing's wrong.'

'Oh come on.'

'I'm just tired, that's all.' He rubbed his eyes. 'Jenny's got the mumps and we were up all night with her, I didn't get much sleep.'

Lorna's frustration softened into sympathy. She liked Richard and his wife, and their little girl too. But she knew she was right, the show *was* a great idea; it was just her timing that stank.

'I'm sorry to hear that,' she said, gathering up her script and stuffing it back into the duffel bag. 'Poor little kid. Poor you! Be sure and ask Helen if there's anything I can do to help.'

'I will,' he promised, but she sensed that his attention had already drifted away.

When Lorna was gone, Richard contemplated the happy family photograph beside his desk diary. Put on a lavish new production by a novice writer? Not a chance, however much he might want to. Not with the Arts Forum and the local council both threatening to withdraw their subsidies. Not with all his savings uselessly invested in this theatrical dinosaur.

He picked up the photograph. Helen and Jenny were relying on him. Why on earth hadn't he just given in and become a dentist, like every other Craddock since the barber-surgeon who'd sawn off Nelson's arm? Now he and the Jasper were hurtling ever faster towards financial oblivion.

And there was damn-all he could do about it.

On Wednesday, Claire was just biting into a BLT baguette when the phone on her desk trilled into life.

'Operations Manager, can I help you?'

'Cousin Geoffrey here.'

'Sorry,' she said. 'It's really good of you to make the offer, but I still haven't made up my mind.'

*

It was April Fool's Day at Brockbourne Hall, and it showed.

Orion – the lead guitarist formerly known as Brent Lovelace – coaxed a pensive arpeggio out of his acoustic guitar. 'The way I see it is this, right? We're going to chase out all the evils of the Millennium, OK, and, like, welcome in the New Age of Universal Love.'

Carefully laying down his guitar, he slid nimbly off the boardroom table. In his pointy hat and yellow and black striped cloak, he looked like something out of *The Hobbit*. Claire exchanged looks with Alun Williams, the Entertainments Manager, willing him not to burst out laughing. To his credit, he simply smiled nervously and said, 'Oh?' in a slightly panic-stricken kind of way.

'So,' said Claire, doing her best to go with Orion's cosmic vibe, 'you see this Millennium solstice gig as a kind of major spiritual experience, do you?'

Orion's right arm described a high arc through the air above her head. 'The Age of Grace will descend,' he intoned. 'And the children will reunite with the Mother and her Divine Plan.'

Out of the corner of her eye, Claire could see that Alun was quivering with suppressed hysterics. But Orion was far too high on his own rhetoric to be offended. His voice dropped to a mystical whisper. 'And at last, *all things* shall be as one, in a state of eternal spiritual harmony.'

'Fascinating,' gulped Alun, grabbing his glass of water and draining it.

Orion smiled, relaxed and shook out his unkempt, yard-long hair. He was middle-aged and smelled of goats. Claire could hardly bear to be in the same room with him. A girl should not have to come face to face with her first schoolgirl crush; not twelve years on, when he'd turned into Bilbo Baggins's weirder brother, and definitely not without chocolate.

Somewhere out in the grounds of the Hall, a peacock screeched at the top of its voice. It was probably peeing itself laughing.

Alun cleared his throat. 'So ... er ... where exactly do I come in?'

Orion poked a spindly finger in his chest. 'You, my man, are the one who is going to make it all happen.'

'I am?'

Orion swished around the boardroom table, declaiming about ley lines and stellar coordinates, astral power nodes and the occult force of the Earth's vibrations. 'So you see, it's crucial, there's no other way.'

'I'm sorry,' said Claire, frankly baffled. 'I don't quite follow.'

The pagan megastar let out an impatient sigh. 'Look, sister, it's like the stone circle, right?'

'What stone circle?' demanded Alun.

'The one that used to be here. The one they destroyed back in the eighteenth century when they vandalised this place.' Seeing only looks of blank incomprehension, Orion jabbed a finger at the map of the Brockbourne estate on the boardroom wall. 'Here, see? It was even bigger than Stonehenge.'

Claire followed him over to the map. 'A prehistoric stone circle? What, there, in the middle of the car park?'

'Exactly there, my friend. And that's where you're going to rebuild it for the gig.'

'What!' exclaimed Alun, spluttering water down the front of his shirt.

'We'll put our stage up there, right in the middle of the stones. Think of the power, man! Course, it'll have to be an exact replica. You'll have to bring in the right kind of stones from the west of Ireland, and they'll have to be worked by hand, none of your circular saws an' that.'

Alun blanched. 'I can't do that!'

'It might be rather ... difficult,' agreed Claire.

Orion's smile froze to his face. 'Man, you're gonna do it or we're not even going to step out on that stage, you got that?'

Claire cursed the day Alun had ever thought of persuading Facade to play 'the biggest Millennium gig in the world – ever'. She forced herself not to lose her rag. 'But why?'

'Because the Mother wills it.'

'What about a polystyrene replica?' hazarded Alun. 'I'm sure we could make it look quite realistic.'

'I don't believe I'm hearing this! It's a holy stone circle, right? A *stone* circle. And that's what it's gonna be, OK?'

'Come on, Orion,' pleaded Alun. 'We can't build an enormous stone circle right in the middle of the car park, just for you!'

An expression of beatific radiance spread across Orion's face. 'Oh yes you can,' he said. 'And you know why? Because I'm Brent Lovelace, and come December I'll have fifty thousand free-spending As, Bs and C1s queueing at your gates, just to see me.'

On Friday, just as she was getting ready for bed, Claire had another call from Low Common Farm.

'How much?' She stifled a giggle. 'Oh Geoffrey, I'm sorry, I really am. But you'd have to put a nought on the end of that before I'd even think about it!'

Before he'd had a chance to protest, she put the phone down, and went back to wrapping up the woolly jumper in pink pig-patterned paper. Would Ted appreciate it? The hell he would; but he needed it.

And that was what mattered.

Chapter 7

'Dad?'

A crying child in the background muffled the voice on the other end of the line. 'Helen darling, I think Izzy needs changing again, you couldn't just ...? Thanks.' Then the voice sounded again, more clearly this time. 'Sorry, I didn't quite catch what you were saying.'

'It's me, Dad. Claire.' She cradled the receiver between chin and chest, and snuggled more comfortably on to the sofa. Through the little leaded windowpanes of her flat she could see right across the grounds of Brockbourne Hall, to the plumply-rolling hills with spring sunshine glinting on their fresh green grass.

'Claire, sweetheart, how are you?'

'I'm fine.'

'How's the job? Not bored with it yet?'

She ignored the tease. 'The job's fine. Dad, I've got some news for you. Great-Aunt Mary's died and left me her cottage.'

There was a short silence. In the distance, Claire could make out a young woman's voice, singing softly to a baby: 'Round and round the garden, like a teddy bear ...'

'Dad, are you still there? What do you think? Do you understand what's going on? What am I going to do?'

'Whoa, steady on, let me sit down. Say that again. Your mother's Aunt Mary's left you her *what*?'

'Her cottage. That's exactly how I reacted when the solicitor rang me up. I thought it had to be some kind of mistake, but it wasn't.' A tiny note of accusation crept into Claire's voice. 'I tried ringing you all last week, but you were never in.'

'Ah, no, well we wouldn't be. Sally and I took off for a few days in the Lakes, you know how it is when you both finally manage to get the same week off work. And of course, it was great for Izzy. She stroked her first moo-cow!'

Claire felt a twinge of jealousy, and immediately felt ashamed of herself for being so childish. Her father had brought her and Peter up for years and years, all on his own; why shouldn't he marry a girl two years older than his daughter and start a second family? Anyhow, on the couple of occasions they'd met, Claire had rather liked Sally; not that it was any of her business to pass judgement on her father's new wife. She was glad that he was happy, truly she was. It was just surprisingly difficult sharing Dad after all these years. Especially with a brand-new stepsister.

'That's nice,' she said, hoping he hadn't noticed her hesitation. 'Dad, can you explain any of this? Why would Mary Willenhall leave me her house? I don't even remember meeting her, at least, not really.'

She heard the rasp of fingers on stubble, and visualised her father rubbing his chin, the way he always did when he was working something out. Dad's chin sprouted stubble at a phenomenal rate; even at eight in the morning he had a five o'clock shadow. As little kids, she and Pete had always tried to wriggle out of his bristly bear hugs. Now she would have given anything for one of them.

'You definitely did meet her – but just the once, I think. Yes, that's right. Your mother and I weren't getting on very well. In fact we split up a few months later. Anyhow, I was keen to give things another go, so we left you and Peter with your Great Aunt Mary while we went away for the weekend.'

'Did you? I wish I could remember properly.'

'Turned out to be a waste of time in the end, of course. Mind you.' He laughed. 'The old girl was quite taken with you. Said

71

you were just like her when she was a kiddie, and twice as stubborn.'

'She never did!'

'Oh yes, that's one thing I do remember. And now she's gone, has she? That's sad. Still, I suppose she must have been getting on a bit.'

'Late seventies, the solicitor said. Do you remember anything else about her, Dad?'

For some reason she couldn't quite define, Claire was desperate to know something, anything, that might forge some link with her aunt. Being left Paradise Cottage was like being left the intimate diary of a stranger's life and being unable to decode a single word of it.

'Only that she didn't mix much with the rest of the family, not even the Willenhalls. And she was a widow, of course.'

'I thought she never married.'

'Oh, she was married all right, but he died young. The cottage was her husband's. After he died she kept it like a shrine.'

Claire could hardly believe what she was hearing. 'A shrine! Dad, the place is completely decrepit! The roof's falling in, there's stuff growing up the walls. You should see the state of it. In fact—'

A young voice called to her father on the other end of the line. 'We're right out of Pampers, darling. You couldn't . . . ?'

'Yes, of course. Just give me a mo, Claire's on the phone.'

'Oh, really? Say hello to her from me.'

In the distance, a door closed 'Sally says hello,' said Terry.

'I heard. Dad, about Paradise Cottage. Pete's coming down next weekend and we're going to look over it together.'

'Good idea,' approved her father. 'I always knew it'd come in handy, having a civil engineer in the family.'

'Yes, I'm sure it will when he qualifies, but Dad, why don't you come along too? To the cottage. I'd really value your advice.'

'Ah. I'd love to. The thing is . . .'

A small seed of desperation was germinating inside Claire's heart. She wanted this to happen much more than she ought to, much more than was reasonable; because if it happened, if Dad came, it would prove something vital to her.

'It'd be lovely to see you again, Dad. It's been ages.'

Terry gave a sigh. 'I know love, but the thing is, I've promised Sally we'll take Izzy up to Middlesbrough to see her parents next weekend, and you know what doting grandparents are like.'

'Oh,' said Claire. 'I see.'

'You do understand?'

'Yes. Yes, of course I do. No problem, it wasn't important. Next time, eh?'

'Next time, for sure.'

It was always next time, thought Claire. All those years he'd fought tooth and claw for her and Pete, being both Mum and Dad to them, and now, quite suddenly, he never seemed to have time for either of them any more. It was understandable, natural even; but not easy to accept, even when you were supposed to be grown-up and perfectly capable of sorting out your own life.

'Tell you what,' said her father. 'Take a photo of the cottage and send it to me. And keep in touch, OK?'

'OK.'

'Terry darling,' called the woman's voice, more tense now. 'I really do need those Pampers.'

'Just going. Got to go now, Claire, see you soon. Love you lots.'

'Yeah. Love you too.'

And she listened to the click as the line went dead.

At last the Russian trainees were packing their bags to fly back to Moscow; but Mattie Sykes was not the happiest of bunnies.

'Have you any idea how long it took me to track down that balalaika ensemble?' she demanded. 'In Gloucestershire? And all those blokes in furry hats?'

73

Claire tried to look sympathetic. 'Of course we have. But think. If you were on a training course in Moscow, would you want your leaving party to consist of fish and chips and Morris dancing?'

'I might,' said Mattie defensively.

'Get real Mattie,' boomed Mel. 'All those Russians wanted was to get rat-arsed, eat burgers and go shopping. Just like normal people. That's why they all pissed off to Birmingham for the day.'

'You call that normal?' commented Michael Tang, picking up his car keys and putting on his jacket. 'Some of us have more respect for our minds and our bodies.'

Three pairs of eyes watched him in silence as the door closed behind him.

'Wanker,' sniffed Mel. 'Who does he think he is? Always going on like he's better than everybody else.'

Mattie grunted. 'According to Michael, he is.'

'Only in his dreams.'

Claire shrugged. 'Well personally, I don't care what rubbish Michael comes out with, as long as he sticks to his management training courses and keeps his nose out of my job.'

Mel laughed. 'As if he'd lower himself. Can you imagine him running the lost children tent at the Country Fair? It'd be like C Wing at Parkhurst.'

Mattie leaned over her to press a button on the photocopier. 'I wouldn't know, I'm sure, I've never had the pleasure. But the Russians seem happy enough, I guess that's the main thing.'

'I'd forget the Russians if I were you,' advised Claire. 'We've got fifty timeshare salesmen arriving tomorrow, remember.'

A collective groan ran round the office.

When Claire clocked off it was well after seven. That was the problem with living on-site; it was much, much too easy to hang around doing overtime. Even when she got back to her flat and closed the door on it all, she always half expected the phone to ring with tales of overflowing drains and double-bookings in the banqueting hall.

What she didn't expect to find at the top of the stairs was a very drunk Russian, snoring on her doorstep; a lacy purple uplift bra dangling round his neck like a laurel wreath, Aston Villa baseball cap askew on his cropped brown thatch, pockets stuffed with cans of lager.

She stood and stared down at him, debating what to do and trying to remember his name. 'Mr . . . ' It came. 'Ulyanov?'

One eye blinked blearily open.

'Mr Ulyanov, are you all right? Shall I call your friends to help you back to your room?'

The other eye opened with a flick. 'No, not friends! They are not my friends.' A bear's paw of a hand clamped itself to Claire's leg. 'You are my friend, Miss Claire. You help me, yes?'

Oh no, thought Claire; he's completely pickled and maudlin with it. She smiled and – gently but firmly – unclamped Mr Ulyanov's fingers from her flesh. They promptly reattached themselves to the hem of her skirt. 'Mr Ulyanov, please.'

He used the skirt to haul himself to his knees. 'They say I must go back,' he said, in a gust of beery breath.

'To Moscow? Yes, that's right. You're flying back in the morning.'

The Russian shook his head so vigorously that his hat fell off. 'No, no, not go back. Not want to go back.' Doglike, the eyes appealed to her compassion. 'You help me stay, *da*? You get me asylum?'

'Mr Ulyanov,' she replied firmly, yanking her skirt free, 'I think you've had too much to drink.'

Another vigorous shake of the head. 'Not too much. Not drink enough to forget. Moscow, she have nothing for me.'

'I'm sure that can't be true,' protested Claire. Though from the look on Mr Ulyanov's face, it probably was.

'My wife, she run away with other man, a richer man, *da*? She take my children away, they hate me now because I am not rich. You understand, Miss Claire?'

Claire groaned inwardly. All she'd wanted was a nice hot shower and a plate of five-cheese tortellini, and instead she was copping for the contents of Mr Ulyanov's tortured soul. 'Come on,' she said, helping him to his feet and propping him against the doorframe like a carpet remnant. 'I think you'd better come inside and I'll make you a nice black coffee.'

Mr Ulyanov's mood did not lighten much, even with two mugs of Alta Rica and half a packet of digestives inside him. 'I not go home,' he insisted. 'I stay here.'

'But you can't,' Claire repeated patiently, waving his passport in front of his bleary eyes. 'Your visa expires next week.'

'I get asylum, yes? I fill in form. You help me.'

Her hand hovered over the telephone, debating whether to call Security now or let him sleep it off and preserve some vestiges of his dignity. He'd be bound to regret all this in the morning. And there was something terribly pathetic about this middle-aged Russian; something hapless that reminded her faintly of Ted Merriman.

'You don't really want to stay here,' she coaxed. 'You wouldn't like it. No, really, you wouldn't. It's not your home.'

Ulyanov's head sank slowly into his hands. He was slightly more sober now, but very morose. 'My wife ... my children ... It was not like this in the old days.'

'The old days?'

'Sometimes I think, the old days, they were not so bad. I was a young man, I was in the Party, I had respect. Now ...' He threw up his hands. 'Now I am nobody.'

'That's not true! Why would they send you here unless you had respect? Why spend all this money training you?'

He wasn't listening. 'In the old days ...' He wiped his nose on the purple lace brassière.

Claire leaned forward in her chair. 'You can't live in the past, Mr Ulyanov. You know you can't. You can't just run away from things and never face up to anything.'

Claire Snow, amateur psychologist, she thought as he slumped there on her sofa, head hanging down and shoulders hunched, looking for all the world like a dejected vulture. But then she thought, it's true. About the past. It screws us all up, one way or another. Either you're desperate to recreate it, or you're determined to rebel against it. Whichever way you pick, you're so busy looking back that you never manage to take a single step forward.

She thought about Dad and Sally and the new baby; and about Paradise Cottage and the old lady she scarcely remembered; and then about all the jobs she'd had in the six years since she left school. Living in the past. Was that what she was doing too? Was she going backwards or forwards, or just standing still?

When she looked back at Mr Ulyanov, she saw that he had nodded off. So she took a blanket off the bed and laid it over him. Security could wait. Things would look completely different in the morning.

There were only fifty-six people in the audience for the opening night of *Cabaret*. And one of them was a staff photographer from the *Courant*.

They weren't exactly heading for a box-office record. But the show might still have gone well, if it hadn't been for Glyn Marchant, a teenage heckler and two dozen choc ices.

Afterwards, Lorna could recall every detail with painful clarity. There she was in the chorus line, hoofing across the back of the stage in her fishnets, thanking providence for giving her good legs and ample bosoms – and the show was going OK. Not great, but OK. Sixteen more bars to the interval and Glyn was mincing, flouncing and pouting fit to bust. In fact, if anything he was overdoing it. Perhaps she'd misjudged him; in all fairness, he wasn't making a bad job of being camp. Not as good a job as Worm would have made, naturally, but still.

It was just as she reached extreme stage right and started high-kicking back the other way that she heard the heckling start.

'Bloody pooftah! Look at 'im!'

A nervous titter ran round the auditorium. The leading man froze for a second, nailed his smile back on to his face, and carried on.

Then kids started whistling in the front stalls. 'Get off, you fuckin' useless fairy.'

One thing Glyn Marchant did not take well was criticism. Any kind of criticism. Something must have snapped inside him the moment the first of the choc-ices bounced off his brilliantined head. By the time the fifth and sixth were scudding through the air, he was vaulting off the stage with a face like Armageddon.

'Come here and say that, you little . . .'

There was a high-pitched adolescent squeal as Marchant ploughed into the audience in search of blood. Worm, hamming it up on stage as a club piano player, leapt off the stool in alarm, slipped on a melting choc ice, and toppled into the orchestra pit, knocking himself out on the timpani.

From that moment on, things could only get better. Except, of course, that they didn't.

Lorna pressed the telephone receiver very hard to her ear and shouted down the line. The corridor outside the dressing rooms was not a great place to have a phone conversation, especially not after tonight's performance. The place was in uproar. 'You're sure it's not concussion?'

Worm's voice came back faint and reedy. 'I told you, I'm fine.'

'You don't sound fine.'

'I'll just have a bit of a bruise, that's all. What's going on down there? It sounds like the Brixton riots.'

Lorna glanced over her shoulder. An aggrieved parent had found his way into the 'star' dressing room and the sounds of thumping were floating through the door. 'I think Glyn's having full and frank discussions with that man in the donkey jacket.' She winced as something heavy rebounded off the dressing-room wall. 'Still, it's his own fault.'

'What's all this about him walking out on the show?'

'Oh, if you ask me he just jumped before he was pushed. I mean, face it darling, Richard would have to sack him now, wouldn't he? You can't go throttling the punters.'

'Unfortunately.'

'Worm!'

'Oh come on, don't tell me you haven't been tempted. Hang on.' There was a sound of scrabbling. 'There, that's another twenty p. Are the police down there then?'

'Not any more. The *Courant* took a photo though, I flashed my legs in the background.' She allowed herself a dirty chuckle. 'Look on the bright side. You're Glyn Marchant's understudy. They'll have to let you play the lead now!'

Worm grunted. 'Assuming there's still a show to play the lead in.'

'Of course there is! We're booked in for a six-week run. Look, sit tight where you are. I'll come and fetch you in a taxi as soon as I've got changed, OK?'

'A taxi? Oooh, I must concuss myself more often.'

'Don't get too excited, you're paying.'

Lorna put down the phone and walked back towards the chorus dressing room, which was even smaller than it looked from the outside, a bit like a Tardis in reverse. She was about to go in when, on impulse, she turned round and walked back in the opposite direction, towards the theatre manager's office.

If Glyn Marchant really was jumping ship, someone was going to have to play his part; and she was going to make damned sure that someone was Worm.

The door of Richard Craddock's office was ajar. And Lorna Walsh had always been the kind of girl who listened at keyholes. Not that she had to, because she could hear the voices from halfway down the dingy, brown-emulsioned corridor.

'That bloody fool Marchant.' Lorna recognised the voice instantly. It belonged to Jos Reeve, one of the theatre's trustees. 'What the hell did you think you were doing, taking him on?'

Richard's voice now, quieter, more defensive. 'I told you, we agreed . . . we needed a big name.'

'A big name, Craddock, not a washed-up old has-been. Didn't it occur to you to ask why the TV studios sacked him?'

'He was the best we could afford, Jos. We had to take the gamble and you know it. And now he's let us down.'

'Let us down? It's a bit more than that, Craddock. The front-of-house people tell me every single person who bought a ticket for tonight has been demanding a refund. And when the story hits the local paper tomorrow . . .'

'Yes,' said Richard quietly. 'I know. Marchant's ruined our last real chance to make the Jasper work. Nobody knows that better than I do – I have most of my capital tied up in this place, remember?'

A long, apologetic sigh. 'I'm sorry Richard, I'm not blaming you. But you and I both know it's only a matter of time now. How long do you reckon we can keep this place staggering on?'

'A few months, maybe. If we put everything into it. But we have to be realistic, Jos. The Jasper Kendall Theatre is dying on its feet.'

It was six o'clock on Sunday morning, but Lorna couldn't sleep; which was hardly surprising, given the circumstances.

In the flat below, Candy was reaching the heights of ecstasy for the fifth time that night, with frantically-squeaking bed-springs and a climactic scream that sounded exactly like a smoke alarm going off. As if that wasn't bad enough, in the room above hers Stuart, the eskimo-faced Geordie Buddhist, was setting about his morning devotions. As this involved meditating to a CD recording of a steam train crossing the Andes near Ojos del Salado, there was little chance of a lie-in.

She got up, walked across to the window and opened the curtains. It wasn't as if she felt like sleep anyway. It was still dusky blue outside, but in the garden below Mr Papajian the landlord was arguing with one of his peculiar cronies, the two men lit like thieves by the light spilling out of the ground floor kitchen.

Tea. That was what she needed. And gin. Not necessarily in that order. Maybe she'd make Worm a cup too, and take it to him in bed. As she put the kettle on to boil, she wondered how he'd take to being woken at six o'clock on a Sunday morning. Hopefully, with good grace.

After all, they had a theatre to save.

Chapter 8

Worm was not having any of it.

'This crackpot idea of yours isn't going to work,' he warned Lorna as they sat eating breakfast in the downstairs kitchen. 'And you know that as well as I do.'

'All I know is, you've practically given in before we've even started,' retorted Lorna, defiantly crumbling a chocolate flake on to her muesli. 'As per usual.'

Worm chewed on the end of a croissant. 'That's not true,' he insisted with infinite patience. 'I'm just being realistic. And face it, somebody has to be. This isn't Hollywood, you're not Judy Garland and I am definitely not Mickey Rooney.'

'So?' challenged Lorna, fetching an opened bottle of wine from the fridge and pouring herself a mugful. So what if it was early, she told herself; she had to keep her strength up.

'So you can't just warble, "Hey, let's put on a show!" and expect everything to turn out right. Two people do *not* make a difference, Lorna. They just end up signing on at the dole office.'

'That's complete and absolute bollocks,' replied Lorna sweetly. 'If you want something enough, you just have to get off your backside and make it happen. That's the power of positive thinking.'

'Nope, it's just the power of your over-active imagination.' He crossed his arms forcefully. The body-language translated as:

'Don't bullshit me, Lorna' in foot-high capitals. 'The best we can do now is revive the old magic act.'

Lorna's face crumpled round a mouthful of muesli. 'Aw, Worm!'

'You heard. We dust off the old routines, get out on the streets and start busking again.'

Lorna's jaws started working at double speed. 'No, no, no, no, no.'

'Why not?'

'The magic act? After what happened that time with the guinea pig?'

Worm dunked his croissant in lukewarm coffee. 'Forget about that, Lorna.'

'I doubt the guinea pig will.'

'And forget the guinea pig. If the Jasper's going to close . . .'

'We don't know that for sure,' she reminded him.

He gave a sceptical shake of the head. '*When* it closes and they chuck us our P45s, we're going to need money, and quick. You can write us some new routines, and I'll polish up a few more tricks. It's either that or go back to working in the all-night burger bar.'

Lorna stood up, flicking crumbs off her dressing gown. With Worm's endless legs still tucked under the kitchen table, it gave her a rare height advantage. 'I am not freezing my assets off on some street corner in that leopardskin leotard,' she said firmly. 'And if you think I'm going back to work in that greasy—'

The kitchen door opened and a girl walked in. Completely naked save for the briefest of blue bathtowels, Candy cut a petite but arresting figure. And she richly deserved to be arrested too, thought Lorna; after last night's shameless exhibition.

'Morning.' With the most artless of smiles, Candy padded over to the fridge and took out a plastic bottle of chocolate milk. Two silent gazes followed her as she padded back across the kitchen, closed the door softly behind her and headed upstairs to her room.

'She was at it again last night,' commented Worm, resuming his breakfast.

'I heard.'

'Oh. You too?'

Lorna laughed drily. 'If you were stone-deaf with a bag on your head you could hardly help hearing Candy. You could use that girl as an air-raid siren.'

Worm munched reflectively. 'Adam again, wasn't it?'

'God knows, I've lost track.'

'Come to think of it, I thought I heard her shout out 'Charlie' when she, you know – or was that last Saturday?'

'Search me.' Lorna's spoon made circles in her muesli. 'Have you noticed something?'

'What?'

'You never see them leave, do you? Do you reckon she murders them and hides the bodies under the floor?'

'Probably. Or turns them into Irish stew. Lorna ...' She looked up. 'You can't save the theatre on your own, you do *know* that, don't you?'

She smiled and patted him on the head. 'Who says I'll be doing it on my own?'

'Hi,' gushed the local DJ. 'This is Scott Duprez with more magical Monday morning sounds on Chelt FM.'

Claire groaned, rolled over, jabbed for the off button on her radio alarm. And missed. The radio burbled on.

'... and today I'm in the *hot* seat with Dr Ellie Day, because this morning we're talking about ...'

'Piles,' interjected a woman's cultured voice.

'That's right listeners, it's the Haemorrhoid Hotline with Dr Ellie Day. And our next caller, on line two, is?'

'Lorna,' said a voice that had Claire sitting bolt upright in bed. 'Lorna Walsh.'

'And do you suffer from haemorrhoids, Lorna?' asked the melodious female voice, dripping with sisterly compassion.

'Er, no.'

'But you have a friend who does, right?' interjected Scott Duprez.

'Well no, I don't. Or at least, I do, but Worm'd kill me if I mentioned his name on the radio. Actually, I'm an actress at the Jasper Kendall Theatre. In *Cabaret*.'

Scott Duprez's voice took on an edge of genuine interest. 'Really? So you were there the other night when . . . ?'

'Yes. But that's not why I'm calling. I just thought your listeners might like to know I'm offering a free snog to anyone who comes to see the show.'

'Sorry?'

'A snog, Scott. A free kiss from a hot babe in fishnet tights. Got that?'

'Oh. Right. Well, listeners, remember: you heard it first on Chelt FM!'

'Actually no,' admitted Lorna breezily. 'I've just been talking live on Severn Sound.'

'Thank you caller. And on line three . . . '

It was a great marketing idea, but even Lorna had to admit it wasn't having quite the immediate impact that she'd hoped. On Monday evening there were barely three dozen in the audience at the Jasper, most of whom were middle-aged and female, and half the cast weren't talking to her. It was a real bummer.

Just as she was preparing to go home after the show, a head popped round the dressing room door. It belonged to Charisse, the assistant stage manager.

'There's somebody waiting for you. At the stage door.'

Lorna pricked up her ears. 'Who? Is it press?'

'Dunno. But it looks like you've got yourself a fan club.' With a giggle, she was gone.

Lorna put on an extra lick of red lipstick, checked the seams in her fishnet tights and tarted up her hair before she set off for the stage door. You never could tell, this might be the big photo opportunity that would launch her into international superstardom, like Liz Hurley and *that* dress.

Or on the other hand, it might turn out to be a greasy-looking saddo in an anorak, clutching the sort of cloth cap popularised in Hovis adverts. He was already puckering up before she'd got within ten yards of him.

'Hello darling,' he gurned. 'I've come for me free snog.'

On Tuesday afternoon, just before Lorna set off for the theatre, the phone rang.

'Hi Claire!' trilled Lorna, wafting her wet red nails in front of the storage heater. 'How's the house from hell?'

'Don't ask,' replied Claire. 'And I didn't phone you to talk about houses. I've just seen the *Evening Courant*.'

'Oh yes? Anything good in it?'

'Don't you play the innocent with me, Lorna Walsh. You do *know* you're all over page five, snogging a man in an anorak?'

'What, I only made page five?' Lorna let out a small 'tch' of disappointment. 'Still, at least they used the photo. Worm!' she bellowed down the hall, 'the photo's in the paper!'

Worm's unenthusiastic reply floated through the open door to the TV room. 'Oh whoopee.'

'Go out and buy me a copy will you?'

'Buy one yourself.'

'Don't take any notice of him,' counselled Lorna. 'He's just sulking because I won't go out busking with him.' She sat down on the ancient leather pouffe next to the telephone, and a small thweep of musty air escaped from its punctured sides. 'Did you hear me on the radio yesterday? Fab, wasn't I?'

'Lorna,' said Claire, 'half of Gloucestershire thinks you're a dodgy escort service, and the other half thinks you've got piles. Exactly how is that fab?'

'Don't go all snotty on me. At least people have heard of the Jasper now. And you know what they say – there's no such thing as bad publicity!'

'Lorna sweetie,' replied Claire with humour, 'whoever they were, they were lying.' She switched the phone to the other ear.

'Listen, you know we're going bowling on Sunday night?'

Lorna frowned. 'Don't you *dare* cry off!'

'I'm not. I just wondered if you'd mind somebody else coming with us.'

'Who?' Lorna checked her nails for tackiness. 'Kieran?'

'No. Ted.'

Lorna almost dropped the receiver. 'Ted Merriman! Good God darling, I know you've always fancied older men, but don't you think you've gone a bit far this time?'

'Oh shut up. You know I need to butter him up a bit if I'm going to get anywhere with doing up the cottage, and I can't exactly take him to a posh restaurant, can I?'

'Well, all right,' conceded Lorna. 'But only if Worm can come too.'

Claire had been hoping she wouldn't suggest that. Worm had been banned from every bowling venue for miles around. 'If Worm comes,' she protested, 'we'll have to go all the way to Swindon!'

'It's not his fault he's accident-prone!'

'Hmm. But this time, just make sure you tell him to bowl *under*arm, OK?'

On Thursday lunchtime, Richard Craddock hauled himself across to the Cotswold Cantina.

'It's got to stop, Lorna,' he said, perching on the stool next to hers.

'What has?'

'You know what, Lorna. This nonsense about giving a free kiss with every ticket.'

Her chin jutted stubbornly. 'I've got the Jasper into the papers, I've got us on to local radio, what more do you want? Everybody in Cheltenham's talking about the show.'

'True,' Richard agreed. 'But for all the wrong reasons. I know you're only trying to help, but it can't go on. It's a gimmick, it won't do anything to save the theatre in the long term, in fact all it'll do is turn us into a laughing stock.'

Lorna grunted. 'As if we aren't already.'

The theatre manager nodded sadly. 'Yes, yes, I know. That business with Glyn Marchant . . . But if you persist in doing this kind of thing, it's only going to make things worse in the end. I want you to promise you'll stop.'

'What – right now? Today?'

'Well . . . soon.'

For a moment she almost turned round and said no. Why should she give up, just because he wanted her to? So what if she was an embarrassment to the theatre trustees? There'd be no theatre to be a trustee of, if somebody didn't take a chance and do something radical.

'All right,' she capitulated. 'I'll give up the kissing thing, it's pretty disgusting anyhow. But I'm not just going to sit around waiting for you to close us down, you do realise that?'

He smiled. 'Oh yes, Lorna. I do.' And she got the distinct impression he was glad.

Claire's life had always seemed so straightforward in the past. How on earth had she allowed it to get into such a tangle?

As she waited in the darkened car park at the railway station, she thought about Lorna and her one-woman crusade to save a grotty old theatre. OK, so maybe her own life wasn't quite as bizarre as Lorna's, but it was getting that way. One minute you were comfortably bored and wondering whether to change jobs yet again; the next, your life had turned itself into a mad muddle of mysterious bequests, decrepit tenants and derelict cottages.

Well, it wasn't going to stay muddled for much longer; because she was going to roll up her sleeves and sort it out. With a little help from Pete.

A distant rattle and a distorted voice on the tannoy announced that the Derby train had just pulled in. Claire cleared a patch of misted windscreen and peered out at the herd of bodies streaming out of the front entrance to the station. Was that him? No, too tall; and he'd die rather than wear trousers that colour. What about . . . ? No. Or even . . .

A staccato rap on the passenger window made her jump so high she banged her head on the sunroof. 'Pete!' She leaned across and unlocked the door. 'You nearly gave me a heart attack,' she said with mock reproach, not quite managing to conceal how pleased she was to see him again.

He grinned broadly and flung himself into the car, lobbing his rucksack on to the back seat. Pete was in almost every respect a blonder, wirier, masculine version of herself: or, as their father used to say, five foot six with an eight foot personality.

'I dodged out the back entrance,' he explained, giving her a hug and a fraternal peck on the cheek. 'It's much quicker. Ooh, same car?' he teased. 'I don't believe it! I thought you bought a new one every time you changed your vest.'

She turned on the ignition and eased out of the parking space. 'I've told you a million times, don't exaggerate,' she joshed, poker-faced. 'And the last time I wore a vest was on that school trip to Aviemore – do you remember?'

Pete grimaced. 'Don't remind me. I fell off the dry ski slope and you got measles. And Dad had to come and fetch us both home.'

'Hmm. Some skiing holiday that turned out to be!'

They drove along in companionable silence for a mile or two. 'Anyhow,' said Claire, 'I can't afford a new car, not with Paradise Cottage hanging round my neck.'

Pete tutted and rolled his big blue eyes. Baby blue, thought Claire; no matter how old and venerable he might get, Pete would always be baby brother to her.

'I ask you,' said Pete. 'Talk about ungrateful. Some of us'd give our right arms to be left a cute little country cottage.'

'Not this one you wouldn't,' advised Claire, braking for a red light. 'Anyhow, Great Aunt Mary did leave you something.'

Pete pricked up his ears. 'Hey, top, what is it?'

She tapped the side of her nose. 'Just you wait and see.' The lights changed and they drove on. 'By the way, Paradise Cottage is definitely *not* cute.'

'No? So what's Dad got to say about it then?'

Claire's face fell. 'He hasn't.'

'He's not coming with us?'

She shook her head. 'They're taking Izzy to Middlesbrough to see her gran.' She forced a smile. 'Still, what do I need Dad for, when I've got my own personal civil engineer?'

Pete returned her smile with one of his characteristically cheeky grins. Even at twenty, he still smirked like a naughty six-year-old. 'That's all very well, but I'm a penniless student. I shall want paying, you know.'

'Oh yes? What in?'

'Biscuits. It's no good hiding them from me, sis, I know they're in here somewhere.' He popped open the glove compartment, rummaged around and emerged with half a packet of Jaffa Cakes. 'Aha, gotcha! Thank God, I'm starving. Those railway sarnies don't even touch the sides. Anyhow, it can't be that bad,' he went on through a spray of crumbs.

'What can't?'

'Paradise Cottage.'

'Oh no?' Claire smiled grimly as she pointed the car's nose towards Brockbourne Hall. 'Say that when you've seen it.'

'I aren't never been bowlin' before,' observed Ted as they walked towards the wooden shed at the back of Paradise Cottage. 'S'pose it's just like in *The Flintstones*, is it?'

Claire smiled. She hadn't known Ted long but she was getting used to his obsession with television – *any* television. As a handyman Ted might be only marginally better than a squad of demolition contractors, but the TV set was one appliance guaranteed to be in perfect working order.

'A bit,' she agreed. 'But without the bronto ribs. I'm sure you'll enjoy it.'

The door of the shed was standing ajar. Ted dragged it across the muddy ground, letting in the watery afternoon light. 'There you are,' he said, with a nod towards the interior. 'Just the way she left it.'

'Sis,' protested Pete, sneezing as dust blew into his face, 'that's not a car, it's a chicken coop.'

As if to confirm the definition, a russet-coloured bantam fluttered out through the old banger's shattered windscreen. The car had obviously been sitting in the rickety shed for years, and it was not a pretty sight. Clouds of dust swirled around the rust-pitted bodywork, and there were wisps of straw sticking out of the shattered headlamps.

Ted sprang to its defence. 'Nineteen fifty-three Riley that is, best car I ever drove.'

Pete scratched his head. 'I thought it was Aunt Mary's.'

'Arr, so it were, an' now it's yours.' The old man's eyes misted over. 'Used to take her on outings in it, so I did. Till she took bad.' He patted the bonnet affectionately and two more squawking chickens scurried out of the open door. 'You're a lucky man, Mr Snow.'

Pete didn't look too convinced, but Claire dug him in the ribs. 'Oh. Yes. Right,' he said, as the wing mirror snapped off in his hand.

'You can do it up,' said Claire, smiling encouragement at her brother. 'You could do with a hobby.'

'A hobby!' He laid the wing mirror gingerly on the front passenger seat and stepped back. 'That's one word for it. Well.' He rubbed cobwebs off on his trousers. 'Suppose I'd better get on and take a look at the house then.' He turned round and set off towards the bottom end of the garden. 'Those outhouses all belong to the cottage, do they?'

Ted took a protective stride towards the largest of the stone outbuildings, a squarish, single-storey structure that looked in distinctly better condition than the cottage. 'That's my private workshop, that is.'

Claire took Pete by the elbow and towed him away. She knew better than to separate a man from his shed. 'Let's start on the cottage. And don't pull any punches, OK?'

Dad was right, thought Claire as she stood watching Peter leap all over Paradise Cottage like a labrador pup. It was useful having a trainee civil engineer in the family. But at this precise moment, it was also extremely depressing.

Any fool could tell that there were bits of ceiling missing, and that the staircase really ought to be joined to the wall rather than death-defyingly suspended in mid-air. But it took Pete's trained eye to spot the subtler horrors, like the massive colony of earwigs lurking under the kitchen draining board, or the small tree growing up through the middle of the gas meter. Claire was grateful to Pete, of course she was; but every new discovery added a few more noughts to the totaliser running in her head.

'What's he doin' with that thing?' demanded Ted, as Pete jabbed a six-inch probe into the living-room wall.

'I'm measuring the damp,' he replied cheerfully, as the probe sank right through the plaster and the needle on the display unit whizzed into the red zone. 'Mind you, I don't know why I'm bothering, it's right off the scale.'

'Off the scale? What's that mean?' demanded Ted.

'It means it's no wonder you've got bronchitis, Mr Merriman. What with rising damp, and all that black fungus growing up your walls.'

'Ted,' said Claire when Pete went off to test the upstairs floorboards, 'I think you and I need to have a little talk.'

Ted's tufty eyebrows slid down like shutters over his narrowed, suspicious eyes. 'Talk about what?'

'About you. And this place.' Claire allowed herself a silent prayer to the patron saint of lost causes as her eyes roamed over the rotting plaster, the enamel bucket strategically placed under the hole in the roof, the spongy windowframes that crumbled like fruit cake if you so much as looked at them funny. 'Ted, I really don't think you can go on living here.'

The deep-set eyes blazed accusingly. 'I'm a sittin' tenant, I got my rights.'

'Yes, I know you have. I'm not trying to throw you out, really I'm not, but ...' Come on Claire, she urged herself; you're supposed to be good at this people stuff. Stop making things so difficult for yourself, just spit it out. 'What I'm trying to say is, this place just isn't fit for human habitation.'

'I'm not budgin',' said Ted. 'I've lived here all these years an' I've bin all right, I'm not shiftin' at my time of life.' His words ended in a cough that sounded like lava bubbling up from an undersea volcano.

'Please Ted, listen,' begged Claire, producing a handful of paper tissues from her pocket and stuffing one into his fist. If Paradise Cottage was ever going to be less than disgusting, Ted was going to have to stop using every available bit of floor-space as a spittoon. 'It's not that I want you to leave, it's just that this place isn't healthy for you. Not until it's done up, anyway.'

From overhead came the ominous sound of wood cracking as Pete tried out a few experimental bounces on the bedroom floorboards. Puffs of plaster dust floated down from the ceiling on to the shoulders of Claire's red rugby shirt, and she sneezed into a tissue. Oh please, she prayed, don't let the whole lot give way.

'I'm all right,' Ted insisted tetchily. 'There's nothin' wrong with me.'

'Of course there's something wrong,' she insisted. 'This house is making you ill. Please try and understand. All I'm trying to do is work out what to do for the best.'

'What's best is just to leave me be.'

'I can't do that Ted, surely you can see that.' His expression closed in even more. 'Look, I'm no expert but I can tell it's going to cost a lot of money to put this place right. And I don't have a lot of money. It may turn out that I can't afford to do it, at least, not all at once.'

'Lick of paint, that's all this place needs. Bit of new lino, couple of slates on the roof here an' there. I'll do the job myself, soon as the weather gets warmer.'

'Don't even think about it!' The thought of Ted Merriman clambering about on the roof of Paradise Cottage inspired nothing short of terror. 'I'm afraid it won't work, Ted. This place needs plasterers and plumbers and electricians . . . all sorts.

And if it turns out that I can't afford to pay for them, I'll have no choice. I'll have to sell up.'

She knew he'd take it badly. His head sunk on to his chest. 'You've made your mind up, haven't you? You're goin' to get some lawyer to throw me out on the street. Well get on with it then, I've no money to fight you.'

'No, Ted, you've got it all wrong.'

'You reckon so? Well the way I sees it, it don't matter what words you use, I'm still going to lose my home. I might as well go an' lay myself down in a ditch right now, an' die.'

She placed a hand on his arm. It felt very thin and cold and bony through his shirt and she wondered why he wasn't wearing the nice new Arran sweater she'd sent him. Perhaps he'd been offended by the gesture. It was so difficult to know what was the right thing to do or say where Ted was concerned. Up above her head, Pete was wandering about with his dictaphone, whistling to himself and muttering something about infestation.

'What I've got in mind,' she explained, 'is to do this place up as best I can, sell it for the best price I can get, and give you half of whatever profit I make.'

Ted's head shot up. 'What you say?'

'I think you should have half the profit, Ted. I'm sure Great Aunt Mary would have wanted you to be looked after.'

Ted turned crimson to the lobes of his huge, wrinkly ears. 'You'd give me *money?*' His eyes lit up like Blackpool Illuminations.

'It's only fair. After all, I can manage without it. But we would need to come to some arrangement while the cottage was being sorted out.'

A sudden weight leaned itself against the backs of Claire's legs, and reinforced its presence with sotto voce grunting.

''E's taken to you, has that pig,' said Ted. She wasn't sure if it was a compliment or an accusation.

She reached down to give the pig's back a cautious scratch, but to her surprise her fingers encountered not bristles, but wool. Looking down, she saw with horror that the very Arran sweater she had sent to Ted as a present was stretched grotesquely across Brucie's barrel chest.

'Ted!' she exclaimed, staring down at the distended pullover, its sleeves concertina-ing down the pig's forelegs. 'What have you done!'

'What? Oh arr, the sweater. Had to stretch it a bit like, but I got it on him in the end. Nice an' warm it is an' all.'

'But I bought that jumper for you!'

'For me?' Ted looked first stunned, then nonplussed, then mortified. 'Oh,' he said at length, scratching the bald spot on the back of his head. 'I did think as how it were a bit on the small side.'

Pete was still laughing as they walked into the lounge bar of the Saxon Cross. 'The pig? He really thought you'd sent it for the pig?'

'That's Ted Merriman for you,' sighed Claire. 'Sometimes I think that man lives on a different planet.'

Pete reached the bar and dug into his jeans pocket for some change. 'Pint of best and a . . . ?'

'It's OK, I'll get these. Pint of best and a dry white wine please.' She handed over a five pound note. 'What am I going to do, Pete?'

'About Ted?'

'About everything.'

Pete watched the landlord intently, as though he half recognised him but couldn't quite put a name to the face. 'Well, you were right about the cottage,' he conceded. 'It's not cute and it is falling down.'

Claire winced. 'Falling down as in?'

'Falling down. Ker-splat. One sneeze and the whole thing'll be down on top of your head.' He caught the appalled look on Claire's face and chuckled. 'Well, maybe it's not quite that bad; but boy does it need some work doing on it.'

Claire slid on to a bar stool. 'Go on. Give it to me straight.'

Pete flipped open his notebook and drew in a sharp breath. 'Where to start, that's the question. Roof: knackered. Walls: well, they're standing up but that's about all you can say about them. Timbers: not so much wood, as woodworm stuck together with sawdust. Electrics: let's just say I flushed the toilet and blue sparks shot out of the light switch. Shall I go on?'

Claire took a hefty swig of white wine. 'Oh shit,' she said. 'So now what do I do?'

'Well, there's this guy I know in Sheffield who has his own wrecking ball.' Pete's eyes drifted back to the landlord. 'Sis.'

'What?'

'The landlord. What's his name?'

'I dunno. Neville something. It's over the front door.'

'Not Neville Shute?'

Claire's nose wrinkled. 'I thought he wrote *A Town Like Alice.*'

'Not *Nevile* Shute, *Neville* Shute, with two 'L's. The one who used to bowl for Gloucestershire! Best leg-spinner they ever had.'

The landlord turned round from wiping the optics and extended a hand. 'Somebody taking my name in vain?'

'Oh my God!' Pete frantically wiped his hand on his jacket before accepting his hero's handshake. 'Mr Shute? I used to have a poster of you on my bedroom wall!'

Claire sat back and watched her normally sensible brother turn into Mr Embarrassing. In all her twenty-four years, Claire had never seen anybody quite so star-struck before; not even Mattie when Tony Bennett played Brockbourne Hall.

'Excuse me,' said a voice at her elbow. 'But I couldn't help hearing. Sounds like you've got quite a job on your hands.'

She swung round. A dark-haired, very attractive man with grey eyes that crinkled at the corners was leaning on the bar, a pint of real ale in his hand, an electronic organiser on the bar-top in front of him. The moment she set eyes on him she recognised him. He was the man she'd noticed chatting to the landlord the last time she was in here. It didn't take much remembering; he was the kind of guy you didn't forget in a hurry.

'Sorry?'

He offered his hand. It was long, slim, tanned, with a deceptively light grip. 'Aidan Ross, I live just across the way.'

'Claire Snow.'

He kept hold of her hand just a fraction longer than absolutely necessary. 'Haven't I seen you in here before?'

'You might have done.' She felt secretly flattered that he had noticed her, too. 'I was in here last Sunday.'

'Ah, I thought so.' The smile was more than friendly, with just the faintest hint of the lounge lizard. 'I make it a habit never to forget a pretty face.'

Ugh, thought the feminist half of Claire; but the treacherous other half was thinking, mmm, he's tasty. Tall and dark *and* good-looking. Looks loaded too. Where's the catch?

'So,' he went on. 'You're buying Paradise Cottage?'

She shook her head. 'I inherited it. From my great-aunt.'

'Oh, right.' He nodded sagely. 'Come to think of it, I did hear something about that. Well I must say, from what your boyfriend was saying just then . . .'

'Pete's my brother actually.' She didn't know why it mattered. But somehow it did.

'From what he was saying, it sounds like the old heap's in a worse mess than I thought. You'll be getting the professionals in, of course?'

'Well actually, I don't really have the budget.'

'Ah, so you'll be selling up? Either way I might be interested.' Slipping a hand into the inside pocket of his leather jacket, he took out a business card and flipped it on to the bar-top. It read: 'Aidan Ross Period Homes'.

Oh you might, might you, thought Claire with a flash of resentment. 'What makes you think I'd be interested in selling to you, Mr Ross?' she parried. 'In fact, what makes you think I'd want to sell at all?'

'Please, you must call me Aidan. Everybody does.' His eyes

flicked to her ring finger and away again. She'd already performed the same ritual on him; and there was no tell-tale indentation to suggest a wedding ring - not that that meant anything, of course. She couldn't even imagine why that might interest her. 'Paradise Cottage is going to cost a fortune to put right, and since you've just admitted you don't have a fortune to spend on renovation work, naturally I assumed that—'

'I wouldn't make assumptions if I were you,' said Claire coolly. 'Actually, I haven't made up my mind yet.' And the next few words blurted themselves out before she could stop them bypassing her brain. 'I might even do the work myself.'

Aidan spluttered into his beer. 'You? Do that place up yourself? Great joke, I'll give you that.'

'Who says it's a joke?' she demanded, maddened now and squaring up to fight her corner. 'Why shouldn't I be just as capable of doing it up as anybody else?'

'Why? Surely that's obvious.'

'Sis,' cut in Pete, who had suddenly tuned back in to the conversation. 'What are you on about? You can't even change a—'

'Button it, Petey.' She kicked him under the bar counter. 'Well, Mr Ross?' she demanded, staring right into the crinkly grey eyes. 'Why is it so obvious?'

'Be realistic, Claire love, it's obvious you're a complete amateur.' The smile was distinctly patronising now. 'And that place would be a tough job for a squad of professionals.'

'Oh it would, would it? Well I'm telling you I could do it myself if I put my mind to it.'

'Oh yeah? Well if you're so sure about that, prove it to me. Prove to me you can renovate that cottage.' He stuck his hand in his back pocket and slapped a banknote on the bar counter. 'Fifty quid says you can't.'

And then Aidan Ross threw back his head and guffawed; which was a bad error of judgement, since there was nothing more guaranteed to make Claire Snow do something stupid than to laugh in her face and tell her she couldn't.

'All right,' she said, regretting the words even as she spoke them. 'You're bloody well on!'

The bar fell silent.

'Oh God,' groaned Pete, banging his forehead on the bar counter.

Oh God, thought Claire, five seconds later. What on earth have I just said?

Chapter 9

Worm and Lorna; Claire and Ted. The odd quartet certainly turned heads at 'Nines' bowling alley, particularly as Ted hadn't changed his clothes since mucking out the chicken shed.

'That's a very ... unorthodox bowling style your friend's got,' commented the manager, a man whose hair appeared to have been replaced by a brown carpet tile.

'Yabba-dabba-doooo!' roared Ted, skidding along the floor as the bowling ball hurtled towards the distant pins.

Claire and Lorna giggled. Worm hid his face.

'Another clean strike,' whistled the manager. 'I don't believe it.'

'Well done Ted,' said Claire as the conqueror returned, red-faced and wilder-haired than ever. She slid a dish in front of him. 'Have another ice-cream.'

'Come on Worm,' said Lorna, hauling him out of his seat. 'Our turn.'

Ted eased his joints on to the bench seat and plunged into his second raspberry sundae. 'Told you I could show them young 'uns a thing or two.' He chuckled. 'Mary used to say I were the star of the village cricket team. Mind you, the wicket keeper only had one leg.'

Claire watched him, questions running through her head. 'You were very fond of her, weren't you?'

The grin on Ted's face lost some of its lustre. 'Don't make ice

100

cream like they used to,' he grunted. 'An' these seeds get stuck in me gums.'

Claire persevered. 'And she must've been fond of you.' She paused for him to say something, but he just went on sucking ice cream off his spoon. 'Ted . . . what was she like?'

'She were . . . ' For a moment, Claire thought he was going to reveal some enormous secret; then he dipped into his sundae again. '. . . a lovely woman. That's what she were.'

'Why did she leave Paradise Cottage to me, Ted? I don't understand.'

Ted answered without meeting her gaze. 'How should I know?'

Lorna flung herself back down on her chair and took a swig of beer. 'Rubbish! Absolute rubbish! Did you *see* him?'

Worm helped himself to a bite of Claire's hot dog. 'I thought I did rather well actually.'

Lorna corpsed. 'Worm, you're supposed to hit the skittles, not go round them.' She leaned over and touched Ted on the arm. 'You have another go, Mr Merriman. Go on, show us how it's done.'

She watched with amusement as he launched himself down the alley like a bobsleigh down the Cresta Run. 'I think that's what's called a character.'

Worm licked mustard off his chin. 'He smells a bit ripe. What is it?'

Claire went on eating. 'Chicken manure.'

'Oh strewth.'

'Did you find out anything about your great-aunt?' asked Lorna. Claire shook her head. 'Oh well, maybe there's nothing to find out.' Legs stretched out, sprawled against the back of the seat, she sipped reflectively from her beer can. 'Claire.'

'Hmm?'

'You do know this bet you've made with that Ross man is completely, utterly stupid, don't you?'

Claire put up her hands. 'OK, OK, no need to rub it in. It was the heat of the moment, and I don't like being patronised, all right?'

'All the same,' commented Worm, 'there's no point in taking on more than you can cope with just for the sake of a fifty-quid bet.'

'No,' sighed Claire. 'I suppose I'll have to swallow my pride and get some proper builders in to give me estimates.'

'No suppose about it,' declared Lorna. 'And make sure you get more than one, or you'll get ripped off.'

Claire pulled a face. 'Yes Mum.' Lorna was right though; she couldn't do the work herself, she didn't know one end of a steam stripper from the other. But that didn't stop the idea being appealing. Almost as appealing as waltzing into the bar of the Saxon Cross and demanding her fifty quid prize money off Aidan Ross.

Ted returned, much out of sorts. 'Missed one,' he announced dejectedly. 'Must be losin' my touch.'

'Tell you what, Worm,' said Lorna. 'Cheer Mr Merriman up, show him how crap you are.'

'Thank you Miss Walsh, for that overwhelming vote of confidence.'

Worm was just reaching down to pick up a bowling ball when he noticed the small child toddling past him, the major part of a choc-nut sundae dribbling down the front of its frilly dress. It never ceased to amaze him just how fast babies could travel when they put their minds to it.

'Phoebe!' shouted a harassed woman in a blue T-shirt and leggings. 'Phoebe, come here right now!'

She was heading straight for him, so he dodged to one side. It really wasn't his fault that the manager happened to be standing behind him at the time, or that his right arm happened to lash out and send the shagpile toupee whizzing through the air like a furry flying saucer.

But that was the last time they went bowling in Swindon.

'You again,' grunted Ted as he hoed away at the overgrown vegetable patch, his creaky back bent almost double.

He did not need to turn round to know that Geoffrey

Willenhall was standing by the old henhouse, grinning like a Cheshire cat; or that Geoffrey Willenhall smiling did not make a pretty sight. What's more, he had Eric with him; and Eric was always bad news.

'You know me, Ted,' said Geoffrey. The tone was matey but he managed to make it sound like a threat. 'Like to pay my neighbours a friendly visit now and again. Keep in touch with what's going on.'

Ted's bony fingers did not relax their grip on the handle of the hoe. 'What do you want?' he growled, jabbing the blade into the clayey soil.

The smile stretched another half-inch, drawing Geoffrey's lips into a thin arc that extended right across his wind-reddened face. 'Information – you know, a nod here, a wink there.'

'Well I've got none to give you, so you might as well bugger orf now.'

Far from buggering orf, Geoffrey removed his cap, wiped it across the grubby roof of an old dog-kennel and sat down on the edge of it. 'Come on now, we want to keep this friendly don't we?'

'You're no friend of mine,' retorted Ted, glancing back over his shoulder as he slung a clump of weeds into a bucket.

'Of course, if you want to play silly games with me . . . well, I can play games with you too.' The smile slipped from affably insincere to distinctly menacing; and its meaning wasn't lost, even on Ted. 'Fond of that pig, aren't you?'

Eric had Brucie pinned up against the corner of the work-shop. 'Here piggy piggy,' he coaxed mockingly, jabbing at his hide with the sharp prongs of a pitchfork.

Ted swung round, eyes mad with rage. 'You tell 'im to leave my pig alone, you hear?'

Geoffrey grinned horribly. 'Don't know as I can do that, Ted. Unless you was to turn a bit more co-operative.'

Ted was shaking; whether with fear or anger it was hard to tell. 'What information do you want?' he demanded, keeping the derelict chicken coop between himself and his next-door neighbour.

'About the girl. Claire. I want to know what she's going to do with this place. Is she going to sell up or not?'

Ted pulled uneasily at a tuft of snow-white nostril-hair. 'That's what she said last week when she were up here with that brother of hers.'

Geoffrey's smile crept back, sly as a burglar's dog. 'Good, good, there's a sensible girl. And did she say if she was going to take me up on my generous offer?'

'No, she never said a word. How the hell should I know if she's sellin' to you?'

The reply came spitting back. 'Because you're going to make sure she does.'

The mucky blade of the hoe hovered over the world's biggest dandelion. 'Why?' he demanded. 'What's it to you whether she sells or stays?'

'Never you mind.' Geoffrey stood up. 'But if I were you I'd play ball if you want to keep a roof over your head. Ain't that right, Eric?'

'Right, Dad.' Eric grinned gormlessly, and aimed a kick at Brucie, who promptly sank his teeth into the toecap of his boot. ''Ere, you let go my foot you bastard pig.'

Ted muttered something inaudible, but it bounced right off Geoffrey's thick hide.

'You stop her doing up this place, you hear?' said Geoffrey. 'You make things difficult for her, make sure she can't wait to get it off her hands. You got that?'

'And what if I don't?' demanded Ted.

Geoffrey sniffed the air. 'Is that roast pork I can smell?'

Ronnie Callaghan's Golf Resort was renowned for its relaxing atmosphere, but you would never have known it from the way he was glowering at his estranged wife across the poolside patio.

'You slag,' he snapped, swallowing another indigestion pill.

She returned his venomous glare with a look of stony contempt. 'That's what I love about you, Ronnie. Your witty repartee.'

The patio doors slid open and Ronnie's butler came out on to the patio, carrying a telephone on a silver tray. 'A call for you, senhora.'

'Thanks.' She winked at him, just to wind up Ronnie, and put the phone to her ear. 'Veronica Callaghan here. Oh. Oh *really*? You don't say. Well, well, well.'

When she put the phone down she was smiling.

'So where does this one go then?' enquired Ravi the Site Manager. 'Round ... about ... here?' He brought his Continental Nougat Creme in to land on top of two Praline Delights.

Claire licked melted chocolate off her fingers. 'No, not there.' She consulted her 1784 edition of *Cope's Gloucestershire Antiquities*. 'Further over to the left, next to the Caramel Cluster.'

'It'll never balance on top of that, it's too knobbly.'

She dipped into the box of chocolates. 'Here, try this coconut one, it's flatter.'

All around the panelled walls of the boardroom, former aristocratic owners of Brockbourne Hall glowered disapprovingly from their gilded picture frames. On the polished oval table in the centre of the room lay a scale map of the Brockbourne estate, several boxes of Ledbury's Luxury Assortment, and a pile of multicoloured sweet wrappers. The chocolates that had once been inside the wrappers had been carefully arranged on the southwest corner of the map to form a circle, bang in the middle of the main car park.

'There,' announced Ravi, positioning the last chocolate with a steady hand that had won many games of Buckaroo. 'What do you reckon to that then? Work of art or what?'

'Blinding.' They stood back to admire their joint creation. OK, so it was constructed from chocolate caramels rather than granite boulders, but it managed a pretty good impression of the Brockbourne stone circle, circa 1784. 'I just wish the real one was going to be this easy to build.' Claire swiped another chocolate from the box. 'So, how many standing stones is that alto-gether?'

Ravi checked the figures on his clipboard. 'Er . . . thirty-six enormous ones and nineteen little ones, plus the one that rolled under the table. That makes fifty-six in all.'

'Aargh.' Claire pulled a face. 'Plus a whole new car park.'

Ravi helped himself to one of the standing stones. 'And a new stretch of driveway to get to it.'

'Yeah. And all because Brent Lovelace wants to get in touch with his Mother Goddess.' She seethed. Why couldn't the stupid prat have stuck to getting drunk, groping groupies and fiddling his income tax, like a *normal* rock star?

'If I were you I'd tell him where to stick his standing stones,' counselled Ravi. 'I always thought his records were rubbish anyway.'

'Rubbish or not, he's refusing to play here unless he gets his stone circle, and Brockbourne can't afford to lose the publicity – or the TV rights. Besides, we don't make the decisions, do we?'

'No. We just take the rap when it all goes horribly wrong.'

'This isn't going to go wrong,' replied Claire firmly. 'I'm not going to let it.'

'Oh well,' said Ravi, eating the sacrificial altar. 'At least we've already got outline planning permission to redevelop that part of the estate. And the car park's always flooding, it's about time we moved it somewhere sensible.'

'Hmm.' Claire gazed with awful fascination at her chocolate nemesis, trying to visualise it twelve feet tall and floodlit. Fifty-six massive great standing stones! It was completely ridiculous. 'Do you think we might get a lottery grant?' she ventured, more in hope than expectation.

'Don't make me laugh.'

'Ravi,' she replied sweetly. 'Who's laughing?'

Naomi pushed aside an untidy heap of papers to make space on her desk for Claire's outline budget figures. Through the window behind her right shoulder, Claire watched six unfit-looking executives in tracksuits lope off towards the woods, in pursuit of a Greek god in full combat gear. She wondered how many of them would have fallen into the river by teatime.

'Good heavens,' said Naomi for the fourth time, pushing her round, wire-rimmed glasses back up her nose. 'I take it you've checked these figures thoroughly?'

'Several times.'

'But this *is* an *over*-estimate?'

'Er, no.'

Naomi's eyes turned unnaturally round behind her thick lenses. 'But this is an awful lot of money.'

'I know it is. But that's what it's going to cost, give or take the odd thousand. Check with Ravi if you don't believe me.'

'Oh, I believe you all right.' Naomi sat back in her leather swivel chair, crossing her puffy ankles. 'I just don't think the Board are going to be terribly thrilled about it. Still, if there's really no option . . .'

'Not if we go with the plan as it stands.'

'Then I shall have to put it to them.' Naomi pondered for a few moments, her fingers drumming pensively on the arm of the chair; then her face brightened. 'Alun's a persuasive chap, isn't he?'

'Alun Williams? Yes, I suppose he is, why?'

'Let's send him round to see Mr . . . what does he call himself these days?'

'Orion?'

'That's it, I knew it was something to do with astronomy. Let's see if Alun can persuade Mr Orion to meet some of the cost.'

'Well,' replied Claire, rather unconvinced, 'he can try.' She started as the invisible carriage clock on Naomi's desk struck three o'clock, its high-pitched pinging emerging from beneath a mound of crumpled paper tissues. 'Oh – and here's that monthly budget report you asked me to do for you.'

She handed it over, glad to be rid of it. It had taken her several late nights and wasn't really her job in the first place.

Naomi swiped the tissues into the wastepaper bin and made space on the desk for Claire's report. She flicked quickly through the pages. 'Claire, you are a *star*.'

'It's what you wanted then?'

'Exactly, you've saved my life. I wouldn't have asked you,' she added apologetically, 'only I've had to put everything on hold for Mr Mayberry's latest obsession. Don't suppose you know anything about the three-legged Toad Gods of Wealth?'

Claire frowned. 'No. Are they in the charts?'

'What?' Naomi looked baffled. 'No, no, they're not a pop group! It's Feng Shui.'

'Oh. That.'

'Yes, *that*. Mr Mayberry's developed a thing about the Orient. It's a complete waste of time of course, but you know what he's like.'

'When he gets a bee in his bonnet we all have to get one too?'

'And when he says "jump" ... ' She leaned over the desk, lowering her voice to the sort of hushed whisper women use when discussing their hysterectomies. 'Do you know what he said to the Paraguayan trade minister?'

'No.'

'Yes, well, fortunately neither did the minister. I was inter-preting.' Naomi shook her head in disbelief. 'I'm telling you Claire, that man is Prince Philip in disguise.'

Chapter 10

'Termites,' opined the builder, rapping on the bedroom wall. 'That's your problem.'

Claire didn't know whether to laugh or question her own sanity. 'Termites?' she repeated. 'In Gloucestershire?'

'Bloody great enormous things they are,' confided the builder, hitching up his sagging Wranglers a fraction of a second before they slipped over the crest of his sweaty backside. 'Two inches long, some of 'em.' Catching the look of disbelief on Claire's face, he elaborated: 'Migrating they are, see.'

'Oh really.'

'Really. Come over on Concorde in a potted palm, that's what I heard. There's a colony of 'em in Dorset, I saw it on *South West Tonight*. Ate a whole three-bed semi they did.'

Claire followed Mr Mackenzie round the house, listening to a hundred tales of insect-related horror, each less believable than the last. Had she really thought this was such a good idea? She would take a long weekend from work, phone up a load of local builders, and get them to quote for working on the cottage. Simple, surely. Except that every builder within twenty miles of Lilcombe Magna was apparently mad, lecherous, dishonest or all three.

Mr Mackenzie prised open the rusted catch of the airing cupboard door with a screwdriver. Sticking his head inside, he took a long, reflective sniff. 'You're lucky to get me, you know.'

'I am?'

'Oh definitely. I'm an expert, see.'

'What in?'

'Termites.' What else, thought Claire. ''Course,' he went on, emerging from the airing cupboard with a pair of mildewed grey underpants dangling between finger and thumb. 'Some builders'd look at a pretty little thing like you and tell you any old rubbish, just to get your money.'

'Not you though?' enquired Claire with an amused smile.

'Not me, Lord no. Like I said, I'm an expert.'

The Old Rectory could not have been more different from Paradise Cottage. For a start, it had a roof. And there were definitely no pigs snoring on Aidan Ross's king-size futon.

The eighteenth-century, stone-built vicarage stood right in the centre of the village, on the edge of the pocket-sized green; its southern wall shadowed by the short, stumpy tower of St Ogmore's. Since Lilcombe Magna now had to share a vicar with Lilcombe Regis, it no longer needed a rectory, old or otherwise. Never one to miss out on a bargain, Aidan had snapped up the redundant property for a song, promptly fallen in love with it and decided to live in it himself.

It wasn't a pretty house; it was better than pretty. Aidan loved the covetous glances it drew from Sunday drivers as their Astras and Fiestas chugged past its intricate canopied porch and double row of perfectly-proportioned windows, glazed with specially-commissioned handblown glass. Little touches like that cost big money. The Old Rectory was a permanent reminder of Aidan Ross's success.

On this particular warm afternoon he was lounging on a rattan chaise-longue in the vinery, talking to a business contact on his mobile as he worked his way lazily through a bottle of Côtes du Rhône.

'Wednesday? Yeah, Wednesday should be OK. After eleven though, I have to go to that architectural salvage place in Bath – don't suppose you know where I could pick up an Adam fireplace for a good price?'

'Real or repro?' enquired the voice on the other end.

'Real of course. This is a quality job I'm looking to do.'

'For a quality price?'

'Of course!' Aidan flicked through the address file at his elbow. 'You know me, I'm not cheap but I'm worth it. You still on for tomorrow?'

'Yeah, yeah, no problem. Meet you at the track shall I? 'Bout two?'

'Make that one thirty.' Aidan stretched out his long legs, in the pleasant anticipation of an afternoon's motorbike scrambling. 'Only thing is, this may be the last time for a while.'

'Why's that then?'

'Remember I told you I was standing for the local parish council?'

'God knows why, but yeah, I think you mentioned it.'

'Well, so far I'm the only candidate standing; and nominations close on Tuesday morning. I don't suppose I'll have much free time once I'm elected.'

The thin man in the shiny blue suit held a pencil up to the light and screwed up one eye as he tried out different angles against the tumbledown stonework.

'What you need,' he declared, 'Is a nice bit of pebbledashing. Hides a multitude of sins, does pebbledashing.'

Claire shuddered as she pictured the effect of pebbledashing Paradise Cottage. True, it was a horrible little heap, but even horrible little heaps deserved better than that. And just think of the rabid letters it would spark off in the local paper.

'I don't think that's quite . . . ' she began, but Lennie Goodright was in full spate.

'Now, have you had time to look at our brochure?' Something glossy passed briefly under Claire's nose.

'Actually . . . '

'Then you'll know about our special spring deals on UPVC replacement windows and doors.'

111

Plastic doors *and* pebbledash? This time the image that shot through Claire's mind was of an enraged lynch mob, descending on Paradise Cottage at dead of night with flaming torches.

'No,' she said firmly, stuffing the leaflet back into Mr Goodright's top pocket. 'Definitely not UPVC anything.'

'Well what about a nice medieval-style porch with double-glazed stained-glass-effect panels? Or – I know – how about stone cladding? We do a lovely Cotswold range.'

Claire could hardly believe her ears. 'Stone cladding on a stone-built cottage?'

'No?'

'No.'

His face fell. 'I know, it's the building regs, isn't it? That's the trouble with living round here, you can't change your socks without the council sticking its nose in. Tell you what though.'

'What?'

He poked a disparaging finger at a lump of blackened oak. 'We could take out all these old-fashioned beams, knock that wall through, do you a lovely pair of patio doors . . .'

'Thanks Mr Goodright,' said Claire, steering him out of the front door. 'I'll be in touch.'

Ted did not much care for builders, and still less for the thought of them poking around the cottage he had come to regard as his home. Which was why he and Brucie were taking refuge in the village shop.

'Outside please, Mr Merriman,' said the woman behind the counter as the shop bell jangled.

Ted laid a protective hand on Brucie's head. 'We're not doing no harm.'

'Not you, Ted.' She looked up from arranging vanilla slices on a tray. 'Brucie. I've told you before,' she scolded gently, 'I can't have that pig breathing all over my egg custards, it's not hygienic. Besides, there's the smell.'

'What smell? I can't smell nothin'.'

'Gawd help us,' chortled a man behind the magazine rack.

Ted swung round. 'He's clean as a whistle, is my Brucie!'

'For a pig, maybe,' conceded the woman behind the counter. One look at Ted's crestfallen face, and she relented. 'Oh all right, he can stay. But if he puts his snout anywhere near my bacon counter he's out.'

This ritual was repeated almost every time Ted visited the shop. Mollified, Ted ambled across to the magazine rack to look through the pictures in the TV guides. If there had been a TV Olympics, Ted would have come home with a clutch of gold medals.

As usual, Brucie preferred to lounge in the corner by the door, easing his economy-size bottom on to the welcome mat. In this strategic spot, he was ideally placed to be fed titbits from passing shopping baskets; in the course of his regular visits he had developed a taste for everything from jalapeño chillies to doughnuts.

'What's that girl like then?' asked Annie. 'That Claire.'

'All right I s'pose,' replied Ted non-committally.

'I heard as she was havin' the old place done up.'

Ted grunted. 'Builders all over the bloomin' place, a man can't get five minutes to himself.'

The front door jangled. 'This and a meat pie please, Annie.'

'Right you are John. That'll be one seventy-nine.'

The man in blue overalls rummaged in his pockets for change. 'Here you are, Brucie.' He nipped off a corner of pastry and chucked it to the pig, who caught it in mid-air. 'See he's not lost his touch, Ted. Maybe we should field him in the cricket team, Lord knows we couldn't do much worse.'

'That's true,' laughed Annie. 'You've already got Ted.'

Ted muttered something indecipherable. He was absorbed in a centrefold of Carol Vorderman in leather trousers. 'What you say?'

'Fine figure of a pig you got, Ted.'

'Oh. Arr.'

'Regular pillar of the establishment, he is.' Old John munched on his pie as he scanned the notices pinned to the

113

board next to the counter. Amateur dramatics, cheese rolling, jumble sales, the usual village fare. And a poster inviting nominations for the forthcoming parish council elections. 'You heard about the elections then?'

'Just that there's only the one candidate,' replied Annie, obsessively rearranging her cakes so that their corners were precisely aligned with the edges of the tray.

John sniffed. ''Tain't right, you know. '

Tain't democratic. And that Aidan Ross, he's not even from round these parts. Don't see why we should have a man like that telling us what to do in our own village.'

Annie started stacking cream horns. 'That's all well and good, but nominations close on Tuesday, and if nobody else is willing to stand . . . '

Ted looked up. 'You ask me,' he declared, 'my pig could do the job better than him.'

John's gaze shifted from the notice board to Brucie, placidly gnawing on a gas canister marked 'Danger, do not puncture'. A slow smile spread across his weatherbeaten face. 'Your pig, you say?'

Annie laughed. 'Don't encourage him, John.'

'I'm tellin' you it's true,' insisted Ted. 'An' at least he were born in the village, not like some I could name.'

'You know something, Ted,' said Old John. 'You've got a point there.'

'I know I have! Comin' in here, buyin' up half the place, acting like he was lord of the manor.' Stomping over to the counter, Ted slapped down a sliced white loaf and a pound coin. 'You know what, I've a good mind to nominate him myself.'

'What?' laughed Annie. 'Your Brucie — stand for the parish council? Don't talk daft.'

'Daft? I've never been more serious in my life.'

At last, thought Claire: somebody sensible. Someone who understands what it's like to be a single woman trying to get a fair deal in a man's world. Somebody who won't try to pinch my bum and rip me off.

Somebody female.

Alice came highly recommended by the Women's Manual Work Collective. She arrived five minutes early, and went round the house like a one-woman whirlwind, clambering all over the roof, poking about in the drains, running over all the walls with an electrical meter. Best of all, she didn't ask Claire if her husband was in, or demand mugs of tea with six sugars. Claire almost dared to think this might work; if the price was right.

'Well,' said Alice, putting her jacket back on, 'there's a lot of work in this place.'

'But your firm could do it?'

'Oh yes. The only thing is ...' She sat down on the edge of the kitchen table. 'I do like to choose my clients carefully.'

'Carefully? How do you mean?'

'I really must feel that we're on the same wavelength, you see.' Without warning, she seized one of Claire's hands and clasped it between her own. A look of radiant serenity passed across her face.

'I was wondering, Claire. Do you ever think about God?'

It was Sunday morning, and Lorna was having the loveliest of lie-ins. No shows today, nothing to do but laze around.

She wasn't exactly asleep, just dozing on top of the bedcovers trying to recapture the dream she'd just had about Sir Lancelot, a toothbrush and a bottle of baby oil. *Warm* baby oil, ooh yes. She clutched a pillow and tried to metamorphose it into somebody really sexy – Ewan McGregor maybe, or George Clooney, but definitely not that Leonardo di Caprio, who looked like a trans-sexual pixie and was liable to break into an Irish jig at any moment.

Mmm, nice. Just a little higher up, George. But mind the bristles. Sod off Leo, how many times do I have to tell you? I'm not interested.

At first she thought the voices were part of her dream. Then she thought, hang on, one of those voices belongs to Mr Papajian, and why on earth would I dream about *him*?

Her eyes shot open. Mr Papajian was standing at the foot of her bed in his usual beige polyester slacks and donkey jacket, flanked by a well-dressed man and woman she had never seen before in her life. Mind you, at least the two strangers had the goodness to look mortally embarrassed; Mr Papajian was smirking.

'Oh, by the way,' he leered, 'Lorna's extra.'

She shot bolt upright. 'Who the bloody hell . . . ?'

'Er, perhaps we should come back some other time?' ventured the man in the raincoat, backing off a couple of steps.

It was at that moment that Lorna realised that his eyes were not on her face. In fact neither were anybody else's. Which wasn't really surprising, seeing as she was stark naked except for her socks.

'It's yer underpinning, love,' explained Chas Willetts, squinting down into the small hole he had dug outside the outhouse door.

'I can't see anything,' said Claire, trying to follow the wobbling beam of his torch.

'Ah well, takes a trained eye, see.' Chas clicked off the torch and dropped it into his toolbox. 'Great big cracks right through your foundations, mind you that's no wonder, what with all the underground springs round here.'

Claire frowned. 'What underground springs? Nobody else said anything about any underground springs.'

Chas tapped the side of his nose. 'Local knowledge love, local knowledge.' He patted her on the arm and gave her the broadest of winks. 'Don't you worry darlin', you're in safe hands now, know what I mean?'

The public bar at the Saxon Cross greeted Aidan with raucous jeers.

'Well, well.' Chas raised his glass in an ironic toast. 'If it ain't El Presidente.'

116

'Ha ha.' Aidan threw his briefcase on to the floor. 'The usual please, Nev. And one of those bits of microwaved cardboard.'

Nev stuck a pint glass under the beer tap. 'Coming up.' He turned his head to shout through the hatch into the kitchen. 'One pizza, hold the anchovies.'

'You're looking down in the mouth,' commented Aidan. 'Love-life getting a bit too much for you?'

'What love-life?' He opened the till and counted out a handful of change.

'I thought you had three on the go.'

'I did. Till they all found out about each other.'

'Never mind, mate. Plenty more fish in the sea.' Aidan drank the first inch of his pint and wiped a moustache of froth off his upper lip. 'So, Chas, heard about me running for the parish council have we? What do you reckon?'

Chas's pudgy features convulsed with mirth. 'You and politics? You're made for each other. One hand in the till and the other on your—'

'Nev,' Aidan interjected.

'What?'

'Make that two pizzas, I'm building my strength up.'

'Two pizzas? Sure your election budget'll stretch to it?' enquired a man in blue overalls at the other end of the bar.

'Yeah, yeah John, everyone's a comedian tonight,' retorted Aidan good-naturedly. He turned back to Chas. 'You're a long way off your patch aren't you? Or have the building inspectors in Swindon sussed you at last?'

'I'll have you know I'm a highly-skilled craftsman.' It might have sounded more convincing if Chas hadn't been grinning as he said it. 'Somebody round here thinks so anyway, otherwise they wouldn't have called me in, would they?'

'Who's that then?' asked Aidan, interested.

'Oh, some girl at a cottage over the other side of the village. Real wreck it is.'

Aidan set down his glass. 'Not Claire Snow? At Paradise Cottage?'

117

'That's right.' The grin returned, faintly indecent now. 'Not her as well? You dirty dog. Is there a woman in this village you haven't knocked off?'

'I've just spoken to her a couple of times, OK? She seemed a nice enough kid. Got you in to give her a quote has she?'

'Somebody'd obviously primed her on the right questions to ask. Pity really, she was quite clued up.' Chas rubbed his hands and chuckled. 'But not *that* clued up. I spun her this line about the foundations being knackered, and she swallowed the whole thing.'

'What – you mean there's nothing wrong with the foundations?'

'Put it this way, it's about the only bit of that place that *isn't* knackered.' Chas emptied his beer glass. 'Should be good for another couple of thou on the estimate, she'll never know the difference.'

The hatch opened and two rubbery pizzas appeared, piled one on top of the other. Neville slid the plate down the bar, Western-style, and Aidan neatly trapped it with his arm. 'You're a brave man, Chas, I'll give you that,' he said.

'What do you mean, brave? She's only five foot five in her socks.'

'But you did recognise her?'

'No? Should I have?'

Aidan shook his head in disbelief. 'Don't you ever see *Watchdog*?'

'Well . . . sometimes. Why?'

'Answering the phone in the background? Behind Anne Robinson's left shoulder?'

'No – you're kidding!' Aidan crossed his heart with solemn reverence. Chas blanched. 'Oh.'

'Just watch yourself, that's all I say. Place is probably full of hidden cameras.'

'You mean – a set-up?' He pulled off a piece of Aidan's pizza, stuffed it into his mouth and chewed. 'Oh hell. Maybe I'd better revise my estimate downwards a bit.' He consulted his genuine

Korean Rolex. 'In fact if I go now I could get the whole thing knocked out tonight.' He clapped Aidan on the back. 'Cheers mate, I owe you one.'

Neville watched the bar door swing closed behind him, then reached across and picked up the empty glass. 'Well, well, well,' he chuckled.

Aidan looked up. 'What?' he said, through a mouthful of soggy dough.

'Not getting soft are we?'

Long weekends were supposed to be irresponsible and fun, thought Claire. Or at least they were when you were twenty-four years old. You were supposed to go on minibreaks to New York, or lounge around in the nude, covering your sexual partner in luxury ice cream. You were not supposed to get to Monday night thinking thank God, I'm going back to work tomorrow.

By Tuesday morning Claire had decided that being a grown-up was a lot harder than it looked. And being the owner of Paradise Cottage was a very grown-up thing indeed. As she super-vised a gang of workmen decorating Brockbourne's banqueting hall for a wedding party, her mind wandered back to Lilcombe Magna and the gruesome procession that had passed through the cottage since Friday night. The Hammer House of Horror could not have supplied a more disturbing cast of tradesmen.

'Will here do?' shouted a spindly youth teetering on the top of a very tall ladder. A heart-shaped arrangement of silver helium balloons was bouncing against the frescoed ceiling as he strug-gled to tether it in place. 'Only if I lean over any further I'll rupture myself.'

'There's fine, Julian, just make sure you don't le ... ' The words 'let go' were lost in the general chorus of groans as Julian lost his grip and the balloons floated gracefully away, to hook themselves to the underside of a chandelier.

'Prat,' shouted Mel.

Julian clung to the top of the ladder like a stranded kitten. 'Sorry.'

'Just move the ladder and get it back down,' said Claire. 'And get a move on, we've only got two hours, remember?'

Workmen, she thought. Who needs 'em? Actually, you do, she reminded herself. And you need them to submit amazingly low estimates, because if the work costs anything like what Pete thinks it's going to cost, you're well stuffed. You really *will* have to get your dungarees on and do it yourself.

'Actually,' said Julian faintly, 'I don't think I can move.'

'Of course you can move!' yelled Mel, shaking the bottom of the ladder. 'Stop messing about and shift your useless arse.'

Julian turned whiter than a polar bear's bottom. 'No, I *really* don't think I can move.' His knuckles blanched as he gripped the top rung of the ladder. 'I'm stuck.'

So absorbed was everybody in getting Julian off the ladder that nobody noticed one of the side doors open. The staccato tap of high-heeled shoes was almost inaudible above Julian's whimpering and Mel's bellows of 'encouragement'.

In fact it wasn't until Julian was safely back on the ground that anybody noticed there was a stranger in the ballroom.

'Hello,' said Mel, walking towards the door to pick up some more balloons. 'Are you with the wedding party?'

'My God,' said the woman, taking two steps forward and completely ignoring Mel. 'My God it is . . . it's her.'

'Sorry?'

'Weed!'

The exclamation was so loud and so high-pitched that every window in the ballroom bulged outwards.

Claire cringed instinctively, then froze. Then turned round, very very slowly, dreading the inevitable.

'Weed! My own little Weed. The woman was smiling broadly and holding out her arms. She had an orange face, brown arms and silver high-heeled sandals that matched her nail varnish. 'I'd know you anywhere.'

Oh God, thought Claire. So would I. I just don't want to.

'Don't just stand there.' The arms stretched wider. 'Come and give your mum a lovely big kiss.'

120

Chapter 11

The multicoloured party-banner above the door might spell out CONGRATULATIONS, but the atmosphere in the Mulberry Suite was far from celebratory.

Claire glowered at her mother across a vegetarian finger-buffet for two hundred, wondering if it was just faintly possible that this was a bad dream. 'Are you happy now?' she demanded. 'Now you've humiliated me in front of two dozen people?'

Veronica's blue eyes grew even rounder. Claire might have believed their expression of martyred innocence was genuine, if she hadn't known better. 'Humiliate you, sweetheart?' replied her mother, right hand laid across her heart. 'But why on earth would I want to hurt my own Little Weed?'

Little Weed? Claire cringed. As ever, Veronica's timing was perfect: perfectly awful. Even as a little kid Claire had loathed that nickname; and right now it stuck in her throat like a week-old vol-au-vent. 'If you call me that stupid name one more time,' she seethed, 'I swear I'll . . . ' Frustrated by the lack of the right words, she slammed the flat of her hand down on the table. All the individual ramekins clinked together in alarm.

Veronica's bottom lip began to tremble. 'I only wanted to see my lovely son and daughter again, patch things up between us before it's too late.' She scrabbled for a paper napkin and dabbed at the corners of her suspiciously dry eyes without so much as smudging her navy-blue mascara. 'Is that so terribly wrong of me?'

'Oh for goodness' sake,' exclaimed Claire. 'Spare us that old routine, you're not fooling anybody. This is all about Great-Aunt Mary's will, isn't it? *Isn't it*?'

'Claire,' interjected Mattie, her voice full of concern. 'Claire, please.'

'What?' snapped Claire, swinging round in irritation.

'Are you sure you're all right? This isn't like you.'

No, Claire thought, it bloody isn't. After all I'm supposed to be the woman who never loses her cool. But then again, she reminded herself, how often do you come face to face with the woman who ruined your father's life and did her darnedest to screw yours up too?

'Mattie,' she growled, 'what the hell has this got to do with you?'

'Well ... I ...'

'Just shut up and stop interfering.'

Mattie looked wounded. 'I was only trying to help.'

'I expect it's all a bit of a shock for Weed,' confided Veronica in a solicitous whisper. 'Having me spring up again after all these years.' She sounded like a social worker discussing bladder problems. 'I probably should have phoned first.'

'*I* know,' said Mattie, in a voice that reminded Claire of all the infant school teachers she had ever met. 'Why don't I go and make a nice pot of tea, and then you can both—'

'Mattie,' cut in Claire. 'Just go away.'

'I'm sorry?'

'Go. Now.'

'Oh. Oh, all right then. If that's what you want.'

The look of tacit disapproval on Mattie's face cut no ice with Claire. Mattie didn't know Veronica like she did. In fact nobody did, with the possible exception of Pete. She waited for the door to close behind her and the sound of footsteps to fade into the distance.

'That wasn't very nice, sweetheart,' said Veronica reprovingly, helping herself to a toasted almond.

'Nice!' Claire swiped the dish out of her mother's hand and

banged it back down on the pink tablecloth. 'What would you know about nice? You walked out on us on Christmas Eve, or have you conveniently forgotten that?'

Claire's mother twiddled a lock of damson-coloured hair around one gingerbread finger. 'You know it wasn't like that, sweetheart.'

'So what *was* it like?' Veronica opened her mouth, then closed it again without speaking. Claire felt her heart thumping triumphantly against her ribcage. 'What's that? I didn't quite catch what you said.'

'You wouldn't understand.'

'All right then, I'll tell you what it was like. Dad used to cry himself to sleep some nights, I could hear him through the wall. And poor little Pete was only three years old. What do you tell a three-year-old boy when he asks where his mummy's gone?' She paused for breath, some tiny part of her hoping perhaps that there would be a Disney-style last-minute explanation that would make everything suddenly better; but Veronica made no attempt to defend herself. 'It's been seventeen years, Veronica. What the hell possessed you to turn up now?'

'I told you sweetheart, I missed you.' The tawny-lipsticked smile returned to the sun-wrinkled face. 'Is it so wrong to want to see my little girl again, now she's all grown-up and beautiful?'

Yuk. Claire took a deep breath. 'Owen Pendle's tracked you down and told you Great-Aunt Mary left you something in her will. Hasn't he?'

The blue eyes drifted up from the two sugar-paste doves billing and cooing on the top tier of the wedding cake. 'Well yes,' she admitted. 'But that's nothing to do with—'

'Oh come on, don't give me that! You had to come over here anyway, to get your hands on the money, so you thought, while I'm here why don't I sniff round Claire and see if there's anything else in it for me?'

'Weed! The thought never crossed my mind!'

Veronica looked shocked to the core, but only in a daytime

123

soap-opera kind of way. Claire was unmoved. 'I suppose Pendle told you about me being left the cottage, did he?'

'What cottage?' asked Veronica, all wide-eyed innocence.

'You know what cottage. Paradise Cottage, Mary Willenhall's cottage!'

This time, Veronica's look of astonishment was so grotesque it was almost genuine. 'Aunt Mary left you her cottage? But that's absurd!'

'Yes,' agreed Claire.

Veronica's mouth gaped even wider. '*You*? But she only ever met you the once, why on earth would she do that?'

'I've no idea,' replied Claire. 'But it's true, and don't try telling me you didn't know.'

'I didn't!' squeaked Veronica. Her chest was rising and falling with an excess of righteous indignation. 'My God. Mary left you that lovely little cottage of hers, with the orchard and the roses round the door?'

'Actually, it's a total wreck.'

'I can't believe that for a moment. It was such a *darling* little house.'

Claire felt faintly sick. Wreck or not, if she could have transported the cottage, stone by stone, to a place where Veronica would never dream of setting foot (anywhere without a tanning studio would probably suffice), she would have done it there and then.

'Well it's not darling now,' she said, acidly. 'And it's got a pig in the living room.'

'What, a stuffed one? One of those fluffy cushion things?'

'No, a real one. It belongs to the sitting tenant.'

'Oh my God, how disgusting!'

Claire looked her mother up and down. She didn't know what she'd expected to see after all these years, but it struck her as faintly pathetic that a grown woman would sink so low. 'Not as disgusting as you,' she said, with quiet venom.

'Weed!'

'I've got nothing for you, Veronica. And neither has Pete. So

124

why don't you just go back to Portugal and leave us to get on with our lives?'

Lorna was no Hercule Poirot, but even she had worked out that something very, very odd was going on at number sixteen, Jardine Crescent.

It wasn't just the dawn raid by Mr Papajian and his two mysterious companions. There were other things too, like the frequent whispered conversations in the back garden; and when she'd finally come straight out and asked the landlord what was going on, he'd told her it was 'nothing to do with her, or at least nothing she should be worrying herself about'. Well, if that wasn't cause enough to worry in itself, she didn't know what was.

Sunday morning's unscheduled strip show had at least made up Lorna's mind for her. One way or another, she was going to find out what Mr Papajian was up to. She decided to start by talking to all the other tenants in the house; besides herself, Worm and Kieran, there were only five. It wouldn't take long to ask them if they'd seen or heard anything unusual.

She often ventured up to the second floor to share Worm's gas fire and get him to test her on her lines; but she couldn't recall the last time she had crossed the landing to Stuart's flat. The twilight world of the shaven-headed Buddhist trainspotter held little attraction at the best of times, and frankly the picture of a ritual suicide dagger drawn on the door in silver felt tip pen did little to persuade Lorna of Stuart's potential as an all-round bosom buddy.

Not that Stuart had buddies, or at least, Lorna had never noticed any; all the people he knew seemed to be divided into two groups: those he meditated with, and those he headbutted when he'd had too many bottles of Rolling Rock.

It was the middle of the afternoon, but as usual he was dressed in black pyjamas and espadrilles. Lorna found him doing Tai Ch'i, to the accompaniment of a recording of a Deltic hauling nuclear waste wagons through Croydon station.

125

You could say what you liked about Stuart (and people did), but he had certainly stamped his personality on this bedsit. Lorna blinked to accustom her eyes to the smoky gloom created by fourteen joss sticks and a couple of three-foot-tall black candles. It was hard to believe that this black-walled cube of a room was part of the same house as Worm's collection of Star Wars figurines, Candy's ostrich-plumed boudoir or Mr Veidt's amazing assortment of brass instruments.

'I can only give you two minutes,' Stuart announced, stomping over to the CD player and grudgingly turning down the volume half a notch. 'What you want?'

'Oh, you know. Just a friendly chat.' Fat chance of that, thought Lorna. More chance of his head turning green and spouting ectoplasm.

'Too busy, I've got a bhangra album sleeve and a Freemasons' leaflet to design by Thursday.' He nodded in the direction of his computer, possibly the only normal thing in the entire room, though not many people painted their PCs black with silver spots. 'Go on then, get on with it.'

Lorna waited for him to clear a space for her to sit down, but he didn't; so she picked her way through a mulch of screwed-up printouts, noticed the pair of Japanese love-eggs abandoned on the distinctly moist floor cushion, and decided to stay standing up.

'It's about Mr Papajian,' she explained. 'He barged into my room on Sunday morning, with a couple of strangers. Didn't even bother knocking.'

'So what?' shrugged Stuart, sitting down at the computer desk.

'So I was naked at the time.'

'Why didn't you lock the door?'

'That's just it. I did, but he had a master key. I was wondering, has he ever done anything like that to you?'

Stuart cut-and-pasted an elephant's head on to Melinda Messenger's body, then added dividers and a masonic apron. 'What's the point of all this crap?'

'It's not crap, I think he's up to something, and I want to know what it is.'

'Why?'

'Because we live here! Because it's bound to be something to do with us.' She could tell she wasn't getting anywhere, but carried on regardless. 'Well?'

'Well what?'

'Have you heard anything?'

'No.'

'Seen anything then?'

'I told you, no. I don't know anything, I haven't seen anything.'

'Yes, OK, only . . .'

He swung round with a glare. 'Now get out of my face before I make you. OK?'

'Stuart?'

'What now?'

'I thought Buddhists were supposed to be nice, friendly people.'

'Oh piss off.'

Lorna was bloody-minded enough to have persisted anyway, if somebody hadn't chosen that moment to bellow her name up the stairwell.

'Lorna!' She opened the door and walked out on to the landing. 'Lor-naaaa?'

Rubbing incense-smoke out of her eyes, she leaned over the banisters. Candy was two floors below in the downstairs hallway, stark naked except for a floral shower cap, and standing in a puddle of water.

'What is it?' Lorna called down.

'Somebody at the door.'

'Can't you answer it?' asked Lorna.

'Do me a favour!' Candy waggled her small but perky boobs. 'You want me to freeze these off or what? You'll have to do it, there's no one else in.' Candy padded away, leaving a trail of wet footprints on the cracked floor tiles.

By the time Lorna reached the front door a voice was calling through the letterbox. 'Let me in, I know you're in there.'

Lorna stooped down and squinted through the narrow slit. 'Claire?'

'Stop buggering about and let me in.'

Puzzled, Lorna opened the door. 'Shouldn't you be at work?'

Claire tramped in without a word, head down, a big supermarket carrier bag clutched to her bosom, and headed straight down the hallway to the kitchen. 'Claire?'

'Don't ask.' Reaching the kitchen, Claire up-ended the carrier bag on to the table. Out rolled two litres of ice cream, some chocolate cupcakes, a bottle of red wine, a cuddly badger wearing a jumper embroidered with the words 'I've been to Brockbourne', and a toothbrush.

'Just don't bloody ask, OK?'

Naturally, Lorna did ask. Claire had been counting on it.

'Your *mother*?' She whistled. 'How many years is it since you saw her?'

'Not nearly enough.' Claire poured herself another large mugful of Rioja. 'All this time and not a word from her, and then suddenly it's, "Drop everything sweetie, Mummy's home, what do you mean you wish I'd drop down dead?"'

'That's a bit strong, surely,' said Lorna, peeling the silver paper off one of the cupcakes and fashioning it into a hat for the badger.

'Is it?'

'Well ... I know she ran out on you like that, and it was pretty terrible, but you don't actually hate her, do you?'

'Don't I?' The truth is, thought Claire, I don't really know whether I do or not. I just wish she would piss off out of my life. 'She's a horrible grasping bitch and she wouldn't have come within a thousand miles of me if it wasn't for Great Aunt Mary's will.'

'You reckon she's only here for what she can get?'

'I'm sure of it.'

'Not that there's anything for her to get, unless she's seriously into rubble,' pointed out Lorna, sitting the badger on the table. Claire promptly grabbed it and hugged it so hard that its growl came out like an asphyxiated wheeze.

'Oh God.' She dropped the badger and scrabbled in her bag for her mobile phone. 'I've got to warn Pete.'

'Hang on.' Lorna prised the phone from Claire's fingers and put it to one side. 'Don't you think you ought to calm down a bit first?'

'But what if she finds out where he is and turns up on his doorstep or something? You know what Pete's like about Mum. He wet the bed for three years after she ran off with that bloke. Then Dad caught him cutting her head out of all the family photos. It took years for him to come to terms with it, and now this!'

Lorna chose her words carefully. 'He's a big boy now, Claire. He's probably over it by now.'

Claire laughed humourlessly. 'And you know what the sickest thing of all is? She can't understand why I'm not thrilled to see her.' She dragged her fingers through her blonde hair; normally soft and bouncy, today it had the consistency of chewed string. 'Lorna, I need to sleep on this. I was wondering . . .'

Lorna was one step ahead of her. 'You want to stay here?'

'Just for tonight, if that's OK.'

'No problem. If you don't mind being on your own till I get back from the show.'

'Anything's better than going back to Brockbourne. Veronica's probably still hanging around, and I don't think I could cope with that right now.'

Lorna chuckled. 'You? Not cope? That's a new one on me.'

'Do you think I'm being pathetic, running away?'

'Darling,' replied Lorna, helping herself to another glass of wine, 'everybody has to run away sometimes. It's good for the soul.'

When Lorna had gone Claire sat at the kitchen table for a

long time, just thinking. It was strange. She'd had problems in her life before, she must have done; but they had never taken hold of her the way they were doing right now. Or was it that most of them had been other people's problems, work problems, Pete's problems, Lorna's problems? Yes, maybe that was it. It was easy to stand back and cope and be in control when it was someone else's life that was in turmoil. Not so easy when it was no one's mess but your own.

Her pager buzzed and she groaned into the dregs of her red wine. More problems, that was all she needed. She glanced at the display – CALL AIDAN ROSS – and threw it aside. Probably another offer to buy Paradise Cottage off her. Well, whatever he wanted, it could wait.

Time to ring Pete? Lorna was right; she should calm down first. She put her feet up on the table, leaned back and tried to think beautiful thoughts. Maybe one night away from the Hall would change everything. Veronica's lurid coiffure might spontaneously combust; Great-Aunt Mary might return from the grave to reclaim Paradise Cottage.

You never could tell what tomorrow might bring.

Claire was doodling calculations on a jotting pad when Kieran arrived home, weighed down by two enormous wooden boxes of stuffed dates.

'Hello stranger,' he beamed, puckering up for a kiss he didn't receive. He let the boxes fall with a crash on to Mr Papajian's chipped beige Formica. 'Couldn't keep away, huh?'

He nuzzled into the back of her neck but all she could manage was a weak smile. 'What have you got there?'

'Where? Oh, the dates you mean? I've still got a few contacts in Saudi, so I fixed up a rather brilliant deal for the chap who runs the mini-mart in Tanners Street.'

'Oooh, don't tell me you're turning into Pittville's very own import-export tycoon?'

'Not quite,' admitted Kieran, putting on the kettle. 'But it keeps me out of mischief till I can be bothered to get myself a proper job.'

He reached into the fridge for a piece of pork pie. 'Bastard!'

Claire looked up from her figures. 'Pardon?'

'Not you, that bastard Davey. He's been at my pie again.' He thrust the chunk under Claire's nose. 'See? Where that line was? He's had another two inches at least.'

'Tragic,' said Claire.

'Too damn right it is,' agreed Kieran, through a mouthful of minced pork. 'Or it will be when I get my hands on his onion bhajis.'

'Not the pie, I meant it's tragic what living in a place like this does to people. Do you ever think about anything except who's been nicking what from the fridge?'

'Sometimes.' He sidled up to her, dragging a chair with him. 'Sometimes I think about you.' He gave her shoulder a squeeze. 'What's up, kid? Something got you down?'

For a split second she thought of telling him all about her mother. But it was no use, Kieran wouldn't understand. He was far too uncomplicated; his family's idea of dysfunctional was missing Evensong.

'Nothing,' she said dully.

But Kieran was in one of his more perceptive moods. 'Now, now, don't give me that, I can see something's wrong. Tell Uncle Kieran what's the matter.'

His tickling under the chin produced a faint giggle and a swat. 'Don't!'

'What's this then?'

'Shh. I'm adding up.'

Taking no notice, he slipped the paper out from under her nose and read it. 'Ah. This is to do with Paradise Cottage, isn't it? No wonder you're looking so down in the mouth.'

'Yes, well, so would you if you'd just realised how much it'd cost to restore it properly.' She jabbed her pencil into a hole in the table-top where the melamine had chipped away. 'I might even have to sell to Geoffrey Willenhall, isn't that disgusting? To be honest I think I'd rather buy some dynamite and blow the place sky-high.'

'Hang on there, it can't be as bad as all that.' Kieran sat down beside her and slipped a consoling arm about her shoulders. He was really nice when he was like this, thought Claire; when he stopped acting the fool and allowed himself to be just the soft-hearted, decent bloke he was underneath.

'Oh yes it is, these figures just don't add up. Even if I sold the car, and got the biggest bank loan I can afford, and did some of the work myself, I'd still be several thousand short.'

'But if you did do up the cottage properly you could sell it for a big profit, couldn't you?'

'Well ... yes, I suppose,' she conceded. 'If I could find somebody who didn't mind a sitting tenant keeping pigs in the house.'

Kieran waved this minor consideration aside. 'You could get round that.'

'Anyhow, it's all academic if I don't have that kind of money to invest in the first place.'

Kieran sucked the jelly off his pie crust. 'What about if somebody came along and invested, say, half the money you needed?'

She looked at him quizzically. 'Who? Like Father Christmas?'

'No,' he replied, wiping his mouth with the back of his hand. 'Like me.'

Chapter 12

'Raisins,' said Aidan Ross, producing another one from his hip pocket. 'Pigs love 'em.' As if to confirm this, Brucie gazed up at him adoringly, jaws agape, pink eyes bulging with greed. 'There you go, boy.'

He flicked the raisin away across the path and Brucie pursued it into the undergrowth, rooting around with snuffles of porcine ecstasy. Even Ted looked grudgingly impressed.

'How does a builder get to be so good with pigs?' enquired Claire. 'Or shouldn't I ask?'

He grinned as he went on scribbling in his notebook. 'I once built this luxury piggery for the Earl of Burford. Had the seat ripped out of four pairs of trousers before the head pigman gave me a few tips. There.' He handed over the sheet of paper with his jottings. 'It's only a rough estimate of course, but it'll give you some idea of what we could do for you.'

Claire scanned the figures. Aidan wasn't offering any once-in-a-lifetime bargain deals, but then again there weren't any major shocks there either. 'And this would cover?'

'All the major structural works, as we agreed.' He cast another glance over the outside of Paradise Cottage. 'I'd need to subcontract to a specialist firm for the foundations and the underpinning, of course, but I've not found anything too serious there.'

'And after they'd done their bit?'

'I'd take over.' Hands in pockets, he wandered down the path which bordered the cottage, watched with some suspicion by Ted, who had been pretending to weed an overgrown flower bed for the past two hours. 'Not a bad little place really.'

She followed him. 'You reckon so?'

'In an appalling state of course, you've taken a lot on.' He paused to poke at a chunk of crumbling mortar. 'Don't suppose you've had second thoughts about selling?'

'No.'

'Ah well, can't blame me for trying.' He leaned against the wall. 'I'll pop the final estimate through your door tomorrow, if that's OK. Take your time thinking it over, I know it's a big step.'

For all his cockiness, Claire found herself warming to Aidan. For one thing, there was an air of honest competence about him that came as a breath of fresh air; for another, she was newly flush with Kieran's injection of funds; and, last but not least, he was drop-dead gorgeous.

She held out her hand. 'Thanks. If the final estimate matches what you've put here, I think we can shake on it.'

The grey eyes crinkled appealingly. 'Good. Right then, I guess I'd better get on.'

He didn't make a move, and neither did Claire. For several long moments they stood there, in the gathering dusk, just looking at each other. Then Claire gave way to a reckless impulse.

'I was wondering . . .'

'Yes?'

'If you were free . . . I mean, if you're not doing anything else this evening . . . maybe we could meet up for a drink?'

He opened his mouth to answer, and she was quite sure he was about to say yes; but at that moment a little silver sports car roared up to the front gate of Paradise Cottage.

'Aidan! Aidan, sweetie, it's me!' shouted the bimbette with the blonde bubble curls and the knee-deep décolletage. Leaning over, she clicked open the passenger door. 'Come on, we're going to be late!'

'Sorry.' Aidan's smile wavered between smug and apologetic. 'Looks like I'm spoken for. Some other night, maybe?'

Claire watched him swagger off down the path with the distinct feeling that she had just made an idiot of herself. Yeah, right, she thought. Don't hold your breath.

Naomi was working late. And it was all Kenton Mayberry's fault.

As she sat at her desk, composing a particularly tedious e-mail, she wondered how anybody could derive so much pleasure from being unreasonable. But if Kenton insisted on phoning her from Japan at a time convenient to him, there wasn't much she could do but go along with it.

Shadows flitted across her work as somebody ran past the window, calling urgently to someone else, but Naomi didn't bother turning to see who it was. People wandered about the grounds of Brockbourne Hall at the oddest hours of the day and night. If it wasn't trainee sales reps on an all-night orienteering course, it'd be someone arriving late for the Baroque Recorder Workshop.

She was just wondering if Kenton was ever going to ring when she heard running feet in the open-plan office outside.

'Gotcha! Oh dammit. Come here, you slimy little sod!'

Intrigued, Naomi got up and went outside, just in time to see Ravi hurtling through the general office with an enormous butterfly net.

'What on earth's going on out here?'

'Toads.' He bent forwards, hands on knees, gasping for breath. 'They're everywhere.'

She screwed up her eyes. '*Toads*?' It sounded ludicrous, but now that he came to mention it, she could just make out several brownish-green shapes hopping past the coffee machine. 'Ravi, why are there toads in the building?'

'God knows,' he panted. 'But there's hundreds of them. Can't stop, gotta catch them.'

'Ravi, I don't . . .'

135

He loped off into the distance, tripping over a wastepaper bin on his way to the door. Something landed lightly on Naomi's foot and she looked down. Clamped to the toe of her sensible brown lace-up was a rather warty-looking thing about two inches long, with eyes like tiny yellow marbles. Laughing, she bent down and scooped it gently into the palm of her hand.

'Hello little feller,' she said; and the teenage toad riddiped its approval. 'Are you lost? Let's go and find your chums.'

Claire had been looking forward to a mindless evening of TV and jasmine bubble bath; instead of which, she was standing in the foyer holding a bucket of live toads.

'The problem is, they're spawning, ' explained the man from the Wildlife Trust, extracting a toad from behind the reception desk and dropping it into the bucket.

'Ugh,' said Claire, examining her fingers for slime. 'But why do they have to do it here?'

'Ah, well, I expect they were heading for the lake, same as they do every year, and what with all these new buildings being here, it confused them.'

Claire peeped into the seething bucket, thought better of it and jammed the lid back on. 'You mean this is going to happen every year?'

'I am *not* wading into that pond again!' declared Ravi, leaning on his net.

'Me neither,' piped up a female security guard. 'There's nothing in my contract about ponds. Look, these shoes are ruined.'

'Toad tunnels,' announced Naomi, placidly emptying her suit pockets of the wildlife she'd collected. 'That's what we need.'

All eyes swivelled in her direction. 'What's a toad tunnel?' asked Claire, grudgingly impressed by Naomi's hitherto unsuspected rapport with amphibians.

'You run little concrete tunnels under the toads' normal migration route,' explained the wildlife expert. 'Under roads, that kind of thing. That way, they get where they want to go without getting squashed . . . '

'. . . and we don't end up with pondweed all over our new carpets.' Naomi picked up a couple of buckets. 'I'll just go and pop these in the lake then, shall I?'

'It's OK, I'll do it,' said Claire with reluctant altruism. 'You'll get your good shoes wet.'

'No, no,' insisted Naomi with unusual energy. 'Just lend me your wellies, we're about the same size.'

'What I want to know,' said Ravi as Naomi squeezed her size eights into Claire's size six wellies, 'is how the little blighters got in here in the first place.'

'That's a good point,' nodded the wildlife man. 'One or two I could understand, but hundreds . . . Didn't you say the electric doors were locked at six o'clock?'

'That's right,' agreed Claire. 'You can only open them from the inside if you've got the security code.'

'It's an X File,' decided Ravi. 'Like that time it rained frogs in Milwaukee.'

A security guard's head poked round the side of the reception desk. 'Anybody seen Miss Vance? Kenton Mayberry's on the phone from Japan.'

The following morning, Claire was not at her best. Wearily she poured milk on to her Rice Krispies and shovelled a spoonful into her mouth. If only they didn't look quite so much like toadspawn.

'Sorry Pete,' she yawned into her mobile, curling up on her sofa with the cereal bowl. 'You wouldn't believe what I was doing all last night.'

'Puh-leeze,' he begged. 'Spare me the sordid details of your love-life.'

'As a matter of fact I was collecting toads in a bucket.'

'Toads? Is this some kind of knock-knock joke?'

'No, honestly. We had a plague of toads all over the ground floor. Hundreds of them, nobody's sure how they got in.'

'How Biblical. Did you have boils and locusts as well?'

'Pete,' said Claire firmly, 'you're avoiding the issue.'

There was a brief but telling silence. 'No I'm not, there is no issue. Veronica turns up out of nowhere and says she wants to see me, I say go to hell. End of story.'

Veronica, thought Claire. That was what the two of them had called their mother ever since they were old enough to work out that she wasn't coming back. Veronica. Like she was some tiresome acquaintance who'd fallen out of favour with the family, an irrelevance from way back when. Irrelevant she might be. But she was still their mother.

'Pete, what if she turns up . . . ?'

'You didn't tell her where to find me?'

'Of course not. But she might ask somebody.'

'It doesn't make any difference, I'll still tell her to go to hell.' His voice softened a little. 'Look sis, it's not you I'm angry with, it's her. She can't do this to us and I'm not going to let her.'

Claire's spoon doodled a widening spiral in the mess of cereal and milk. 'It's difficult, Pete.'

'I know. It was rotten of her, turning up like that. But she'll soon get the message and go away.'

'I suppose so.'

'We've managed all these years without her, haven't we? Remember when we were kids, and that big lad teased you about not having a mother?'

She laughed. 'And you challenged him to a fight, and he threw you in the river.'

'But I gave him a bloody nose first.'

'Typical Pete. Always talking with your fists.'

'I'll always be here to protect you, sis. Just you remember that.'

Claire's childhood flooded back into her mind, so vividly it almost hurt. Two frightened little kids and their dad; together they'd taken on the whole world and won. But life couldn't go on being a battle forever. Could it?

'How's the course?' she asked, changing the subject.

'OK I suppose. Bit of a struggle making ends meet though.

Last week we ate nothing but lentils and tinned pineapple. Don't you just wish you were a poverty-stricken student?'

'No thanks, I'm already a poverty-stricken house-owner. Oh by the way, you know I told you Kieran's putting money into renovating the house? Well, I think I've decided on a builder. Guess who?'

'That raving evangelical woman with the pamphlets?'

'No way! Aidan Ross.'

'Aidan Ross! But you said he was a swollen-headed chauvinist with his brain in his pants.'

Claire thought painfully of the idiotic bet she'd made, and the bimbette with the silver sports car. 'Yes, well, he probably is. But I've got to be realistic about this, and his was the best quote by far. Besides, I'm choosing a builder, not a boyfriend.'

'Are you sure about that?'

'Pete! I've *got* a boyfriend. Anyway, Aidan Ross isn't my type. Look,' she glanced at her watch. 'If I don't go I'm going to be late for work. I just wanted to warn you in case Veronica gets in touch.'

'Don't worry sis, forewarned is forearmed. Just do one thing for me, will you?'

'What's that?'

'Whatever you do, don't trust her.'

That night, Claire kept her promise to Lorna and turned up for the last night of *Cabaret*.

On the whole, she wished she hadn't; she had a hunch that Lorna felt the same way. It was downright embarrassing, sitting in an audience so small that it had all been crowded into the front four rows to make the theatre look fuller. And it was such a pity for Lorna. The one and only time she'd actually got to play Sally Bowles, and hardly anybody was there to see her do it.

It wasn't that it was a bad production; although you could hardly expect West End quality with a depleted cast, lights that kept fusing and a stage the size of the average built-in wardrobe. But, as Worm pointed out when she went backstage, there were two other shows in town that week; one was half the price, and the other one had full-frontal nudity. How could the Jasper hope to compete?

At the after-show party Petronella wafted about in floaty scarves, kissing everyone and telling them how terribly sad she was to be leaving them for a five-year contract with the English National Opera.

'No really dahlings, totally sad, you know my heart will always be here at the Jasper.'

'And if you'll believe that you'll believe anything,' said Worm, sitting down on the edge of the stage between Lorna and Claire. 'Here, have a prawn cracker. They're free,' he added.

Lorna scooped up a handful. 'Thank God that's over.'

'You were really good,' said Claire. 'Both of you,' she added as the prawn crackers were moved meaningfully away. They returned and she helped herself to some more.

'The question is, what's it going to be next?' Worm swung his heels against the hollow staging.

'I heard it was going to be Chekhov again,' said a stagehand, helping to push a plywood staircase across the stage.

Everybody groaned. 'Well I was talking to Bethany,' butted in a girl in tight white shorts, 'and she said *The Sound of Music*, for sure.'

Lorna mimed sticking two fingers down her throat. 'Well if Richard thinks I'm reprising my Mother Abbess he's got another think coming. I used to wet myself every time I hit that top A flat.'

'Darling,' said Worm drily. 'We all did.'

'The *Sound of Music* would be better than Chekhov, surely,' reasoned Claire. 'All those kiddies – their mums and dads would be bound to turn up to see it, wouldn't they? You'd have a full house every night.'

'Exactly,' said the girl in the shorts. 'Bums on seats, that's what it's all about.'

'Philistine.'

The door at the far end of the auditorium swung open and

Richard Craddock appeared at the back of the theatre. 'Here we go,' said Lorna. '"You've all done very well, bad luck about the show . . ."'

Worm picked up the refrain. '". . . now go home, sleep it off, and we start rehearsals on Tuesday." I've heard it that many times I can recite it off by heart.'

A ripple of laughter ran round the assembled throng. 'So what's the next show going to be, Richard?' somebody called out. 'Godzilla on Ice?'

No answering smile cracked the mask of utter gloom on the theatre manager's face.

'I don't know how to say this,' he began, stopping in the middle of the aisle and gazing round the theatre as if he was seeing it for the very first – or last – time. 'In fact, I don't think there is an easy way, so I guess I might as well just come out with it.

'I'm really sorry everybody, and I didn't want this to happen, but there was nothing I could do. I'm afraid the Jasper Kendall Theatre has had it. The trustees have just voted to close us down.'

It was one o'clock in the morning, and the Cotswold Cantina was hosting a wake.

Behind a drawn-down blind advertising refried beans, Les Lynch was dispensing tequila and sympathy to the half-dozen survivors of the Jasper's after-show party. The atmosphere was dire. Claire would gladly have headed home hours ago, but every time she got up to leave, Lorna threatened to tell everyone about the time she'd lost her knickers on Paddington Station. Besides, Lorna had had several over the eight. If somebody didn't get her home safely, she'd probably wake up in Pittville Park tomorrow with a toilet seat round her neck.

Depositing an empty bottle of Wigan's finest tequila-style spirit on the counter, Les turned up the hotplate and gave the five-litre pan of bubbling red goo a hearty stir. 'Anyone for any more chilli?'

Silence.

'There's plenty left.'

Shoulders drooped. Eyes glazed. Somebody let out a loud and pungent fart. Taking that as an expression of interest, Les waved his dripping ladle over a stack of empty polystyrene trays. 'Half-price?'

'Les,' said Kelly, the girl in the white satin shorts, 'I thought you said you *liked* us.'

'I'll throw in a free gherkin.' Sure enough one emerged, green and slimy, from a murky jar next to the till. But still there were no takers.

The percussionist, a man whose bald head was as flat and shiny as one of his conga drums, peered blearily into his plastic cup. 'There's no worm in this.'

Lorna raised an eyebrow. 'Thank heavens for small mercies.'

'Where's my worm?' He waved his cup belligerently. 'I want a worm.'

Les dropped the gherkin into his cup. 'There you go Rog, on the house.'

Roger scowled. 'It's not wriggling.'

Les raised his eyes to the heavens, picked up the cup and gave it a good shake. 'See? It's wriggling now. More tequila anybody?'

A half-dozen plastic cups appeared from nowhere. Claire took this as her cue to escape. 'I really ought to be going Lorna, I've got forty-nine Japanese exchange students in the morning.'

Lorna clutched at her arm. 'You can't go, you're not pissed yet.'

'I can't get pissed,' Claire pointed out, unclamping Lorna's fingers. 'I'm driving, remember? All I've had is Coke. Besides, I wouldn't touch that gut-rot if you paid me.'

'Bloody shame.' Lorna shook her head tipsily, and another four hairpins pinged out of her unravelling hairdo. 'Bloody shame, not getting pissed.' She rubbed a hand across her face, smearing her plum-coloured lipstick. 'Go on, have a drink, it'll put hairs on your chest.'

Claire extracted the cup from Lorna's fingers and put it firmly down on the shelf by the window. 'I think you've had enough already. Come on, let's go.' She tried sticking her hand under Lorna's arm and hauling her to her feet, but her ankles were twisted round the legs of the stool and it was like trying to prise a limpet off a rock.

'God I'm depressed,' groaned Worm, chin resting on his hands, elbows propped up on the counter.

'So what's new?' said Kelly, tossing another free drink down her throat. 'You're always depressed.'

'No I'm not, I'm only depressed when I'm in here.' Worm turned baleful eyes on the proprietor. 'Les, why am I always depressed when I see you?'

Les slid a wooden spoon down the back of his trousers and scratched his buttocks reflectively. 'Because you're jealous of my success?' he ventured.

Charisse the ASM chortled. 'Or 'cause you're so suave and sophisticated?'

Worm thought for a moment. 'Nah,' he decided. 'It's because I know I'm going to get the shits.'

Claire turned her attention back to Lorna, who was huddled over a bottle of tequila like a mother hen incubating a chick. 'Come on, put your coat on, it's time for beddy-byes.'

Lorna stroked the bottle lovingly. 'I've got to do something,' she said. 'I've got to *do* something. Nobody understands.'

Claire resigned herself to at least another half-hour of maudlin reminiscences. They'd already had How I Nearly Played the Lead in *Thomas the Tank Engine*, Why I Turned Down Christopher Biggins, and How I Almost Got a Standing Ovation in Dumfries. Reluctantly she hoisted her bottom back on to her stool. 'What do you mean, nobody understands?'

'About me. About my career.' Claire took a closer look at Lorna and saw that she was not quite as drunk as she sounded. 'I'm twenty-six, Claire, I've done nothing!'

'You've done loads,' protested Claire.

Lorna dismissed the suggestion with a wild shake of her

shaggy mane. 'No, no, I haven't. Nothing *good*. Nothing that matters. I was going to be a star by the time I was twenty-five, and look at me!'

Claire slid an arm round her shoulders. 'There's still plenty of time to be a star.'

'No there isn't. It's hopeless, I've blown it.' Lorna's gaze dropped down to her attractively substantial bosom. 'They asked me to do Page Three once, you know. Said I could be a sensation with a pair like these.'

'Did they?' Claire regarded her best mate's chest in an entirely new light. 'You never said.'

'That's 'cause I told them where to shove their photo shoot. Oh no, I wasn't going to prostitute my boobs all over their scummy little tabloid, just for a few quid and five minutes in the spotlight. I was going to be a proper star.'

'Quite right too,' said Claire.

Lorna sniffed. 'Quite right my arse, I should've taken the money and run.' She undid the top button of her shirt and peered down the front of it. 'And now even you bastards are going droopy on me. I'm telling you Claire, I'm over the hill.'

There was no point in arguing with Lorna when she was in this kind of mood. The only thing you could do was go with the flow. 'All right, so you're a bit too old to be a Page Three girl, so what? Be a star at something else.'

'Like what? A star checkout girl? A star floor-scrubber?'

'A famous actress, that's what you've always wanted to be.'

'The theatre's closing, Claire, or haven't you noticed?'

'There are lots of other theatres.'

'And thousands and thousands of other actors.' Lorna's shoulders sagged in a very un-Lorna-like way, aiming her bosoms at the floor. 'Be yourself, everybody said; they'll love you. Well, I've been myself and they don't. End of story.'

Claire sighed. 'So ... oh I don't know ... be somebody else,' she said, recklessly.

Lorna's back uncurled slightly. 'What?'

'Somebody else,' she repeated, feeling slightly foolish. 'If people don't like you as you are, change who you are.' She caught the incredulous look on Worm's face. 'Yeah, yeah, I know, stupid idea.'

'Be somebody else?' To Claire's surprise, Lorna's eyes lit up. 'Stupid? You're a genius!' Sitting up straight, she banged the empty tequila bottle on the counter. 'Drinks all round, Les. Claire's paying.'

Chapter 13

The following evening, Claire was sitting in Kieran's room when his mobile rang.

'Kieran Hart . . . oh.' He looked taken aback.

'Problem?'

He waved her aside and went on talking. 'Well, yes, she is, but . . .' He put his hand over the mouthpiece and hissed, 'It's your mother.'

A cold hand clenched at Claire's guts. 'What!'

'How did she get my number?' demanded Kieran.

'God knows.' Her expression turned thunderous. 'Oh bloody hell, this is all I need.'

'Shall I tell her to . . . ?'

'No, give it here, I'll tell her myself.' Claire grabbed the phone and rolled off Kieran's Ikea sofa-bed, ready to do battle. 'Veronica? Veronica, what the hell do you think you're doing?'

'Weed, darling!' gushed Veronica. 'I hope your friend doesn't mind me calling you on his number, only you forgot to give me yours.'

'Actually, I didn't forget,' snapped Claire. 'And how did you get this number, anyway?' she demanded.

Veronica chose to ignore the question. 'He's got a lovely voice, darling. Ever so sexy. And Kieran's such a nice name.' She rattled on at breakneck speed. 'Now, you simply have to tell me: is he as handsome as he sounds on the phone?'

Claire reddened as she looked across at Kieran and flashed him an embarrassed half-smile. She mouthed 'Sorry.' Then, getting up, she walked across to the other side of the room. 'Veronica, stop this right now!'

'Stop what, darling? I'm only taking a mother's natural interest in her daughter's love-life. Is it serious between you two? Or are you still playing the field?'

Claire's knuckles whitened. 'This is none of your damn' business.'

'Oh, I understand. He's listening in. Never mind, I can tell you're very fond of him. You must be if he's investing in the cottage. Did I hear somewhere that his father's a farmer?'

Claire's jaw dropped. 'Who have you been talking to about me?'

'You could do worse, you know. How many acres does he have?'

'Veronica,' said Claire, finally gathering her wits. 'What is this about? Why have you phoned me?'

Veronica's voice became even more syrupy. 'Just to have a lovely little chat, sweetheart.'

'Oh really. What sort of "lovely little chat"?'

Go on, thought Claire; tell me what it is you're after, you grasping cow. You wouldn't be phoning me if you didn't want something.

'Oh, just about Aunt Mary's cottage.'

Aha, thought Claire. Now we're getting to the punchline. But if you think you're screwing a single penny out of me you've got another think coming.

'Oh what a surprise,' she said sarcastically. 'What about it?'

'Well, you did mention that you go down there every weekend, so I thought I'd just let you know I'm definitely free on Saturday so I'll be able to come along with you and Kieran. Won't that be lovely?'

'Shit,' said Claire as she switched off the phone and handed it back to Kieran.

'Bad news?'

147

'My mother is *always* bad news.' Claire flopped back down on to the sofa bed, picked up a curry-stained cushion and pummelled hell out of it. 'She's only gone and invited herself to the cottage on Saturday.'

'Ah,' said Kieran. 'Oh well, I suppose she was bound to want to see it sooner or later.'

'Later would be nice,' grunted Claire. 'About two hundred years later. And it's got abso-bloody-lutely nothing to do with her, either!'

Kieran sat down on the sofa, pulled off Claire's left shoe and started massaging her foot. 'How's this feel?'

'Fantastic. Where did you learn to do it?'

'I dunno really. But it works a treat on egg-bound hens.'

Claire lay back and wriggled her toes luxuriously. She couldn't remember the last time anybody had pampered her; she was always far too busy steering skilfully round other people's egos to think about doing indulgent things for herself. It was really nice having somebody to do it for her.

If she was honest, she hadn't been at all sure about Kieran when Lorna introduced them – he'd come across as far too rough and ready, and not really her type, whatever that was. But since he'd offered to invest in the cottage their relationship had been taking significant strides forward. For a start, Claire's spare toothbrush now lived in Kieran's sponge bag.

'Aidan's mates are starting at the cottage on Wednesday,' she fretted, surfacing through the warm pink fuzz of pleasure. No matter how much fun she might have, the spectre of Paradise Cottage was never very far away, thumbing its nose at all her attempts to forget it.

'Shut up and lie still,' he scolded, giving her big toe a reproving tweak. 'Are you sure it's wise, getting involved with this Ross bloke? He looks like a shyster to me.'

'I know he can be a bit . . . full of himself.'

'A bit!'

'But he knows what he's doing. And he quoted a fair price.'

'Hmm, well, let's hope you're right. I've got a lot of money tied up in that cottage, you know.'

'So have I, don't remind me.' She tried to relax but it was really, really difficult. 'Oh Kieran . . . '

'Lie still.'

'Ow! I can't, I'm wondering what they'll be up to while I'm at work. And then there's Ted. We've got to move all his stuff into the workshop. And the pig! What about the pig?'

'Let me worry about that,' ordered Kieran.

'I'm not worrying, I'm just wondering.'

'Well you can stop that as well, because I'm going to be there to make sure nothing goes wrong, OK?'

She opened one eye and gazed adoringly at him through the fronds of her collapsing fringe. 'You will? All day?'

'Yes, I shall spend the entire day in that horrible cottage with Ted and Brucie. Underpinners, bricklayers, deathwatch beetle – let 'em all come, I'll take care of everything, I promise.'

'Wow,' purred Claire, for once happy to delegate the whole damn thing to anybody who wanted it. 'My hero.'

'Too right. I ask you, does that deserve a medal or what?'

She grinned and pulled him down on top of her. 'I don't know about a medal, but it definitely deserves a snog.'

'Come on mate,' urged Aidan, shuffling from one foot to the other. He nodded towards the white panel-van with its cargo of impatient builders, parked in the lane outside Paradise Cottage. 'This lot want to get started this side of the Millennium.'

'All right, all right,' growled Kieran. 'I'm doing my best, OK?'

'Want me to have a go?' enquired Aidan, a half-smile playing about his lips.

'No! Just get on with your job and I'll get on with mine.'

'Chance'd be a fine thing,' replied Aidan, heading back towards the van. 'Better put on another brew lads, looks like we could be in for a long day.'

'Leave everything to me, Claire. I'll deal with Ted, it'll be easy.' Kieran cringed at the memory. He could just imagine the

149

look on Claire's face when she found out about this fiasco – and it wasn't much fun being made to look a prat in front of Mr Smug Features, either.

He rattled the door handle so hard it threatened to come apart in his hand, but the back door of Paradise Cottage remained resolutely locked.

'Ted?' he yelled through an inch and a half of rain-warped pine. 'Ted, are you in there?'

A few more seconds passed. The gang of builders watched in amusement from the safety of their van, passing round tin mugs of tea and Penguin biscuits. Aidan was starting to look edgy. Kieran tried to keep the note of desperation out of his voice.

'Ted!'

At last a muffled voice responded. 'You still there then?'

'Of course I'm still bloody here!'

'What you want?'

Kieran could feel his teeth clenching in frustration; any harder and they'd probably shatter into crazy paving, cartoon-style. 'Ted, are you going to stop playing silly buggers and unlock this door?'

'No,' came the blunt reply. 'And it's Mr Merriman to you.'

Stubborn old git, thought Kieran. If it'd been up to him, he'd have slipped the builders a few quid to 'accidentally' break down the door and forcibly relocate Ted to his workshop at the bottom of the garden – on which good money had been wasted turning it into a snug temporary home. But Claire had made him promise to handle Ted with kid gloves, and in his more rational moments he had to admit she had a point. Like it or not, Ted Merriman had legal rights and 'Cruel landlord evicts irritating but harmless old codger' would not look good splashed across the local paper.

Time to swallow his pride. He took a deep breath, knelt down and lifted up the edge of Ted's homemade pig flap. If Brucie could squeeze through it, maybe he could too. Or maybe not, he thought as his new leather jacket snagged on the rough-sawn edges of the hole. He sat back on his haunches, cursing, and inspected the damage. As if to rub salt into the wound, at that moment Brucie sauntered across the back yard, trotted past him and eased his pink hairy bulk through the hole, leaving the flap clattering in his wake.

Gales of muted laughter drifted across from the van.

'Bastard pig.' Kieran lifted up the flap for a second try, and this time a wet pink snout pushed itself lovingly into his face. 'Eurgh, get off!' He flailed disgustedly at the snout and a long slobbery tongue extracted itself from his ear. 'Ted ... Mr Merriman ... *please* be reasonable.'

'I'm not comin' out and that's that,' retorted Ted defiantly. Kieran had the distinct impression the old boy was enjoying this. Brucie's round pink eyes peeked inquisitively through the flap. He could have sworn that damned pig was laughing too. 'I know my rights, you can't throw me out of my home.'

Kieran sighed. 'Nobody's trying to throw you out,' he protested. 'All we're asking you to do is move into your nice cosy workshop for a little while, so the builders can make the cottage safe.'

'There's nothing wrong with my cottage.'

'Nothing wrong! It's a deathtrap. And it's not your cottage, is it? It's Miss Snow's.'

Ted chose to ignore that crucial point. 'Look here,' he continued, 'what's goin' to happen to me after the work's done? You tell me that.'

We're going to find a devious yet scrupulously legal way of getting rid of you, that's what, thought Kieran; but he could hardly tell Ted that – he hadn't even brought Claire round to his way of thinking yet. That girl was way too soft-hearted for her own good.

He crossed his fingers behind his back. 'Nothing's going to happen, Mr Merriman. Just unlock this door and we can talk about it.'

There was a long, rather promising silence. Then ...

'Bugger orf. An' take your builders with you.'

Kieran stood up to the accompaniment of ironic cheering. As

151

he turned round, brushing mud off his knees, he saw that the builders had been joined by a motley assortment of grinning villagers, lined up along the front wall like spectators at a bare-knuckle fight.

'That's right,' commented Aidan with heavy irony. 'You tell him. Don't take any nonsense.'

'If I want your advice' replied Kieran curtly, 'I'll ask for it.' Then he wondered what the bloody hell he was going to do next.

Claire glared daggers at Kieran as they manoeuvred a huge, pig-chewed armchair out of Paradise Cottage.

'What's that you said? "Leave it all to me, Claire, it'll be a piece of cake"?'

'Yes, yes, all right,' grunted Kieran, aiming a kick at Brucie who was running about wildly, convinced that the whole thing was some wonderful new game designed just for him. 'No need to rub it in.'

'I'll be in deep shit if Naomi finds out I'm not at the dentist, you know. We've got fifty-six standing stones being delivered to the Hall today.'

'For the stone circle? Hope your loony friend Orion's suitably grateful.'

'He'd better be.'

'Here, let me help you with that,' volunteered Aidan, pausing from supervising the builders to take one end of the armchair from Claire.

She flashed him a grateful smile. 'Thanks Aidan.' Picking up yet another box of Ted's peculiar possessions, she followed the chair on its slithery progress across the garden to the work-shop. What a smelly old man like Ted could want with a Corby trouser press was beyond her, not to mention the lava lamp and the collection of Delia Smith cookery cards; but he'd made it perfectly clear that he wasn't going anywhere without them.

'Looks like you owe me fifty quid,' Aidan grinned over his

shoulder. In the background, builders were throwing rubbish into a skip.

She pulled a face. 'OK, no need to rub it in.'

'Well, it was a silly bet anyway,' he said. 'I mean, a girl like you, on your own? No chance.'

That riled Claire a bit, but not as much as it riled Kieran. 'She's not on her own, she's got me.'

Aidan looked unimpressed.

They slithered on. It was a cold, windy day but Claire could feel her skin start to prickle with sweat. 'I hope this isn't going to take long,' she panted, with a glare aimed at Kieran. 'I've got the Southern Regional Clowns' Convention to sort out.'

'The *what*?'

'Red noses, stripey pants, collapsing cars? Believe me, you don't want to know.'

Brucie squealed delightedly as he galloped round the garden, describing lunatic circles and kicking up great gobbets of mud. 'Bloody thing,' panted Kieran, lashing out with a gumboot. 'Where's Ted gone? Why can't he keep that blasted animal under control?'

They reached the workshop and he nudged open the door with his knee. 'In here?'

'Just to the right,' Claire directed him.

The armchair forced its way through the door of the work-shop, leaving a tuft of horsehair on a jutting nail, and Claire dumped her box of assorted oddities on to the square of blue carpet. It was hard to see why Ted had been reluctant to move in here; it was much cosier than the cottage, didn't smell nearly as peculiar, and the electrics were almost modern.

'It's not Brucie's fault he's all excited.' She smiled indulgently as the pig nudged in ahead of them. 'He thinks it's a lovely big game, don't you sweetie?'

Kieran stared at her, aghast, as she reached down and gave Brucie's ear an affectionate scratch.

'*Sweetie*? You've changed your tune haven't you? What happened to the slavering brute with the fangs of doom?'

153

'Well.' Claire felt slightly foolish. 'I've just got to know Brucie a bit better, I suppose. He's quite cute really.'

'And intelligent,' cut in Aidan, on his way out of the door. 'Don't forget intelligent.' He disappeared out into the garden.

'He's a *pig*!' said Kieran, as if that explained everything.

Claire looked up, wondering for a moment if they were talking about Brucie or Aidan. 'So?'

'So he stinks to high heaven, he's got filthy habits, and the sooner he's a string of sausages the better.'

Claire put her hands over Brucie's ears. 'How can you say that? He's not like that at all, he's even house-trained.' She reconsidered. 'Well, almost.'

Kieran perched on the arm of the chair. 'Listen, my dad's a farmer, you don't know pigs like I do. Surely I must have told you about the piglet that ate its own testicles?'

Claire withdrew her hand abruptly from Brucie's snout. 'Kieran, I think I'd remember!'

'There my dad was, castrating this litter of piglets . . .'

'Do I want to hear this?'

'It only took a second or two to . . . you know . . . pick their pockets, and then he drops the bits on the yard floor, see, and . . .'

'Bits!'

'Well, he's just done the last piglet and when he turns round for a minute to wipe off the knife, the disgusting little beast's only run off and gobbled up its own . . .'

'Gee, thanks Kieran,' said Claire, feeling faintly queasy. 'I really needed to know that.'

'So,' said Kieran. 'You can see why I never could stand pigs.'

There was a jaunty rat-a-tat-tat on the workshop door.

'Afternoon folks. Hard at work are we?'

It was Cousin Geoffrey's loathsome voice, a voice Claire could definitely have done without. She turned round slowly, giving herself time to rearrange her face into a guarded smile.

'Oh, it's you. Geoffrey. How nice.'

'*Cousin* Geoffrey now, don't forget we're family.' He slapped her on the back with such violent bonhomie that he almost knocked her head-first into the armchair. 'This your young man is it?' He looked Kieran up and down, and the grin broadened into a smarmy leer. 'Well, well, right pair of lovebirds aren't you? You never told me you was courting, Claire.'

Claire stifled a retch. Brucie bared his teeth, emptied his bladder on to Geoffrey's wellingtons and stalked out, squiggly tail held high.

Kieran stuck out his hand. 'Hi. Kieran Hart.'

'Geoffrey Willenhall, Low Common Farm.' He shook his foot, unconcernedly sprinkling Ted's rag rug with pig-wee. 'Me an' Claire are neighbours now, aren't we, cousin?' Claire's smile strained at the corners. 'Old Ted's leading you a merry dance I see. Looks like he's got you runnin' about like headless chickens.' He wandered about, picked up the lava lamp, glanced underneath it and put it down.

'Not at all,' said Claire defensively. 'In fact we're all getting along fine, aren't we Kieran?'

He looked up, startled. 'What?'

'Fine. Us and Ted and the builders. We're *fine*. Aren't we, Kieran?'

'We are?' Kieran caught the warning glint in Claire's eye. 'Oh yes, we are. Definitely. Salt of the earth is old Ted Merriman. And that Aidan Ross. Top guy.'

Cousin Geoffrey peered into an elephant's foot umbrella stand, then a Pooh Bear cookie jar and the empty grassbox of a brand-new hover mower. He guffawed. 'That's one way of puttin' it I suppose. Though there's them as'd call old Ted a bloody nuisance.' Thumbs in the pockets of his greasy waistcoat, he gazed out of the window at the cottage, its roof sagging like the spine of a broken-down old carthorse. 'Don't know why you're bothering with all this titivatin'. Old wreck wants knockin' down.'

'Really?' said Claire flatly.

'Oh, definitely. Matter of fact, I could sort that out for you if you wanted.'

155

'And you wouldn't just be saying that because you want to get your hands on the land?'

Geoffrey grinned. 'Would I want to do down my own family?'

'I don't know,' replied Claire coolly. 'Would you?'

He ignored the jibe and went on wandering round the room, picking things up and scrutinising them as though he was viewing lots in a bizarre auction. 'Now, if you was to listen to me . . .'

Claire knew what was coming next. The hard sell. Ears firmly closed, she filled a kettle from the tap by the door and lit the Calor gas stove. 'You'll have to excuse me,' she said brightly. 'I'm just going to ask Ted if he wants a nice cup of tea.'

Ted was not difficult to find. All Claire had to do was follow the trail of empty crisp packets that led to the living room, where an old man and a lop-eared pig were sitting side by side, engrossed in *Teletubbies*.

'Time to go, Ted,' announced Claire brightly.

Ted sank a little further into the derelict settee. 'Not ready,' he mumbled.

'There's a nice mug of tea waiting for you in the workshop,' she said, invitingly. 'And I've put the fire on for you.'

Ted grunted. 'I'm all right here.'

'No you're not.' Claire said firmly. 'The builders need to start work and they can't take up the floor if you're sitting on it, can they?'

She took a step forward and a Jaffa Cake squelched under her right foot. On the screen, the Tubby Custard machine had just exploded, and the Noo-Noo was racing about hysterically, trying to clear up the mess. It would have its work cut out in Paradise Cottage, thought Claire.

'I'm going down the shop later,' she coaxed. 'Can I get you anything?'

At this, Ted showed a flicker of interest. Claire hadn't known him long but she'd already worked out that Ted's favourite hobby, after watching TV, was spending money. Nothing else could account for the complete works of Jeffrey Archer, or the novelty thimble collection.

'Mebbe.'

'What then? Some cake? Another packet of biscuits?'

He considered for a moment. 'All right, Garibaldis, mind. An' a pound of lard. Fer me chest.'

Claire resisted the urge to squirm. '*Lard*?'

'Best thing in the world fer keepin' the cold out, is lard. Plenty of lard an' a red flannel vest, an' you're set up till July.'

'Right,' said Claire, making a mental note. 'Lard. Now, shall we get on with moving you across?'

'Not yet.'

Time was pressing on. Soon, even Naomi would notice she wasn't anywhere near Brockbourne Hall. She switched to a different tactic: emotional blackmail.

'Come on Ted,' she urged. 'You can't change your mind now. You *promised*.'

'I never.'

'Oh yes you did.'

Ted let out a sigh of defeat. 'Oh all right, p'raps I did. But if I'm goin' down the workshop I'm taking me spare telly with me.'

'Of course you are.' Relieved, Claire reached for the remote control but Ted got to it first.

'Not right now,' he hedged. '*Baywatch Nights* is on in a minute.'

'Morning, Miss Snow.'

'Morning.' Claire closed the door of the village shop behind her and waved a slightly self-conscious acknowledgement to the three old women huddled round the pillar box. By lunchtime it would be all round the village that Mary Willenhall's great-niece had bought a pound of lard and a tube of Preparation H. It took some getting used to, being an object of local curiosity.

'Hello there.' The terribly posh lady who ran the riding

school came striding by, shopping basket swinging in time to the click of her heels on the pavement.

'Hello, Mrs . . . ?'

'Waverley, Amanda Waverley. You must call me Manda, everyone does. I hear you're having some work done up at the old cottage.'

'Some renovations, that's right.'

'Well I won't say it's not long overdue.' Manda produced an ornate business card from her handbag. 'When you've finished, you simply must give my interior designer a call. Guido's absolutely marvellous. Charges a hundred an hour of course, but he has such a fabulous way with Roman blinds.'

She'd hardly got another twenty yards across the village green when Annie from the shop came running after her. 'Miss Snow! Miss Snow, you forgot your lard.'

'I'll forget my own head one of these days.' She slipped it into her carrier bag. 'Thanks.'

'Settling in, are you?'

'Well, I've not actually moved in to the cottage.'

'No, course not, it's a miracle old Ted can stand it in that place, the state it's in, let alone normal folk. You ask me, it's a wonder he's not gone down with something nasty.' Annie stepped back and looked Claire up and down. 'Well, if it ain't the truth!'

'What?'

'You're the living spit of your Great-Aunt Mary when she was a girl, anybody told you that?'

Only the entire population of Lilcombe Magna, thought Claire. 'I think somebody did mention it.'

'Well, if you're half as good a woman as she was, you'll not be doing so bad.'

Claire carried on across the village green to St Ogmore's. She'd been putting off this moment, but the need kept gnawing away at her and it wouldn't be put off any longer. The need to see the only thing that really remained of Mary Willenhall. Her grave.

158

The squat little church gave the lie to the theory that old equalled beautiful. Built for sturdiness rather than grace, it was not so much a poem in stone as a bad limerick. What's more, the money had run out halfway through building the tower, and a former impecunious squire had pawned the stained-glass windows.

The grassy graveyard lay at the east end of the church, a higgledy-piggledy arrangement of lichen-covered stone slabs, interspersed with the odd weeping angel and rugged cross.

'Mornin', Miss Snow,' said Old John, sitting on the corner of a tomb puffing away at his pipe. 'I were wonderin' when you'd show up.'

'You were?' Can everybody in this village read my mind, she wondered.

'Stands to reason you'd want to pay your respects.' The verger stood up, stretching his ageing joints. 'She's over by the wall, I'll show you.'

There wasn't much to see of Mary Willenhall's grave; not even a headstone. Only a mound of fresh flowers which made Claire's shop-bought bunch of daffodils look positively puny. She gaped. 'Who left all these?'

Old John shrugged. 'Folks round about thought a lot of Mary. Wonderful woman she was. Remembered a lot of the village folk in her will, you know.'

'She did?'

'Loved people she did, see. 'Specially kids.' He gazed into the middle distance. 'Terrible sad she was, not havin' any of her own, what with her husband dying young.'

'Oh. I see, poor Aunt Mary.' Claire laid her daffodils on the mound of tulips and narcissi. 'And what about Ted Merriman? Where does he come in?'

Old John sucked on the stem of his pipe. She could tell he was thinking, forming every word carefully before he said it. 'He were company for her,' he said. 'A Barnardo's boy.'

'More than just a lodger then?'

'Aye, a real friend to her he was. Like an old married couple

159

they were, but Mary started spendin' more and more time away from Lilcombe, and Ted ... well ... he's a bit simple, you know. Can't manage money, can't keep house to save his life. Needs someone keepin' an eye on him.' He scraped around in the bowl of his pipe, shielded it against the breeze and relit it. 'Got the pig 'cause he were lonely, see.' He shook his head sadly. ''Tis a terrible thing to lose your family, an' die old an' alone.'

'Now don't get me wrong,' said Geoffrey, helping himself to a mug of tea. 'She's a lovely girl, is Claire, but you know the ladies.' He gave Kieran's shoulder a matey nudge. 'Not like us, are they? Get these daft ideas into their heads and it's the devil's own job to shift 'em. Take my Emmy ...'

Kieran smiled uncomfortably. 'Yes. Yes, I suppose so. But Claire's nobody's fool.'

Geoffrey held up his hands, as though horrified at the very suggestion. 'No, no, 'course she ain't. Very smart young lady is our Claire. But old Ted's got her wrapped round his little finger, see.' He shook his head sadly. 'And I don't like to think of one of my own bein' swindled by that crafty old beggar.'

Kieran sat down on the edge of the workbench that had been scrubbed down and pressed into service as a temporary table. It was ever so snug in here, with its gas fire, kitchenette and single bed: a kind of dream shed, the sort of home from home a man could get passionate about. Geoffrey had a point: it was completely wasted on Ted Merriman.

'I don't think we'll have any more trouble from Ted,' ventured Kieran. 'Not now Claire's had a chat with him. He likes her.'

'Oh, I'm sure he does,' chuckled Geoffrey. 'I mean, don't we all, eh? But that don't mean he's goin' to play her straight, does it?' His pink-rimmed eyes flicked towards Kieran's. 'Any more than that Aidan Ross is.'

Kieran pricked up his ears. 'What do you mean? About Ross?'

'Oh, nothing,' replied Geoffrey casually. 'But if I was you I'd be wonderin' why he's falling over himself to work on this place.' He picked up a small wooden box, shook it and put it down again. 'So – you've put some of your own cash into this place, have you?'

'How did you know that?' asked Kieran uneasily.

Geoffrey shrugged. 'Oh, you can't keep nothin' to yourself in a place like Lilcombe Magna. If a cow farts it's all over Gloucestershire by dinnertime.'

He burped reflectively, rasping a pudgy hand over his close-cropped beard.

'Thing is, like I said, I don't like to see honest folk squanderin' their time and money, and believe me, your money's wasted on that old heap.' He cocked his head towards the house. Kieran wondered if he meant Paradise Cottage or Ted; most probably both. 'Now, you know I've had my eye on this bit of land,' Geoffrey went on.

'So I've heard. But it's not for sale.'

'Believe me, you should take me up on my offer, you'll not get a better one, no matter what that Ross tells you.'

'Maybe so,' replied Kieran. 'But it's Claire's house and it's her decision.'

'So persuade her.' Geoffrey's smirk was seedily suggestive. 'Bet you could get round her easy as pie if you put your mind to it, resourceful young feller like you. Who knows, you might even persuade me to up my offer. Not that I'm promising nothing, you understand.'

'I know selling up now seems like the easy way out,' conceded Kieran, 'but the cottage will be worth a lot more once it's done up.'

'Maybe.' Geoffrey picked Ted's breadknife off the table and started scraping the dirt from under his fingernails. 'Maybe not. I mean, I'm only interested in the land, aren't I? Don't matter how much you do up that cottage, how many folk'll want to buy it with *him* in it?'

Kieran suppressed a brief shudder of panic. The thought of

161

what Ted and Brucie could do to a sensitively restored bijou Cotswold residence was enough to break your heart. Ted slaughtering chickens on the limed-oak worktops ... Brucie having a nice hot soak in the whirlpool bath ... Pig-droppings floating in the bidet ...

No! Kieran brought himself up short. He and Claire had been over this a dozen times; and – sitting tenant or not – Ted Merriman was not going to hold them to ransom.

'Don't you worry about Mr Merriman,' he said firmly. 'I'm sure he'll be amenable to a bit of persuasion.'

Geoffrey chortled. 'A few quid in his back pocket, you mean? You're an optimist, boy, I'll give you that.'

'Oh, I'm sure it'll be worth all the trouble in the end,' said Kieran. Out of the corner of his eye he watched Ted staggering out of the cottage, his beloved TV set clasped to his bosom and the power cable dragging in the mud behind him. 'Yeah,' he said again, as though to convince himself it was true. 'It'll definitely be worth it in the end.'

Cousin Geoffrey wiped the breadknife on the seat of his corduroys and tossed it back on top of a stack of currant buns. 'Best be off,' he announced. 'Can't stand around chatting all day. You think about what I said though,' he called back over his shoulder. 'Sell up to me, you'll not regret it.'

He went off whistling down the path, acknowledging Ted's mute scowl with a mocking wave.

That night, Claire couldn't sleep. She lay alone in her little bed at Brockbourne Hall, listening to the distant sounds of a private party in the Tewkesbury Suite.

No matter how she tried to empty her mind, Old John's words kept playing over and over again. ''Tis a terrible thing to lose your family, and die old and alone.' But Veronica's not old, she told herself. And she's not alone either, she's got a husband back in Portugal. Why can't she just go back there and leave me and Pete in peace?

It didn't wash; not quite. OK, so maybe Veronica really was a grasping bitch, interested in her kids only as long as there was something in it for her. Then again, maybe she was telling the truth. Maybe she genuinely did want a reconciliation before it was too late.

Claire rolled herself up in the duvet, winding herself into a tight little cocoon. It's no good, you've got to let go, she told herself. You've got to give her a chance to show her true colours.

It's the only way you'll know for sure.

Chapter 14

Up till now, Veronica had gone through life believing there was no such word as 'no', but Owen Pendle didn't seem to share her philosophy.

She uncrossed her legs in a long, slow slither of seven-denier Lycra, and wondered vaguely if he was gay. He must be. Forty-five or not, there wasn't a normal man alive who could resist a flash of Veronica Snow's thighs.

'Oh please,' she pouted.

The solicitor shuffled the papers on his desk but did not look up. 'I really am sorry, Mrs Callaghan . . . ' He didn't sound it.

'It's Snow now. But you can call me Veronica,' she added winsomely.

'Like I said, Mrs Snow, I'm sorry, but rules are rules.'

'Ah, but you know what they say,' she coaxed. 'Rules are made to be broken. I'm sure we could, you know, come to some arrangement.'

The sternly professional expression solidified on Pendle's face. 'I'm a solicitor, Mrs Snow, not a used car dealer.'

'Of course not.' She laughed at his little joke, though she had the feeling it wasn't meant to be one. How could it be, when the wretched little man had no sense of humour? If she hadn't been so desperate she'd have told him where to stick his bequest. But desperate she was, since everything had gone so horribly wrong with Ronnie. She leaned forward, treating him to a good deal more cleavage than he deserved. 'Look,' she said. 'Can I speak my mind?'

Pendle's impassive mask concealed a trace of unease. 'Go ahead. But I really can't bend the rules, you know. The terms of Mary Willenhall's will are quite specific.'

'But I really need this inheritance!' she protested. 'Ever since Ronnie threw me . . . I mean, since I left Ronnie, well, things haven't been easy for me. My divorce settlement's going to take forever to come through. The plain fact is, I haven't got enough to live on. You don't want to see me thrown in the gutter do you?'

Pendle remained resolutely unmoved. 'Perhaps you could get a temporary job?' he suggested. 'Until things are sorted out.'

Veronica stared at him, aghast, wondering if this was another of his humourless little jokes. Work? My God, she hadn't done that since she was sixteen, and even then she'd spent more time ogling the manager.

'This is not fair!' she blurted out. 'That bequest is rightfully mine!' So's Paradise Cottage, she added in silent resentment, but there was no point in arguing about that, seeing as she couldn't afford to challenge the will.

'Once you fulfil the conditions, yes. As I said, they are very specific.'

'But the old woman was obviously ga-ga! I mean, it stands to reason, she'd never have left Paradise Cottage to Claire if she wasn't,' pleaded Veronica. Pendle didn't react. 'And I've bent over backwards to do what Auntie Mary wanted, haven't I?' she wheedled. 'I've really, really tried.'

Pendle's left eyebrow twitched; it was the only sign of emotion on his sublimely slappable face. 'So,' he said. 'If I was to pick up this telephone now and call Claire, she'd tell me the two of you have buried all your differences?'

Veronica's frozen smile developed several microscopic cracks. 'Well . . . I mean . . .'

'And what about Peter? Have you made things up with him?'

'I know what my son's name is, thank you,' snapped Veronica.

She squirmed on her hard chair. 'Look, things aren't completely ironed out between us yet, I admit that, but I've arranged to see Claire tomorrow. At the cottage. Now are you satisfied?'

Owen shook his head and smiled. 'Not quite. But it's a start.'

A man was hanging off the scaffolding that surrounded Paradise Cottage. 'This all right here then, Mr Hart?'

Claire got in before Kieran had a chance to answer. 'Not there, over to the left. And this is *my* cottage, so you can ask me next time, OK?'

She turned back to her drawings, well aware that the builders were making rude gestures behind her back. Well let them. It was utterly infuriating being ignored, just because you were a girl. As if it wasn't bad enough that they assumed Kieran was in charge, some of them had even started deferring to Ted. But this was *her* cottage, not theirs; and nobody was going to tell her what to do with it.

A massive drill whined as the bit churned through solid stone. Claire tried to concentrate on the task she had set herself: redesigning the cottage gardens. At this stage it was all pie in the sky of course; but it was something to do while the house was in turmoil, and now that she'd started she was finding it all rather exciting. The few old photographs she'd managed to track down provided a good general impression of how the cottage grounds had looked in their heyday, forty or fifty years earlier; Claire had made up her mind that that was how they were going to look again.

She called to him across the garden. 'Kieran.'

He looked up from prodding a long stick into the soggy earth. 'Hmm?'

Claire pointed to a bushy tuft of foliage. 'Do you reckon this is a plant or a weed?'

'Christ knows. If it was up to me I'd take a flame-thrower to the whole lot.'

'Don't say that!' She caught sight of a grumpy face pressed up against the workshop window. 'You'll upset Ted.'

'Tough. Anyhow, what's the point of doing up the garden? Whoever buys this place will only dig it up and start again.' He plunged his stick into the ground again. 'I'm sure it's here somewhere, it's got to be, it's on the map.'

Claire walked over. 'How can you *lose* a cesspit?'

A playful spring breeze flicked at the plans as Kieran tried to smooth them out flat on the rotting wooden lid of the coal bunker. They were an elderly photocopy of some tatty Victorian sketches that had turned up in the Council basement, and the interpretation was so free it was difficult to tell which way up they were meant to be.

'You can't,' replied Kieran irritably. 'The damned thing's got to be under here somewhere. If there wasn't so much bloody rubbish . . . ' He aimed a bad-tempered kick at a frayed sheet of corrugated plastic, missed and winced as his toes crunched into a decrepit garden roller.

'Now, now, temper, temper,' soothed Claire, turning the plans the other way up. She jabbed a pencil at the crumpled paper. 'Do you think that's meant to be the coalshed or the outside privy?'

Kieran glanced down, still rubbing his toes. 'God, I don't know. Could be a gravy stain for all I can tell.' He sat down on the garden roller and drew in a deep breath.

'What are you up to now?' enquired Claire, inspecting the remains of a stunted Old English rose bush. 'Trying to locate the cesspit by smell?'

'No, I'm steeling myself to tackle this lot.' He gazed around him. 'Just look at it!'

She raised her head and surveyed the cottage, the yelling workmen swinging about on the scaffolding, the complete chaos that was all down to her. It wasn't as if she hadn't seen builders before, dozens of times; but they'd never been *her* builders, working on *her* little house. It was warm for early May, and although the house was a wreck, in the timorous sunshine the stones looked lived-in and friendly. A feeling of immense optimism stole over her.

'Great, isn't it?' she beamed.

Kieran's jaw dropped. 'Great – this?' He scanned the scene, trying to locate some small thing to be enthusiastic about. 'What – having squads of hairy-arsed builders knocking holes in your walls?'

'God Kieran, you're such a romantic.'

'Oh, so you mean the rampant rising damp and the en suite landfill site?'

'No, I meant this. The cottage. Don't you think it's sort of . . . pretty?'

'Oh, *pretty*.' Kieran's eyes flicked heavenward to the tattered black binbag fluttering like a vulture from an overhanging branch. 'That. I thought you meant something important.'

Claire pursed her lips. 'It is important.'

He grinned. 'Yeah, you're right.' He rubbed his hands together. ''Cause you know what pretty means.'

'Do I?'

He tweaked her nose playfully. ''Course you do. Pretty means profit.'

'Actually . . . ' began Claire. Then she stopped.

'Oi Kieran mate,' yelled the man with the drill. 'OK if we knock off for ten minutes?'

'Yeah, sure. Actually what?' Kieran lifted up a bottomless plastic dustbin, revealing a pile of gravel and two empty plant pots. 'Good God, what did your auntie want with all this junk?'

'Who knows?' Claire kicked the toe of her boot into the soft earth. She felt irrationally excited, like a silly kid. 'But don't you ever find yourself wanting to hold on to it?'

'To the junk?'

'To Paradise Cottage.'

'Hell no.'

'Not even a little bit?'

Kieran's expression hardened. 'Not even a bit so small you'd need an electron microscope to see it.' He looked at her down-cast face and relented, putting a reassuring arm round her shoulders. 'It's a festering heap, Claire, you know that.'

'Yes, but . . .'

'And there's no changing that. But soon it's going to be a well-disguised heap that we can sell at a nice fat profit.'

'I suppose so.' Claire frowned. 'But what about Ted? We still haven't really thought about him.'

Kieran waved away the objection. 'Don't you worry about Ted, he'll see sense.' He threw the dustbin into a nearby skip and turned away. 'Anyhow, come on. We've still got to find the—'

He took one step forward and his left leg disappeared up to the knee, with an almighty squelch and a subterranean belch of foul-smelling gas.

'Shiiit,' groaned Kieran.

Claire laughed. 'I think you just found the cesspit.'

This was not one of Claire's more enjoyable Sunday after-noons. How could it be, when its highpoint was a royal visit from Veronica? Claire had secretly prayed that Brucie would sink his teeth into her chargrilled leg and send her running screaming back to the Algarve. Unfortunately her prayers had not been answered; Veronica seemed to be having a whale of a time.

'I know it's in a shocking state now, but I can see it's going to be absolutely *darling*,' enthused Veronica as Claire reluctantly took her on a tour of the building site, eerily silent until tomor-row morning. 'All roses round the door, just like it used to be in the old days.'

'What I'd really like to do is get the gardens back to the way they were in Great-Aunt Mary's time,' ventured Claire. 'Of course, it might not be poss—'

'Oh *absolutely*! What a wonderful idea.' Veronica wafted through a patch of stinging nettles without any apparent ill-effects. 'Honeysuckle here, and a little lily pond over there. Oh, and you *must* have lots and lots of hollyhocks, you can grow them up against that wall.'

Claire sneaked a peek at her watch, ducked under a line of

Ted's vests and entered the kitchen. 'Didn't you say you had to be somewhere?'

'Me? Oh no, don't you worry, I'm all yours this afternoon.'

'Oh.'

Standing in the middle of the kitchen, Veronica pivoted on her three-inch heels, arms aloft as though she was about to conduct all the kitchen cupboards in four-part harmony. 'I remember now. There was a lovely green Aga in here – you *will* get an Aga, won't you, Weed? And antique pine units, you don't want anything too modern. I'll come and help you choose something suitable.'

Claire cringed. Kieran stood smirking in the doorway, little clouds of white plaster-dust nestling in every available orifice. 'I doubt there'll be any money for an Aga,' he said. 'We're working to a tight budget, aren't we . . . ' He gave a camp little pirouette. '*Weed?*'

She stuck out her tongue at him. 'You've got plaster-dust in your bum crack,' she retorted. 'Come on Veronica, I'll show you upstairs.'

But Veronica wasn't listening. She was too busy recreating some kind of fantasy centrefold from *Perfect Homes*. 'Exposed beams *here*,' she intoned, her eyes closed and her fingers wiggling in the air. 'They're a must-have. And lots of copper saucepans for the ambience, and one of those wooden airing racks to hang bunches of fresh herbs from . . . '

'Veronica!'

'Of course, your Auntie Mary had a real coal fire in the parlour but you can always get one of those gas ones, if you pay the extra for a good one you can hardly tell the difference.'

Claire seized her mother by the sleeve of her impractical white jacket and tried to nudge her out of the kitchen, but Veronica made a beeline for the window. 'I remember now. A rose arbour, that's what she had. English roses and clematis. Just there, do you see? Where the pig's eating that dustbin liner.'

Kieran peered over Claire's shoulder. 'Stupid animal, with a bit of luck he'll choke on it.'

170

'That's not a dustbin liner he's eating,' Claire said serenely. 'That's your leather jacket.'

Kieran disappeared down the garden in a flurry of oaths, but even the thrilling sight of a tug-of-war was not enough to jolt Veronica out of her reverie.

'Irises in the marshy bit down the bottom, and lots of wisteria climbing up the front wall – oh, and you can knock down that horrible shed the old man's living in and build a lovely gazebo. The old place'll look just the way it did when your Great-Aunt Mary was young. No, even better!' She clapped her hands together in ecstasy. 'Won't that be perfect?'

Claire managed a feeble smile. 'Very nice. But I don't think you quite understa—'

'Of course I understand, I'm your mother!' Veronica faced Claire, her eyes shining. 'And once the cottage is done up properly, we can all move in together, and be a proper happy family.'

Something huge and heavy lurched inside Claire's head, fell over, and passed out. 'What did you say?'

'It'll be lovely! You, me and Peter. Just like it used to be. We'll go shopping together, and out to the theatre, and I'll show you what clothes to buy to make more of yourself, and—'

'Just hold it right there!' Claire halted the speeding train of her mother's fantasies. 'Did you say what I thought you said?'

Veronica smiled kookily and gave her daughter's cheek a pinch. 'Silly girl! You heard. You just can't believe it's really going to happen, can you? Us together, after all these years. I can hardly believe it myself.'

'Too right I can't,' retorted Claire, taking a step backwards. 'Because it isn't!'

Veronica pursued her across the kitchen, armed to the teeth with relentless smiles. 'Of course it is, Weed. It has to, don't you see? We've lost so much time!'

Give her a chance – thought Claire – how could I have been so stupid? 'I don't believe I'm hearing this!'

The smile acquired a hint of contrition. 'Oh, I've been a hopeless mother to you, I know that now, but that's why you

171

have to let me put things right, don't you see?'

Claire's throat was dry and hoarse with disbelief. 'Put things right? By living with me?' The words rose to an inaudible squeak.

'Yes, Weed – as a proper family!'

A pig squealed somewhere down the bottom of the garden. Claire felt like squealing too. 'Veronica,' she enunciated, very slowly and clearly, 'we are not and never have been a family. The sooner you get that straight in your pea-brained head, the better.'

Veronica's smile froze but did not fade. 'Weed, darling, I know you're angry with your mummy.'

'You deserted us, or have you conveniently forgotten that?' Veronica did not reply. 'You abandoned us and there's no going back.'

'Darling, don't be silly, there's always—'

'Shut up!' Claire felt tears trembling behind her eyelids as she fought to get the words out. 'You stopped being my mother the day you walked out on Dad, and you are never, *ever*, going to live under any roof of mine!'

When your boss was obsessed with Feng Shui, your father didn't return your calls, and your long-lost mother wanted to take over your life, what could you do but phone your darling baby brother? Claire had to admit it was good to talk to him again, even if he did insist on having the last word.

'Peter,' she warned, wriggling her feet into her fluffy slippers, 'if you say "I told you so" one more time . . .'

'But I did tell you so,' he pointed out, not unreasonably. 'The minute you told me she was back I knew she was going to be trouble. Oh, but big sis had to know better, didn't she? "We've got to give her a chance," you said. "Maybe she's changed." Changed! I ask you.'

'She might have done,' said Claire defensively.

'Oh yeah! That's like saying Dracula might have taken up knitting. And now look what's happened – the old witch wants

172

to move in and play happy families! Well don't say I didn't warn you.'

'Oh shut up, baby bruv. I'm the one who's supposed to be always right, not you.'

Claire carried the telephone across the room, snuggled down into the window seat and gazed out over the grounds of Brockbourne Hall. One big building site, that's what her life was turning into; if it wasn't collapsing drains in Lilcombe Magna, it was mechanical diggers churning up the car park at the Hall, and bits of megalith everywhere you looked. And then, just to crown everything, there was Veronica.

'Look,' said Pete, 'I know you wanted to think the best of her, but you've got to face facts: Mum's a total cow.'

Mum. A tiny pang of doubt kept resurfacing in the big black lake of Claire's resentment. Surely nobody could be entirely horrible, not even Vile Veronica. 'She keeps saying she just wants to make it up to us for all the bad stuff in the past.'

'Does she bollocks,' snorted Pete. 'She just wants to stir up trouble. And you can tell her she needn't bother writing me any more letters, I'll only bin them.'

Claire curled her legs underneath her on the cushioned seat and nestled into the snug angle of the oriel window. As she talked, her breath misted up one of the little mullioned panes, and she drew a picture of a heart on it; it turned out rather lopsided, not unlike the way Claire was feeling right now.

'I expect she'll give up and go back to the Algarve soon,' she said hopefully.

'I expect so. As long as you don't start inviting her round for tea and crumpets.'

'As if!'

Why did it have to be like this? she wondered. Why can't I have a normal mother? Why does Veronica have to treat me like some kind of doll, something to love when she feels like it and then forget about for another seventeen years? She traced a second heart, overlapping the first, shaded it in and impaled both of them on a wilting arrow. 'The cottage is coming along,

173

anyway,' she said, by way of a change of subject.

'Great. So how far have you got with it?'

'The underpinning people have sorted out the wobbly front wall, and there's scaffolding everywhere.'

'So structurally it's not too bad?'

'Well, no; Aidan seems to think it'll be OK. Only trouble is that's all there is to it – a structure. It's like a Lego box with nothing inside it. And the money's running out fast. What do you reckon we should do next?'

Pete considered. Claire smiled to herself as he lowered his voice to the rather squeaky bass he thought made him sound older. She hadn't the heart to tell him it made him sound like Scooby-Doo.

'Well there's the electrics,' he mused. 'But if I were you I'd start with the plumbing. It sounds like the four-fifteen from Paddington when you turn on that kitchen tap. And all that pipework's solid lead, you know.'

'Lead!'

'Yup, it'll all have to be replaced. Toxic, you see. Come to think of it, it's no wonder old Ted's half barmy.'

Claire visualised the last few quid dripping through a hole in the bottom of her bank account. It was funny how you never thought about money until you started running out of it. If she'd had all the dosh she'd squandered on Kurt Geiger handbags and Curly-Wurlies, she could probably afford to renovate Paradise Cottage three times over.

'Oh God,' she groaned, 'this is going to cost a fortune.'

'Not if you get a mate to do it on the cheap.'

'A mate? I wish.'

'Claire, you idiot, I'm talking about me! If you can wait a month it'll be the Long Vac. I could come and help out for a week or two if you like. I'm quite good with plumbing.'

Claire perked up. 'That'd be great!'

'It'll have to be the first couple of weeks mind, I'm off trekking across Nepal in July.'

'Nepal?' laughed Claire. 'I thought students were supposed to be hard up. Dad bailing you out is he?'

'No,' replied Pete brightly. 'You are.'

If that giggly Scottish bint on the TV can do it, so can I; that was what Claire had told herself.

She'd supervised the maintenance crews at Brockbourne Hall often enough; she'd watched the builders leaping all over Paradise Cottage with their lump hammers and drills, making the whole thing look suspiciously easy. Hey, she knew the name of every hammer in Aidan Ross's toolbox. Why *shouldn't* she do it herself?

It had seemed like a great wheeze when she enrolled over the telephone; but once she was actually there, Singles Night at the DIY superstore came as quite a shock. As if being chatted up by a man in NHS glasses and combat trousers wasn't weird enough, who should she walk straight into but . . .

'Worm!'

The silly grin on Worm's face faded into the look of a panic-stricken haddock. 'Claire! What are you doing here?'

The small, plump woman he had been trying to impress turned suspicious eyes on the new arrival. By Claire's reckoning she was at least a decade older than Worm and one ear was an inch higher than the other. 'Here, who's she then?'

She stuck out a hand. 'Claire Snow, pleased to meet you.'

'You his girlfriend then?'

'No!' interjected Worm, with a look of horror.

The woman sniffed. 'That's what Bernie said, and he had two wives in Llandudno.' With that she stalked off towards the complimentary nibbles and the man in the combat trousers.

'Well thanks a bunch,' grunted Worm. 'I was well in there.'

'Yes, but did you want to be?' She glanced towards the display of power tools. 'You never said you were into DIY.'

Worm looked sheepish. 'Yes, well.'

Poor Worm, thought Claire. He has a secret thing for Lorna, Lorna has a thing for every bloke in the world but him. He'd do anything to meet girls. *Any* girls. Ah, bless him.

'I'm here to pick up a few DIY tips,' volunteered Claire as the gaggle of assorted singles drifted towards the demonstration area. 'I thought I might do some of the work on the cottage myself.'

'What does Kieran reckon to that then?'

'He doesn't reckon anything, 'cause I haven't told him,' she confessed. 'I want to get seriously good at this before I go public. I was going to ask Lorna to come with me, but she'd only blab to Kieran.'

'Thank God you didn't. If Lorna saw me in a place like this I'd never hear the last of it.' Worm slid into a seat between a middle-aged lady and a girl in a very tight white crop-top. He put on his best pulling smile, which was irresistibly reminiscent of Freddy Krueger. 'Room for a little one, ladies?'

The lesson began. It was all terribly basic, and Claire began to wonder if she shouldn't have started off with something a bit more ambitious. After all, it wasn't as if she was a *complete* novice, and the girl in the crop-top didn't even know a combination plane when she saw one.

'This is from our latest range,' announced the man in the carpenter's apron, holding up a sugar-pink power drill. 'Very popular with the little ladies, styled for maximum elegance, and of course, not too difficult to manage for the less powerful physique.'

'Sexist pig,' muttered Claire, who was not often given to outbursts of feminism.

'Sorry?' said the man in the brown coat, pausing in his demonstration. 'Did somebody ask a question?'

All eyes turned on her. 'Er, nothing. Just clearing my throat.'

Worm left off juggling tester pots of red paint, leaned over and poked her in the back. 'Claire was wondering if she could have a go with that jigsaw, weren't you Claire?'

She mouthed back an obscenity, but Worm just winked and went on juggling, much to the delight of the girl in the white crop-top. 'Actually, I . . .'

The man in the brown coat beckoned her down, like a

contestant on *The Price is Right*. 'That's what I like to see, the lovely ladies taking an interest.'

Oh well, thought Claire, tugging her terribly practical sweat-shirt down over her hips; now's my chance to show them how it's done. How difficult can it be, cutting a straight line in a piece of MDF?

'That's right dear,' patronised the man in the brown coat. 'Make sure it's nice and steady in the vice. Now, when you switch on, be sure that you—no, hang on! Not yet!'

Claire stared down at the S-shaped line she had just cut. 'Oops.'

'Never mind dear.' The manic smile was ever so slightly strained as he turned the board round and repositioned it in the vice. 'Try again. And this time, hold on tight.'

She started again. And this time things were going great. This was easy, she didn't know why people made such a fuss about it being difficult. The only drawback was, the instructor was guiding her hands so tightly that he was practically doing the job himself. 'It's OK,' she announced. 'I can manage this bit by myself.'

'Sure?'

'Sure.'

'OK then, just follow the line.'

She must have lasted all of two seconds before the saw shot off sideways, taking her with it and slicing a neat blue triangle out of the instructor's brand-new uniform trousers.

'Look on the bright side,' said Worm as she gave him a lift home to Pittville. 'At least you didn't draw blood.'

Claire glared balefully through the windscreen as a builder's van cut her up at the lights and sailed past, complete with a cheery wave. 'Yeah, and at least I didn't drop red paint all over that girl's white top.'

Worm slid a little lower in his seat. 'Don't remind me.'

They drove on for a little while, Claire lost in gloomy thought. 'DIY?' she said. 'You can shove it.'

'Not hooked then?'

'What do you think?'

'*I* think,' said Worm reflectively, 'that we ought to keep schtumm about this evening.'

'Worm,' replied Claire, 'that's the first sensible thing you've said all night.'

Chapter 15

Election fever hit Lilcombe Magna with all the force of a wet tissue.

In fairness, old Mr Crowatt's son Desmond would have been the automatic choice to succeed his father on the parish council, until his homemade distillery took the roof off the sub post office. Consequently the over-sixties' vote had swung sharply against him, as they now had to take a return bus trip to Lilcombe Regis every pension day.

Which left only two candidates in the race: Aidan Ross and Brucie. And since Brucie was a pig who couldn't even sign his own proposal form, the outcome was fairly predictable.

Nevertheless the lounge bar of the Saxon Cross was packed on election night, if only because Thursday night was quiz night and there was a yard of ale on offer.

Feet stamped impatiently as Neville Shute stepped up to the microphone to announce the result.

'As returning officer for the parish of . . . '

Groans ran round the bar. 'We don't want none of that crap, Nev. Just give us the result.'

'Yeah, the pub quiz is half an hour late already, an' I've been bonin' up on South American mammals.'

Ted sat at the bar, bent low over a pint of Old Irregular. Snout buried in a packet of his favourite salt 'n' vinegar crisps, Brucie munched unconcernedly, apparently oblivious to the dramatic tension of the moment. Aidan glanced repeatedly at his watch and tapped his fingers impatiently on the bar counter. 'Come on Nev, let's get this thing settled so I can buy everybody a free drink.'

'All right then.' Neville coughed, scrunched up his official speech and stuffed it back in his trouser pocket. 'The winner is . . .'

Somebody burped.

'. . . the pig!'

A cheer went up, almost drowning out Aidan's protests. 'What? What do you mean?'

Neville shrugged. 'Like I said, the pig won.'

'Don't be ridiculous, it's a pig! It's not even eligible to stand.'

'As a matter of fact,' replied the landlord, 'there's nothing in the rules that says a pig can't stand. I checked. You just have to live in the parish, that's all.'

'Where's our free drinks then?' called out one of the regulars.

Aidan felt several dozen pairs of eyes bore into his back. He turned round and met them with a smile so tense, it hurt. Reaching reluctantly into his back pocket, he took out a fifty-pound note and slapped it down on the counter with a muttered 'Bastard yokels'.

'So – how many did I lose by?'

Neville started pulling pints. 'You don't want to know.'

'Oh yes I do.'

'All right, have it your own way.' The crumpled sheet of paper found its way into Aidan's hand. 'There you go. The pig slaughtered you.'

Aidan stared at the figures, still faintly hoping this was some kind of bad joke. But he knew it wasn't. Only in Lilcombe Magna could a pig carry off ninety-eight per cent of the vote.

'But *why*?' That was the question that burned to be answered. 'Why, Nev? I just don't understand it.'

Nev sighed and clapped him on the shoulder. 'Face it Aidan, old son,' he confided. 'The people round here just don't like you.'

While Aidan was facing facts and Claire was soaking in a long bath at Brockbourne Hall, Veronica was paying Cousin Geoffrey a social call.

She'd been dreading it, terrified of losing face; but the funny thing was that now she was sitting in the front parlour at Low Common Farm, she actually felt quite at home.

'More tea, Veronica?' asked Emmie, abnormally pleasant as she wielded the gaudy rococo pot with its gold scrolled handle and lots of hand-painted roses.

'Don't mind if I do – oh, what a lovely tea service.'

'Like it do you?' simpered Emmie. 'It's real bone china you know. From abroad.'

Emmie certainly appeared to be warming to Cousin Veronica, a woman who shared her unimpeachable taste – though it did take a while to get used to the pickled walnut complexion. Round Lilcombe Magna, folk's faces tended to be either luminous red from windburn or shroud-white from uninterrupted childbearing.

'Nice to see you again, Veronica,' said Geoffrey, helping himself to three sugars. 'Plannin' on sticking around are you?'

'Well.' It was difficult to say this in a way that didn't make her look pathetic, but she was going to manage it somehow. 'That rather depends on how things go with my Claire.' Veronica lowered her voice to an appropriately caring whisper. 'You know how it is, Geoffrey, I haven't seen much of her and Peter these past few years.'

'Few?' grunted Geoffrey. 'Must be more like twenty.'

Veronica winced. 'Anyway, what I want to do now, more than anything, is rebuild my relationship with her – you know, be a proper mother to her and Pete. And I thought, if there was some way I could stay around here, I'd have lots of opportunities to see her.'

'Go and fetch us some more of them Mr Kiplings,' prompted Geoffrey. Emmie disappeared like a well-trained ewe, closing the door behind her. Geoffrey, noticed Veronica, was smirking.

181

'I've seen the will you know,' he commented, popping a buffet pork pie into his mouth. 'All of it.'

'What!' Veronica's eyes narrowed. 'How?'

Geoffrey tapped the side of his nose and grinned. 'Ways an' means, Veronica, ways an' means. Made interesting reading an' all.'

Veronica's heart sank. 'Ah.'

He chewed slyly. 'Look, girl, why don't you just admit you're only doin' this for the money?'

Veronica shot bolt upright on her chair. 'I don't know what you mean!'

'Don't come the innocent with me, Veronica, I know your game. If you don't get real friendly with Claire, you don't get your hands on Auntie Mary's bequest.'

Veronica was bright enough to know when she'd been out-manoeuvred. What was the point of denying it? It was obvious he knew everything already.

'All right,' she sighed. 'I admit it. If I can't patch things up with Claire, I'll not see a penny from that will.' She felt a stirring of indignation. 'But is it so wrong for a mother to want to see her little girl?'

Geoffrey slipped a protective arm round her shoulders, gave her a cousinly hug and tried to look down the front of her dress. 'It's all right. You can come and stay here if you want.'

She looked up, stunned. 'I can? Really?'

'No problem. You can have all the "opportunities" you like to cosy up with Claire.' He chuckled. ''Course you can, you're family. An' I got a feeling you're goin' to fit in round here just fine.'

I wish Claire was here, thought Lorna as she herded the residents of number sixteen into the downstairs kitchen. She'd know how to handle this lot. But Claire was doing something urgent with overhead projectors, and besides, this wasn't Claire's problem.

'Is everybody here?' she asked, above the din of scraping

chairs. Nobody bothered answering. 'Fine. Talk to yourself, Lorna, why don't you.'

She looked round, ticking off a mental checklist. There was Davey, sitting on the worktop, boots swinging, chewing gum; Mr Veidt was hovering in the doorway, nervously cradling a toilet brush; and the odd boy from the attic was humming the theme tune from *Ready, Steady, Cook*. Kieran was in the corner with a radio glued to his ear, and as for Stuart . . . well, Stuart was his usual epitome of malevolent chic.

'I hope this isn't going to take long,' said Worm, edging nearer the door. 'Only I've got a bath running.'

Lorna grabbed him by the shoulder and plonked him back on his chair. 'It'll take as long as it takes.' She clapped her hands, schoolteacher style. A couple of heads bobbed up. 'Is everybody ready?'

'What's this all about anyway?' asked Davey, folding another stick of gum into his mouth. 'If it's that dead rat in the microwave, it wasn't me.'

Heads turned. 'What dead rat?' demanded Stuart.

Davey went on chewing.

Stuart's lip curled. '*What dead rat*? I did my miso soup in there this morning!'

Lorna cleared her throat. 'Never mind all that, listen. Kieran and I thought we ought to call a tenants' meeting, because—'

Kieran waved his hand for her to be quiet. 'Shh, the football results are just coming on.'

Lorna glared. 'Kieran!'

Davey bounded across the kitchen on invisible springs. 'How did Villa do?'

'And Vimbledon?' cut in Mr Veidt, much to everyone's surprise. 'Did Vimbledon vin?'

Stuart was half out of his seat. 'Some of us,' he intoned darkly, 'have better things to do than sit around listening to *Final Score*.'

'What about my bath?' whimpered Worm, his bottom lip starting to quiver.

Lorna felt a rush of righteous indignation. This bunch of losers deserved to be left to the tender mercies of double-dealing landlords and evil property barons. For two pins, she'd have given up trying to get through to them – only this was her home too, and she liked it; besides, the Jasper was doomed and these were the only cheap digs in Pittville.

'I said listen!' She hammered on the kitchen table with the nearest available object, which happened to be a tin of Spam. That grabbed their attention for a couple of seconds. 'It's about Mr Papajian,' she said. 'I think he's up to something.'

'Wimbledon, three . . .' announced Kieran.

Mr Veidt's face lit up.

'. . . Liverpool, four. Sorry mate.'

'Up to what?' demanded Davey. 'Ripping us off, you mean? He can't put up the rent, you know. Not without going to the tribunal.'

'It's not about the rent. Though actually I'm not sure,' admitted Lorna. 'It might be.'

'Well that's as clear as mud,' observed Stuart sarcastically.

'Oh darling, I'm so bloody sorry,' snapped Lorna. 'And I suppose you can explain exactly what's going on, can you?'

'No,' he admitted.

'Then button it. The thing is, I think we need to talk to Mr Papajian about this. Urgently.'

The odd boy took an inhaler from his pocket and squirted it up his nose with a horrible slurping sound. 'Why?'

Lorna's exasperation fizzed like space-dust. 'Because we live here, that's why! Don't you care about what happens to this place?'

Several sets of critical eyes focused on the drab paintwork, the sagging polystyrene ceiling tiles, the whole devastating beigeness that screamed 'end of season sale at B&Q'.

'God no,' replied Stuart. 'I'm only living here to experience the negative *chi*.'

'Oh you are, are you?' retorted Davey. 'Well you can go and experience it in a cardboard box for all I care, but if Papajian's doing the dirty on us I want to know, right?'

'Right,' echoed Mr Veidt, with an emphatic nod. A murmur of lukewarm agreement ran round the kitchen.

'Right,' sighed Lorna, relieved. 'So – is everybody agreed?'

'About what?' asked the odd boy, waving his inhaler to the beat of some imaginary tune.

'About what to do. Do you want me to approach Mr Papajian and ask him straight out what his plans are? Or does somebody else want to do it?'

Everyone promptly tried to look as if they were somewhere else. 'Be my guest,' said Stuart.

Kieran called across to Davey. 'Villa won mate, two-nil.'

'Ace.'

'Let's take a vote on this,' said Lorna.

'Hang on,' said Davey, 'where's Candy? She ought to be in on this too.'

'Perhaps she hev gone out,' suggested Mr Veidt.

'No, she's definitely in,' replied Worm. 'I saw her go into her room ten minutes ago.'

'Oh all right,' sighed Lorna. 'I'll go and get her. But don't anyone dare move, OK? I'm not rounding you all up again.'

Lorna stalked off across the hall. Flipping Candy. Flipping everything. She raised her hand to knock on the door, but her knuckles stopped suddenly, half an inch short of the lime green paint. The most bizarre noises were coming from inside Candy's room; bizarre, but instantly recognisable as the kind of low, satisfied moaning that belonged on the soundtrack of a Continental skinflick.

Oh not again, thought Lorna, with a twinge of jealousy. How could one person spend so much time having sex? She waited for the moaning to approach a pulsating climax of passion, then hammered very loudly on the door.

'Candy! Candy, are you in there?'

There was a brief pause. 'What is it?'

'It's Lorna. About the tenants' meeting. We're about to vote.'

A split second later the door opened and Candy emerged,

fully dressed and infuriatingly unembarrassed. 'Hi. Have you been waiting for me?'

You dark horse, thought Lorna, trying unsuccessfully to peek into the room before Candy snapped shut the door. I wonder who this latest boyfriend is. And why haven't we seen him around? Come to think of it, why don't we ever see any of your boyfriends?

Before she had a chance to ask, the front door opened.

'Afternoon, ladies.'

'Mr Papajian! Just the person I wanted to—'

He brushed past, waving his furry hat. 'Not now, not now, I am busy.'

Undeterred, Lorna pursued him right down the hall, into the kitchen and through the back door into the garden. 'Mr Papajian, it's important.'

Behind her, a crowd of faces were pressed up against the kitchen window, jostling for position. Mr Papajian bent down to inspect a row of beetroot. 'What is it?'

'It's about the house,' she said. 'And all these people you've been showing round lately. They didn't look like new tenants to me. Besides, we haven't got any vacancies.'

'Ah,' said Mr Papajian, flicking dust off his astrakhan collar. 'You must mean my business associates.'

'Is that what they are?' Lorna bit the bullet. 'The thing is, some of the tenants are worried about what you've got planned for this house. We think you ought to tell us if there's something we should know.'

Mr Papajian nodded thoughtfully. 'Perhaps so.'

'Perhaps what?' demanded Worm, arriving on the scene.

'My bones are getting old,' he said. 'I would like to retire to somewhere warm and sunny.'

'Retire? When?'

'Very soon. Which means, my dear, that I have decided to sell this house.'

At that climactic moment, Candy's voice floated up the garden from the house. 'Worm!'

He spun round. 'What?'

'Get in here and turn your bath off! It's flooding through the kitchen ceiling.'

In times of tribulation, chips could be a great comfort.

Lorna and Kieran sat in the TV room, working their way through the world's biggest takeaway, while Worm droned on about how cruel life was and how chips didn't taste nearly as nice as they used to.

'I am just sooooo depressed,' he moaned.

'Give it a rest mate,' urged Kieran.

Lorna swigged Irish stout straight from the can. 'Eat your chips.'

'How can you eat at a time like this?' He picked up a chip, watched it wilt and dropped it back into the tray. 'Look at me! No job, and now no home.'

'Come on, it's not quite that bad,' pointed out Lorna, trying to cheer him up. 'Not yet, anyway.'

'No?'

'Well look on the bright side. At least they can't throw us out of here till our six-month tenancy's up.'

If anything, Worm looked even more morose. 'True. Trouble is, mine's only got a month left to run, hasn't it?' He sighed. 'No job, no home ... no shoes ...'

Kieran laughed, choking on a battered sausage. 'Oh yeah, get out your violins, Worm's a poor barefoot orphan.'

Worm's response was to wrench off his right trainer and wave its flapping sole under Kieran's nose. 'See? No shoes!'

Kieran coughed and pushed the trainer gently away. 'Yeah, OK, you've made your point. Honestly though, you two need to lighten up. When Claire gets here she'll think she's come to a wake.'

Lorna and Worm exchanged looks. 'Lighten up, he says!'

'You're an insensitive git, Kieran Hart,' commented Lorna. 'You could at least try to look upset.'

'Too right,' grunted Worm. 'Whatever happened to solidarity?'

Kieran slurped down his last chip and wiped the grease off his chin. 'It's nothing to do with solidarity. Like I said, I don't see the problem, not when there's such an easy way out of this.'

Lorna was so intrigued she put down her can of beer, sat back and folded her arms. 'An easy way out. Right.'

'Right.'

'Don't tell me, you've booked us all into an en suite dosshouse round the back of the corporation dump.'

Kieran chuckled. 'Wrong. Better than that.'

'It had better be,' remarked Worm, helping himself to Lorna's beer. 'So, what's this amazing master plan then?'

'Me and Claire buy this house, and everybody gets to stay here!'

Lorna gaped. 'This is a joke, right?'

'Nope.'

'So you and Claire are really eccentric millionaires?'

'Hardly. But if we sell Paradise Cottage to Claire's cousin Geoffrey, we should have enough to put down a deposit on this place and make up the rest with a mortgage. This place'll be a much better investment than that old heap.'

'An investment?' Worm's nose wrinkled. He contemplated the incredibly kitsch plastic storm-lantern dangling from the swirly Artexed ceiling. 'It is?'

'Oh definitely. Bags of potential.'

Lorna leaned forward. 'And Claire'll go for this, will she?'

'Of course she will, she's a sensible girl.'

'I thought you two had had another of your little spats.'

This irritated Kieran more than it ought to have done. 'Who told you that?'

'Oh nobody. I just noticed she didn't stay over last night.'

'Well we're fine, OK? And I know she'll think this is a great idea.'

'What's a great idea?' asked a voice from the doorway.

Kieran swung round, a slightly nervous smile on his face. 'Oh Claire! Hi!'

'Why don't you tell her, Kieran?' asked Lorna, settling herself back in her chair.

Claire was puzzled. 'Tell me what?'

Chapter 16

Veronica did not enjoy taking advice, but this time she needed it. The big problem was, when it came to taking advice about Claire, there was really only one reliable source: her ex-husband.

The phone rang for a long time before somebody answered. 'Four-five-six-one-two.'

She took a deep breath. 'Terry? It's me.'

There was a long moment's hesitation on the other end of the line. Then, '*Nicks?*'

Nicks? Ugh. She'd loathed that nickname twenty years ago and she didn't like it any better now. But Veronica swallowed down her annoyance and forced a smile into her voice. 'That's right Terry, it's me. Veronica.'

'Good God. How long has it been? I thought you were in – where was it?'

'The Algarve. But I'm back now.'

'Oh. That's . . . nice.'

The voice was perfectly amiable, but there was a definite edge to it. A woman's voice in the background called out, 'Who is it darling?' and Terry called back, 'Nobody important, dear, just somebody from the office.'

She couldn't suppress a smile. After all this time, she still had the power to get him hot under the collar.

'It's all right Terry,' said Veronica. 'I'm not going to turn up on your doorstep and upset the happy home. I just wanted to ask you something. About Claire.'

The edge of nervousness became an edge of suspicion. 'I don't want Claire hurt, Veronica. Her or Peter.'

'No, no, of course not,' she soothed. 'Look, I'll be straight with you. Some of the things that have been happening to me lately ... well, to be honest they've made me take a long hard look at my life and I can see now what a mess I've made of it.'

'You can?' She could tell he was surprised; impressed even.

'Oh, absolutely. The thing is, through my own stupid fault I've missed out on all those precious years with the kids, and I guess I just want a chance to get close to them again.' She twirled the telephone flex round her fingers. 'I thought maybe you could help me.'

'I don't know, Nicks,' said Terry soberly.

'Please, Terry. I don't know where else to turn. All I want is some advice, somebody to help me mend fences with Claire.' She was on a roll now. 'Who knows: if I can be a better mother, maybe the rest of my life will start sorting itself out.'

'Tell me what?' repeated Claire, shrugging off her jacket.

Lorna stretched out her foot and jabbed Kieran in the ribs. 'Go on then. Tell her.'

But Kieran wasn't paying attention. Neither was Worm. They were far too busy staring, open-mouthed, at a point somewhere behind Claire's head. To be fair, it wasn't every day the young Deborah Harry wiggled into your front room in a black PVC minidress. Even better, she was carrying popcorn and a six-pack of Tizer.

Shedding the fluffy blonde wig and several dozen hairgrips, the new arrival revealed an even cuter halo of tight black bubble-curls.

'Hiya.'

The accent was somewhere west of Salford, but Worm couldn't have cared less if she'd just landed from Mars. He was grinning like a maniac.

191

'Er ... h-hi there,' he stammered, in a futile attempt to sound casual. 'Wow. Tizer.'

Six cans and a jumbo bag of popcorn landed on the Seventies coffee table. Worm's eyes bulged another couple of millimetres as 'Debbie' shoehorned a hand down the front of her dress.

''Scuse us a mo, me left one keeps sticking to the inside.' Something squeaked against bare plastic. 'There, that's better.' She tugged down her hem, to little effect. 'Don't suppose somebody could show me where the bog is? I'm bursting for a pee.'

'Yeah. Sure. I'll show you.' Worm leapt up and headed for the door like a stud whippet, tripping over Kieran's feet in his hurry to be helpful.

'Pathetic,' sniffed Lorna as 'Debbie' trotted off up the stairs. 'Did you *see* that?'

'I'll say.' Kieran lay back in his chair, swung his legs round and draped them over the arm. 'What I want to know is, are they *real*?'

Claire threw the popcorn at his head. 'You can be really disgusting sometimes.'

'Only sometimes?' He winked. 'Must try harder.'

'Her name's Murf.' Claire retrieved the popcorn. 'I met her down the Arts Centre. And you'd better mind your manners or I'll deck you.'

'Murf?' There was an edge of disdain in Lorna's laughter. 'Sounds like dandruff shampoo.'

'It's short for Murphy, I don't know what her first name is. She's in that Blondie tribute band I told you about.'

'Oh, *right*.' Kieran pulled Claire down on to his lap. 'Any good?'

'Not bad. Mind you, she's wasted doing Debbie Harry impressions.' Claire helped herself to a handful of popcorn. 'So. What's this big dark secret nobody's telling me?'

Lorna looked at Kieran expectantly. 'It's about this house.'

Kieran paused, then snatched the popcorn back from Claire and crammed a fistful into his mouth. 'Not now, it can wait.'

'No it can't!' Lorna objected. 'The thing is, Claire, you know we've been worried about what Mr Papajian's been up to?'

'Yeees.'

'Well he came round today. And he's definitely selling the house.'

'Oh dear. So you were right.'

'Looks that way. God knows what's going to happen to us.'

'Apparently we're Mr Papajian's pension plan,' said Kieran drily. 'Isn't that touching? If it wasn't for us, he couldn't afford his lovely new condo in the Florida Keys.'

'But Kieran's got an idea,' cut in Lorna, her eyes not leaving his face. 'Haven't you, Kieran?'

'Well, yes,' Kieran admitted, with a hint of reluctance.

'What kind of idea?' Claire flipped the ring-pull on a can of Tizer. 'And what's it got to do with me?'

'He thought maybe you could club together and buy it.'

'Sorry? Buy what?'

'This house.'

Tizer slopped down the front of Claire's French Connection top. 'What!'

'He's got it all worked out,' said Lorna reassuringly. 'At least, that's what he told me.'

'Oh he did, did he?' Claire's blue eyes locked firmly on to Kieran's. 'And when exactly was he planning on telling me?'

Claire was taking it out on Mr Papajian's kitchen units.

'Haven't you got *anything* in this place?'

Lorna gave the question a moment's consideration. 'We've got cockroaches.'

'Cockroaches. Great.' She slid open a drawer crammed with scrunched-up carrier bags. 'But no corkscrew, right?'

'No.' Lorna followed Claire round the kitchen at a safe distance. 'Somebody must've nicked it, you know what it's like. Besides, the only booze I can afford these days comes in two-litre plastic bottles.'

Claire slammed the door of another wall unit with such force that a box of breakfast cereal overbalanced, fell off the top and scattered cornflakes all over the kitchen floor.

'Oh, arse.'

She opened a door with no handle and peered into the mildewed gloom beneath the sink. There seemed to be nothing down there but a bottle of Happy Shopper bleach, two headless Action Men and a sprouted potato. So this was communal living, was it? Well you could keep it.

'Where's the dustpan and brush?' she asked, her voice echoing in the subterranean gloom of the cupboard.

'There isn't one,' admitted Lorna.

Claire emerged, banging her head on the U-bend. 'Of course there is – what about that horrible yellow thing with hardly any bristles?'

'Oh that? Davey got pissed and sort of melted it in the oven.' Lorna got down on her knees and started unconcernedly scooping the cornflakes back into the box. 'Shift your feet.' She glanced up. 'Don't look at me like that!'

Claire recalled all the times she'd eaten breakfast in this kitchen since she'd started going out with Kieran. Cornflakes, usually. It didn't bear thinking about. 'You can't just bung them back in the packet!' she exclaimed.

Lorna waggled the box in Claire's face. 'Look, they're Kieran's,' she said enticingly. 'They've got his name on the box.'

'In that case, don't let me stop you.' Claire abandoned the wine bottle on the kitchen table. 'Oh, sod the Chardonnay, I'm putting the kettle on.'

'Fine.' Lorna intercepted the flex as it headed for the wall socket. 'But I wouldn't plug it in there.'

'Why the hell not?'

'A bit of water got in the socket when Worm accidentally set that fire extinguisher off, it might not have dried out yet.' She carried the kettle to the other side of the kitchen, plugged it in and picked the least offensive mugs from the selection racked up on the draining board.

Claire held up a mug shaped like a pair of pink buttocks; inscribed across them in curly gold letters were the words 'Hello

Cheeky'. 'Go on Lorna, remind me. Why am I going out with a man who likes to drink his coffee out of somebody's bum?'

Lorna sighed. 'Kieran's not that bad, Claire.'

'Oh yes he is.'

'He's just a bit . . . thoughtless.' She hunted through Worm's stash of recycled teabags for one that hadn't gone mouldy.

'That's the understatement of the year.'

'I don't know why you're getting so het up about this. You *never* get angry, remember?'

'Oh ha ha, very droll.' Lorna was annoyingly right though. Claire couldn't remember the last time she'd been this mad at anybody. Well, anybody but Veronica.

Lorna sniffed the teabag surreptitiously. It had a faint tang of well-rotted compost, but hopefully no one would notice. 'Anyway, it's my fault really,' she said.

'How do you work that one out?'

'Kieran wouldn't have told you if I hadn't made him.'

'Oh yes he would,' retorted Claire. 'He'd just have got me drunk and incapable first.' She flopped down on a Sixties bentwood chair, which promptly listed over on to its two truncated legs. 'Stop trying to defend him.'

'I'm not.'

'Yes you are. And it's not going to do any good.'

'You're still mad at him?'

'Bloody furious. Mind you, knowing Kieran he probably hasn't even noticed yet.'

Lorna flicked the kettle switch and sat down opposite Claire. 'Oh, I think he's got a shrewd idea. I mean, it's not every day your main squeeze calls you a lump of putrescent slime, is it?'

'Unless you're Stuart.'

'Well, yeah. Unless you're Stuart. But then who'd squeeze him?'

A faint smile crossed Claire's lips. 'Putrescent? Did I really call him that?'

'And the rest. I seem to remember balls and barbeques being mentioned too.'

'Well whatever I said, he deserves it.'

Lorna arranged mugs on a tray. 'You know he didn't mean to get up your nose, don't you?'

'He never does, does he?' said Claire bitterly. 'It's just this natural talent he has.'

'I really don't think he realised. He was so fired up he was sure you'd think it was a great idea.'

'Well I'm sorry but it's not. It's crap. In fact it's the crappest idea I've ever heard.'

'You reckon?' Lorna tapped her fingers softly on the table top, breaking up the thin encrustation of dried-on Pot Noodle. 'I thought it . . . well, I thought it might be worth thinking about. I mean, these houses fetch quite a lot when they're done up, don't they?'

'That's not the point!'

'No. No, I suppose you're right. And I know he shouldn't just have assumed you'd agree. But I just thought, seeing as the two of you are going to sell the cottage soon anyway . . .'

It was exactly the wrong thing to say. Claire looked up, a warning flash in her blue eyes. 'Sez who?'

Lorna was taken aback. 'You, actually.'

'If I sell up, it'll be my decision. Not Kieran's, not anybody else's. It's my cottage, Lorna.'

'I know it is. But he's putting money into it,' Lorna pointed out. 'I suppose he thinks he has a stake in it now.' She cocked her head quizzically. 'What do you mean, *if* you sell? I thought that was the whole point of doing it up.'

Claire got up and poured boiling water into the teapot. Her head felt fuzzy, and it was starting to ache. Rows, she hated them. 'Yeah,' she sighed, 'you're right, of course it is.'

'But just at the moment you feel like thumping Kieran into the middle of next week?'

'Too right I do. Who does he think he is, acting like he owns me or something?'

'You don't think you're exaggerating a bit?'

'No I don't.' Claire didn't add that the row with Kieran had stirred up something at the back of her mind, childhood memories of her mother taunting her father, of huddling at the top of the stairs with Peter, listening to their parents arguing about money. She snatched up the tea tray with its assortment of chipped Garfield mugs.

'Not even a teensy-weensy bit?'

'I might have guessed you'd take his side.'

'Me? Why?'

Claire nudged the door open with her foot. 'Oh come on, you'd be over the moon if I threw all my money into this place.'

'I might,' admitted Lorna. 'But that doesn't mean . . .'

'You're my best mate, Lorna. You could be six years late with the rent and I still wouldn't evict you, would I?'

Lorna groaned. 'I just thought Kieran had a point, that's all. Obviously I was talking out of my arse.'

'Obviously. And I'm not jacking in Paradise Cottage just so Kieran can play Monopoly with real hotels.'

Unnoticed, Kieran had sidled up. 'Need anything doing in the kitchen?' he asked hopefully.

'No.'

'I'm good at humble pie.'

Claire pushed past him with a stony glare.

'Oh hell, she still hates me,' said Kieran dejectedly. 'Well thanks a bunch Lorna, you really dropped me in it.'

'At least I didn't accuse her of being premenstrual!'

'She must be,' he protested. 'Buying this place is a great idea.'

'Kieran,' she said, sticking a dishmop in his hand, 'have you ever considered a career in the diplomatic corps?'

'Resting', they called it. Well that was a joke, thought Lorna as Worm dragged her down to the Arts Centre at the crack of dawn.

'Wasn't it kind of Murf to fix us up with this cheap rehearsal room?' enthused Worm, doing a headstand against the wall.

Lorna fortified herself with another swig from her Thermos. Murf, Murf, Murf. That was all she'd been hearing since last night. Murf this, Murf that. Murf's so gorgeous, Murf's so talented, Murf can do no bloody wrong. He'd only met the girl once, and already he was ga-ga over her. Mind you, that was Worm all over. It was just as well he had Lorna to keep his feet on the ground.

'Give it a rest Worm, all she did was give you a phone number to ring.'

'She's really nice though, isn't she?'

'If you like that sort of thing.'

It was obvious that Worm liked that sort of thing very much indeed: he continued to beam like a transfigured saint. The sooner he gets into that girl's pants the better, thought Lorna. Worm was never lucky in love. The quicker this latest one bonked him, chucked him and broke his heart, the sooner he could get over it and life could get back to normal.

'Indian clubs,' he panted, as his T-shirt fell down over his face, exposing a chest so skinny it looked like a double row of bicycle racks.

Lorna lifted up the hem. 'What did you say?'

Worm waved an arm. 'Clubs. The silver ones. I want to see if I can juggle four at once.'

'You can't even do three the right way up.'

'Go on. No, not all at once! One at a time.'

She threw one at him and it hit him on the knee. 'Sorry.' She really was doing her best to concentrate, but her heart wasn't in this busking thing at all. For one thing, she'd gone to all the trouble of writing a brilliant new script for the act, and all Worm had done was grunt and say it was 'fine'. For another, she was sick to the back teeth of hearing about Murf.

On top of all that, she couldn't help wondering if it was worth all the hassle. Contrary to urban mythology, future Broadway superstars were seldom talent-spotted fire-eating in Swindon shopping centre. No matter how hard she tried, Lorna couldn't make herself view this as a good career move. At least when you did night shifts for Les Lynch you got time and a half and all the pickled gherkins you could eat.

'How am I doing?' demanded Worm, struggling to keep two clubs in the air, let alone four.

'Your face has gone red.'

'But do I look as if I know what I'm doing?'

'No, you look like you're having a stroke. What if there isn't a handy wall to lean up against?' she enquired.

'You'll just have to hold on to my legs.'

Lorna contemplated Worm's spaghetti limbs, bare, white and extremely hairy in his 'stylish' shorts. She did not relish the prospect of having those rancid trainers rammed up her nose. 'I'm still not wearing that leopardskin leotard,' she warned him.

'Aw, come on.'

'No.'

'But you look so good in it.' Worm righted himself in a tumble of Indian clubs.

'You mean it makes my tits look massive.'

'Exactly! Doesn't half pull in the punters. Do you want us to make money, or not?'

Another explosion of noise shook the pink plywood walls, making the light bulb jiggle on the end of its bare flex. The Arts Centre was not what you'd call a luxurious establishment; it was freezing in winter, roasting in summer, the walls were paper-thin, and the all-day workshop next door was so loud it might as well have been in the same room.

Worm cocked an ear. 'Sounds like the primal scream group are really getting into it.'

'Since when did roaring like a constipated rhino help you to find your inner self? I mean, I'm all for the holistic approach, but . . . ' Worm gave her iron-hard neck muscles a squeeze, and she yelped. 'Ow!'

'Maybe you should try a bit of primal screaming. Might help you lose some of that tension.'

'I am not tense!'

'Yes you are, you're totally uptight. You've not been doing your Alexander Technique, have you?' he scolded.

'Oh shut up, you sound like my mum.'

The door opened and an elderly man in a paint-spattered smock walked in, carrying an easel. 'Over-sixties' life class?'

'Third door on the right,' said Worm. 'Just past Jazz-Tots.'

'Much obliged, sorry I disturbed you.'

The door closed again, muting the hideously tinny rattle of an untuned piano, backed by the collective drone of twenty-five tone-deaf three-year-olds.

'That's the fourth time we've been disturbed since we got here,' said Lorna, refilling her cup from the flask. 'Any more of this and I'm going home.'

'Oh no you're not. Not till we've been through everything.' Worm took the cup away and handed her a bowler hat and a cane.

She screwed up her nose. 'Oh Worm. Can't we go through the new script?' she wheedled. 'I've written you some great one-liners.'

But Worm had one eye on the clock. 'Murf mentioned she might drop by, did I tell you?'

'Only about a thousand times.' Lorna threw down the script and capitulated. 'OK, let's do this dance routine if we're doing it.'

'Not definitely. Just if she was passing, you know.'

'Yeah. Right.' Lorna switched on the tape, and 'My Kind of Town' blared out. 'Two-three-four.'

'What's "yeah, right" supposed to mean?'

'Nothing. Ow, that's my toe!'

'Sorry.' Worm tapped on the spot, twirling his cane. 'She's really nice though, isn't she? Murf.'

'You've already said that.'

'Have I? Sorry.' Worm was silent for a few bars, then piped up: 'Lorna?'

She high-kicked painfully, wondering how she could possibly have got so out of condition so quickly, and praying that Worm would stop going on about Murf before she felt obliged to wring his neck. 'What now?'

'If you met me, and you were ... you know ...'

'No, I don't know. If I was what?'

'An attractive young woman.'

She stopped in mid-tap. 'Well thank you very much, Brad Pitt!'

Worm didn't even have the good grace to notice his faux pas. 'But if you were, you know, like *really* attractive . . .'

'She's got fat ankles,' said Lorna curtly.

'Who?'

'Murf. I presume we *are* still talking about Murf, seeing as we haven't talked about anything else since we got here.'

Worm looked wounded. 'She's got wonderful ankles!' He shuffled his feet. 'I was just wondering . . .'

'Worm, if you're asking me if she fancies you . . .'

'Actually I was just wondering: do you think she might like me better with a beard?'

Lorna stared at him in utter disbelief for a moment, then burst out laughing. 'A beard? You?' The kids down the hall were laughing hysterically too, to the accompaniment of small feet stomping on bare boards.

Worm looked wounded. 'Why not?'

'Take it from me, it's a really bad idea. No, second thoughts, go right ahead. It'll be the best laugh she's had all year.' The music stopped and Worm went to turn the tape over. Lorna could tell she'd hurt his feelings. Tough. He'd hurt hers too. She softened slightly and trailed him across the room. 'Look Worm, I only meant . . .'

His shoulders were defiantly stiff. 'There's no need to take the piss. You know I'm no good at this boy-girl thing.'

Lorna unscrewed the top off her flask and sat down. 'You can't be any worse at it than Kieran,' she pointed out. 'Don't switch the music on yet, I need a break.'

'Is Claire still angry with Kieran?'

'I think so, I haven't seen her since last night. Course, Kieran's trouble is, he goes about things all wrong.'

'Which is. exactly what I'm afraid of doing.' Worm glanced across at Lorna. 'What's that you're drinking?'

'Just herbal tea.'

He sniffed the air. 'Really? It smells sort of alcoholic.'

'Can't think why,' she said firmly, downing the rest and screwing the top back on. Her fingers were trembling slightly. 'I'd offer you some, but that was the last of it.'

Hands in the pockets of his sagging shorts, Worm wandered across to the only interesting feature in the entire room: a noticeboard plastered with cards, flyers, cryptic messages on tatty scraps of coloured paper. 'There are some house-shares advertised on here, shall I take the details?'

She shrugged unenthusiastically. 'If you like.'

'Hmm. Non-smokers required for friendly house, sounds OK. Nice area, own kitchen, must like snakes . . .'

'That's me out then.'

'How about this one then? In Prestbury?' He peered closer. 'Hang on though, that's gays only. Oh look.' His finger travelled down to a yellow poster decorated with red balloons. 'Did you know they hire out rooms here?'

'Of course I do, we're in one, dimbo.'

'Not for rehearsing in, for private functions. Parties, that sort of thing.' Worm snapped his fingers and swivelled round, a look of sudden illumination on his face. 'That's it!'

'What's what?'

'You hate busking in the street, right?'

'Right.'

'You hate getting rained on and wearing that leotard?'

'Do you really have to ask?'

'What if we could put on our act somewhere nice and warm, and get paid a proper fee for it?'

'Do flying pigs come into this?'

'No.'

'Maximum security mental institutions?'

'No! Children's parties – that's what we should be doing.'

Lorna hesitated for a moment. The memory of Skegness had not quite faded; but on the other hand, her agent reckoned she'd always been rather good with ankle-biters. 'You really think so?'

'It's a huge growth industry, Lorna. Parents are queueing up to offload their little darlings on to a couple of real professionals like us! OK, so we'll have to adapt the act a bit . . .'

'Maybe I could try out some of that new material I've written.'

'Exactly!'

'I could even dust off *Max Turbot, Fish Detective*.'

'And we can get some new costumes made up. Maybe a bunny rabbit, and a clown. Or vegetables. Root vegetables are always good for a laugh.'

'It *might* work, I suppose,' mused Lorna.

'It *will* work.' Worm did a line of back-flips across the bare wooden floor. 'Murf's a professional. Perhaps I'll ask her for some advice.'

'So you're going to do kiddies' parties are you?' Claire munched on a tuna sandwich and gazed out over the daisy-speckled lawns to the river. The sacrificial altar of Brockbourne's partly-built stone circle made a lovely picnic table.

'If the blessed St Murf thinks it's a good idea,' grumbled Lorna. 'I'm telling you Claire, that boy's obsessed.'

Claire eyed up her friend. 'Do I detect a hint of the green-eyed monster?'

'Don't be ridiculous, I just don't want him upset again. You know how useless he gets when he's just been chucked.'

'You'll probably make a lot of money,' reasoned Claire, licking mayonnaise off her fingers. 'In fact, you might even get a bit of work here.'

'You reckon?'

'Well, we do get the odd high-class kids' bash here from time to time. And Alun's always on the lookout for acts for the Kiddies' Fun Festival.'

'Kids. I can't imagine having kids of my own, can you?'

'Not really.'

Lorna picked the shell off a hard-boiled egg. 'I wonder what happened to Rena.'

'Rena who?'

'That tall girl from the sixth form. Last thing I heard she'd got two sets of twins and another baby on the way.'

Claire gaped at the enormity of the thought. 'Five kids before you're twenty-six! Can you imagine *that*?'

'Only as the plot from a horror film.' She bit into the egg. 'Pity we've lost touch with so many of the old crowd. I used to love those massive pub-crawls we went on.'

Claire laughed. 'I bet you did. You were the only one over eighteen, remember?'

'So?'

'So you made us all buy you drinks in return for getting us in past the bouncers.' She sipped her Evian. It was nice to sit out here on a warm May lunchtime and forget about conferences for half an hour. 'Actually,' she said, 'Nadia rang me the other day.'

'What – Nadia with the big nose and the moped?'

'And the boyfriend who used to be a window-dresser at Seuss & Goldman.' Claire chuckled dirtily. 'Do you remember the time they . . . ?'

'Of course I remember! It made the front page of the *Courant*.'

Which wasn't all that surprising, thought Claire. Not many couples got amorously drunk, broke into the bed display in their local department store, and woke up next morning to be greeted by two security men and a camera crew from *Look Southwest*.

'What's Nadia doing now?'

'Selling caravans in Penzance.'

'Oh God, poor girl.'

'Don't feel too sorry for her, she drives a Ferrari now.' Claire wiped her mouth. 'Funny, isn't it? How when you're seventeen you think you're always going to be best mates with all your gang, and a few years later you don't even know where half of them are living.'

'You've still got me,' Lorna reminded her.

'Until Hollywood snaps you up.'

'That's OK, if you're nice to me I'll let you be my personal

204

publicist.' Lorna's eyes followed a burly workman as he walked past, pushing a wheelbarrow, his bare chest glistening in the sun. 'Claire?'

'Mmm?'

'About number sixteen.'

Claire's peace of mind deflated slightly. 'If it's about buying the house with Kieran, I'm really sorry but the answer's no.'

'No, *I'm* really sorry. I shouldn't have got carried away, it was a stupid idea.'

Claire shook her head. 'Actually it's quite a good idea.'

'It is?'

'But it's just not for me.'

There was a brief silence. Somewhere in the distance a skylark shrieked up towards the sun and plummeted down towards the lush green hills.

'This is about Paradise Cottage, isn't it?' said Lorna. Claire didn't answer. 'Claire, what's going on?'

Claire abandoned the last of her sandwich and sprawled out on the warm grass, oblivious to green stains on her beige linen trousers. The sky above was cloudless, sunny blue; but when she closed her eyes all she could see was a blaze of crimson. It wasn't things that changed; it was just that you found different ways of looking at them.

'You know something,' she said quietly, 'I wish I'd never got involved with Kieran.'

'What – over Paradise Cottage?'

It took some admitting, but she had to say it. 'At all.'

'Ah,' said Lorna. 'I did wonder. I mean, you two haven't really been getting on, have you?'

Claire shook her head. 'I'm sick of all the bickering. And it's not just that. I don't want to sell the cottage.'

Lorna looked at her quizzically. 'To spite Kieran?'

'No, nothing like that. I just can't face it.'

'But I thought the first time you saw that cottage, you really hated it!'

'I know. But that was before.' Claire rolled over on to her

front. 'There's something special about the place, Lorna. I know it doesn't make any sense, I just feel the more things we do to it, the more I keep thinking, I want to be here when this is finished. Even if it takes me years to save up the money.'

'I see. I guess.'

'I mean, I'm not saying I'd want to stay there forever. I might want to sell up sometime. But I'd like to be there till it's finished.'

'But I thought you said you couldn't afford the work it needs.'

'I can't. And then there's Ted and Brucie. I know Kieran keeps telling me there's ways and means of getting them out, but I'm not sure I want to. Is that stupidly sentimental?'

'Yes. Probably.'

'You know something? I don't give a stuff.'

Lorna scratched her head. 'Does Kieran know about this?'

'Not yet,' admitted Claire. Right now, she didn't even want to think about it.

'Don't you think you ought to? He's got a lot of money invested in that cottage.'

'Don't remind me.' Claire's face sank on to her fingers, outspread in the warm, sweet grass. Her voice was muffled. 'Either I find some way of paying him his money back, or he's going to force me to sell up.'

'It might help if you were on speaking terms,' observed Lorna.

'You think I'm barmy, don't you?' said Claire, sitting up. 'You think I should be signing up to Kieran's plan for world domination.'

'No,' declared Lorna, taking herself by surprise. 'Funnily enough, I don't.'

Chapter 17

Find a nice, cheap place to rent in Cheltenham? thought Lorna. We've more chance of landing a six-month season at the London Palladium.

House-hunting had not started well. Apparently it was a 'bad time of year' to be looking, but frankly it was always a bad time of year if you were a couple of out-of-work actors. Students, darn 'em; it was all their fault. No sooner had all the hotel management trainees gone off on their summer placements than hordes of foreign language students descended on the town, flashing great wads of fifty-pound notes.

Which was how she and Worm came to be flat-hunting on the Bluebell Estate. Lorna gazed dolefully at the steel-lined front door in front of her, and the three boot-sized dents at the bottom of it. A funny smell had pursued them up four flights of stairs and showed no signs of giving up the chase; she wondered if it could have anything to do with the dark, wet stuff seeping out from under the threadbare doormat.

'No way,' she said, striking a red line through the sixth address on her list.

Worm snatched the pen out of her hand. 'You can't cross a place off without even looking at it!'

'Worm, I don't need to.' Lorna grabbed him by the arm and turned him round so that they were both peering down over the balcony. From their vantage point, up on the fifth floor of a

Sixties block so bleak that the Council had had to pay somebody to take it off their hands, they had an excellent view of three concrete cows, a graffiti-daubed post box and a burned-out Ford Capri. 'Look at it! It's Beelzebub's back yard.'

'It could be worse,' argued Worm. 'And it's cheap.'

'Cheap?' retorted Lorna. 'Oh yes, I wonder why. Don't suppose it could be anything to do with the fourteen muggings and the race riot?'

'Don't exaggerate.'

'I'm not, and you know it.' She laid a hand on Worm's arm. 'Couldn't we just wait a bit?'

'No.'

'Pretty please? Just till the money starts coming in from the kids' parties?'

'We can't afford to.'

'But we've got our first party tomorrow,' she reminded him. 'If it goes well, we might pick up lots of other gigs. And if we wait till we've saved up a decent deposit, we can afford to get something fit for human habitation.'

Worm pressed the doorbell. 'If we wait much longer, we'll be sharing a park bench.' He rang again. Nothing happened, so he hammered on the door with his umbrella.

Lorna glowered. She hated it when Worm was right. 'I am *not* living here.'

A little square panel opened near the top of the door and a single bloodshot eye peered out from behind bottle-end glasses. 'Yes?'

'Mr Gruber? We've come to look at the flat.'

The door opened, to the accompaniment of many bolts being drawn back.

'Worm,' warned Lorna, as the stench of decomposing flesh hit her full in the face. Too late. Two seconds later Mr Gruber was standing on the doorstep, carving knife in one hand, severed sheep's head in the other.

'Come on in,' said Mr Gruber. The sheep said nothing. 'You did say you was animal lovers, didn't you?'

208

The following afternoon, still flat broke and flatless, Lorna and Worm put on their smiley faces and set off for the Green Café, down the bottom end of the High Street.

It wasn't quite the Old Vic. But as she squeezed into her Auntie Banana costume in the stockroom, amid sacks of organic lentils, Lorna reminded herself that it was very kind of Worm's mate-of-a-mate to wangle this gig for them. No, honestly, it was. Really, really kind to arrange for them to entertain the kids at her little boy's birthday party. Just don't think about Skegness.

Remember you're a pro, Lorna, she told herself sternly when the first spoonful of carob mousse hit her square in the eye. These are not spoiled little bastards; they're lovely, cuddly, sweet little kiddie-winkles and before they leave here they're all going to love you to bits. Or die. Besides, if you can survive strippers' nite at Heckmondwike Working Men's Club, you can handle this bunch of amateurs.

Mind you they were an odd lot, she thought as they reprised 'Bananas in Pyjamas' and Worm moved into his magic routine. Very odd. And that was just the parents. Who *was* that peculiar girl with the shocking lime-green hair and the small, curly-headed boy dressed head-to-toe in orange Lycra?

'Not again, Dylan,' urged the girl, as the small boy sabotaged Worm's fourth card-trick in a row.

The small boy turned to protest. 'But Mummy . . . '

Mummy flashed an apologetic smile at Worm. 'Sorry, mate. He's mad on Jonathan Creek, this one. Dylan,' she said sternly, 'Let the nice man win one, will yer?'

'But Mummy, I know where he's put the card, it's up his—'

Lorna stepped in, bent down and shoved a lollipop in the child's mouth. 'But the other children don't know, do they?' she pointed out, in a whisper that managed to be both coaxing and threatening. 'So it can be our little secret, can't it?'

Dylan's mind had to work hard on that concept. Finally he pushed the lollipop to the side of his mouth. 'OK.'

Thank God for that, thought Lorna. There's always one.

After that the rest of Worm's tricks went down rather well, and Lorna started to relax. She wasn't exactly *enjoying* herself, perish the thought; but if you discounted the miniature Einstein, they weren't the worst kids in the world, and as an audience they were gratifyingly easy to work.

She stood up, called for silence and – much to her surprise – got it. Once she had their rapt attention, she made great play of twiddling one of the dials she'd glued on to the front of her costume. 'Eee-ooo-eee,' she carolled, doing a pretty good impression of a radio tuning in. It wasn't the Teletubbies, but it was the closest you could get without being sued. Fascinated little eyes widened as she segued through several different voices before settling on a Country 'n' Western drawl.

'An' now, friends, thuh Great Wriggletto will eat – yes, I said EAT ...' She gestured grandiosely. '... a BALLOON GIRAFFE! Thank yuh very much.'

The kids went wild and flocked round Worm, in the innocent childlike hope that the nice man would choke to death on his own balloons. As Lorna was straining to remember the Heimlich Manoeuvre, a smart-looking dark-haired lady leaned over to talk to Dylan's mother.

'Mandy, this has got to be the weirdest kids' show I've ever seen!'

Mandy chewed gum. 'Good though, ain't it?'

'Very good. Very ... original.'

'I can't remember the last time my Dylan sat this still, it's brilliant.' Mandy nudged her friend and confided, ''Course, it's all down to that Auntie Banana, you know. She writes all their shows.'

Kieran might have had the decency to be heartbroken, but all he seemed to care about was his investment.

'I *am* going to get all my money back?'

She rounded on him as he followed her into the gutted living room of Paradise Cottage. 'No, Kieran, I'm planning to run off to Rio with Brucie and blow the lot on pig-nuts. Of course you're going to get your money back!'

'When?'

'Soon.'

'How soon?'

'For God's sake Kieran, we've only just split up! I haven't thought about it.'

Kieran did not look best pleased. 'You'll have to put the cottage on the market straight away.'

'It's my cottage, Kieran. I'll do what I want with it!'

'All right then. How else are you going to get the money to pay me back?'

'Somehow.'

'Somehow's not good enough, I need it now!'

Aidan knocked softly on the doorframe. 'Sorry to bother you, folks.' He handed Claire a sheet of paper. 'I've worked out those figures you wanted. Sorry it's not less, but it's the best deal I can do under the circumstances.'

Claire took a peek. It wasn't great but it was more or less what she'd expected. 'OK. So this is what I owe you so far?'

He nodded. 'We can't leave the walls half-finished, it would-n't be safe. But once that's done we'll suspend all work on the cottage. You're sure that's what you want?'

Claire avoided Kieran's gaze. 'I don't have much choice. I can't afford to do anything else to the place until things are sorted out, money-wise.'

Kieran swaggered up to Aidan. 'She'll be selling up now, so it looks like you'll have to find some other mug to make money out of.'

'Oh shut up, Kieran, don't be so bloody juvenile!' She turned back to Aidan. 'Thanks. I appreciate this.'

'No problem. And, er, if you do think about selling . . .'

Claire was just explaining, more from bravado than genuine optimism, that she was definitely *not* being pushed into selling up, when a shadow fell across the window.

'Coo-ee!' Veronica waved through the cracked pane. 'Can I come in?'

211

There was little point in saying no, since she was already skipping over the threshold in her cream crocheted two-piece, one of Emmy Willenhall's best china cups in her hand.

'What do you want?' demanded Claire, in no mood for social niceties.

'Just a cup of sugar dear,' trilled Veronica, her cheeks dimpling with secret pleasure.

'A what?'

'A cup of sugar.' She laughed. 'We're neighbours now, Weed darling. I've just moved in with Emmy and Geoffrey. Isn't that wonderful?'

So it was on the small side; but it was nice. Very nice, for a flat above a newsagent's shop. Recently redecorated too, to judge from the strong smell of paint and paste. Now this, thought Lorna, is definitely more like it.

'What about the traffic?' enquired Worm, shading his eyes against the sun and squinting down at the main road. 'Doesn't it get noisy round here?'

The young Asian newsagent joined him at the window. 'Oh, no, the traffic is no problem. The double glazing cuts out most of the noise, you see? And of course, you are very handy for the shops and the buses.'

'And the rent you quoted in the ad, that's right is it?' ventured Lorna. 'I mean, there's no mistake? It is that much per month?'

'Yes, yes, per month. That is quite right. You think it is too much?'

Lorna and Worm exchanged looks of disbelief. Had they really found that rarest of animals, the landlord with no idea of how to rip people off?

'No,' said Worm truthfully. 'It seems very fair.'

This is it, thought Lorna. This is finally it. She wanted to get a word in edgeways and say, 'We'll take it,' but the landlord was still babbling on about what a nice little flat it was, and how it was a shame it had been empty for so long.

'It has?'

'Beautiful wallpaper don't you think?' He patted it admiringly, raising his eyes to the smart new light-fitting that hung from a beam across the ceiling. 'The decorator has done a very fine job, you'd never think poor Mr Timpson had been hanging from that beam for three whole weeks before anybody noti—'

He stopped, noticing that his two prospective tenants were edging towards the open door.

'Did I just say the wrong thing?'

The appalling woman with the Mrs Thatcher hairdo shuffled paperclips on her desk, doing her darnedest not to make eye contact with Lorna. In return, Lorna did her best to look bedraggled.

HomeQuest was, after all, a housing charity; and if she wanted to wangle herself some help she needed to look like a charity case. This, she told herself, was going to be the most challenging role of her career to date.

'Address?' snapped Mrs Moncrieff, reluctantly selecting a form from her desk drawer.

'I told you.' Lorna sniffed miserably into a grimy hanky she'd borrowed from the odd boy in the attic. 'I won't have one soon, I'm being thrown out on the street.'

'Your address *now*.'

Lorna flicked an unbrushed ringlet over her shoulder, exposing a fraction more cleavage than she'd intended; she'd settled on the low-cut Indian top with the tassels in the hope it would give her the air of a stateless asylum-seeker without the passport problems.

'Sixteen, Jardine Crescent,' she confessed.

Mrs Moncrieff's eyes narrowed to suspicious slits. 'Jardine Crescent? That's in a very desirable area.'

'You haven't seen the house.' Lorna managed a consumptive cough worthy of Little Nell. 'There's mould all up the walls. And cockroaches, you should see the size of them.'

Mrs Moncrieff laid down her pen. 'Miss . . . '

'Walsh.'

'HomeQuest is a charity, Miss Walsh. Our policy is to assist only the truly needy.'

Lorna looked up into the stony face with Bambi eyes, defying Mrs Moncrieff's heart not to melt. 'I *am* the truly needy. Please help me, I've got nowhere else to go.'

The old harridan harrumphed but reluctantly went on filling in the form. 'Age?'

'Twenty-six.'

'Single?'

'Yes.'

'Pets?'

Lorna crossed her fingers under the desk. Dog wasn't a pet, he was an infection. 'No.'

'Occupation?'

At the last moment, Lorna stopped herself replying 'Actress'. That sounded much too prosperous and middle-class. Unemployed? Yes, but unemployed what? She hit on a suitably bohemian compromise.

'Street entertainer.'

Mrs Moncrieff's monstrous gaze swept her up and down, lingering disdainfully on the chipped nail varnish, holey tights and the Mount Vesuvius of all cleavages, erupting abundantly out of Lorna's low-cut top.

'Street entertainer?' she said, through tightly-pursed lips. 'Well I've never heard it called *that* before.'

Birds chirruped and cats dozed in the sunshine as Claire drove up Jardine Crescent and parked outside number sixteen. It was a perfect June morning, or it would have been if it wasn't for Paradise Cottage, and Kieran . . . and Veronica.

But, she wasn't the only one with problems; and at least she had a roof over her head. Two in fact, if you counted the cottage's interesting mosaic of cracked tiles and tarpaulins. And a day's strawberry picking with Lorna and Worm would cheer them all up, it always did.

She gave a quick blast on the car horn. Nothing stirred. Finally Dog wandered out of the shrubbery, cocked his mangy leg over the gooseberry bushes and wandered off again. Still there was no sign of Lorna.

Ten past. She'd promised faithfully to be ready, and now Claire would have to go inside and drag her out of bed. No sooner had she got one leg out of the car than the front door of number sixteen burst open. Lorna came bouncing down the path like a manic Afghan hound, wrenched open the car door and leapt into the front passenger seat.

'Claire, sweetie, you'll never believe what's happened!'

'Go on, surprise me,' said Claire. 'No wait, let me guess. You're going to pay me back that twenty quid.'

'That's not very nice!' protested Lorna, momentarily deflated. 'You know I will as soon as I can.'

'Sorry. Go on then, tell me what's happened.'

Lorna turned all smug and mysterious. 'Shan't,' she flounced. 'You'll have to wait till Worm gets here.' She opened the glove compartment, rooted around and unearthed half a tube of Werther's Originals. 'What's the latest on the love-life?'

'There isn't one. Kieran's a scumbag.'

'Your mother?'

'Don't ask. You know,' reflected Claire, 'I never thought I'd envy you . . . '

'Me! Good God woman, you're mad.' Lorna leaned over and popped a sweet into Claire's mouth. 'I'm telling you kid, if it wasn't for Worm keeping my head together these last few weeks, the little men in white coats would have been round for me long ago.'

'Oh look,' said Claire through a mouthful of butterscotch. 'Speak of the devil.'

Worm was loping down the driveway, but Lorna didn't look best pleased to see him. Or maybe it wasn't Worm she was scowling at, but the girl hanging on to his arm.

'Oh hell,' muttered Lorna. 'Not Murf.'

'Hiya!' Murf gave a breezy wave. Everything about her was

bright and sexy and energetic, thought Claire; even her braless boobs seemed to be on springs.

Worm was wearing the gormless expression of a fourth-former who has just discovered how to undo girls' bras one-handed. 'Hi Claire, hi Lorn. Anybody mind if Murf comes strawberry-picking too?'

''Course not,' said Claire, with one eye on Lorna.

Lorna grunted and flopped back in her seat, arms folded aggressively across her chest.

They set off down the road, Murf sharing private jokes with Worm on the back seat and Lorna pretending not to sneak the odd backward glance in the vanity mirror.

'So what's this good news you were going to tell us?' asked Claire, breaking the awkward silence.

'It doesn't matter,' sulked Lorna.

'What news?' Worm sat forward and stuck his head between the seats. 'Go on, spit it out.'

Lorna demurred. 'I'll tell you later.'

'Oh go on,' urged Claire. 'I could do with cheering up.'

'So could I,' chimed in Murf. 'I broke a nail this morning.'

'Well, all right,' relented Lorna. 'If you really want to know, I just had a phone call from my agent.'

'Oh great,' said Worm. 'You up for another murder victim on *Crimewatch UK*?'

'No! Listen.' She turned to Claire. 'Do you remember just after I left school, when I had that thing about being a pop singer?'

'You mean when you blagged your way into doing that session work with the Wombles?'

'The Wombles!' snorted Murf.

'Yeah, well, forget the Wombles,' said Lorna firmly, 'I'm talking about that novelty record I did lead vocals on.'

Claire clicked her fingers, trying to remember the song. It was a very, very long time ago, had spent one week at number eighty-three in the charts, and was so excruciatingly bad that even Chelt FM's 'Nostalgia Hour' hadn't played it since 1991.

'Something about Spiderman, wasn't it?'

'Batman.' Laura transformed herself instantly into a squeaky New York bimbette: 'Batman is a hunk,' she sang, 'but Batgirl's much much cooler . . .'

Murf joined in the chorus, very loudly, and fluffed all the high notes. Which made Lorna feel instantly much, much better. 'That was *you*?' Murf said, aghast. 'I thought it was Madonna in disguise.'

'Well it was me,' said Lorna proudly. 'And now it turns out there's this Japanese production company . . . anyhow, to cut a long story short they've used the song on the soundtrack of a Manga film.'

'Manga?' puzzled Claire. 'What's Manga?'

'Some cartoon rubbish, who cares,' replied Lorna. 'The main thing is, Manga means moolah! There's a big fat royalty cheque in the post, Claire – looks like I'm finally in the money!'

Chapter 18

Claire was thoroughly fed up. How could so many things conspire together to make her life so complicated? And that was exactly what it felt like: one big conspiracy, a plot whose sole purpose was to do her head in.

First all the trouble with the cottage, then the split with Kieran, not to mention Veronica turning up at Paradise Cottage like a persistent bad smell . . . and now Dad.

It had taken the best part of a week to build up the nerve to do this. To do the one thing she'd always promised herself she'd never do: ask her dad for money. Claire's independence had always been the thing she prided herself on most, the thing she wore like a talisman, to protect herself from hurt. And now, when she'd finally admitted she needed his help, Dad was doing the one thing she'd been so certain he would never do.

He was letting her down.

'Dad,' she repeated, hugging the receiver to her ear, 'about the money?'

Again, he breezed right past the question as though he hadn't even heard it. 'You're sure you're keeping well?'

'Well, yes, I suppose,' said Claire, momentarily thrown. She was standing by her bedroom window, watching a man and a woman walking towards the 'Homes and Families' exhibition, pushing twin babies in a buggy. 'But about this loan for the cottage. It wouldn't be for long, just until—'

'The thing is, your mother was quite worried about you when I last spoke to her.'

Claire's jaw dropped. 'You've spoken to Veronica? Behind my back?'

Terry sounded sheepish. 'Not behind your back, sweetheart, it wasn't like that. She just phoned me out of the blue.'

'When?'

'Oh, I don't know. A few weeks ago, does it matter?'

It matters to me, thought Claire. It matters to me more than I can say; and if you can't understand that, how can you ever understand me? 'What did she want?'

'Want?'

'Oh come on Dad, she must have wanted something. That's the only reason she ever gets in touch.'

Terry paused. 'Claire, sweetheart, about this money you need. You know I'd love to help you, only . . . '

'Dad . . . '

'. . . only I've got a lot of, you know, financial obligations right now, what with Sally and the new baby.'

The new baby. Pain tightened around Claire's heart. Daddy's new Claire, she thought to herself; Daddy's new daughter who's newer and brighter and better than you in every way, because her mother's not Veronica. In that moment Claire realised she had never felt real jealousy before, not like this.

'OK,' she said.

The little family reached the exhibition hall. Claire watched the young man hold the foyer door open while the woman pushed the buggy inside. Slowly it closed behind him and they all disappeared. Smiling.

'I'm sorry, Claire, really I am. I mean, if there's anything else, anything at all . . . '

'Sure. Fine.'

'Come to think of it, have you considered asking your mother to help you out?'

'What! Ask Veronica for a loan!'

'I know things have been bad; but that husband of hers in

Portugal sounds well off, and I really do think she's got your best interests at heart, you know. Why don't you give her a chance?'

Give Veronica a chance? The phone burned in Claire's hand; she wanted to slam it down on him. But there was one thing she had to know first. 'Dad.'

'Yes, sweetheart?'

'She told you, didn't she?'

'Told me what?'

'That she was moving in with the Willenhalls.'

'Well, yes. I think she did mention it.'

'Oh she did, did she? Isn't that just great? Pity she didn't bother telling me.'

She crashed down the receiver and hurled the phone across the room. Then, for the first time in years, she cried.

'Oh Lorna, I'm so happy for you,' wailed Worm, and burst into tears.

Lorna rolled her eyes and topped up his glass of Malibu. 'There, there, just you sit in the corner and get pissed, OK sweetie?'

'Don't mind Worm,' said Davey. 'He's only happy when he's miserable.'

Lorna was having a party. Which meant, in practice, that the whole of number sixteen was partying with her, since she had borrowed Stuart's hi-fi (one scratch on it and you die), Worm's life-sized cutout of Darth Vader (hey, what's yours is mine), Davey's CD collection (what do you mean you don't like Metallica? Everybody likes Metallica) and Mr Veidt's very ancient video recorder.

For reasons best known to himself, the odd boy from the attic had elected to serve drinks dressed as Dracula, while Kieran had decorated the TV room with Manga posters, and Candy had donated a plate of homemade canapés. She claimed they were shaped like bats, but frankly they looked more like Stilton-flavoured willies, which probably said a lot about Candy.

Claire felt positively unimaginative with her M&S crostinis

220

and bottle of Pinot Noir. And frankly, she wasn't even remotely in party mood. Dad, Veronica, the cottage, Kieran ... lately there hadn't been much to celebrate. She was only here so as not to rain on Lorna's parade.

'I've got it, I've got it!' squealed Lorna as she rushed into the room, boobs fighting to get out of her red fleece minidress. She looked, thought Claire, like Mrs Santa's naughty sister.

'Got what?'

'It! The film!' Lorna ripped shrink-wrapped plastic off a video cassette. 'The studio just biked it over – look, it's got my name on the credits and everything!'

'Quick, put it on!' exclaimed Kelly, Lorna's fellow bit-part player from the Jasper. Everybody clustered round the television set.

'How does this thing work?' Lorna wondered aloud, peering at the archaic controls on Mr Veidt's video player. 'Everything's in German.'

'Here, let me.' Claire reached out for the video, but Lorna whisked it playfully out of reach and clasped it to her ample bosom.

'I was thinking,' she teased, 'maybe we ought to watch my other video first.'

'Lorna,' moaned the assembled throng.

Roger the percussionist tore himself away from Lorna's extremely potent rum punch. 'What other video?'

'My showreel,' she enthused. 'It's got clips of me playing fifty-three different corpses. Or is it fifty-five? I suppose it depends on whether triplets count as three. Anyway, it's got everything from *CrimeScene Southwest* to *Sharpe* – they even put me up in a proper hotel for that one, you know! Room service and everything.'

'Corpses? No thanks, this sounds bad enough.' Claire made a grab for the video, missed and Davey intercepted it.

He scanned the label, turned the cassette upside down and made another attempt to decipher it. 'Here, this is in Japanese!'

'Let me have a look.' Stuart took it from him. '*Aqua Hero*

Honey,' he read, tossing it back to Lorna with a contemptuous sniff. 'I thought you said this was the cutting edge of contemporary Japanese cinematography.'

'It is!' Lorna thrust the cassette into Claire's hands. 'Go on, stick it in the machine thingy.'

'So what's this wonderful film about then?' demanded Murf, nibbling daintily on a bagel chip.

'Well, I haven't actually seen it,' said Worm, 'but apparently there's this teenage punk mermaid with water-defying rayguns, who fights demons in an underwater space city . . .'

'Oh, right,' said Stuart. 'Gritty realism.'

Lorna ignored the sarcasm. '. . . and when she's not being a superhero she hangs out at the mall with her friends and has a secret identity and everything. Don't look at me like that, it'll be good!' She waved an uncertain finger at the display. 'Which one's play?'

'This one,' said Claire. The tape started whizzing at a phenomenal rate. 'Oops no, must be that one.'

'Oh yes.' Lorna pressed the button and arranged herself in pole position on the sofa. 'Ladies and gentlemen, I give you: *Aqua Hero Honey*!'

Claire curled up on the floor, and Dog came and leaned his smelly, hairy body against her. The credits rolled. Sure enough, a punk mermaid flashed across the screen, two enormous guns blazing through the water. 'Batman is a hunk,' trilled the irritatingly-familiar tune. And Lorna sang along, with one eye on Murf, 'but Batgirl's much much cooler.'

'Hey!' exclaimed the boy from the attic. 'It really is Lorna singing!'

Kelly gave her a hug. 'Ace!'

'So how many thousand did you get in royalties?' enquired Kieran, turning his head to look at Lorna.

She grabbed one of Candy's Stilton willies and bit the end off. 'None of your business.'

'Aw go on, tell me.'

'A nice fat cheque. Just as well, seeing as the Jasper's closing.'

'They've cut you in for a percentage then?'

'Japanese and English rights, yeah.' Lorna posed, hand on hip. 'What is this, twenty questions?'

Davey whistled. 'This Manga stuff's massive in the States.' He grinned. 'Hey Lorna, will you marry me?'

She grinned and threw him a vol au vent. 'No.'

'Pity. I could quite fancy being a kept boy.'

They all sat and watched in silence for ten minutes. Claire strained to get the hang of the plot, but as far as she could tell there wasn't one. Mr Veidt sipped sweet sherry and scratched his bald head. 'Lorna, forgive me, but vat exactly ees happening here mit ze big mask on ze head?'

'Yeah,' said Kieran. 'Why's the boyfriend wearing all that diving gear?'

'Because he's human and she's a mermaid,' said Claire. 'It's obvious.'

'Is it? How do you work that one out?'

'Well put it this way, he's got legs and she hasn't.'

'So how does he shag her then?' puzzled Davey. 'If she's got no bits?'

It didn't get any better. Five minutes later, even Lorna was wilting. Reaching down the side of the sofa cushions, she drew out another video with a flourish.

'Fifty-five assorted corpses, anyone?'

The vote was unanimous.

'I'm not even sure why I'm telling you this,' muttered Claire to nobody in particular. She couldn't decide which was worse: feeling silly, or feeling sorry for herself.

'Why doesn't matter,' said the voice. 'Relax, let it all out.'

'But this isn't like me,' she protested, 'telling my problems to a stranger! I don't *do* all that huggy-feely counselling stuff.'

'Listen, it's easier telling things to a stranger. Just close your eyes and concentrate on the eternal mother's power, OK? And let it flow . . .'

'Couldn't I just . . . ?'

'I said *relax*!'

That was a lot easier said than done. Claire surreptitiously eased her left buttock off the cold stone slab as pins and needles ran down her leg. It was half past four in the morning, and here she was, sprawled on the altar in the middle of the stone circle at Brockbourne Hall, still dressed in her pyjamas. Gazing up at the brightening sky, she watched the last of the stars go out and marvelled at Brent Lovelace's powers of persuasion. One thing was for sure. This was the first and last time she was welcoming in the summer solstice in fluffy pink mules, spreadeagled on a lump of granite.

'How much longer?' she asked, trying to raise her head. A hand firmly pushed her back down on to the slab.

'It's nearly time.'

'My bum's going to sleep.'

'Shh, never mind your bum. Concentrate. Open your heart to the blessed spirit of the solstice. And tell me what's going wrong inside your head.'

She wriggled her tingling toes. Thank God Orion hadn't invited the world's press to photograph him consecrating the new Brockbourne Henge. This was one publicity opportunity she was happy to pass over.

'It's nothing really,' she said, rather unconvincingly, the way old people do shortly before launching into a monologue about their bunions.

'Sure it is,' scoffed the man who called himself Orion. 'Like, if it was nothing that'd really explain why you were crying your eyes out when I came to fetch you this morning.'

Claire let out a short, irritable puff of breath. It annoyed her that Brent Lovelace had caught her at a low ebb. It was unprofessional but, more than that, it had left her feeling vulnerable.

'All right, it isn't exactly nothing. I'm just tired, that's all. Tired and . . . and a bit . . . er . . . ' The word stuck to the inside of her mouth, as though it was ashamed to come out.

'A bit what?'

'Lonely.'

224

Lonely? she thought. What have you got to feel lonely about? You've got stacks of friends, and hardly a day goes by when you don't talk to dozens of different people. OK, so half of them don't even know what your name is, but ... She paused, waiting for Orion to say something profound, but he didn't.

'I'm tired of being a tower of strength all the time,' she moaned. All the bad stuff was coming out now; now she'd started she couldn't stop. 'Always there whenever there's a crisis, always making sure this place doesn't grind to a halt.'

'And people take you for granted, right?'

'Too right they do. It's, "Oh, Claire'll sort this, Claire'll take care of that, we can all go to hell in a handcart, but Claire'll still be there to make sure there's enough pitchforks to go round."'

'I'm sensing a lot of anger here. A lot of, like, righteous pain.'

By now, Claire was too fed up to feel embarrassed. 'It just gets me down sometimes, you know? You sort out everybody else's shit, but when you've got some of your own, what happens? Everybody vanishes.'

'Yeah, right. We had times like that in the band. 'Course, dropping all that acid didn't help.' Orion placed something small and heavy on her stomach. 'Don't move.'

She tried to take a squint at whatever it was, but couldn't see a thing without sitting up. 'What is it?'

'Just another crystal. It'll channel all the power into, like, your spiritual energy-centre.'

She located the crystal with an exploratory finger. 'What – my spiritual centre's in my appendix?'

He pushed her hand firmly away. 'I said don't move! You'll disrupt the meridians.' Claire grumbled but lay still as he re-adjusted the crystal and put another on her forehead. 'What about your family?' he asked.

'Don't talk to me about family. My mother doesn't give a damn about anybody but herself, and my dad ...'

'Bad karma, huh?'

'Not good.' It felt painful just to think about Dad. All those teenage years they'd seen through together, her and Pete and

Dad. Just the three of them against the world, never needing anyone but each other. It had felt, at times, like the only certain thing in her life; and now it was gone. 'He's got a second family now, he doesn't need me and Pete giving him grief.'

'Pete?'

'My brother. He's great but he's just a kid.'

'So ask your friends.'

'To sort out my life? I can't. I'm the one who never has any problems, that's what they always tell me. And then there's the money.' She stared blankly up at the sky, by now a rich turquoise with pinkish streaks.

'You have to pay this guy Kieran back, right?'

'Right. Either I borrow the money from somewhere or I have to sell Paradise Cottage.' She jerked her head sideways, trying to work out what the strange noises were. 'What are you doing?'

'Nothing. Just preparing myself. Go on. You're selling the cottage, right?'

'Wrong!'

'But hey, if you've got no bread . . .'

'I'll find it. Somehow. I just don't know how yet, OK?'

Claire's thoughts drifted to Lorna. Lorna who had just paid a cheque for sixteen thousand, seven hundred and forty-five pounds, thirty-two pence into her bank account. Even allowing for the overdraft that was already there, that made for an awful lot of spare dosh. Except, of course, that it wasn't spare. It was all Lorna had in the world, all she had to live on until she got another acting job, and who could say when that would be?

The awful thing was, she was sure Lorna would let her have it if she asked her for it. Because Lorna was a mate, a *real* mate, not like the others. And that was precisely why Claire couldn't do that to her. What if something went wrong and she lost the money? That was the kind of guilt you couldn't live with.

'Hail!' shouted Orion suddenly.

Claire sat bolt up upright and the crystal fell off her head. 'W-what?'

'Not yet, lie down.' Orion was prancing around the middle of the circle, a sprig of mistletoe in one hand, an upturned builder's hard hat in the other. In his floaty white robes and pointy hood, he looked like a cross between Isadora Duncan and the Ku Klux Klan. 'Hail to thee, blessed earth mother!' He swung round in a swirl of chiffon, gesturing with the mistletoe. 'Lie down, you're supposed to be the sacred sacrifice.'

'Brent ...' She noticed the nasty-looking curved dagger stuck through his belt.

'Orion.'

'Whatever. This is not *The Devil Rides Out*, and if you come near me with that knife ...'

'Chill out, it's only, like, symbolic, OK?'

Unconvinced, Claire swung her pyjama-clad legs over the edge of the stone and sat there, fluffy mules swinging. As a concession to Orion she retrieved the crystals and balanced one on each knee. 'So – what happens next? You do a little dance and we go home?'

'We wait for the sun to rise' The mistletoe quivered excitedly as the strip of brightness on the horizon grew broader and pinker. 'There! See? I told you it was going to work!'

Suddenly the sun crested Brockbourne Ridge , and by some trick of magic or physics or both, a kaleidoscope of rainbows threaded through the stone circle.

'It's amazing!' gasped Claire, genuinely flabbergasted.

'Praise! Praise to the mother spirit!' Laughing wildly, Orion upended the contents of the hard hat over his head, drenching himself with brackish water from the boating lake.

He's finally flipped, thought Claire. 'What did you do that for?'

Shaking back his scraggy wet mane, Orion grabbed her by the arm and pulled her to her feet. 'It's consecrated now.'

'Oh. Good.'

'Come on.'

'Where to?'

'Your flat.' He winked in an ageing rock-star sort of way. 'You can cook me breakfast.'

But breakfast didn't happen. Because at that moment something came roaring down the hill from the Hall. Something dayglo yellow, with a noisy engine and two wheels that spat divots of mud and grass in all directions.

'Whoo-hoooo!' screeched the motorcyclist, head down, leering demonically over the handlebars.

Orion gaped at the motocross bike as it sped towards them, ploughing an erratic furrow across the bumpy grass. 'What the hell?'

'Oh no,' groaned Claire as the familiar features hove into view. 'That's Julian. And he hasn't got a licence!'

By some miracle Julian, although pissed as the proverbial fart, did not actually crash into a lump of granite or kill anybody. The bike screamed into the stone circle, executed a couple of incompetent wheelies, ran over Orion's discarded hard hat and toppled over.

'You stupid prat!' seethed Brent Lovelace, all trace of cosmic oneness disappearing. Grabbing Julian by the shoulders, he hauled him to his feet and yelled in his face. 'Look what you've done to the blessed earth mother's temple!'

Julian grinned through an alcoholic haze. Behind him, a trail of churned-up grass extended all the way back from the altar stone to the rose garden. 'Fuckin' brilliant.'

'Julian,' said Claire sternly. 'This is *not* fucking brilliant, it is wanton vandalism. Have you any idea . . . ?'

He belched beer fumes. 'Yaaaa. Go fuck yourself.'

'You,' snarled Brent Lovelace, 'are a festering little tosspot.'

'So wotcha gonna do about it, big boy?' slurred Julian, swaying on uncertain feet. 'Nuffink, that's wot you're gonna do about it.' He jabbed a finger in Brent Lovelace's face. 'An' why? 'Cause I'm Julian fucking *Mayberry*, that's why.' He laughed. 'You can't do nuffink to me.'

'Oh yes I can,' replied Orion, delivering a headbutt that laid Julian out cold. 'I can do *that*.'

For a woman who had just come into a sizeable chunk of

money, Lorna was feeling mighty glum. She'd tried ringing Claire for a girlie heart-to-heart, but her mobile was switched off. OK, so it was only eight in the morning but best mates were supposed to be there for you, twenty-four hours a day. And Worm was less than useless. Worm had *her*.

She pushed soggy Sugar Puffs round her bowl, trying to ignore The Mallard going for yet another speed record on Stuart's hi-fi system. At least the steam train recordings masked the sounds of frenzied shagging coming from Candy's room. Shagging? thought Lorna gloomily, her thoughts drifting once again to Worm and Murf. You're only jealous. Just 'cause the last thing you pulled was a Christmas cracker, and you didn't even get a bang out of that.

There was half a bottle of Bailey's sitting on top of the bread-bin. Lorna wondered fleetingly what Bailey's tasted like on Sugar Puffs, and might well have given it a try if Kieran hadn't crashed into the kitchen on the end of a giant pair of folding doors.

'Christ, hurry up mate,' urged a muffled voice from the hallway. It sounded like Davey's. 'I think I've ruptured myself.'

'Steady as she goes, left hand down a bit. OK, put her down . . . now.'

The doors shuddered to earth, half in and half out of the kitchen.

'You can't leave them there,' said Davey, limping over them with one hand clasped to his groin. 'Can he, Lorn?'

Lorna munched apathetically. 'Can he what?'

Davey nudged the doors with his right boot. They were ancient, warped and covered in globs of dried cement. 'These. He can't leave 'em here, somebody'll come a cropper.'

'It won't be for long, just till I shift them. Anyway, they won't fit anywhere else.' Kieran grabbed a pint of orange juice from the fridge and downed it in one. 'You coming out for a McDonald's, mate? It's two for one with that coupon.'

Davey explored his groin with tentative fingers. 'Bloody hell mate, I think I can feel a bulge.' Hand still on the offending spot, he waddled over to the table. 'Put your hand on here, Lorn, and tell me if it sticks out when I cough.'

Lorna snatched her hand away. 'That's the worst chat-up line I've ever heard.'

'How about it then?' asked Kieran.

'I beg your pardon?' said Lorna.

Meanwhile, Davey had unzipped his trousers and was peering distractedly down the front of his underpants. 'Oh God,' he wailed, 'one's bigger than the other. That's the last time I help you nick stuff out of skips.' He looked up. 'How about what?'

'Breakfast.'

'Nah, don't fancy it mate.' Davey limped towards the door. 'Think I'd better have a lie-down, I've got a box of live bacteria to bike to Coventry this afternoon.'

He disappeared. Kieran picked up a discarded spoon and helped himself to a mouthful of Lorna's cereal. She slid the bowl sideways as he came in for a second helping, and his spoon clattered into the table-top. 'Get your own.'

'I've run out of cornflakes.'

'I thought you were going out for a McDonald's.'

'No point, is there?' Kieran rummaged in the archaeological sub-strata at the bottom of the fridge, and took out half a tin tray of takeaway chicken dhansak. 'Might as well save the coupon till there's two. Don't suppose you . . . ?'

'No.'

'Not like you to turn down free food.' Kieran sat down at the table, spooning cold curry into his mouth. 'Something's up, isn't it?'

She gritted her teeth. 'No.'

'Yes it is, I can tell. Your boobs are are all droopy and you haven't brushed your hair.'

Lorna glared. 'Well thank you Dr Freud.' She killed a Sugar Puff with the edge of her spoon and watched the two halves of its severed corpse float off in different directions. 'Do you *have* to eat with your mouth open?'

Kieran shovelled some more in. 'Shorry.' He offered the tray. 'Want shome?'

'Just eat it and go away, will you?'

Kieran contemplated the pile of papers and opened envelopes at Lorna's elbow. 'What are all those then?'

'Nothing.'

He craned his neck to read the address labels on the top envelopes. 'Ariel Fanshaw? Mr P J Quimby? Who are they then? And why are you reading their mail?'

She gathered them up, compacted the whole lot into a big, untidy ball, and shoved it into her shoulder bag. 'Nobody. And it's none of your business.'

'All right, all right, I only asked.' He sat in silence for a little while, glancing at her from time to time as though choosing his moment carefully. 'Lorna . . .'

'What?'

'I'm definitely thinking of putting in an offer on this house.'

Lorna's head jerked up in surprise. 'You can't!'

'Why not? Papajian's not signed on the dotted line yet.'

Lorna waved her hands about. 'Because you haven't got enough money, and because Claire's not interested.' She cocked her head on one side. Was there something in the Claire-Kieran saga that she'd missed? 'She isn't interested, is she?'

'I'm not talking about buying it with Claire.'

'But your money's tied up in the cottage.'

'It soon won't be, she's promised to pay me back. The thing is, once I've got my money back I'll have almost enough capital to negotiate an affordable mortgage on this place – but not quite. And then there's the deposit. If I want to get this place I'll have to move fast and put some hard cash on the table.'

Lorna picked up her spoon and went on eating. 'That's that then, isn't it? You're stuffed. Unless Claire sells Paradise Cottage to that horrible cousin of hers, and I can't see that happening, can you?'

'Not necessarily stuffed,' Kieran corrected her. 'Actually, it all depends on you.'

'Me? How?'

'You like living here, don't you? And you'd like to go on living here?'

She was there before him. 'Oh I get it. You're trying to get your hands on my royalties! You want me to hand over the only bit of security I've got, just so you can be a property tycoon.'

'You'd be one too,' he pointed out. 'You'd have a share in the house, according to how much money you put in. And your name on the deeds. And you'd get a share of income from the tenants while we were doing the place up.'

'Income . . .'

He must have sensed her wavering, because he homed in like an aardvark on an anthill. 'Think about it, Lorna. Make that nest egg work for you. Miss out on this, and you're going to regret it for the rest of your life.'

Kenton Mayberry was furious.

'Look at him!' he roared, incandescent with rage. 'Look what that – that drug-addled *lunatic* has done to my son!'

Julian Mayberry dangled on the end of his father's arm like a saggy overcoat on a peg. Blood had caked on his upper lip and chin, giving him the appearance of wearing a red goatee beard. 'He hit me Dad, he bloody hit me.'

'Shut up Julian, you've made enough of a prat of yourself already. Well Lovelace, what've you got to say for yourself?'

'Believe me, man, you don't want to hear it.'

Naomi interposed herself between the two warring factions. 'Mr Mayberry . . . Orion . . . please. It strikes me there are faults on both sides here. Kenton, your son should definitely *not* have been drunk in charge of that motorbike.'

Mayberry quivered with rage. 'At least my son doesn't go round headbutting defenceless youths!'

'I think it would be best if you apologised, Orion,' urged Claire.

'What – apologise to *him*? He desecrated the earth mother's temple, man!'

'Oh, for Christ's sake!' snapped Kenton Mayberry.

Orion tossed his shaggy head. 'Don't you lay your phallocentric Judaeo-Christian ethic on me, man.'

Claire towed Orion into the general office. Through the thin partition wall, she could just discern Naomi pointing out to the chairman that Orion's Millennium gig could not, repeat not, be cancelled; that it meant vast amounts of profit for Brockbourne; and that the TV proceeds alone would keep the Hall going for the next six months.

'Listen,' said Claire, 'I know Julian's an idiot.'

'At last somebody talks some sense.'

'But you can't go round headbutting people just because they're idiots. The hospitals would be overflowing. Can't you just apologise?'

'I want everything putting back the way it was. And an apology. And I want the temple reconsecrated.'

'I'm sure Naomi can sort all that out. Please, just a teeny-weeny apology.' She did her best to look winsome and vulnerable. 'You can keep your fingers crossed behind your back.'

'Look sister, I'll think about it, OK? But if I get any more shit from this Julian guy . . .'

She breathed an immense sigh of relief as the door of Naomi's office closed behind him. The rest was up to them.

'There has to be a better way of dealing with this,' commented Michael Tang, who had been observing from a distance.

She nodded. 'Before Kenton Mayberry runs the whole damn show over a cliff?'

'Exactly.'

Chapter 19

Claire wasn't sure how it had worked, but maybe Brent Lovelace had had a point after all. Maybe it really was the cosmic force of the summer solstice, channelling its energies into her brain; maybe it was just the fact that she'd talked and someone had listened. Either way, she could feel herself beginning to see things in perspective again.

What you give out you get back, that was what life was supposed to be about. Orion would have called it karmic adjustment or some such New-Age gobbledigook, but the name didn't matter. Some people went through life giving out lovely warm furriness wherever they went, and getting lovely warm furriness back. Veronica, on the other hand, gave out trouble. That was the only thing she seemed to have a real talent for: cutting a swathe through other people's lives, sowing discord.

Well, now it was payback time.

Veronica seemed genuinely touched by Claire's invitation to visit her at the cottage.

'Weed darling,' she beamed as she hitched up her skirt and hopped over the hole in the kitchen floor. 'This is so lovely.'

'Lovely?' Claire looked about her dubiously, at the crumbling horsehair plaster, the gutted cupboards, the almost complete absence of ceiling.

'No, not this kitchen, silly. Us! Together! I was beginning to think you were going to stay angry with your poor mummy for ever.'

Claire did not wince, flinch or pull a face. If Veronica could play the loving mother–daughter reunion card, so could she. 'I'd like to make you a cup of tea,' she said apologetically, 'but the only safe electricity we've got is in Ted's workshop.'

Veronica's smile took on a slightly nervous edge. 'That pig's not nosing about is it?'

'No, no, it's OK, he's at a parish council meeting.'

'A what? Oh, you mean that silly election thing. Haven't they sorted it out yet?' Once reassured that Paradise Cottage was pig-free, Veronica looked mightily relieved. 'Anyhow, I didn't come here to talk about pigs, Weed.'

'No, nor did I.' Claire picked her way through the builders' debris, across the hallway and into the front room. 'Mind where you step, some of the floorboards are rotten. Oh, and if you go upstairs don't flush the loo, the cistern falls off the bracket.'

Veronica lowered the seat of her white denim jeans, very gingerly, on to an upturned tea chest. Her eyes fixed on a dangling black loop of electrical cable, hanging out of the wall like a lurking mamba. 'The old place is in rather a state, Weed. It looks worse than it did before the builders started.'

'I know,' Claire agreed. 'And it's such a shame to leave it like this ... I know you wanted Great-Aunt Mary's cottage to be just like it was in the old days.' She shook her head. 'But you know how things are.'

Veronica took off her sunglasses and speared them into the purple bird's-nest of her hair. 'Well, I have offered to give you a hand, darling, but you just don't seem to want your mummy's help.'

That was Claire's cue. 'I've changed my mind.'

'Sorry?'

'I've changed my mind. I'd like you to help me.'

The smile grew broader, then hesitated and took on a puzzled air. 'How, darling? What exactly did you want me to do? Only I'm no good with hammers and things, your father

235

once sent me out for a tin of striped paint.'

'I'm not talking about DIY.'

At this, Veronica looked relieved. 'I could help you redesign the garden maybe, do a few watercolour sketches.'

'What I really need right now is money,' said Claire, hardly believing she was actually doing this, calling Veronica's bluff. 'I have to pay Kieran back his investment and I need more capital to finish the renovations. Otherwise I'll have to sell up, and I'm just not prepared to do that.'

Veronica swallowed. She looked quite pale underneath her tan. 'Couldn't you just get back with Kieran, sweetie? He's such a lovely boy.'

'Kieran and I are finished. I couldn't keep on going out with him just because he had money, could I?'

'Well . . .' said Veronica doubtfully. She caught Claire's eye. 'No, I suppose you're right.'

'Actually, Dad said I should ask you for a loan.'

This was not an easy thing to say, and Claire's heart was pounding. How on earth would she feel if Veronica actually said yes? Relieved because she wouldn't have to sell the cottage, or horrified because she'd be in debt to her mother?

Astonishment turned to horror. 'Terry did?'

'Oh yes. He said you'd been telling him how much you wanted to do something to help, you know, bring the family closer together.'

Veronica's face went through half a dozen different expressions. 'Oh. Well. Yes. I think I may have said something . . .'

'And he said you told him you're really well off since you remarried, so a few thousand pounds shouldn't be a problem.'

'A few thousand?'

'It would really get me out of a hole. And you'd get it all back.'

Veronica was on her feet. 'Oh Weed darling, I'm so sorry, but I can't.'

She looked so uncomfortable that Claire felt almost mean. 'But Dad said . . .'

'I'd love to help you out, I really would; but all my money's tied up in Portugal right now. I can't get at a penny of it, in fact I've hardly enough to live on. That's why I'm staying with your Cousin Geoffrey.'

Claire pursued Veronica as she backed away towards the door, and in her haste to escape one gold sandal disappeared abruptly into a gap in the floorboards. 'Ow.' She tugged at it and the heel came off. 'Stupid thing.'

'You couldn't call the bank or something?'

'It's all in Ronnie's name. And, Ronnie's away, you see, I wouldn't know how to contact him.' There really was a most peculiar pallor beneath Veronica's tan. 'You know I'd help you out if I could Weed, of course I would.'

'But of course, you can't.' How did I know you were going to say that? thought Claire, a bitter stab of pain running through her. She realised that once, just once, she would have liked to be proved wrong about her mother.

'Not at the moment anyway.' Veronica hovered on the threshold, varnished fingernails digging into her gold clutch bag. 'Weed, sweetie, Cousin Geoffrey tells me he's made you a very generous offer.'

'I am *not* selling to Cousin Geoffrey.'

'I know it's not what you wanted, darling, but at least the cottage would still be in the family.'

Claire's composure slipped. 'Oh yes! For about five minutes, till he bulldozed it to make way for a new slurry pit. You said you loved this place, Veronica. You told me you wanted to help me turn it into a cosy little shrine!'

'Well . . . yes, but . . .'

'But that was before I asked you for money.'

'That's a horrible thing to say!'

'But it's true.'

'Don't be silly, you know don't mean that.' Veronica glanced at her watch. 'I'm so sorry darling, I have to go. I told Emmy I'd be back by nine.'

'Don't let me keep you.'

237

Veronica was already limping away across the garden on her one good heel, stopping every few steps to shake the mud off it. She didn't turn round till she reached the garden gate, and by then she had had time to glue the smile back on her face.

'You know, you really ought to think about Cousin Geoffrey's offer,' she said. 'It's obvious all this stress is getting to you, you poor darling. And after all, it's only a cottage.'

'Tried to get money out of you, did she?' Geoffrey sank his teeth into a sixth chicken drumstick.

Veronica picked a caterpillar out of her salad. 'It's obvious she only invited me there so she could ask me for a loan,' she said. There was a note of sadness in her voice. '"Just a few thousand", she says. A few thousand! As if I could even if I wanted to.'

Geoffrey chuckled. 'Heh, heh. You got to hand it to the girl. Chip off the old block if you ask me.'

'What was I supposed to say? I could hardly tell her I've not got a penny to my name. And now she hates me more than ever.'

Geoffrey squirted ketchup all over his peas, scooped them on to a slice of bread and marge and stuffed the whole lot into his mouth. 'How much, you say? A few thou?'

'It might as well be half a million, I haven't got it.' Veronica stabbed disconsolately at a radish.

Geoffrey ruminated. 'It's all right girl, stop worrying. I'll give it you.'

'Give me what?'

'The money.' His long pink tongue deftly licked a blob of margarine off his chin. With all that ketchup dribbling from the corners of his mouth, thought Veronica, he looked like a chubby rustic vampire. 'I'll give it you, an' then you give it her, right?'

Veronica exchanged mystified looks across the table with Emmy Willenhall. 'I think your dad's goin' funny in the 'ead,' ventured Emmy to Paula.

'Dad,' piped up Eric, 'If you're tryin' to get rid of Cousin

Claire an' the old man, what you want to go givin' her money for?' His slobbish face grew sly. 'Why don't you let me an' the lads torch the place? That'll shift 'em double-quick.'

Geoffrey dealt him a fierce back-hander across the ear. 'You sure this one's mine, Emmy? He's got the brains of a turnip. Look, I'll spell it out, OK? I give your Auntie Veronica the money, an' she gives it to Claire and says it's from her. You with me?'

'No,' said Eric. 'Still can't see why you're givin' her money.'

Neither could Veronica, but she wasn't daft enough to say so.

Geoffrey put his head in his hands. 'Because then,' he enunciated very slowly and deliberately, 'your Auntie Veronica will have a stake in the cottage, won't she? And that's one step closer to me gettin' my hands on the place.'

An hour later, as Claire was getting ready to drive back to Brockbourne, her mobile rang.

'Wonderful news, darling!' Veronica's voice trilled over the phone line, very high-pitched and excited.

Holding the receiver at a safer distance from her ear, Claire walked out into the garden to get a better signal, and perched herself on the wall that separated the cottage from the lane. 'What news?' she asked suspiciously.

'About the loan, Weed darling. I've got all that money you need.'

Claire nearly dropped the phone into the flowerbed. 'What did you say?'

'The loan you wanted. I rang Ronnie, and he said no problem, he can arrange it all.'

Something lurched inside Claire's chest. Oh my God, she thought; this isn't supposed to happen. You're supposed to ask, she's supposed to turn you down flat, and then you congratulate yourself on being right about her all along. Only you weren't right, were you? And if you take that money ... if you take that money, how the hell are you ever going to get Veronica out of your life?

239

'Weed?' said the voice on the end of the line. 'Weed, are you still there?'

Veronica put the phone down and turned round.

'Well,' she said, a tremble in her voice. 'I did it.'

Geoffrey rubbed his hands together. 'Emmy, fetch me that single malt, I feel like celebrating. Veronica, help yourself to a glass, one of the big ones.'

'There's something bothering me,' said Veronica as Geoffrey poured out the whisky.

'Oh?' He took a long, satisfying sip. 'What's that then?'

Veronica settled herself on to the Willenhalls' leather sofa, put down her glass and folded her arms. 'Paradise Cottage,' she said. 'Why do you want it so much?'

'Oh, you don't want to go worryin' your pretty head about that,' scoffed Geoffrey.

'Yes I do,' she retorted. 'And this time I want the *real* reason.'

Chapter 20

Geoffrey leaned back, rested his muddy boots on the white marble fireplace and went on talking.

'Old Mary, she promised that cottage to my poor dead ma, so she did.'

Veronica was unimpressed. 'So?'

'So it were rightly hers, and it's rightly mine now. Stands to reason.'

'I don't get this.' Veronica's surgically-enhanced nose wrinkled, pulling the corners of her mouth into a peculiar grimace. 'You mean – that's all there is to it?'

'What d'you mean, *all*?' growled Geoffrey.

Whoops, thought Veronica, back-pedalling furiously. 'Well, what I meant was—'

'That cottage was promised.' Geoffrey's finger wagged an inch from her face. '*Promised*, you got that?'

'Er, yes.' She pushed the finger gingerly away as though it might explode at any moment. 'Of course I have, but . . .'

Geoffrey drained his glass and stuck out the empty for a refill. 'Come on woman, make yourself useful.'

Emmy banged the bottle down on the mantelpiece with a silent scowl, and stumped back to the shapeless knitted thing that was destined for the tombola stall at Saturday's village fete. Geoffrey refilled his own glass with singularly bad grace.

'That cottage is mine,' he repeated with murderous precision.

'Mine and nobody else's. Ain't that right, Emmy?'

Emmy grunted into her purple knitting. ''Tain't *hers*, that's for sure.'

Geoffrey banged his hand on the arm of his chair. 'Exactly! Can't have strangers coming into the village and stealin' what's rightfully ours, can we?'

For someone who was about to get exactly what he wanted, Kieran looked less than ecstatic.

'You're making a big mistake Claire,' he said, as the summit meeting was convened around number sixteen's beer-stained coffee table.

'The only mistake I made was getting involved with you,' she retorted, turning to Veronica. She took a deep breath. 'Let's get this over with.'

Veronica hung back with unusual reticence, the cheque quivering hesitantly between thumb and forefinger. 'Weed darling, you have thought about this, haven't you?'

'Of course I have.'

Davey shuffled on the sidelines, hands in the zipper pockets of his leathers. 'Well if that's that I'll be off then.'

Claire halted him in his tracks with a basilisk stare. 'Don't you dare move, you're a witness. I don't want Kieran turning round next week and saying I still owe him money.'

'As if I would,' protested Kieran. 'You've got me all wrong.'

'Have I?'

Kieran looked baffled that anyone could think ill of him. 'Look Claire, why don't we give this another go? We could be good together. Think of all the money we could make.'

Claire plucked the cheque from her mother's hand and waved it in front of Davey's face. 'Witness?'

He shrugged. 'Sure. Whatever.'

'There you go then, Kieran.' She presented it to him. 'All you have to do is give me a receipt and we're quits. OK?'

'If that's what you want.'

'It is.'

So that was all there was to it, thought Claire as she sat alone in the kitchen, contemplating Kieran's scribbled receipt. He'd even missed the 'i' out of her name; which just about summed up the depth of their relationship.

'Weed,' said a small voice behind her.

She raised her head. 'Hi.'

Veronica dawdled on the threshold, fingers fiddling with the clasp on her clutch bag. 'Mind if I come in?'

'Be my guest.' She felt a sudden surge of unaccountable warmth towards this stranger who was supposed to be her mother. 'Thanks, Veronica.'

'Whatever for?' Veronica sat down, less than elegantly, on the chair with the uneven legs.

'For the loan.' For once, she didn't have to force the smile. 'You really got me out of a hole, I appreciate it.'

Go on, Claire willed her mother silently; look smug. After all, you've got me where you wanted me. But Veronica did not look smug; frankly, she looked positively uneasy.

'Weed . . .'

'Is something wrong?'

'Are you *sure* you're doing the right thing?'

Veronica's concern surprised Claire. Maybe it was faked, but if so it was pretty convincing. 'Oh yes,' she replied. 'Absolutely sure.' She smoothed her fingers across the crumpled receipt. 'I'm just not sure if it's the *best* thing.'

When Claire got the letter from Pete, she knew she was in deep trouble. For days she'd been steeling herself to tell him about Veronica and the money, without ever quite getting round to it. Now he was about to turn up on her doorstep with a sleeping bag and a plumber's wrench.

Ten to three. Zero hour was approaching, and Claire was dreading it. She checked her arsenal of ammunition: three swiss rolls, four packets of Jaffa Cakes and a copy of 'Grand Theft Auto' for the Playstation. If that didn't butter Pete up, nothing would. Maybe she should have asked Lorna to come round too, he liked Lorna. But that would have meant telling Lorna about the deal she'd struck with Veronica, and then she'd have to put up with being called an idiot twice in one day.

Footsteps climbed the stairs. Then a key turned in the lock. 'Hello? Anybody in?'

It wasn't Pete, it was Mattie Sykes. 'Oh, sorry, I thought you weren't in so I used the pass key.'

'That's OK, what's the problem?'

'Need you ask? It's that flaming Julian again.'

This is all I need, thought Claire. The only total cretin in the whole of Brockbourne, and he has to be the boss's son. 'Go on, tell me. What's Daddy's little helper done this time?'

'Only lost track of that stuffed polar bear. Naomi wondered if they might have delivered it here by mistake.'

'Why would anybody lug a polar bear up three flights of stairs?'

'Don't ask me, there's no accounting for—agh!' As Mattie turned to go she collided with a great clanking rucksack, festooned with pots and pans. 'Oh, hello Pete.'

'Hi,' said Pete, righting Mattie and slinging his rucksack on to the antique chair by Claire's front door. 'Sorry about that, don't know my own strength.' He pushed up his sleeve and flexed a muscle. 'Feel that.'

Mattie laughed. 'I'll be down in Admin if any polar bears turn up.'

'Right you are.'

'Polar bears?' quizzed Pete.

'Best not ask.' Claire steered Pete into the flat, nudging the door shut with her foot. 'Help yourself to food,' she said, adding enticingly, 'I've got jam swiss roll.'

'Actually I'm not that hungry,' he admitted, unprecedent-edly. Peeling off his fragrant climbing socks, he rolled them into a ball and headed them deftly into the fruit bowl. 'I had a box of doughnuts on New Street Station. Could murder a beer though.'

Beer, thought Claire, fetching him a can of export lager from the fridge. Damn, why didn't I buy more beer? It wasn't that long since he'd been padding around with his nappy round his ankles, toting a bottle of infant formula. She slung him the can, but he fumbled the catch and it landed on the floor.

'Poor old sis,' grinned Pete, scooping it up and bouncing on to the sofa. 'What a girlie. Never could throw straight to save your life.'

'Sexist pig.'

'Realist, more like. Remember that time we were playing French cricket on the beach at Weston, and you knocked that man's false teeth out?'

'I wouldn't have done if you hadn't ducked.'

'I had to, you'd have had my head off!'

'That's a rotten lie!' She barged Pete off the sofa and he slid off the end, dragging her with him in a laughing heap. 'Pete,' she said when the laughter subsided, 'I've got something to tell you.'

Upside-down on the carpet, he looked up at her suspiciously. 'You're not pregnant, are you?'

She hit him with a scatter cushion. 'No!'

'Thank God for that, I'm too young and sexy to be an uncle.'

'Says who?'

'Says me.' He sat up. 'Hey, the cottage hasn't fallen into a disused mineshaft or something? I knew I should've checked the land survey maps for old mine-workings.'

'No. But it is about the cottage. And . . .' She swallowed, suddenly very embarrassed. 'Veronica.'

All Pete's good humour evaporated instantly. 'What's the old witch been up to now? I hope you sent her packing.'

Claire sat cross-legged on the floor, picking at the pile on the carpet. How on earth was she going to explain to Pete what she'd done, when frankly she was having trouble coming to terms with it herself?

'Pete,' she said, 'you know I split up with Kieran? And he wanted his money back?'

'Yeees.'

'And I didn't want to sell Paradise Cottage, but I hadn't got any money to pay him back with?'

'Uh-huh.' Pete gestured, nudging the story forward. 'And?'

'Well, I tried everywhere I could think of to borrow the money, but nobody wanted to help me. Not even Dad.'

'So you *are* selling up? Oh sis, you could've told me, I needn't have bothered coming.'

She waved at him to shut up. 'No, I'm not selling up. I'm borrowing the money.'

'But you said—'

'Dry up Pete, this is difficult enough as it is.' She took a deep breath. 'Veronica offered to loan me the money. And I said yes.'

Pete fell backwards on to the carpet. 'No,' he said flatly, staring up at the ceiling. 'No, you wouldn't do that.'

'I had to, Pete. I had no choice.'

'Oh Claire, how could you be so stupid? The old cow's taken you in good and proper, hasn't she? And now she's using this as a ruse to force her way back into our lives.'

'No, she hasn't taken me in,' said Claire firmly, more certain than ever that she had done the only thing possible. 'But selling Paradise Cottage would mean losing everything I've put into it so far. And I'm sorry Pete, but I just can't do that.'

Claire stood in the empty shell of Paradise Cottage and stared at the impressive growth of green moss on the bedroom wall. 'It's got to be a damp problem,' she declared sagely.

Lorna laughed. 'Even I can see that, you div, it's dripping wet!'

Claire prodded experimentally at the moss. It was positively luxuriant. 'Maybe I should forget all about renovations and just turn the place into a paddy field,' she mused.

Lorna flung out her arms, so violently that the floorboards twanged beneath her feet. 'Ah yes, I can see me doing the TV adverts now: "Paradise Cottage Basmati Rice, for the great taste of organic pig poo."'

'You're more cheerful today,' observed Claire.

'So would you be, if you'd just earned sixteen thousand quid for doing nothing.'

'True.' Claire sighed. 'Instead of which I haven't got a bean, I'm in hock to my mother, and I've got an entire eco-system developing on my bedroom wall.' She squinted up at a damp patch on the ceiling. 'I bet there's a leak.'

'Did I tell you?' Lorna went on, not really listening. 'Worm had an argument with Murf and she threw a trifle at him.' She giggled. 'It was the funniest thing I've seen since Darren's tights split in *King Lear*.'

'I'm *sure* it's a leak.' Claire stood on tiptoe and tried to touch the patch, but it was out of reach. 'Maybe I should go up into the loft and check the water tank.'

This interrupted Lorna's account of cleaning custard out of Worm's ears. 'You? Go up there? You're kidding.'

That touched a raw nerve. If there was one thing Claire was heartily sick of, it was being told she couldn't do things. 'Why shouldn't I fix my own water tank?'

'Well *excusez-moi mademoiselle*, but you're not exactly Handy Andy, are you?'

Claire pushed her DIY class fiasco to the back of her mind. It was a one-off, it didn't count. 'I could be if I wanted. Besides, I've got no money. How am I going to get this place fixed up if I don't learn how to do things myself?'

Lorna shook her head. 'Why don't you wait for Pete to do it?'

'Pete's gone off pot-holing in Cheddar Gorge.'

'Still sulking, huh?'

'You know what he's like. He'll come round in the end.'

'So wait until he does. Why don't we just pack up? I thought you wanted to go down the village fete.'

'I do. Later.' Claire was already manhandling the stepladder out on to the landing. 'Hold the bottom, I'm going up.'

'Claire, you're a maniac.'

'Just hold it steady. And hand me that torch, it'll be dark up there.'

With a bravado that masked a heart of pure jelly, Claire climbed up the steps and prised open the loft hatch, dislodging a half-hundredweight of dust and dead spiders.

'Ugh!' squealed Lorna, darting to the other end of the landing.

'Don't let go of the ladder!' spluttered Claire. 'I'll fall off!'

Lorna returned reluctantly, shaking cobwebs out of her hair. 'If this sets off my allergy, it's all your fault,' she said darkly.

'And if I fall off this ladder, it's all yours.' Claire poked her head through the hatch and switched on the torch. 'My God, there's all sorts up here. Old wind-up gramophone, dressmaker's dummy, couple of beaten-up oil lamps, they might come in useful. Oh yuk, what's that?'

'Well, what *is* it?' demanded Lorna after what seemed an eternity.

'It's OK, it must've been dead for ages.' Claire crawled in through the hatch. 'Ah, there's the water tank, over there. I'll just go over and see if I can tell where the leak's coming from.'

Once she was actually in the loft, things were much less daunting. For one thing, glimmers of daylight crept in through the temporary roof covering, muting the absolute darkness to a friendlier twilight. Now all she had to do was get from one side of the loft to the other . . .

A thought occurred to Lorna. 'Claire?'

'What?'

'Whatever you do, don't step off the—'

'Aaaaah!'

'—joists.'

Letting go of the ladder, Lorna rushed through into the bedroom, to be greeted by the sight of two writhing legs dangling down through the ceiling.

'Oh shit Claire, are you OK?'

'Lorna!' came the plaintive cry from up above. 'I think you'd better go and fetch Aidan Ross.'

St Ogmore's summer fete was one of the undisputed highlights of Lilcombe Magna's social season – if you discounted the

Scouts' jumble sale and the annual mole cull. Where else could you throw wet sponges at the vicar, play Bat the Rat with real rats, and buy a fifty-six-pound sack of goat droppings?

'You,' said Aidan sternly as they sat down outside the tea tent, 'are a very silly girl who deserves a sound spanking.'

Lorna winked broadly at Claire. Claire's expression set somewhere between grudging gratitude and abject humiliation. 'Don't you dare even think about it,' she warned.

'You ready to order then?' enquired Annie, taking out her pad and pencil.

'Pot of tea for three please,' said Claire.

'And a plate of cream scones,' added Lorna. 'It's OK Aidan,' she said. 'Have anything you like, this one's on Claire.'

Annie scribbled on her pad. 'Cream ... scones. See your mother's gettin' into the swing of village life,' she commented, nodding over to the Bat the Rat stall, where Neville Shute was showing a giggly Veronica exactly how to perfect her grip.

'Isn't she just,' agreed Lorna, nudging Claire's elbow. 'Just look where she's got her hands.'

Claire hardly dared look. It was bad enough having Veronica as a next-door neighbour and business associate, without being forced to watch the progress of her dalliance with Neville Shute. For a middle-aged, allegedly married woman, Veronica had an embarrassingly active love-life.

'Claire,' said Aidan, pouring out three cups of tea, 'you do realise what you did back there was worse than stupid?' Claire nodded dumbly. 'And you could have come out with a damn sight more than just a few bruises on your backside?'

'Yes, all right, I know.' She slapped clotted cream on to a scone and tried not to think about the colour her bottom would be in the morning. 'But what was I supposed to do – wait for divine providence to come along and do the cottage up for me? I'm skint, Aidan. If I don't sort the place out myself, nobody's going to do it for me.'

'What about Pete?' cut in Lorna. 'I thought he was going to help.'

'A bit, maybe, if he ever stops sulking. But Pete's not going to be there all the time, is he?'

Aidan bit into a scone. 'OK, so you want to do the cottage up yourself.'

'Correction. I *have* to.'

'Whatever. I understand that. But you have to be realistic about it. Say what you like, you're an amateur. You don't know what you're doing, and that's dangerous. You can't do it without supervision.'

Over the tannoy, Old John was announcing that Councillor Brucie would shortly be starting the sack race. 'And all competitors for the Waggiest Tail to the show ring please.'

'Supervision!' Claire tossed her head. 'And who's going to supervise me?'

Aidan smiled. 'Me.'

Lorna and Claire staged a perfect demonstration of synchronised jaw-dropping.

'You!' exclaimed Lorna.

'Yes, me.' Aidan captured his paper napkin as a gust of wind blew it off his lap. 'Look, I know I said you were hopeless and we had that stupid bet on, but I admire what you've done. You've worked hard, you've got guts. If you want me to, I'll help you whenever I've got free time, show you what to do and how to do it safely.'

Claire could hardly believe she was hearing this. 'And what's in it for you? What's this going to cost me?'

'Pay me what you can afford.'

'This is a wind-up, isn't it?' said Claire.

'No, I mean it.'

'Face it Claire,' said Lorna. 'You're not going to get a better offer than that.'

There had been some bad times lately, sure there had. Sometimes she hadn't thought she'd ever get through them, too often she'd resorted to the gin bottle to blot them out. But things were starting to go right now, she could feel it in her bones. Today, Lorna was on a high.

'Four encores!' she exclaimed, bounding into the nice big suburban bedroom that was doubling as a dressing room. 'I can't believe it.'

Worm wrenched off his teddy-bear head, flung himself full-length on the bed and lay there, red-faced and panting. 'Today forty screaming four-year-olds, tomorrow the RSC?'

'Don't knock it, Worm, kids are the worst critics in the world, and they loved us.' She bent over. 'You couldn't undo my head, could you? I think there's something caught in the poppers.'

Worm disentangled a yo-yo from Lorna's neck. 'There you go, should come off now.' He flopped back, wiping sweat from his brow. 'I'm not knocking it, I'm just saying there's a limit to what you can do with "The Teddy Bears' Picnic".'

'Well, yeah.' Lorna flopped down next to him on the bed. The bear suits were so huge, there wasn't much room for manoeuvre. 'Budge over.' She wriggled into the space vacated by Worm's right paw. 'I've been thinking about developing the act.'

Worm opened his mouth to say something, but Lorna was already warming to her theme. It was impossible not to feel excited, with all those kids still raising the roof downstairs, and two repeat bookings already in the bag. And she had her wonderful secret to tell him: all about the new script she'd been working on without letting him know. It was the very best thing she'd ever written, and she'd written it just for Worm.

'We should do some promotions,' she said. 'I was talking to Claire yesterday, she could get Mattie to give us loads of advice . . . and if we get ourselves some new costumes, she might even book us for the Kiddies' Fun Day. What do you reckon?'

Worm said nothing.

'Worm?' She nudged him.

'Oh. Yeah. Great.'

'What's up?'

'Nothing.'

251

Lorna folded her fat, furry arms. 'Typical Worm,' she said. 'You get a standing ovation and all it does is make you more miserable.'

'I'm not miserable,' said Worm defensively. 'Just ...' He paused for a moment. Downstairs, somebody was pounding out 'Yellow Submarine' on the piano, fortissimo, but you could still make out the childish cries of 'Auntie Banana! We want Auntie Banana!' 'Lorna.'

'Mmm?'

'About the house. Are you going to buy it with Kieran?'

Lorna shrugged. 'Search me.'

'It's a big risk.'

'I know.'

'What if you lose all your money?'

She rolled on to her side. 'I won't.' She chuckled and tweaked his nose. 'I know you, you won't let me. It's like being followed round by your own personal bank manager.'

Worm looked profoundly uncomfortable. 'Lorna, there's something I've got to tell you. I might not be around much longer.'

Lorna gaped. A dozen gruesome diseases paraded through her mind, all of them fatal. 'Oh my God, Worm! What's wrong with you?'

'Wrong with me? Oh no, not that, I'm not ill. I'm just going away.'

She blinked. 'Away? Away where?'

'I'm not sure yet.' Worm's discomfort mutated into guilt. 'I know I should have told you sooner, and I'm really sorry, but I didn't make my mind up until yesterday.' He swallowed. 'The thing is, you know Murf and I ... ?'

Murf, thought Lorna, her heart suddenly leaden. So that's what this is all about.

'I know you've been sharing bodily fluids, yes,' she said with forced brightness. 'What about it?'

'She and the band are moving on in a fortnight's time. Going on tour. I want to go with her.'

Lorna's head whirled with sudden, awful realisation. Worm was in love. He couldn't be in love, not Worm, not now. He couldn't up and walk out of her life, just when the act was starting to come together. He couldn't desert her, he couldn't! Not when she needed him to stop her life falling to bits all over again.

'Oh,' she said. 'I didn't realise you liked her *that* much.'

Worm looked desperate. 'I know it's really bad timing, and I'm really sorry.' His eyes searched her face. 'You're angry with me, aren't you?'

She looked back at him, remembering all the times they'd shared – the dismal dressing rooms, the wet street corners, the dole queues. It was hard to resent a man who'd once spent his last fifty p on a woolly hat to keep her head warm when she had earache. Well, it was a tea cosy really, but the thought was there.

For his sake, she smiled. 'Of course I'm not angry, I'm just glad you've found someone.'

'And you'll manage?'

'Darling, I always manage.'

'I'll keep in touch. And you'll still have Claire . . .'

'Yes,' she said quietly. 'I'll still have Claire.'

And she hugged Worm for all she was worth, and he hugged her back; far too relieved to notice that she was crying, and that they were not tears of joy.

Chapter 21

Claire gazed up at the distant, cockeyed chimney stack of Paradise Cottage, its cracked terracotta pots listing at a crazy angle. Funny how a teeny-weeny little country cottage could feel like Canary Wharf when you were about to climb up it.

'Do *not* forget this.' Aidan jammed a bright yellow hard hat on to her funky new hairdo. The hat was so tight it made her ears sting. 'Oh, I padded it out a bit,' he added, 'seeing as you've got such a tiny head.'

She grimaced. 'Thanks.'

He jumped up on to the bottom row of scaffolding planks. 'Come on then, better make a move in case it starts raining again. And be *careful*, OK?'

Aidan swung up the scaffolding tower like Tarzan on Viagra. Huh, thought Claire. Macho show-off. Well anything he could do, she could do better. Not.

She hung back, one foot on the ladder, the other still reassuringly planted on terra firma. Come on idiot, she scolded herself. If you could manage the climbing wall at sixth-form college, you can manage this. Ah yes, that was all well and good; but the climbing wall didn't wobble in the breeze, did it? Nor had she been wearing these very, very tight, circulation-strangling trousers, in the misguided conviction that showing off her bum was more important than being able to move her legs. She didn't know why she was trying to impress

Aidan Ross anyway; she didn't even like him that much.

'You all right?' he called over his shoulder.

That riled her into action and she scrambled after him up the ladder. 'Of course I'm all right, why shouldn't I be all right?'

'No reason, I just thought maybe you were a bit scared of heights. Maybe we should have got you a safety harness .'

She sniffed. 'I'm fine!'

Then, just as she was beginning to think this was a piece of cake, her left foot slipped off the rung. This is it, she thought with alarming clarity as her foot flailed about in empty space; I'm going to die – and I'm wearing Donald Duck knickers.

'Aaah!' A heart-stopping second later, she regained her footing.

Aidan peered down from his perch, several yards above. 'Watch your footing, and don't muck about on the ladder, it's dangerous.'

She glowered up at him as she heaved her way up the rest of the ladder. 'I already worked that out, thanks.'

When it came to showing off, Claire realised, there was no point even trying to compete with Aidan. By the time she reached the eaves he was effortlessly swinging from one hand, inspecting what remained of the guttering.

'This list your brother made out isn't all that bad,' he admitted. 'For a student.'

'What's wrong with students?' demanded Claire, leaping to Pete's defence.

Aidan laughed. 'Plenty, why d'you think I dropped out of college?'

She smiled up at him with barbed sweetness. ''Cause you failed all your exams?'

If she'd hoped to ruffle his feathers, she was sorely disappointed. He just went on picking ancient tennis balls and birds' nests out of the down-spout. 'Actually, no. I walked out the week before my finals. It was that or miss out on my first big property deal.' He stood up. 'Hey, come up and look at this.'

'It's OK,' said Claire, clinging to the top of the scaffolding and trying not to look down. 'I can see from here.'

'No you can't.'

'Yes I can.'

'All right then, what can you see?'

'Er . . .'

He beckoned. 'Come on, just take your time, it's perfectly safe.'

With a deep breath she stepped off the nice solid scaffolding plank, took Aidan's proffered hand and—

'Not on there! Use the crawler boards! We don't want a repetition of last week, do we?'

Red-faced, Claire extricated her left foot from the rafters. Damn damn damn damn damn, this was going all wrong! 'The boards. Yeah. Right.' As suavely as anybody could with bits of roof slate sticking out of their sock, she scrambled up the roof and joined Aidan, sitting astride the ridge.

'What am I looking at?' She gazed down at her feet. The roof below her was in an even worse condition than she'd feared. Numerous slates were missing, there were two holes above the back bedroom, and several small trees seemed to be growing out of the loft. 'Oh my godfathers, look at the state of it!'

'What?' Aidan looked round. 'No, not the roof, look at the view!'

She blinked and followed his pointing finger. The heavy grey rainclouds were still lumbering over the hills, but the sun had broken out from underneath, casting dramatic moving patches of light and shade over the Gloucestershire countryside.

'Wow,' she said, because no other word would do. 'It looks even better from up here.'

'"Earth has not anything to show more fair,"' quoted Aidan, taking out a packet of wine gums and offering her one.

'"Dull would he be of soul who could pass by, a sight so touching in its majesty,"' murmured Claire, astonished that she could remember the poem and more astonished still that Aidan had ever heard of it. 'Wordsworth.'

'Never could stand Wordsworth,' commented Aidan. 'All

256

those idiot boys and leech-gatherers.'

'Yeah . . . I mean no. Me neither.'

'I'm more of a Ted Hughes man myself.'

'Are you?' Astonished, Claire took a sweet from the packet. 'Aidan, how does somebody like you end up plumbing in toilets?'

There was a half-smile on his lips. 'Somebody like what?' He didn't wait for her to answer, which was just as well as she couldn't think of anything sensible to say. 'As a matter of fact, I like my job. No, I love it. I love spotting something that's got potential and turning it into something everybody's fighting to get their hands on.'

'Like Paradise Cottage?'

'If you like. Though I wouldn't push the point, this place has potential like rats have fleas.' He squished the sweet between his teeth. They were strong and very white, straight out of a tooth-paste advert. 'Mind you, the thing I love best about my job is making money.'

Any illusions Claire had started to have about Aidan were instantly dispelled. 'Money? I might have guessed. In the end, everything boils down to money.'

His broad shoulders shrugged unconcernedly. 'What's wrong with money? I mean, I admit it: nothing turns me on like a nice fat profit margin.' She looked at him, and saw that he was observing her out of the corner of his eye.

'Well . . . almost nothing.'

It was afternoon, but the curtains were drawn in Lorna's room and the lights were on low. She was hosting a teddy bears' picnic (by invitation only), and she was the only person invited. To be brutally honest, it wasn't so much a picnic as a lock-in. Lorna had been holding them several times a week lately; they were rapidly turning into the centrepiece of her social life.

She downed another snifter of peach schnapps, and slammed the empty glass down on the floor in front of Paddington Bear.

'Try to drink me under the table, would you? Take that, you furry little bastard.'

The world was a perverse place, that was one thing she'd learned over the past few weeks. When she'd had nothing but debts to her name, she'd been Miss Popularity. Now she was loaded, she couldn't give the stuff away. Her best mate wouldn't take it, her business partner was deserting her for a painted floozie, and as for her job, well, what job? The Jasper had closed its doors for the last time after today's matinee, these days she couldn't even get a job playing a cadaver, and that, frankly, was all folks.

Sitting cross-legged on the carpet, she grabbed Humpty and forced him to listen. 'Do you know how I feel?' she demanded with uncharacteristic aggression.

Humpty nodded his head vigorously. He had no choice in the matter.

'Bloody lonely, that's how I feel.' She wiped a hand across her eye but all it did was smudge her mascara and come away dry. Typical. She couldn't even cry to order any more. '*Bloody* lonely. D'you know?' She jabbed a finger at his button nose and his expression seemed to grow even more alarmed. 'I bet I couldn't even get a shag at an orgy.'

She refilled Paddington's glass, held it rather unsteadily to his plastic nose, then downed the lot. He wouldn't have appreciated it anyway. The stupid little runt preferred marmalade sandwiches and cocoa.

Refilling the glass, she drank another toast. 'To absent friends. The bastards.'

Kieran found her curled up on a pile of floor cushions, leafing morosely through her photograph album.

'It's a bit dark in here,' he observed. 'Shall I draw the curtains?'

She sat up awkwardly, struggling to get him into focus. She could have been a bit tipsy; but then again, everything looked blurry when she forgot to put her contacts in. 'Who invited you?'

Undaunted, he wiped the dust off Lorna's old cabin trunk

and sat down on it. 'I wouldn't have bothered you, only you said you'd give me a decision today.'

She peered at him, uncomprehending. 'What?'

'About the house, Lorna. Buying this house.'

'Oh – *that*.' She waved it away. 'Yeah, OK, let's do it.'

Kieran looked stunned; then elated; then suspicious. 'You're saying you definitely do want to buy this place with me?'

'Yes.'

He picked up the empty Archers bottle, sniffed it and put it down again. 'And you do know what you're saying?'

Exasperated, she got up on her knees, shuffled across the room and practically bellowed in his face. 'Yes! Yes, I want to buy this house, OK? Now piss off and leave me alone, I don't want to talk about it right now.'

He left. Lorna glanced at the photograph album, then closed it. Great idea, she told herself. Buy your own house.

At least that won't leave you.

Aidan was whistling to himself that evening as he sauntered into the lounge bar of the Saxon Cross.

'The usual?' enquired Nev.

'Make it a double brandy, I've had a good day. Oh, and get Aggie to do me a salmonella special, will you?'

'Aggie,' Nev called through the hatch. 'Make that two lasagnes.' He went on polishing glasses. 'Good day, eh?'

'Not bad.'

'So you're in a good mood then?'

Aidan sipped his brandy. 'Depends what you're going to ask me.'

Neville put up his hands, a picture of injured innocence. 'Now, did I say I was going to ask you anything?'

'Nev, mate, I can read you like a book. What is it, need your DPC redoing on the cheap?'

Nev put down his glass cloth and rested his elbows on the bar top. 'It's about the cricket. Some of the lads are meeting down at the nets tomorrow afternoon.'

Aidan pulled a face. 'I told you Nev, I've got a lot on my plate.'

The landlord chuckled dirtily. 'Yeah, and I bet I know what it is. It's that Snow girl, isn't it?'

'Don't talk bollocks,' replied Aidan with a disarming smile.

Nev persisted. 'I thought you didn't like them with brains.'

'And *I* thought we were talking about cricket.' Aidan put down his glass. 'I haven't got time, Nev, I told you. I've got a lot of work on right now.'

A couple of townies entered the bar, enthusing loudly about 'decorators' pieces' and 'Tarq's loft conversion in Wapping'. Everybody stopped talking for a few seconds to stare at them, decided they weren't worth bothering with and went back to playing dominoes.

'About this cricket practice,' said Nev.

The townie woman approached the bar. She was tolerably pretty, thought Aidan; but peculiarly unappealing with it. Perhaps his tastes in women were changing. 'Excuse me, Mr . . ?'

'Shute.'

'That simply gorgeous antique settle we passed on our way in . . .'

Aidan and Nev exchanged glances. 'What's she after?' piped up Old John, chomping peanuts at the end of the bar. 'That ratty old thing you nicked from the—'

'Have a pint, John,' said Nev, promptly shutting him up. 'On the house.' He leaned on the taps. 'The settle you say?'

'That's right, Marcus and I were wondering if we could buy it from you. We have this friend . . . '

'I'm afraid it's not really for sale. Sentimental value, you know. Been in the family for generations.'

The woman's face fell, but Marcus stepped swiftly into the breach. 'We'd make you a fair offer.'

'Well I couldn't possibly accept less than two hundred,' said Neville promptly, with a sly wink at Aidan. 'Like you said, it's a bit special.'

Aidan watched in amusement as his smooth-tongued friend

flogged yet another piece of worthless tat to yet another pair of amateur antique dealers. It happened, on average, once a week in the summer months, usually after an episode of the *Antiques Roadshow*. Of course, no real harm was ever done. The punters always went off thinking they'd conned an innocent yokel out of his inheritance, and Nev pocketed a few more quid for the cricket pavilion restoration fund.

'One of these days my son,' commented Aidan, 'you are going to land up in court.'

Nev counted the twenty-pound notes, rolled them up and stuffed them in his shirt pocket. 'They said it was an antique, remember. I never said a word! Now, are you coming to nets tomorrow or not?'

'Not. I've got my accounts to do.'

'But you are turning out for the team, aren't you?'

'No.'

Nev threw his hands up in exasperation. Old John gurgled expressively into his pint. 'Aidan, you've got to! You can't miss this one, it's the game of the year!'

Over the years, the annual cricket fixture between Lilcombe Magna and Lilcombe Regis had turned into something of a grudge match. It was a matter of local prestige. According to Lilcombe Magna, Lilcombe Regis had way too high an opinion of itself; even its lofty name was based solely on the fact that George III had once spent two weeks chained up in the local asylum. By contrast, the mighty Lilcombe Magna could boast two witch-hunts, a plague pit, and Britain's biggest-ever epidemic of sheep scab. As far as as the regulars at the Saxon Cross were concerned, it was simply no contest.

'Nev,' began Aidan. Then he realised that Neville was smiling at somebody behind him. He half turned, to see a middle-aged woman with iridescent nail varnish and a figure that wouldn't have disgraced someone twenty years younger. The disturbing thing was that he found Claire Snow's mother vaguely fanciable. He dreaded to think what that said about him.

'Veronica, sweetheart,' purred Neville, in full Leslie Phillips mode, giving her a smoochy kiss on the lips. 'What can I get you?'

'Just a small port and lemon.'

'Coming right up, *chèrie*.'

Veronica let out a girlish giggle and flashed Aidan a flirty smile. 'Isn't Neville a scream!'

Aidan looked around him, scoping out his escape route. Wasn't that Geoffrey Willenhall over in the corner? Why yes, it was. And he'd obviously spotted Veronica and wished he hadn't, because he kept glancing across at her and looking extremely furtive. And wasn't that Ted Merriman he was sitting talking to? Must be, there was a pig in a jumper sitting at his feet. Well, well, two deadly enemies sharing a pint together. Aidan found village politics very intriguing.

''Scuse me,' said Aidan, picking up his drink. 'I just need to see somebody about something.'

Nev called after him, 'But what about the match?', but Aidan had already escaped.

As he approached the table Geoffrey got up, snatched up his greasy cap and headed for the door. Aidan was only in time to catch the parting shot: 'You do as I say, you hear? Don't you go rockin' the boat.'

Hmm, thought Aidan, as Geoffrey shouldered roughly past him and out on to the green. Fascinating.

Brucie lumbered across to Aidan on eager trotters, and conducted an exhaustive body-search. 'Ouch. Sorry Brucie, no crisps in there.' He eased the sharp teeth away from his groin. 'Evening, Mr Merriman.'

Ted looked even more morose than usual. 'Bugger orf.'

'Yeah, bugger orf,' agreed a man with one eye and a stained vest, aiming a dart at Aidan's head. 'Oi can't see the dartboard.'

Ah well, thought Aidan, squeezing into the one remaining seat in the corner. He raised his glass in an ironic toast to the much-mutilated Phil Collins poster above the dartboard. Another day for you and me in paradise.

★

Claire was feeling extremely foolish and more than a little embarrassed. More than that, she was annoyed with herself for letting it happen. She'd set out to impress Aidan Ross, and what had she ended up doing instead? Making a total and utter prat of herself. Well, one thing was for sure: it wasn't going to happen again.

Paradise Cottage might have its share of problems, but at least it wasn't Brockbourne Hall. The Hall was a bit like the Forth Bridge: no sooner had you finished installing, painting, mending or maintaining something than you would invariably have to start all over again. That was why the Hall had its own private army of maintenance men. As Claire walked across to their little den, a Portakabin behind the kitchens, she wondered why this hadn't occurred to her before. After all, she was technically their boss; she really ought to have a better grasp of what they did all day.

The door was ajar so she didn't bother knocking.

'Morning everybody,' she said, coughing as she stepped into a hot fug of cigarette smoke and stewed tea.

Never in her life had she seen such a collection of guilty expressions. A deck of cards vanished like lightning under the table.

'We're still waiting for the parts,' said Roy the foreman, jumping up so quickly he banged his knee on the underside of the table. 'Ow, darn.'

'What parts?' enquired Claire.

Another middle-aged man elbowed Roy in the ribs. 'Shut up, you. Miss Snow doesn't want to hear you blathering on, does she lads? She wants to see some happy smiling faces.' All six guilty expressions metamorphosed into terrible fixed grins. It was so painful to see that Claire almost burst out laughing. 'Right. What can we do for you today? Boiler blown again, has it?'

'Not exactly.' She glanced around the room. 'How long is it since I paid you a visit? Must be months.' And that mouldering coffee cup hasn't moved since the last time I came, she noted.

Mind you, the calendar was new. Her eyes lingered only briefly on Miss July, who was feeling the heat so badly that she had had to remove everything but her T-shirt and cool off in front of a fire-hose.

'There's not been a complaint has there?' asked Roy the foreman, looking distinctly worried.

'Not as far as I know. I've just been thinking ... I'm in charge of operational maintenance here, and it strikes me I really ought to be taking a more hands-on approach.' Jaws slackened. Roy's cigarette fell off his bottom lip and burned a hole in his bib and brace. 'I've decided to help you out with some of the routine maintenance work.'

'You? Help us?' Elderly engineers stared at each other with expressions of blind panic.

'That's right. And as I've got a couple of hours free this afternoon, I thought I'd start today.' She rubbed her hands together. 'So. What have you got for me?'

A horrible silence spread through the room. Then all eyes fixed on a chinless youth, half hidden behind a copy of *Loaded*.

'Damian,' said Roy. Heads nodded.

Damian let out a faint whimper and sank another couple of inches into his chair. 'Me?'

'Yes, you.' A heavy paw landed on his shoulder. 'Damian'll show you the ropes, won't you lad? He's due to flush out the radiators this afternoon.'

Claire could hardly wait. And she was sure the feeling was mutual.

Chapter 22

The atmosphere in the Cotswold Cantina was not its usual relaxed, friendly self.

'Excuse me miss,' ventured a timid boy in a hooded sweat-shirt, holding out his plastic tray. 'Can I have another student special?'

Lorna snatched his tray and threw it in the bin. 'No. Next?'

Claire had her work cut out to keep up with her friend as she stomped up and down behind the counter, flinging chilli and refried beans about with alarming inaccuracy. One thing was obvious: Lorna was not happy in her new job.

'Lorna, I'm worried about you.'

'Why?' Lorna banged down a bowl of tortilla chips. 'Ninety-five p. Go away, I'm fine.'

'No you're not. I've never seen you so twitchy. I've been here half an hour and you haven't stood still for ten seconds. It's like watching "Roobarb and Custard".' A suspicion nagged at her. 'Are you angry with me?'

'Why would I be angry with you? I mean, it's not as if you've been here often enough to get up my nose, is it?'

Ah, thought Claire. So that's that. She thinks I've been neglecting her, and maybe I have. Some days, all she thought about from waking up to crawling into bed was Paradise Cottage. 'Lorna, I'm sorry if I haven't had much time . . .'

'There's nothing to be sorry about. But I'm busy, OK?' She

swabbed away at an imaginary stain on the counter. 'I haven't got time to stand around and chat.'

Claire surveyed the half-empty Cantina. 'Lorna! What are you up to?'

'I'm not up to anything.'

'Are you upset about Worm then?'

Claire thought she caught a flicker of something behind Lorna's eyes, but it was so hard to tell when your best mate was an actor. 'Why should I give a damn about him? He's got his life, I've got mine.'

'It's like you're keeping something from me.' Lorna turned away but Claire caught her by the sleeve. 'Lorna, what's the big secret? Please tell me.'

Lorna paused, threw down the cloth and relented. 'Well . . . all right then.' A slightly brittle smile lit up her face. 'What would you say if I told you you're not the only person in this Cantina who owns a house?'

'I'd say that vagrant over there must be richer than he looks.'

'Claire, I'm serious. You are looking at the official co-owner of number sixteen, Jardine Crescent!'

'Oh my God, you're not serious.'

'Kieran and I struck a deal with Mr Papajian yesterday.'

The look on Lorna's face said 'Please tell me I've done something wonderful'; but best mates don't tell lies that big, and Claire couldn't conceal her dismay. 'You mean – you and Kieran? With the money you got from the Batman record?'

'That's right. I've put the deposit down, and Kieran's arranging the mortgage.'

A very loud inner groan sounded in the cavernous silence of Claire's brain. All those tortured hours she'd spent agonising about whether or not it would be wrong to ask Lorna for a loan, and all along Kieran, damn him, had been feathering his own nest without a second thought.

'Lorna,' she declared, 'you're insane! That money was all you had to live on until you get another acting job.'

Lorna's face set into a stubborn scowl. 'I've got this job here.'

'Yeah, two shifts a week. That's not going to keep body and soul together, is it?'

'There's my share of the rents from number sixteen, I'll get by.'

'What sort of a share?'

'A fair one,' replied Lorna defensively.

'Oh Lorna. What have you done? Why didn't you talk this over before you did it?'

All Lorna's pent-up emotion came bursting out at once. 'You're supposed to be my best mate, Claire! I thought you'd be pleased for me.'

'I *am* your best mate!'

'Oh sure.'

'And I'd be pleased to bits if I thought this was a good idea, but – but it's crazy!'

'Why?' demanded Lorna bitterly.

The vagrant shuffled over with his plate and a fistful of two-pence pieces. 'Got any more?'

Lorna threw a ladleful of red goo on to the empty plastic tray and pushed him away. 'Why is it crazy? Just because I want it?'

Claire seized on a faint hope. 'Is it too late to get out of the deal? Couldn't you just tell Kieran you've changed your mind?'

'But I *haven't* changed my mind, why should I? Number sixteen's an investment.' Lorna played her trump card. 'Just like Paradise Cottage.'

'An investment!' retorted Claire. 'A money-pit more like. Have you any idea how much money I've wasted on that place?'

'Three senior citizens' taco meals please,' barged in a man with a flat cap. 'And a labrador.'

'Four pounds fifty, and you can't bring that dog in here.'

'But Les always—'

'I don't care what Les says.' Lorna jerked a thumb. 'Out. Now.'

She's losing it, thought Claire. This time she's really losing it and all I'm doing is making things worse. 'Lorna, do you really think you're in a fit state to be making decisions about money?'

Once again, it was absolutely the wrong thing to say. Lorna

267

swung round, eyes blazing. 'Oh I see. It's OK for Claire to own a house, 'cause Claire's got a nice respectable job. But it's not OK for Lorna, oh no, 'cause Lorna's a scummy wastrel who ought to be squatting in a rat-infested tenement.'

'I didn't mean that at all!' insisted Claire. 'You work really hard Lorna, much harder than I do – of course you deserve to own your own house.'

'As long as I don't buy one with your precious ex-boyfriend, right?'

'That's totally irrelevant!'

Or is it? wondered Claire. Why am I so convinced that Lorna's doing the wrong thing? What if she's right, and I'm just smarting because my nose is out of joint? But Claire couldn't imagine being jealous of anything Kieran might do. The one thing that really bugged her was the shameless way he'd taken advantage of Lorna's one big piece of luck – and worse, that he hadn't even needed to because she, Claire, had already paid him back all the money she owed.

'Please listen to me,' pleaded Claire. 'I'm just worried about you, I've been worried about you for ages.'

'Well don't bother, I don't need it,' snapped Lorna, knocking over a box of plastic forks.

'It's just that you might have told me. We could have talked this over.'

'Like you talked it over with me before you accepted Veronica's filthy lucre?' Lorna threw the barbed comment over her shoulder like a well-aimed missile.

Touché, thought Claire. 'Yes OK, maybe you're right about that, but surely—'

'Let's be honest about this, Claire,' Lorna went on, ignoring her attempts at self-justification, 'you've hardly been near me the last couple of weeks, except to try and get me to help you renovate that damn cottage. The only time anybody bothers with me these days is when they want something.'

'That's not true!' Claire protested. 'And I thought you seemed happy to help.'

'Oh, effing ecstatic,' spat Lorna, jamming a handful of plastic forks back into their box. Not for the first time, Claire caught the pungent reek of extra-strong peppermints on her breath.

'You've been on one of your binges, haven't you?'

Lorna rounded on her with a ferocity that was almost frightening. 'So what if I have? I'm telling you Claire, I'm not giving up my one chance to own a house just 'cause you want to get your own back on Kieran.'

Claire was at hair-tearing point. 'But I don't!'

The dripping ladle thrust itself in Claire's face. 'Just sod off and leave me alone.'

It wasn't until Claire was long gone that Lorna added, in a soft whisper, 'You might as well. Everybody else has.'

'I just don't know what to do about Lorna,' said Claire, sneezing into a dust-filled tissue. Right now, Paradise Cottage seemed to consist entirely of dust – well, the bits that weren't mould or decaying timber.

'There's nothing you can do,' replied Aidan, hammering the last nail into the roof timber and testing it for rigidity. 'There, that should hold. It just needs treating for worm.' He sat back on his haunches. 'If she's a real mate, she'll know you meant well.'

'And if she doesn't?'

He gave a philosophical shrug. 'There's no accounting for people. It's her life if she wants to screw it up.'

'That's a bit hard isn't it?'

'Life's hard.' He held out his hand. 'Dr Ross's counselling clinic is now closed, that'll be fifty quid plus VAT.'

She laughed and threw him an oily rag. 'If I had fifty quid I definitely wouldn't be giving it to you. Is that that then? We've finished for now?'

'What do you mean, we? I don't remember you sorting out the roof timbers or replacing those damaged slates.'

'Yes, fair enough, but who plumbed in that new cold water tank?' she pointed out, proud of the new skill she had recently acquired from Damian.

'Upside down,' Aidan reminded her.

'All right, all right, don't rub it in. I got it right in the end.'

'Only after I showed you how.'

'It's all very well for you,' she sparred back. 'You didn't have to pick things up from an apprentice plumber who's only just got the hang of changing a tap washer. And at least I'm trying.'

'Very.'

'How did I know you were going to say that?' She crawled towards the loft hatch, this time taking care to keep on the joists. 'Right, I'm going down. Ted said he was bringing us some tea.'

Aidan shuddered. 'Do I have to drink it?'

'He'll be upset if you don't. And we don't want him barricading himself in the coalshed again, do we?'

Admittedly Ted's version of tea bore little resemblance to the traditional beverage. But even that treacly substance was welcome when you had a throat full of plaster-dust and splinters in your dungarees.

'Ah.' She looked down through the loft hatch and saw that Brucie was standing right underneath, his front trotters resting on the second rung of the ladder. 'Brucie love, you couldn't just move over?'

Brucie's large yellow teeth gnawed lovingly on the third rung.

'Please, Brucie. Shift your bum, there's a good boy.'

No reaction.

'Er . . . walkies?'

The gnawing paused briefly, then resumed.

'What's the hold-up?' enquired Aidan.

The sound of eagerly scrabbling trotters drifted up towards the hatch.

'It's Brucie, he's trying to climb up the ladder. I daren't climb down or he'll have my ankles again.'

'I know how to shift him.'

'How?'

'Food. That pig's obsessed with its belly.' Aidan opened his toolbox, unwrapped a blueberry muffin and waved it tantalisingly through the open hatch. 'Din-dins, Brucie.'

This provoked a squeal of interest.

'Told you. Stand back.' Aidan pushed her firmly to one side and drew back his arm. 'Here Brucie boy, fetch!'

Aidan spin-bowled the muffin right along the landing and down the stairs; and the pig flew after it in a miniature earthquake of hairy pink flesh.

'Brung you some tea,' remarked Ted when Claire and Aidan finally made it downstairs. He jerked his grizzled head towards two pint mugs steaming on the living room windowsill and proffered a chunk of grubby muffin. 'Want a bit? Pig's only licked it.'

'Just eaten thanks,' said Aidan, surreptitiously tipping his mug out of the open window. 'Nice tea.'

Claire sat on the window ledge, sipping tea and trying to puzzle things out. 'Something's not quite right about this room,' she announced after due deliberation. 'Shouldn't there be a fireplace or something in here?'

'Weren't never no fireplace since I've been here,' said Ted.

Aidan was already walking round the room, tapping the walls with his knuckles. 'A fireplace, yes, of course there would.'

'No there ain't,' insisted Ted. 'There ain't nothin', you can see for yourself.'

'It'd be in this wall here, wouldn't it?' Claire pointed at the wall opposite the window.

Aidan shook his head. 'No chance, that wouldn't line up with the chimney stacks.' He rubbed his chin thoughtfully. 'Unless of course . . .'

'There ain't no point looking,' said Ted, by now distinctly edgy. 'You won't find nothing behind there.'

Aidan put up his hand. 'Shh.' He tapped again. 'Hang on, I think we've got something here, it sounds hollow. Claire, hand me that club hammer.'

'Why?'

'Why do you think? I'm going to open up the grate.'

'You can't go doin' that!' exclaimed Ted, lurching forward like a road protestor diving in front of a bulldozer.

'Aidan,' said Claire, 'he's right. You can't just go knocking great big holes in my walls!'

Aidan spat on his palms and picked up the club hammer. 'Do you want a nice old-fashioned fireplace or not?'

'Well, I suppose . . .'

'Yes or no?'

'Yes, but . . .' She thought of all the terrible disasters outlined in her DIY manuals: the houses that had fallen down and squashed their feckless owners to a bloody pulp. 'What if it's a load-bearing wall?'

'Don't be silly.' At the very first swing the hammer hit the wall with an undramatic thud and disappeared into a hole beyond, taking a large chunk of plaster with it. Aidan gave the wall a light kick and several more bricks toppled into the hole. 'There you go, didn't I tell you?'

'Is that it?' asked Claire, mildly disappointed.

'Whoever bricked it up didn't use the right cement, it's as soft as butter. Didn't put an airbrick in either, that's against building regulations.'

A couple more solid swings and the last of the bricks tumbled away, leaving a hole just big enough for a pig to crawl into.

'You come right here Brucie, you hear?' Ted made a grab for his collar and dragged him back, just in the nick of time as an enormous pile of soot came tumbling down the chimney. 'I don't know, knockin' down folks' walls, causin' a load of trouble . . .'

When the dust had cleared, Aidan crouched in the big old fireplace and shone his torch up into the darkness. 'Heck of a pile of soot,' he coughed. 'Chimney can't have been swept in years. Not bad condition though, and this stone fireplace must be a few hundred – hang on.' He felt up above his head. 'There's something up here.'

Claire and Brucie kept their distance. Ted looked apprehensive. 'What is it?' asked Claire. 'A bird's nest?'

'No, something solid. It's half blocking the flue.' He reached in and arm and drew the object out. 'Hey, will you look at that!'

'An old-fashioned cashbox!' exclaimed Claire. 'Go on, open it – let's see what's inside.'

Aidan blew off the soot. 'Damn, it's locked and there's no key. I'll have to jemmy it open.'

'You'll do nothin' of the sort!' Ted suddenly snatched the box from Aidan's hands. 'Keep your thievin' hands off my property.'

Claire stared at him in amazement. 'That's *your* box? But you just said there was nothing there!'

'Just you keep your hands off, you 'ear? An' don't you go pokin' your noses into what don't concern you.'

And with those parting words Ted Merriman turned tail and walked right out of Paradise Cottage, with the cashbox tucked firmly under his arm.

Candy was very apologetic.

'You know how it is, Claire,' she said. 'If Lorna won't ring you, I can't make her. I don't think she's here anyway,' she added. 'There's no answer from her room.'

Claire sighed. 'All I want to do is check that she's all right.'

'Don't worry,' Candy reassured her. 'I'll put a note under her door, shall I? Telling her you called? Then maybe she'll give you a ring when she gets back in.'

'Thanks Candy, you're a pal.'

''Bye then.'

''Bye.'

Candy hung up and came back into the kitchen. 'You know, Lorna,' she said, 'whatever this thing is between you two, you really ought to patch it up.'

Lorna was not in any mood to be lectured. 'If I want advice from you, I'll ask for it.'

Candy poured herself a glass of milk. 'Want some?'

'Milk? Ugh, no.'

'You know, Claire sounded really worried about you.'

Lorna grunted dismissively. 'Yeah, well, there's a difference between sounding worried and really being worried, isn't there? She's just going through the motions.'

'But you've always been such good mates.' Candy put her glass down on the table and cast a critical eye over Lorna's shopping. There wasn't much to it really: just a family bag of Wotsits and a six-pack of export lager. 'Is that all you bought?'

'What's it to you?' Lorna's expression dared Candy to make something of it.

'Nothing,' she replied, picking up her glass of milk and heading for the door. 'If you want to do that to your body, it's your funeral.'

When she had gone, Lorna walked out into the hall and reached for the telephone. She hesitated, picked up the receiver and dialled the first three digits of a number.

Then she put the phone down and walked away.

A couple of weeks later Claire and Aidan were in the front room of Paradise Cottage, working through Pete's checklist.

'Right,' said Claire, 'So that's the roof sorted out, then there's the damp course, and the rest of the repointing . . . this is going to cost an arm and a leg.'

'Not if you really are going to do it yourself. All you need is plenty of time and patience.'

She smiled sweetly at him. 'And a bit of help from somebody who knows what he's doing.'

'Something tells me I'm being taken advantage of.'

Claire felt a teensy twinge of guilt. 'I do appreciate what you're doing, you know,' she said. 'I mean, if you hadn't been here to help me get my act together . . .'

'Oh, I'm sure Veronica would be happy to lend a hand,' he said with humour.

She shuddered at the very thought. So far, mercifully, her mother had been an agreeably silent partner in all of this. 'Don't. Veronica doing DIY? Do you want me to have nightmares?'

He laughed. 'Don't worry, I think Veronica's the kind of

person who gets other people to do things for her.' He contemplated the pile of rubble still littering the floor in front of the newly-opened fireplace. 'You're going to need a fire-surround. If you want I can keep a lookout for something tasteful when I do the rounds of the architectural salvage places.'

'OK, thanks. But nothing fancy. Frankly I can't afford a fireplace at all, but seeing as you've made a bloody big hole in my wall . . .'

'You'll thank me when the BBC are filming Thomas Hardy in your sitting room.' Aidan nudged a brick with the toe of his boot. 'I wonder what was in that cashbox. Do you think it really was Ted's?'

'I suppose it must be. He obviously knew it was there all along.'

'Of course, technically speaking it's yours, seeing as it was on your property.'

'I suppose so. But I don't want to make a fuss right now. Anyhow, I'm damn sure he didn't want us to find it.' She started piling the bricks up into a neater pile. It was a job she should have done ages ago, but there always seemed to be something more important to do, and the early August heat didn't help. 'I wonder why?'

Aidan consulted his watch. 'Can't stay any longer I'm afraid, the rest will have to wait. If I'm not at nets by half past, Nev'll send the lads round to haul me out.'

'You mean you actually let him twist your arm? After all that fuss you made?'

'It's the same ritual every year,' he admitted. 'He asks me to play, I say no way, but he knows I'll end up in the team. I've no option really.'

She hauled out two more bricks. 'I don't see why.'

'It's a man thing.'

'Oh, *right*.' She pursed her lips. 'Don't tell me – the honour of Lilcombe Magna is at stake.'

'Well, that and three months' free beer in the Regis Arms.' Aidan snapped his metal tape measure back into its case and slipped it into his pocket. 'I don't suppose you fancy coming to watch me play?'

'Me? Watch a cricket match? Ugh, I had enough of that when Pete was in the school team.'

'You'll enjoy it.' He saw the expression on her face and laughed. 'No really, you will!'

'I suppose I could come.' Claire had to admit she was slightly tempted. 'But cricket's so boring!'

'Boring? That's what Adrienne always used to say whe—' He stopped short.

Claire dropped a brick on to the pile and straightened her back. 'Who's Adrienne?'

A cloud seemed to pass behind Aidan's eyes. 'My . . . er . . . sister.'

She frowned. 'But you're an only child.'

'Who told you that?'

'You did.'

They looked at each other for a few seconds, each waiting for the other to break the silence. Then Aidan let out a long, slow breath.

'Actually, Adrienne's my wife.'

Claire blinked, for a moment thrown completely off balance. 'Your *wife*?'

'Yes.' He swallowed. 'Sorry, I probably ought to have mentioned it before, only I—'

She cut him short, not about to let him see what a fool she felt. 'There's no need to explain, really,' she said with forced brightness. 'After all, it's none of my business is it? It's not as if there's anything between us.'

Chapter 23

'I really don't know why you're apologising, Aidan.' The scene replayed itself a dozen times in Claire's head as she drove through town towards Pittville. 'What does it matter if you've been married before – or even if you're married now? I mean, it's not as if we're *seeing* each other.'

Like it or not, the words had a hollow ring to them. No matter how she framed them, they added up to embarrassment on both sides. And it was no good trying, she just couldn't reason herself into a nice platonic, back-slapping, matey kind of relationship with Aidan Ross. Even if he did think a damn sight too much of himself. You couldn't avoid the fact that they were working on Paradise Cottage together. What had started out as an uneasy alliance had become something . . . She squirmed inwardly, not wanting to admit the word into her consciousness.

Something *intimate*.

The clock on the dashboard read half past eight. Lorna *must* be at home. According to Les Lynch she hadn't been in to work for days, and she wasn't in any of her other usual haunts, either. It's no good pretending you're not in, Lorna, she said to herself as she drew up outside number sixteen; I know you too well.

Claire got out of the car, just remembering to retrieve the box with the chilli banana pizza that was Lorna's absolute favourite. A peace offering. She hoped it would do the trick.

As she reached the gate she noticed that the front garden was littered with black binbags, cardboard boxes and the remains of what looked like that horrible beige Utility fireplace from Davey's room. Hmm, thought Claire. Lorna can't be in *that* bad a state if she's started doing up the house. Maybe she's just been playing hookey from work to help Kieran with a spot of DIY.

A yelling voice drifted out of an upstairs window. 'And you can keep your fuckin' rent rebate, I'm out of here!'

Moments later the front door juddered on its hinges and Davey stomped out, carrying the petrol tank off a 1000cc Moto Guzzi. Kieran was in hot pursuit.

'C'mon mate, we can talk about this.'

'Don't you fuckin' "mate" me, you fuckin' cu—' Davey stopped short when he saw Claire standing there, family-size pizza box cradled to her chest. 'Hi Claire. Tell this wanker to get off my back will ya?'

Claire's eyebrows rose a fraction. Davey and Kieran at each other's throats? This was interesting. More than that, it was unprecedented. They'd always been thick as thieves.

'What's up?' she asked Kieran as Davey stomped off to sling the petrol tank in the back of a white panel van. 'Lovers' tiff?'

Kieran moved her firmly aside and went after his discontented tenant. 'Davey, mate. You know as well as I do, that room of yours is a crap-hole. I've told you I'll halve the rent while I'm doing it up, what more do you want?'

Davey threw him a dirty look. 'Claire, you tell him.'

'Tell him what?'

'Tell him he can't play Mr Big Bastard Landlord and expect the rest of us to just lie down and take it. And that's why I'm moving out.' Reaching in the pocket of his leathers, he lobbed a bunch of keys into the tainted undergrowth. 'There you go – and you're welcome to 'em.'

Claire smiled sweetly at Kieran. 'I think you got the gist of that. Or shall I translate?'

Kieran looked daggers. 'You're enjoying this, aren't you?'

She didn't answer, though it was quite true. After all the bother with Paradise Cottage, it was curiously satisfying to watch Kieran having property problems of his own. In the distance, Davey was throwing the last of his stuff into the back of the van.

'I take it things aren't going too smoothly with the tenants?' she enquired.

'Of course they are, everybody's fine, it's just Davey. Just 'cause you tell a bloke you don't want him taking his bike to pieces on the carpet any more . . .'

'But you used to help him strip it down!'

'Yeah, well, that was in the days when the carpet didn't belong to me.'

'And Lorna,' Claire reminded him, watching him scrabbling about in the undergrowth. 'It belongs to Lorna too.'

Kieran grunted. 'For all the use she is. Ah – gotcha.' He scooped up the keys and dropped them into his pocket.

'About Lorna . . .'

He wasn't listening. 'I'll give Davey a couple of days to cool down. If he hasn't seen sense by Thursday, I'll put a card in the post office window. Shouldn't take long to let the room.'

'What – with you demolishing it around their ears?'

'Don't exaggerate, I'm just doing a bit of redecorating.'

She followed him up the steps and into the house. The hallway was littered with tins of paint and lengths of dado rail, and somebody had made a half-hearted attempt at repairing the mosaic of cracked red, white and blue tiles.

'Nice, isn't it?' gestured Kieran. 'Or it will be when I've finished with it.'

'Hmm. Very patriotic. Really going to town on this place, aren't you?'

'I told you I would.' He smirked. 'You missed out on a great business opportunity, Claire. When it's finished, this place is going to make me a pile.'

'Oh is it? And what about Lorna?' she reminded him for the second time. 'What does she reckon to all this?'

He shrugged. 'Fuck knows.'

Claire followed him up the stairs. 'What? You mean to tell

279

me you haven't even discussed this with her?'

'How can I? When she's not got her head stuck down the bog throwing up, she's locked in her room boozing herself senseless. Half the time she doesn't know what day of the week it is.'

Claire gaped at Kieran's sheer insensitivity. How, in God's name, had she ever managed to find this man even remotely appealing? He made Aidan look like St Francis of Assisi, married or not. 'And I suppose you just leave her to it, do you?'

He looked at her over his shoulder, puzzled. 'What am I supposed to do? Join in?'

By now they were standing on the landing outside Lorna's door. 'Is she in?'

'I suppose so.'

'But you don't actually know, right?'

'I'm not her nursemaid, Claire. *You're* supposed to be her best mate, remember?'

That stung. She stung back. 'Yeah, and you're supposed to be her mate *and* her business partner.'

'So?'

All at once, the suspicions Claire had had for some time coalesced into a concrete certainty. 'So, I paid you back what I owed you before you signed the contract on this place. I bet you had all the dosh you needed, without taking a penny of hers. Didn't you?'

'Well . . .'

'You did, didn't you! And you never let on to Lorna.'

'No,' admitted Kieran, but he didn't look the least bit guilty about it. If anything he looked smug. 'As a matter of fact I didn't. But then why should I?'

'Why?' gasped Claire. 'Because that money was all she had, that's why!'

'And I gave her a chance to invest it in something with a guaranteed return. What other chance would someone like Lorna have to get into property?'

'Kieran,' said Claire icily, 'If anything bad happens to Lorna because of you and your stupid . . . ' She pummelled on Lorna's door. 'Lorna! Lorna, it's Claire, I know you're in there.'

Nothing.

She tried the handle, but it wouldn't turn. 'Damn, she's locked herself in. Lorna!' she yelled through the keyhole, but there was no response. She straightened up and turned to Kieran. 'Where's the pass key?'

'Papajian took it with him.'

'Oh, wonderful! Right then, break this door down.'

Kieran looked at her as though she had just proposed demolishing Buckingham Palace to make way for a landfill site. 'I can't do that!'

'Why? Too weedy, are you?'

'Don't be stupid.' Kieran turned on his heel and disappeared into the toilet. 'I'm not forking out for a new lock.'

Mel had done a lot of odd things since she started working at Brockbourne Hall, in fact no two days were ever quite the same; but she still felt self-conscious shouting into a sewer pipe.

'Claire! Claire, it's Mel.'

Claire's voice boomed back, weird and echoey. 'I think I've got it, I'll be out in a minute.'

'Get a move on will ya? It's important.'

Mel shifted from one foot to the other, increasingly agitated. Finally Claire emerged from the sewer access tunnel like a panto genie from a trapdoor. Mel recoiled a couple of paces. It wasn't so much the sight of her boss paddling about in soiled yellow waders as the awful stench that accompanied it.

'Strewth, what *is* that?'

'I'll swing for those clowns,' panted Claire, hurling a bright red size twenty-eight shoe on to the grass. Out of the corner of her eye Mel thought she saw something crawl out of it; but she took care not to look too closely. Claire bellowed back down the hole. 'Damian!'

'Uh?'

'You found the last bit off that collapsing clown car yet?'

'Is it yellow?'

'Thank God for that.' She clambered squelchily out of the hole, peeling off her gloves. 'Here, take these will you?'

'No ruddy fear.' Mel retreated another couple of feet. 'Claire . . .'

'Mmm?'

'Shouldn't you leave this sort of thing to the plumbers?'

Claire laughed. 'If it was up to me, I'd send the entire Marketing Department down there for a fortnight. The clowns' convention was their stupid idea. So – what's this amazingly important problem?'

'It's Naomi again.'

Claire grunted. 'What now?'

'The TV crew turned up to do that interview about the stone circle.'

'Yeah, so?'

'So Naomi's so busy running round after Kenton flipping Mayberry that she can't do it, and Mattie's off-site today. I'm not kidding Claire, these TV blokes are so pissed off it's unbelievable, you've got to do something quick.'

'Why can't Michael do it?'

'Would you trust Michael?'

'Oh all right, I'll do it.' She pushed a sewage-stained wisp of hair behind her ear. 'Where are they?'

Too late, she saw Mel's eyes fix on a point somewhere behind her head.

'Oh shit Claire, they're coming this way. And don't look now, but the camera's running.'

The August heat was so tropical that Claire's hands were sticking to the steering wheel. Why oh why oh why did all the road signs give directions to absolutely everywhere except where she was going? She remembered now why it was so long since she'd been to Swindon: she valued what was left of her sanity. If the town of Swindon had a coat of arms, it would have to be a mini-roundabout rampant, balanced on a traffic light.

She wouldn't be here at all if it wasn't for Lorna. Well, Lorna's parents. She hadn't seen them for years, not since she and Lorna were spotty teenagers with matching Kajagoogoo haircuts, but she doubted the Walshes would have changed much. People like that never did.

Claire had fond memories of Ken and Renee Walsh. As a kid, they'd been the closest thing to a normal family unit she'd ever experienced. Unflappable, unshockable, and incredibly stable, that was the Walshes. No matter what you got up to, no matter how bad it was, there was absolutely nothing that could not be put right over a cup of PG Tips and a Munchmallow.

They would know what to do about Lorna.

Funny how things looked bigger when you were a child. As she drew up outside the little Fifties ex-council semi, with its topiary chicken and highly-polished wheelie bin, she was struck by how small it was. How on earth had Mum, Dad, Lorna and her three siblings all managed to cram themselves into that tiny little box, and never once resort to axe murder?

A pair of shears was clipping away methodically at the topiary chicken's tail feathers as Claire got out of the car; and she could just make out the smooth shininess of a bald, suntanned head. Good old Ken, she thought with a smile. He always did love his garden.

'Mr Walsh, how are you?'

The rest of the head popped up, egg-smooth, perfectly round and garnished with a narrow fringe of fine, mouse-brown hair. A smile blossomed. 'Claire!'

Claire's jaw dropped. '*Tim?*'

The Walshes' eldest son emerged from behind the chicken, hand extended in greeting. In his Littlewoods short-sleeved shirt, polyester slacks and nylon socks which blended seamlessly with his dung-brown sandals, Tim Walsh was thirty-two going on sixty. Was this really the same Tim Walsh who had positioned mirrors under the biology mistress's chair so they could all see if she was wearing knickers?

'How are you? You're looking great,' enthused Tim. 'Do

you still wear those pink and white dungarees?'

'Er . . . no. I think I got rid of those in about 1986.'

'You did? Oh, that's a pity, you looked just like Kiki Dee. Only blonder, of course.' His shoulders heaved with private mirth. 'Oh look, here's Dad.'

If Claire had not been so flabbergasted, she would probably have corpsed at the sight of Ken and Tim Walsh in their identical shirts and trousers, looking identically bald and identically nerdy.

'Claire, Claire, it's lovely to see you after all these years.' As Ken gave her a peck on the cheek she noticed that his beloved Brut aftershave seemed to have been sidelined in favour of TCP. 'Hope Tim's been minding his Ps and Qs, he's a bit of a lad is our Tim.'

'Don't worry,' she smiled. 'He's been the perfect gentleman.'

Tim beamed. 'We were talking about the old days.' He made it sound like the Dark Ages. 'Claire looks lovely in that skirt, doesn't she, Dad? It really shows off her legs.'

Ken chuckled and slapped his son on the back. 'I don't know Claire, you can't take your eyes off our Tim for a second, the ladies won't leave him alone.'

'Really?' That required a stretch of the imagination, particularly as there was a massive carbuncle on the back of Tim's neck and the crutch of his trousers was swinging just above his knees, like an empty hammock.

'Still, can't let him monopolise you, can we?' Ken towed her up the garden path, through the freshly-painted gate and in through the back door. 'Renee can't wait to see you again. Renee love,' he called out. 'She's here.'

A small, neat woman emerged from the pantry, wiping her hands on her apron. Her wispy brown hair was tinged with grey, but she had changed little from the way Claire remembered her. In fact, wasn't that the exact same Crimplene dress she'd worn the day they all went for a picnic at Bourton, and Lorna stole a duck and brought it home? Or maybe Renee just had a wardrobe full of them.

'Claire!' She embraced her with floury hands, leaving white handprints on her new blue skirt. 'Claire, you're so thin!'

'Am I?' Claire pinched a couple of inches of flesh, which – like Hamlet's – had always seemed a good deal too solid for her liking. 'I hadn't noticed.'

'Much too thin, we shall have to feed you up. The kettle's on. Ken, bring that plate of rock cakes. Claire, you do still like Munchmallows?'

Some things, thought Claire, never change.

Renee busied herself clearing a space on the glass-topped coffee table. The furniture hadn't changed much either: same brown vinyl suite with orange stretch covers, same nylon carpet that gave you a shock if you walked across it in your socks. On the mantelpiece a photo in a silver frame had captured a smiling family group circa 1982: at the back were Renee and Ken, and in front of them Tim, Stephen and Jessica – all frightfully neat and as alike as peas in a pod. Last but not least there was Lorna, wild-haired and gurning at the camera, like a Muppet in a gingham frock. On the Readicut rug in front of the gas fire dozed a fat labrador, like a sandbank in a sea of royal blue wool. It was like entering a time warp.

'You met Tim then?' said Renee.

'Yes. He's very ...' Don't say bald, Claire told herself. Whatever you do, don't say bald.

'Good-looking? Yes he is, isn't he?' Renee was radiant with maternal pride. 'He followed Ken into Associated Gas Pumps, of course. Doing very well he is, too. Now all he needs is a wife.' She winked. 'He always did carry a torch for you, you know.'

Claire's blood ran cold. That was something she would rather not have known. 'Did he? I always thought he preferred model boats,' she said, helping herself to a Munchmallow. Perhaps she could make herself so fat that even Tim would find her unfanciable.

'Of course, Jessica's a senior cashier in Stroud now,' added Ken, as though that equated with being President of the International Monetary Fund. 'And our Stephen designs pedestrian precincts for West Midlands County Council. Nice steady jobs.'

'Yes, you must be very proud of them.' Claire fought to steer the conversation in the right direction. 'About Lorna. What I told you on the telephone . . .'

Ken took a placid slurp of tea, mused for a second, then added another sugarlump. 'You don't want to worry about Lorna.'

'Heavens no!' exclaimed Renee, sitting down opposite and shunting the rock cakes towards Claire. 'She's a little minx is our Lorna. Even when she was little she was always playing up and trying to get herself noticed. Do you remember that time she rang home and said she'd been kidnapped into white slavery?'

'Don't I just,' laughed Ken. 'And the time she found out Ken Russell's address and hid in his wardrobe.'

'But Mrs Walsh,' protested Claire. 'This is different. I can't help being worried about her. She's lost her job, her friend Worm's gone off and left her.' She played the ace up her sleeve. 'And I'm pretty sure she's drinking heavily, too.'

Ken and Renee looked at each other, and for a moment Claire thought she had got through. 'Silly girl,' tutted Renee. 'Wasting her money like that. It's not as if she's got a regular wage coming in.'

'But you know what these bohemian types are like, dear,' cut in Ken. 'It's part of the life, isn't it?'

'It's not just the money she's spending,' insisted Claire. 'I think Lorna's drinking because she's unhappy.'

'Unhappy?' laughed Ken. 'Our Lorna's never been unhappy in her life. Happy-go-lucky, that's our Lorna.'

'But she *is*! Ever since she bought into the house.'

Renee's ears pricked up. 'Our Lorna's bought herself a house?'

'A share of one, yes, but—'

'She never has!' Renee threw up her hands delightedly. 'Well I never thought I'd live to see the day. Ken, can you believe that? Our little girl's seen sense at last.' Another two rock cakes clattered on to Claire's plate. 'Come on, eat up. And then tell us all about this lovely house of Lorna's.'

It was hopeless, Claire could see that now. Ken and Renee were so used to Lorna being 'bohemian' that they would never understand that she was genuinely in trouble. As she drank her tea and half-listened to Ken reminiscing about Lorna's first spacehopper, Claire's mind drifted to her next move. There had to be one. She'd only ever seen Lorna this self-destructive once before in her life; that had been the time she climbed on to the Co-op roof and Worm had had to talk her down.

Worm. She snapped her fingers. That was it. Somehow she was going to have to find Worm.

For some unaccountable reason, the annual St Swithin's Day cricket match never actually took place on St Swithin's Day. But no matter when it was held, you could be sure that it would rain; a fact which added to the overall impression that this was not so much a game as a macho test of endurance. In case batting among cowpats in a thunderstorm wasn't bad enough, even the most arthritic of farmers could acquire a bowling style which sent the ball flying down the pitch at seventy miles an hour and bounced it up again exactly at testicle height.

As Claire watched from the safety of Veronica's oversized golf umbrella, it became obvious why Nev had been so desperate to get Aidan on the team. The boy could take pain.

Veronica screwed up her face in vicarious agony as yet another ball powered towards the crease and made contact with a sickening thud. 'Oh Weed darling, that must *hurt*!'

'Bound to,' agreed Claire, wishing she had heeded Ted's warnings and brought her own umbrella. It wasn't much fun being Veronica's captive audience.

Through parted fingers, Veronica peered fearfully at Aidan as he limped back to the wicket. 'I hope he's wearing ... you know ... *protection*.'

Claire coloured up. 'I beg your pardon?'

'Your friend Mr Ross. He is wearing one, isn't he?' Veronica went all coy. 'I mean, I do hope he's got his bits and bobs covered up.'

'I wouldn't know, I'm sure!'

'Of course you would! Come on Weed darling, you can tell Mummy. I know you two are smitten with each other, why make a big secret of it? And he *is* quite a catch.'

'Veronica, for the last time, there is absolutely nothing between us.'

But Veronica wasn't paying attention. She was waving brightly to Nev, who blew her a kiss from the beer tent. Although Nev had been unprecedentedly out for a duck, he had spent the rest of the game selling overpriced alcohol to the boozy village crowd gathered around the saggy old cricket pavilion. Even if Lilcombe Magna lost the match, Nev would be nicely in profit.

Another black cloud shuffled forwards over the horizon, further darkening the sky. The crowd hushed its drunken heckling as the bowlers changed. Even Claire, who was proud to say she knew sod all about cricket, could tell that things were getting tense.

By her calculations Lilcombe Magna only needed one more run to win. Surely victory was a certainty? Ah, but Aidan was being partnered by tail-ender Ted, whose batting style consisted of closing his eyes and whirling the bat round like the sails on some primordial windmill. And next up was Lilcombe Regis's own demon bowler, Seth Everthorpe, a man with a heart of stone, and the physique of a ten-ton truck.

Bowler and batsman glowered at each other across twenty yards of thistles and cow muck. Everthorpe spat on his palms and cracked his knuckles, one by one. Right on cue, the sun peeped apocalyptically from underneath a coal-black cloud, thought better of it, and went back in again.

'Wouldn't want to be in Aidan's shoes,' commented Old John, emptying half a pint of cider down his throat. 'Hope the poor bugger's made his will. You know, I once seen that Seth Everthorpe bowl the head clean off a sparrow.'

The massive legs pounded, the arm whirled shoulder-high, and the first ball flew off the wrist – hitting Aidan square in the chest. Veronica gasped. 'Oh, the poor man!'

'Remember,' Claire reminded her, 'that's the man who once spent three hours hanging from a timber frame by his armpits.'

'He did?' Veronica's face registered even greater admiration. 'Why on earth would he want to do that?'

'Somebody nicked his ladder on a roofing job.'

Claire was secretly rather impressed too, but she was damned if she was going to admit it, especially to Veronica. She focused her attention on the game. Seth's second ball missed the wicket by a hair's breadth, the third hit Aidan on the knee, and the fourth was a no-ball that whistled past the curate's nose and laid out the vice-president of the Mothers' Union.

It wasn't until the fifth delivery that Aidan finally managed to make his bat connect with the ball, more by accident than design. It fairly whizzed through the air to mid-off, where Brucie, who up to now had snored peacefully through the match, promptly woke up, trotted over, raised his snout to the heavens and . . .

Caught it in his mouth.

'Oi,' chorused the Lilcombe Regis fielders. 'Git that pig orf the pitch!'

'Owzat!' roared Seth Everthorpe hopefully.

'Don't talk daft,' retorted Ted. 'You can't be caught out by a pig.'

'Besides,' cut in Aidan, 'He's on our team, not yours.'

'Then he shouldn't be on the darned pitch!'

Lilcombe Magna held its breath.

The umpire, a rat-catcher from Little Woodingham, tried to prise the ball from Brucie's jaws. They merely clenched a little tighter. He prodded the pig with his toe. 'You. Orf.'

He jerked his finger towards the distant pavilion. Brucie gazed up at him adoringly, sank his teeth a little deeper into the ball and did not budge an inch.

The Lilcombe Regis players gathered round, all offering advice.

'Git a crowbar.'

'You're mad, you are. Git a new ball, more like.'

'Poke him in the arse, he'll drop it quick enough.'

'Oh, right. An' have him bite me bloody arm off? No bloody fear.'

Meanwhile, Aidan and Ted waited anxiously by the wicket, Ted crimson-faced and wheezing like a punctured whoopee cushion.

At last the umpire raised his arm. 'Not out. The run stands. I declare Lilcombe Magna the winners.'

The crowd went crazy. Seth Everthorpe kicked a hole in the side of the tea tent. Brucie stood up, shook himself and waddled away, dropping the cricket ball into a nice ripe cowpat.

'Good man, Aidan.' Nev slapped him on the back and handed him a beer. 'You're a ruddy hero, that's what you are.'

Aidan beamed, clearly delighted with himself. 'Not bad, eh? Seeing as I haven't played since this time last year.'

Claire decided his balloon needed puncturing. 'Six not out, you call that good?'

He knocked back half the beer. 'I do when the whole team only made seventeen.'

Neville laughed and slipped a proprietary arm round Veronica's waist. 'Yeah, one four, two singles, three cuts and eleven bruises. Now that's what I call a beautiful game.'

And that was where the day might have ended, if Aidan hadn't decided to acknowledge his adoring fans. As he took off his cap and executed a low, sweeping bow, the smirk on his face suddenly changed to something far more grotesque.

'Oh no.' He froze, bent in two like a hairpin, one hand clamped to the small of his back. 'I'm stuck.'

'Ha ha, very funny,' said Claire.

Neville seized his arm and tried to make him stand up straight. 'Come on mate, stop arsing about, there's a pint waiting for you in the Cross.'

Aidan let out a pained whimper. 'Well it'll have to go on waiting. I'm not kidding, Nev. I really have done my back in.'

★

The Old Rectory was quite a house. The first time she'd seen it, Claire had somehow expected it to be tackier, more ostentatious, less sympathetically restored. It was almost a disappointment to find that it was perfect. Something deep inside her kept on wanting to find excuses not to like Aidan Ross. After all, he'd made it quite clear he was married and unavailable.

Claire didn't quite know why she had come back to Aidan's house anyway, but since half the village had turned up to gawp it seemed the place to be. Besides, Aidan's back had seized so solid that it had taken half a dozen of them to load him on to Seth Everthorpe's sheep trailer, get him back home and dump him face down on his antique Persian rug.

At least old Dr Milner had managed to straighten him out a bit, though his methods were unconventional to say the least.

'Just a little thing I picked up in India,' he said dismissively, as he whipped off his shoes and socks. Then he started walking up and down Aidan's spine, to the accompaniment of cracks, groans and pizzicato yelps of agony. 'Far better than all your painkillers and your steroid injections.'

'Isn't it a bit dangerous?' enquired Veronica doubtfully.

The ancient doctor waved away the suggestion. 'I only ever saw a chap paralysed once,' he said, 'and that was only because he kept wriggling.'

'I should keep still if I were you, mate,' counselled Nev. 'So, doc, he'll be right as ninepence when you've done this, will he?'

'Well, yes and no. He'll have to stay flat on his back for a few weeks, of course.'

'A few weeks!' squawked Aidan, the sound muffled by the thick pile of the rug.

'I thought the new idea was to keep things moving if you injured your back,' ventured Claire.

Dr Milner snorted his contempt for modern medical science. A loud crack emitted from Aidan's neck. 'Load of westernised nonsense. Ayurvedic manipulation and plenty of bed rest, that's what he needs. Take my advice young man, rest up for six weeks and you'll be right as rain. Go jumping around in this condition, and I'll not answer for the state of your coccyx.'

'But I can't . . . ' wailed Aidan. His protests were silenced by a final jab from Dr Milner's big toe.

'Stay there tonight, don't move an inch, and I'll be round in the morning.'

'He can't stay on the floor!' exclaimed Veronica.

'Best place for him, dear lady, you take it from me.' Dr Milner stuffed his socks in his pocket, slid his bare feet into his shoes and snapped his fingers for his jacket. 'Now come on everybody, show's over. Let's leave the patient to get some rest.'

Claire was last out of the room. She was desperate to avoid another of Veronica's invitations to 'a bite of supper and a little nightcap at the farm'. She was just wondering whether she ought to lurk in the bushes until Veronica had gone, when a low groan from the carpet made her turn round.

'Are you all right?' she enquired.

'Do I look all right?' came the faint reply.

Claire stifled a smile. It wasn't nice to mock the afflicted, even when the afflicted spent half his life mocking other people. She crouched down. 'Can I get you something?'

'Not unless you've got a spare spine about your person.'

'Sorry.'

She stood up to go.

'Claire.'

'Yes?'

'I don't want you doing anything silly, you hear?'

'Silly? I'm not with you.'

'To the house. On your own. Listen, it's important.' He turned his head carefully round in a painful attempt to look up at her. 'I don't want you doing something foolish like trying to do the house up while I'm not around to keep an eye on you, you got that?'

You self-important sod, thought Claire. 'I'm not some fragile little woman, you know,' she retorted.

'I never said you were.'

292

'I'm perfectly capable of managing on my own. What's more, I'm going to prove it!'

Aidan let out another groan. And this time it had nothing to do with his back.

Chapter 24

'You can't route it that way, man, no way!' Brent Lovelace picked up the toy Morris Minor and plonked it on the other side of the stack of empty coffee cups. 'You'll, like, disrupt the cosmic power lines.'

Magnus the architect promptly grabbed the toy car and tetchily repositioned it on the map, right next to the stone circle. 'The access road *has* to follow this precise route, Mr Lovelace.'

'Orion.'

'Mr *Orion*. I've explained it to you six times already.'

Claire gritted her teeth so hard one of her fillings cracked. She, Brent and Magnus had been closeted in the boardroom half the morning, and so far all they'd decided was that Brent was going to wear silver trousers for the Millennium gig.

'Are you two ever going to stop bickering and come up with something constructive?' she demanded. The rock star went on looking self-righteous; the architect, anally retentive. Magnus continued forming a convoy of toy cars across the paper landscape of the Brockbourne estate. 'Well, are you?' she repeated.

'I suppose you *could* route it through the old deer park,' Magnus conceded. 'But you'd be adding thousands to the cost.'

All the bells on Brent Lovelace's hat jingled in horror. 'Thousands of cars and coaches? Driving right through the deer park? That would be, like, total carnage, man.'

'There haven't been any deer in the park since 1947,' Claire reminded him. It had been a bitter winter that year, with meat on the ration; but legend had it that there had been no shortage of fresh venison in Brockbourne village.

'I'm not talking about deer, I'm talking about trees! You can't drive a road through the lungs of the blessed earth mother.'

Magnus threw up his hands. 'Jeez, Claire, doesn't this guy have a psychiatric social worker or something?'

'You wanna take that back?' suggested Brent. 'Or shall me and the boys just move the gig to Stonehenge?'

'Oh for pity's sake.' They were as bad as each other. Claire would dearly have loved to bang their heads together, but contented herself with pouring out three more mugs of coffee. Come to think of it, all this coffee probably wasn't helping any of them to reach a mutually-acceptable compromise – her head was pounding, and she felt as jumpy as a prawn on a barbie. 'Guys, please. This is all so unnecessary.'

'I thought you were on my side,' complained Brent.

'I'm not on anybody's side, I'm just the referee.'

The door opened and Naomi's head popped round it. Claire noticed that a button had dropped off her blouse, revealing a couple of inches of sensible longline bra. 'Er ... hello, Mr Orion. Sorry to butt in ... Could I have a quick word, Claire?'

Half reluctant, half relieved, Claire made her excuses and escaped into the corridor. 'More problems?'

'No, well, not exactly. Actually, I wanted to apologise about that business with the TV crew.'

Naomi looked genuinely contrite, but Claire was in no mood for pussyfooting round the issues. 'Yes, well, you really dropped me in it this time,' she said.

'I do realise that. But you know what Mr Mayberry's like about his working brunches.'

'I don't care! You were still booked to do that interview, not me.' Claire recalled the utter humiliation with mounting annoyance. 'I wasn't even briefed. And have you ever conducted a TV interview with your wellies full of sewage?'

'I know it must have been difficult.' Naomi raked her fingers through her unmanageable hair, leaving it sticking up in comical tufts. 'But you always handle these things so well . . . I had every confidence . . .'

'That's as maybe,' Claire retorted. 'But I shouldn't have had to do it, should I? I'm Operations Manager, I'm nothing to do with PR. *You're* the one who's supposed to give out the soundbites.'

Naomi drooped. In that off-yellow blouse and green skirt she looked like a wilting dandelion; but Claire was determined not to feel sorry for her, not this time.

'These things never used to happen when you ran my life for me,' Naomi said wistfully. 'Since you inherited that cottage, you never seem to have the time . . .'

Claire's brow furrowed. 'I beg your pardon!'

'When you first came here, you used to do everything for me – it was wonderful. Those little notes you used to stick on my lunchbox so I didn't forget things. And I could always rely on you to get things dry-cleaned, or clean out the cat's litter tray if I was working late.'

'Naomi!' exploded Claire, 'even if you asked your secretary to do that you'd be pushing your luck, and I am *not* your secretary!'

'B-but you always used to . . .'

'Yes, well, maybe I used to do a lot of things I shouldn't really have been doing. Maybe I've finally come to my senses.'

'Claire!'

'Listen Naomi, I know you think I'm only here to mop up after you and everybody else who can't tie their own shoelaces, but in case you didn't realise, I happen to have a proper job of my own!' Claire found herself jabbing a finger at Naomi's startled face. 'And every time I have to waste half a day looking for your left shoe, or ringing the fire brigade because Julian's got his head stuck in the railings, that job doesn't get done.'

'You've never said any of this before.'

'No? Well perhaps I should have done.' Something inside Claire told her she'd said quite enough, but she was hot, sweaty, pissed off and looking for somebody to take it all out on. 'Look, I know you spend half your life carrying the can for Kenton effing Mayberry' – Naomi flinched – 'but that's no excuse for passing the buck to me every bloody time!'

Naomi looked like a frog trying to swallow a very large wasp. 'Right,' she said. 'I see. Well, you've made your point very . . . emphatically.'

'Good.'

Horrible silence.

'I shan't trouble you any more, I can see you're busy.'

'Fine. I'll get on with my job then.'

'Right.' And then Naomi backed off, caught her sleeve on a protruding nail and clattered off down the corridor, silk scarf trailing behind her.

Oh no, thought Claire as her adrenaline-fuelled indignation ebbed away. What have I done? 'Naomi, wait!' she called, but the door swung shut in her face.

When she went back into the boardroom Brent and Magnus were glaring at each other across the table, like contestants in a staring competition.

'Worked anything out?' she enquired.

'What do *you* think?' snapped Magnus.

Today just got better and better.

In a way, Naomi was right. Claire didn't have time to run around after her any more, not now she had Paradise Cottage to think about.

'You sure you're all right up there?' wheezed Ted, manfully trying to steady the ladder as it flexed under her weight.

'Fine,' she called back, not daring to look down.

It was a very tall ladder, all things considered; and it didn't just wobble like the scaffolding, it *bent* like a mizzenmast in a force-ten gale. What if it snaps? she wondered, cursing her vivid imagination. What if Ted lets go to scratch his nose and the whole thing falls over sideways? She had a sudden, crystal-clear vision of herself describing a flailing arc through the air, only to land headfirst – and horribly mutilated – in the holly bush behind Ted's workshop.

No, she told herself firmly, I am *not* going to fall off this ladder, and I am *not* going crawling to Aidan, and begging him to hurry up and get better so I don't have to do this all on my own. I am not a pathetic whingeing girlie: I am Claire Snow, and I am a big, strong, brave bunny with *balls*.

'Brucie!' hollered Ted as Claire tried to mark the position of the gutter outlet with a plumb line and a pencil. 'Brucie, you stop that, you hear?'

She dared a swift downward glance, only to wish she hadn't. Brucie was sticking his head out of the bathroom window, desperately straining to give the plumb bob a helpful nuzzle.

'Brucie, don't you *dare*!'

Fending off the pig with a swipe that merely unbalanced the ladder even more, Claire cursed the day she had ever bought Brucie that rubber ball to play with. Instantly hooked, he had quickly become totally obsessed with any and every vaguely spherical object he could lay his trotters on, from Seville oranges to alarm clocks.

'Ted! Ted, he's trying to eat my plumb line!'

'Oh heck,' said Ted. 'I'd better go inside an—'

'No!' she shrieked as the ladder sprang backwards with a sudden elastic boing. 'Don't let go of the ladder!'

'Then how am I goin' to stop him?'

A voice pierced the panic-stricken silence. 'Weed!'

Marvellous, thought Claire. My mother. This is all I need.

'Weed, darling! What on earth are you doing up that ladder? What if you fall off?'

'Oh look,' said Ted, for once clearly impressed. 'Brucie's runnin' orf.'

Lucky Brucie, thought Claire. Out of the corner of her eye, she observed a pink squealing torpedo scurrying frantically to its favourite hiding place behind the old henhouse. Well, at least he wasn't molesting the plumb line any more. Perhaps Veronica had her uses.

'What do you want?' she called down.

Veronica came and stood underneath the ladder, a pint of milk in one hand and a frozen chicken in the other. 'I was just on my way back from the village shop, then I saw you up there.'

'Well you've seen me, now you can go away.'

'Weed! That's not very nice. What are you doing?'

'Putting up some new guttering. Now please, go away, I can't concentrate with you standing there.'

Veronica did not budge. 'You can't do that! Not on your own. You're a girl!

'Tough. I'm already doing it.'

'But you'll fall off!'

This was getting tedious. 'I am *not* going to fall off.'

Ted's voice floated up. 'Shall I put the kettle on then?'

Ted's horrible blood-red brew loomed before Claire like Banquo's ghost. A sudden brainwave came to her. 'Veronica?'

'Yes, Weed?'

'If you want to do something, why don't you make us all a nice cup of tea?'

It was six o'clock in the evening, the frozen chicken was defrosting on the kitchen windowsill of Paradise Cottage and the pint of milk was rapidly turning to cheese. What's more, Veronica had still not gone home. The really weird thing was that Claire didn't mind.

'Here's your box of screws, dear,' Veronica chirruped, holding the plastic box out of the bathroom window. 'Do you want the big ones or the little ones?'

A row of plastic clips clenched between her teeth, Claire shook sweat-bedraggled hair out of her eyes. 'The gig ground gones.'

'Pardon?'

She spat out a clip. 'The big round ones, the ones with the rounded heads.'

'Oh, you mean these, dear? Why didn't you say so?' Veronica beamed with success as she pounced on exactly the right screws.

'You know, Weed, I'd never have thought it, but this Do-It-Yourself thingy is quite fun, isn't it?'

By eight o'clock Brucie was flat on his back in the yard, snoring, with all four trotters sticking in the air like an upturned table; Ted was grumbling loudly about his lumbago; and Claire was fighting a losing battle with the last length of plastic drainpipe.

Veronica, on the other hand, was fresh as a daisy.

'Weed darling, you look done in. Why don't you let me?'

Claire climbed down the ladder and took a swig of water. She stared at Veronica's white Capri pants and expensive Lycra top, already blotched here and there with solvent cement. 'You? Go up there?'

'Why not?'

'Because you've hardly stopped going on about how danger-ous it is, that's why!'

''Sides,' said Ted, nodding towards Veronica's espadrilles. 'you can't climb ladders in them, you'll break your neck.'

'What, the shoes? They're no problem, Weed takes the same size as I do, don't you? Come on, darling, take off your boots.'

Which was how Veronica came to be the one balancing on the ladder, hammering home the last section of guttering, while Claire steadied the bottom of the ladder and Ted looked on in grudging admiration.

'There you are!' Veronica exclaimed, leaning back to admire her handiwork and almost toppling backwards. 'I told you, easy!'

It wasn't even remotely straight, and there was a big gap between the downpipe and the hopper head, but the way she was feeling right now, Claire would have settled for upside down and inside out.

'That Veronica may be a rum 'un,' Ted declared. 'But you know somethin? She's not *all* bad.'

It was very late, and Ted and Brucie had long since retired to the relative comfort of the workshop. Claire peered at her watch, the dial barely visible in the feeble glow from the Calor-gas lamp. She really ought to make the effort to drive back to Brockbourne, but she was too darn knackered to move.

'Why don't you stay the night with me at the farm?' offered Veronica. 'I'm sure it'd be all right.'

'No thanks,' said Claire hastily. 'I think I might just kip down on the floor here.'

They were sitting on upturned tea chests in the front room, sharing a last cup of tea. To her own surprise, Claire had offered to make it. All things considered, it was the least she could do.

'You are *happy*, aren't you?' said Veronica out of the blue.

Claire gave a hollow laugh. She was too exhausted to pretend. 'What?' she said. 'With a cottage falling down round my ears, a love-life that's going nowhere, a best friend who's having a nervous breakdown and a boss I've just publicly slagged off? Oh, delirious.'

Veronica looked startled. 'I didn't realise.'

'Yes, well, why should you?'

There was a short silence.

'Because I'm your mother, Claire. I know you don't think much of me, but whatever else I am, I'm still your mum.'

They looked at each other in guarded silence for a few moments.

'That's the first time you've called me Claire since you came back.'

'I know you hate it when I call you Weed,' admitted Veronica. 'I do try to remember, it's just a habit, I suppose. Weed was what I called you when you were little, and you never seemed to mind then.'

'Actually I did mind. A lot.'

'Oh. I'm sorry.'

'Besides, that was a long time ago.'

'Yes.'

Claire fiddled nervously with her empty mug. There was

301

something else that needed saying, something that wasn't easy to put in words. And she wasn't even sure she wanted to.

'Thanks for helping today,' she said, forcing out the words. 'You really made all the difference.'

'That's OK,' beamed Veronica. 'I didn't mind, I enjoyed it.'

Claire smiled. 'Thanks.' And then the last word just spilled out of its own accord. 'Mum.'

Some things couldn't wait, and this was one of them.

First thing on Monday morning, Claire cornered Naomi in her office.

'I'm quite busy right now – is it important?' Naomi sounded far frostier than usual, far more . . . professional. And she'd sewn the button back on her blouse. It was quite a chilling transformation.

'Actually, yes it is. I wanted to apologise. For those things I said last week.'

Naomi raised her hand. 'Don't. There's no need.'

'But . . .'

'You didn't say anything I wasn't already aware of. Let's just say you brought a few things to the surface.' Naomi picked up her pen. 'Now, if that's everything I really need to get on with this report.'

Taken aback, Claire hardly knew what to say. She'd never seen Naomi like this before, and she wasn't sure she liked it. 'Right, OK. I'll be off then.'

'Oh, there is just one other thing.'

'Yes?'

'You're off to that conference next week, aren't you? Make sure you draw up full briefing notes before you leave.'

Full briefing notes, thought Claire miserably as she closed the door behind her. We all know what that means: make sure you make things nice and easy for your successor. There might not be a job for you when you get back.

'So how's your friend?' enquired Aidan, stumping painfully

across the room and helping himself to a grape from the fruit bowl.

'Lorna? I don't know, she won't answer my calls.'

'That's bad.'

'I thought I might try and track down her mate Worm – you know, the actor?'

'The one who ran off with the Blondie girl? Are you sure he wants to be tracked down?'

'I don't much care if he doesn't. It's the only thing I can think of to help Lorna.' She watched Aidan return to his armchair, leaning heavily on his walking stick. 'I thought Dr Milner said you had to lie on your back for six weeks.'

Aidan pulled a face. 'No chance. I've got a physio coming in twice a day. She says if I do my exercises I should be back at work in a fortnight.'

'Is that wise?'

'The business won't run itself.' He sat back in his chair, plucking grapes off the bunch. 'I've been hearing things about you.'

'Oh yes? What sort of things.'

'Bad things. About you climbing ladders and putting up guttering all on your own.'

Claire's mouth set in a firm line. 'Who blabbed? Was it my mother?'

He chuckled. 'Come on Claire, you know what this village is like, and I should think half of Lilcombe Vale could see you balancing on the top of that ladder.'

'So I suppose this is where I get the big lecture, is it?'

He threw up a grape and caught it in his teeth. 'Nope.'

'You mean, you're not going to tell me I'm incapable of changing a lightbulb without male supervision?'

'Not at all, you did well.' He leaned forward. 'Just be careful, OK?'

Claire shrugged off his concern. 'At the moment,' she confessed, 'falling off ladders is the least of my worries.'

He cocked his head on one side. 'Problems?'

'Believe me, you don't want to know.'

Aidan split the rest of the bunch of grapes and tossed her half. 'Try me,' he grinned. 'I could do with some entertainment.'

Chapter 25

'Welcome to Results 2000!!!' screeched the flyer. It sat on the teak-veneered vanity unit with integral hairdryer, next to the conference agenda, room service menu and complementary sewing kit. Welcome to it? thought Claire with a yawn. Too damn right they are.

It was six forty on a muggy August morning, and all sane people were snuggled up under their duvets, two by two. But Claire was alone; and the dual carriageway under her window was already filling up with stressed sales reps, on their way to flog prefabricated conservatories to people with more money than sense. At least they're going somewhere, she reminded herself with uncharacteristic gloom, as she watched the cars swish by. Not like my life.

The laughably-named Golden Island Conference Village was already stirring into life and Claire had long since given up any hope of sleep. Her next door neighbour, a hypochondriac with alarming toilet habits, had been flushing incessantly since two am, and the boozy crowd from Northern Bowls had filled in any gaps in the performance with raucous renditions of 'Four and Twenty Virgins'.

Padding wearily out of the shower, she sat down on the end of the bed and contemplated her revised CV. Concentrate girl, she told herself. This could be important. Who knows, when you get back to Brockbourne Hall you might be out of a job.

Not that she was going to lose any more sleep over it, she reminded herself. Not even if the worst did happen and Naomi slung her out on her ear. In fact, maybe she'd resign anyway; it was about time she got herself out of this all-too-comfortable rut. OK so the pay wasn't bad and the flat was nice, but it was only a job – and she'd been in it far too long already. Keep moving on, that's what she'd always told herself. If her parents' break-up had taught her anything, it had taught her that. Never let yourself get tied down, never stay in one place long enough to get too attached to it ... and never get too involved with any one person.

Well, that might be a workable philosophy as far as Brockbourne Hall was concerned. But what about Paradise Cottage? What about all these new responsibilities she'd heaped upon herself? Ted, Brucie, the building society, Veronica ... and that was just the start of it. And now she'd got into renovating the cottage she knew she couldn't stop; it had become an addiction – a horribly expensive one. Had she made the biggest mistake of her life, allowing herself to fall in love with that disastrous old heap of rubble? Probably. Not to mention getting into serious debt with a mother she hardly knew.

Well, it was too late to back off now. If she lost her job, that would be a problem; but hey, problem-solving was what Claire Snow did best. She chewed on the end of her free monogrammed biro. A proper action plan, that's what she needed.

A distant rumble of thunder made her raise her head and look out of the window. The sky was threateningly dark; the wind was getting up; and on cable TV, a weatherman dressed as a deep-sea diver was sticking a black zigzag right on top of Lilcombe Magna.

Claire's imagination ran riot as she thought of the lopsided little cottage, and all that jerry-rigged guttering. Silly though it might be, she had the feeling that if only she could actually be there, she could keep the whole thing together with a sheer effort of will. If it had worked on Brent Lovelace and his silver trousers, why not on roof tiles and cement?

She smiled. You're a control freak Claire, that's what you are. Then she cleared the screen and started again from scratch. It was no good just tinkering. What she needed right now was a brand-new CV, the best she'd ever had. There were people at this conference who could give her a job.

And this time next week, she might just be looking for one.

By Tuesday morning the weather over Lilcombe Magna had taken a decided turn for the worse.

Veronica and Geoffrey stood by the fence which divided Low Common Farm from Paradise Cottage, watching the wind repeatedly lashing one end of the guttering against the eaves.

'Heh, heh, heh,' chuckled Geoffrey, rubbing his pudgy hands together. 'Just look at the state of that. Won't last five minutes in this weather.'

Veronica turned up the collar of her borrowed Barbour jacket, and found herself willing the guttering to stay put. It wasn't just the proprietorial pride of having put in some of the screws herself; it was something else. A very different sort of pride. The pride she'd felt a few days ago when she'd watched Claire clinging on to that ladder even though she was obviously scared half out of her wits.

She wondered. Was that what motherhood was supposed to feel like? She had nothing to compare it with, since she'd never felt anything like it before, neither with Claire nor Pete. But this new feeling was oddly . . . satisfying.

'Geoffrey,' she said slowly.

'When that lot comes down round her ears,' he gloated, 'she'll be beggin' me to take the old heap off her hands. Fact is, if it weren't for that old bugger Merriman, I'd hop over this fence right now and help it along a bit with me hammer.'

'That's not very fair,' Veronica found herself saying. 'That's vandalism.'

He seemed to find the concept hilarious. 'Me, a vandal? That's a good 'un.' He gave his cousin a congratulatory pat on the back. 'You're a sly one, Veronica. Offerin' to lend a hand with the guttering and then deliberately buggering it up like that.' He guffawed. 'Couldn't have done the job better meself.'

Veronica wanted to tell him to shut up, that she hadn't meant to do anything of the sort; but she said nothing. She was thinking again. About how proud she'd felt, and how much nicer it had been than getting a new Hermès scarf or a sunbed session, or messing around with that brown-limbed fitness instructor from Ronnie's health club. Thinking about all the money she'd been taking off Geoffrey to give to Claire . . .

And as she watched the wind screeching round the eaves of Paradise Cottage, other emotions set in, ones she'd seldom felt before: sudden, gut-wrenching spasms of panic and remorse. She couldn't betray Claire like this. Not her own daughter.

She simply couldn't.

On Wednesday afternoon, after the optional session on Acts of God and Other Emergencies, Claire executed stage one of her new action plan: Make Useful Contacts.

Unfortunately this meant crawling up the backsides of some of the most boring people in the universe; but Claire was up for it. More to the point, she had to be.

'Go on, have some more champagne,' urged the cockney millionaire with the bleached-blond mullet, insistently refilling her glass as they stood talking at his trade stand.

'Well, I don't usually . . .'

He nudged her fingers aside and filled the glass so full that only surface tension stopped its contents slopping out. 'Champagne,' he said, taking a satisfied slurp straight from the bottle. 'Don't ya just love it? Trace!' He clicked his fingers and an apprentice Baby Spice appeared, all pink mohair and fishnets. 'Another bottle for my guest.' He watched her trot away on towering platform trainers. 'Nice girl, we're getting engaged on her sixteenth. Bit dim, but she's a bit of all right between the sheets.'

Claire coughed into her champagne and the bubbles prickled all the way up her nose. 'About this job you mentioned . . .'

'The job, right.' He winked broadly. 'I like a girl who's keen, if you know what I mean.' A hand festooned with chunky gold rings whipped a glossy brochure out of the inside pocket of his Paul Smith jacket. 'There you go, Glitterball Holdings, that's me. I own the Honeytrap, Mistress Mantis, Spanky-Panky, the TankTop, all the top fetish clubs.'

'*Fetish* clubs?' She peered dubiously at full-colour snapshots of people in crotchless silver pants, boogying on down like kids at a fourth-form disco. 'I didn't realise.'

The teenage fiancée arrived with more champagne, and received an affectionate pat on the bottom. 'Don't have to be one to make money out of 'em do ya, know what I mean? Mind you, Tracey's partial to a bit of rubberwear, aren't you Trace?'

Tracey giggled imbecilically. 'Only the pants mind, I don't like the masks an' that.'

Claire began to wonder if she had led an abnormally sheltered life. 'And these clubs – they're all over the country are they?'

'Abroad mainly. Ibiza, Amsterdam, Rio de Janeiro . . .'

Hmm, thought Claire, visualising herself toasting nicely on a sunkissed beach. Maybe I could stretch a point. For Rio. 'And you're looking for some kind of business manager?'

'Something really hands-on, if you get my drift. Hurr, hurr.' He mimed the hands on Tracey, and Claire edged a fraction further away. 'Just my little joke. I'm expanding big-style over the next eighteen months, see, and I want somebody I can trust to run my biggest club yet. It's going to be quite something.'

'But I don't know anything about nightclubs.'

'You've done events management though, haven't ya? This'd be a piece of cake.'

He produced a photograph of a vast building site, sandwiched between what looked like a derelict biscuit factory and a breaker's yard.

'There ya go, Claire. The Pink Playbox, Stockton-on-Tees. Whaddya reckon?'

On a normal Thursday evening, Aidan would have been down

the Saxon Cross exercising his right arm. Instead of which, he was all alone in his front room, wincing along to an over-fifties' stretch-'n'-shape video. It was all very well the physio telling him it was 'positively the best thing for your back, Mr Ross,' but it was also seriously uncool. He could only pray that the cricket club crowd didn't decide to pay him a surprise visit on their way back from the pub and catch him exercising along to Angela Lansbury. He would never live it down.

Sound turned down, legs and arms cautiously stretching, he wedged his mobile between ear and shoulder and waited. A voice said, 'Hang on a minute, I think he's in the bath. Pete? Pete, phone!'

The receiver thudded down. After an age, a second voice came on the line. 'Steve, you tosser, if this is about—'

'Pete Snow? It's Aidan.'

'Aidan who?'

'Aidan Ross, I live near your sister.'

'Oh. Right. *That* Aidan.' The voice took on a note of anxiety. 'There's nothing wrong with Claire is there? I mean, she's not ill or something?'

'Why don't you come here and see for yourself?'

Pete's tone turned defensive. 'What's that supposed to mean?'

Aidan tried out a tricky stretch and mouthed a silent curse as his muscles all screamed in unison. 'It means, why don't you stop being such a prima donna and get your act together?'

'Who the bloody hell do you think you are?'

'She needs you, Pete. She thinks the sun shines out of your backside, God knows why. Is this how you repay her after all she's done for you? Get your arse down here, Pete. Pronto.'

Switching off the phone, he threw it aside. Stretched. And fell over.

On Friday evening Claire crammed into the El Paradiso Bar with the other conference delegates for a farewell drink. Actually they were sheltering from the storm and it was more of a good riddance drink really, but until tomorrow morning they would all stay studiously chummy. It might be part of the assessment.

Claire sat by the bar with Tony, a colourless man who made up for it with a love of Dayglo socks.

'My dog doesn't understand me,' he mused dully.

'Your *dog*?'

He nodded sadly. 'Imported him from China, didn't I? Blasted thing only understands Mandarin.' He peered into his empty glass. 'Alcohol's a depressant you know.'

'I know.'

'Ruins your liver.'

'Yep.'

'Fancy another?'

'OK. But this one's my shout.'

Claire paid up and they drank on in companionable silence. She was feeling sorry for herself, and Tony was right: the three large glasses of Baileys she'd downed weren't helping matters.

She looked across at Ingebjorg the traffic planner, plastering her Arran-clad bosoms against the windows as the wind tried to hammer its way through half an inch of toughened glass. You had to hand it to those Norwegians: they might all be permanently on the brink of suicide, but they sure knew how to get drunk.

'How many's she had?' marvelled Tony, sipping on a dry white wine.

'I dunno. Eleven or twelve, I lost count.'

'Blimey.' Tony gazed longingly at her taut Nordic buttocks. 'What a woman.'

Claire had other things on her mind. Like Brockbourne Hall. And the job Phil Flowers had offered her. The money was fantastic, but then again, what was the point of having enough money to do up the cottage if she was never there to see it? And did she really want to inhabit a twilight world of fat vicars in PVC basques?

'Have you ever been to Stockton-on-Tees?' she asked, dimly aware that she must be getting tipsy, because Tony's socks were starting to look quite nice.

311

Tony tore himself away from Ingebjorg's bum. 'Where?'

'It's near Middlesbrough.'

'Dunno, can't remember. Why?'

'Oh, no reason. Is it nice?'

Tony pondered. 'I think it's got a brewery.'

'Oh.' Claire took out Phil Flowers' business card and contemplated it. It was holographic silver with purple high-lights, a bit like his hair. What would Lorna do in this situation? she wondered, and suddenly felt guilty that for the last week she'd hardly given a thought to her best friend, who like as not was equally pissed and even more depressed. Not having Lorna around to listen to her moans was like having a limb amputated. She'd never realised that before. Then again, it had never happened before.

She would just have to make her own decisions. Maybe she'd ring Phil Flowers on Monday. She looked at the card for a moment, then dropped it into the fish tank. Second thoughts, she wasn't that desperate.

'I've got a property maintenance business,' announced Tony. 'In Rhyl.'

'That's nice.'

'Are you kidding?' He jabbed a finger at the TV screen over the bar. 'Look at that – it's a flipping monsoon out there. Half my seafront bungalows'll be under water by the time I get back.'

The weathergirl smirked. '... and a warning of severe gales and possible flooding in all areas across the southwest of England ...'

Lightning forked across the heavens. Ingebjorg continued making love to the plate-glass window. 'Good storm!' she enthused, toasting it with a bottle of Tia Maria that bounced off the glass and hit her on the chin.

Beyond Ingebjorg, a picnic table flew past at head height.

Claire let out a dry sob. It was the only dry thing for miles around. 'Oh God, my guttering.'

She would probably have gone on to bore Tony with all the tragic details if the local TV news bulletin hadn't suddenly grabbed her by the shoulders and yelled in her face.

'. . . and there was blood in the boardroom today as controversial local tycoon Kenton Mayberry was ousted from the board of Brockbourne Hall . . .'

'What's that? Turn the sound up!'

The barman obliged.

'. . . it is understood the new chair will be anthropologist Dr Naomi Vance . . .'

Claire was so dumbstruck that she dropped her complimentary tapenade nibble right down the front of her bra.

The next morning, Claire didn't bother going back to Brockbourne Hall; she just headed straight for Lilcombe Magna. Whatever disasters the storm had wrought on Paradise Cottage, she wanted to see them sooner rather than later.

The storms had died down overnight, and the sun was beaming over the rainwashed Cotswolds like a naughty boy who knew you couldn't prove he'd weed in Grandad's wellies. Cottage roofs shone, their slates glassy-smooth with moisture. Perfect little cotton wool puffs of cloud sailed across an ocean of perfect turquoise blue. Even the sheep looked clean.

It was still only breakfast-time when Claire drove up the lane to Paradise Cottage, and there was not a sign of life.

'My *God*!'

She stepped out of the car and clapped a hand over her mouth. The impossible had happened. To her utter amazement and disbelief, not one roof slate had shifted, not one inch of plastic guttering had detached itself from the fascia.

Paradise Cottage was miraculously intact.

I don't believe this, I just don't believe this, thought Claire, pushing open the gate. But it was true: even the wonky bit Veronica had installed had stayed put. As she walked towards the house something very large and noisy detached itself from a puddle and came trotting towards her. At first glance it appeared to be made entirely of mud, except for two pink eyes and a double row of slobbery yellow teeth.

313

She took a step back. 'Brucie boy . . .'

He trotted nearer.

'Brucie, no.' She searched her memory for useful pig-training tips. '*Stay.*'

Brucie paused, cocked an ear, then launched himself at her with little squeals of affection.

'Hang on a minute . . . urgh!'

Too late, the pig bounded up on its hind legs and plastered her with muddy kisses. Oh well, she thought as she wiped the sludge off her skirt; it was a welcoming party of sorts.

Claire wagged a reproving finger. 'Bad boy Brucie, naughty piggy.' Reaching into her bag, she took out an indestructible chewy bone she'd blagged off the Dogz-R-Us delegate. 'Here, happy unbirthday.'

Tail wiggling furiously, Brucie sat down on his haunches, inspected the bone, and bit it clean in half.

The door of Ted's workshop creaked open.

'Well Oi'll be darned,' said Ted, scratching the top of his head through his wild white thatch. 'That pig's pleased to see you, an' no mistake.'

Two more figures emerged into the open air: first Aidan, still walking like a robot but minus the stick, and behind him . . . Veronica.

'What are you doing here?' exclaimed Claire. 'And why are you wearing those silly dungarees?'

Veronica looked embarrassed, then coy, then mysterious. 'We've been talking,' she said.

'You mean *you* have,' retorted Ted gruffly. 'You never *stop* talkin'.'

Veronica ignored the dig. 'We've been talking,' she repeated. 'About this place.'

A red warning signal lit up inside Claire's head. 'If Geoffrey's put you up to this . . .'

Aidan stepped forward. 'It's nothing to do with Geoffrey. We just think we ought to help you a bit more than we have been doing.' He poked Ted in the ribs. 'Don't we, Ted?'

Ted looked gruffly at his boots. 'I'll just go and muck out the chickens.'

'The chickens can wait,' said Aidan, hauling Ted back by the collar of his threadbare waistcoat.

'We know you wanted to do it all yourself, love,' cut in Veronica. 'But we'd like to help. Or at least, I would.' The smile was a slightly nervous one. 'If you'll let me.'

Claire stood dumbfounded. Before she had a chance to think of a suitable reply, someone else came round the corner of the cottage, a ladder balanced on his shoulder, a pencil stuck behind his ear.

'Hello sis,' said Pete sheepishly, leaning the ladder against the wall. 'A little bird told me you could use some help. Will I do?'

To say it had been a funny old week would be a massive understatement. It wasn't every day you learned how to fit an RSJ *and* turned down a job in Stockton-on-Tees.

But even the weirdest weeks had to end, and that meant returning to Brockbourne Hall. Not that anything was any clearer when she got back on Monday night: nobody seemed to have a clue what was going on.

As she got ready for work on Tuesday morning, Claire wondered if turning down that job had been such a terrific move. Rolled steel joists did not come cheap. And just when she'd dared to hope that Naomi had decided to forgive and forget, there was a curt phone message via Michael: 'Eight thirty sharp, Naomi's office. Don't be late.' Everyone knew eight thirty meetings were never great news. And the message Mel had slipped under her door was no more reassuring: 'Good luck in your new job.'

Claire had no option but to prepare herself for the worst. Not that it *would* be the worst, not by a long chalk. You couldn't really say you'd made it as a human tragedy until your story appeared as a 'Letter From The Heart' in *Take A Break*.

She took a deep breath, checked her tights for ladders, and knocked respectfully at the door of Naomi's office. That was a first. Usually people just barged in, and (unless forewarned) tripped over a clutch of old umbrellas, or a heap of books about shamanic practices in the Navajo Indians.

'Come.'

To Claire's surprise, the door opened smoothly. All the umbrellas were in the umbrella stand, and the books were piled up, more or less neatly, on one corner of the desk. Naomi was sitting behind them looking, if not entirely organised, then definitely like somebody who thought she ought to be. She had even removed the Mexican finger-trap from her in-tray, and that had been there the day Claire came for her first interview. Hmm, thought Claire. Naomi has been possessed by a race of houseproud aliens. Scary.

Worse still, Michael Tang was sitting next to Naomi, looking insufferably smug, like the cat who got the whole damned dairy. So that was it. Naomi had moved up in the pecking order, but Michael was the power behind the throne.

'Hello Claire,' said Naomi pleasantly. 'Please. Sit down.'

Claire lowered her bottom on to the chair, automatically sweeping her hand across the seat in case the cat was asleep on it; but there was nothing there, not even the usual mulch of white fur. This was spooky.

'Coffee?'

'Er . . .'

'Chocolate Hobnob?' Not from a tatty packet either, noted Claire as she took one, more from amazement than appetite. A nice new shiny tin, and not a trace of teethmarks on the chocolate.

'Thanks.'

'I expect you've heard about the recent boardroom changes here at the Hall?'

'Yes. I hear congratulations are in order.'

'There is a lot of work to do,' said Michael solemnly.

Naomi scratched her nose with a chocolatey finger, leaving a brown smear across her cheek. 'After our, ah, discussion last week, I did a little asking around.'

'Oh?'

'Clearly I've had my head in the sand for far too long, relying on other people to be my eyes and ears. I had no idea Kenton Mayberry had annoyed so many people. The fact is, Claire, that's when I – that is, we – decided that there would have to be some changes around here.'

Claire saw no point in waiting for the axe to fall. 'Please, can't we just get this over with?'

Naomi regressed, momentarily, to her usual befuddled expression. Even the inscrutable Mr Tang looked faintly bemused. 'Surely you want to hear details of the Board's strategic plan?' said Naomi.

'Not especially,' confessed Claire.

'Why not?' demanded Michael. 'Don't you *want* to be Assistant General Manager of Brockbourne Hall?'

Chapter 26

Me? Assistant General Manager of Brockbourne Hall?

Well strap me, thought Claire. Just when you're wondering how best to sort out your life, along comes some *deus ex machina* to sort it out for you – whether you like it or not.

As yet, she hadn't actually got round to saying yes. There simply wasn't the time to mull things over. Not with four conventions, two missing guest speakers, and a nasty outbreak of something spotty in the kitchens. All these things, and the cottage, and even her own muddled life, Claire could just about get her head round. The question was, who was going to sort out Lorna?

Murf's band proved surprisingly difficult to locate, mainly because – for some reason best known to themselves – they had recently changed their name to UltraFox. Light began to dawn when Claire finally tracked them down to a function room above the Blind Pedlar, Worcester's cheapest and most infested rock venue.

Neil the rhythm guitarist had certainly changed since she last clapped eyes on him. Clad in an ankle-length beige rain-coat and trilby, with a thin moustache eyebrow-pencilled across his upper lip, he was sobbing hysterically into an overflowing hanky.

'Cow! Rotten little cow!'

Sharp-suited axeman Dominic cooed round him with a box of

man-sized Kleenex. With his curly hair ruthlessly Brylcreemed to his head, he had a look reminiscent of a Mafia undertaker. 'There, there, calm down. You'll only give yourself one of your heads.'

Claire let the door swing shut behind her. 'What's going on? Where's Murf?'

The reaction was immediate.

'Don't you say that name in here!'

'Bloody cow.'

'What's it to you, anyway?'

Claire adopted a slightly different tack. 'Actually it's not really Murf I'm looking for, it's Worm.'

Brows furrowed. 'Worm? Who the 'ell's Worm?'

Baz the percussionist stopped picking his nose with a drumstick. 'That'll be Martin,' he said, examining a bogey from several different angles before wiping it off on his trousers. 'That wussie she's got trailing around after her.'

Hollow laughter. 'Oh, him. Stupid git, should've known better than to get mixed up with her.'

'I was wondering,' began Claire, but Neil was already going off on one.

'Snotty bitch, walking out on us just when things were going great.'

'Yeah,' sniffed Baz. 'Booked solid for months we were. Six Christmas parties *and* an Eighties Weekender at Burnham-on-Sea. But that's not good enough for Princess bleedin' Murf, is it? Oh no, she has to sod off and leave us in the lurch.'

'Ah,' said Claire. 'So that's why you're . . . ?'

Baz plucked at his Oxfam raincoat. 'Dressed like a bunch of bloody flashers? Yeah. Ultravox tribute band my arse.'

'What other option did we have?' reasoned Dominic. 'At least we know all the songs. It was either that or Depeche Mode, and you know I'm allergic to PVC.'

'I could have done Tony Hadley,' protested Neil. 'No problem!'

'Oh yeah,' grunted Baz. 'What was it you wanted to call us? *Spam*-dau Ballet, very droll.'

'I was just wondering,' cut in Claire, 'if you happened to know where Murf's gone.'

The bickering ceased momentarily. 'Some pervy nightclub in Bristol,' said Dominic. 'It was Bristol, wasn't it?'

Heads nodded. Baz spat into the fire bucket. 'The Spanky-Panky. She's got herself some poncey residency there ... performance art or some such crap.'

The Spanky-Panky? That was a name you couldn't forget in a hurry, and Claire had definitely heard it somewhere before. The memory clicked into place. Oh bugger, that was one of Phil Flowers' clubs. In fact ... didn't he say he lived in Bristol?

'Thanks,' said Claire, turning to go.

'Hang on a minute,' said Dominic, with sudden eagerness. 'Do you sing?'

'Only in the bath. Why?'

'Don't suppose you know the words to "Heart of Glass"?'

The evenings really started drawing in towards the end of August, and with all the extra hours she was having to put in at the Hall, Claire hardly had any time for herself, let alone Paradise Cottage.

It was thoroughly frustrating. Still, she told the cottage as she patted its nicely-repointed wall, we got you sorted out in time for winter, didn't I promise you we would? You've got a proper slate roof, walls with no holes in them, gutters that almost work. OK, so there's a long way before we get out the Jocasta Innes stencil book, but at least you're going to be safe and snug.

'Come on sis,' urged Pete, bustling past with something electrical. 'Time to put your feet up.'

'*You're* not,' she pointed out. 'You haven't sat down since breakfast. Have a sweet.'

'No time,' he replied, declining the offer of a jelly spanner. 'I haven't fathomed out these electrics yet.'

Claire followed him into the hall, chewing noisily, and watched him running the detector over the walls. 'I don't know why you're bothering, we haven't sorted out the internal walls yet.'

'Safety first, you should know that. Can't cut corners.'

'Yes all right, all right.'

Secretly, she loved it when Pete scolded her, it was like having the big brother she'd always longed for. She adored his middle-aged meticulousness too: this was the boy who used a spirit level on his Meccano. He opened the cupboard under the stairs and switched on his torch. 'If the rest of the wiring is as old as this fuse board, we could be talking miles of flaky spaghetti. And I'm *not* having my favourite sister burned to a crisp, OK?'

'Pete, I'm your *only* sister,' she pointed out with a smile. 'And what about Ted and Brucie? It's all right for them to go up in smoke, is it?'

Pete grinned like a pantomime villain. 'Solve one or two problems, wouldn't it?'

'Pete!'

He patted her on the head like a favourite spaniel. 'Don't worry, when we've finished, this place'll be safe as . . . as . . .'

'Houses?'

'Safer.'

'Where is Brucie, anyway?' enquired Claire as Pete fiddled about with the jumble of loose wires. 'He's been following you around like a lost soul ever since you got here, and now he's disappeared.'

'Hmm?' murmured Pete absent-mindedly from the bowels of the meter cupboard. 'Brucie? No idea. I thought he was with you. What time is it?'

Claire consulted the cement-splattered marble clock balanced on top of a pile of old floorboards. 'Must be nearly seven.'

'Ah, there you are then. Time for *Watchdog*. He'll be glued to the TV with Ted.'

For some reason Claire had never got to the bottom of, Brucie had a thing for people with ginger hair. Anne Robinson, Fergie, even Bonnie Langford, for pity's sake – it was tragic

321

really. He was probably the only animal on earth that looked forward to Chris Evans.

'You know,' she mused, picking at the sixteen layers of paint flaking off the cupboard door, 'Ted's workshop's much comfier than this cottage.'

Pete's head and shoulders emerged, bedecked with cobwebs. 'Thinking of moving in with him?'

'What – share a bed with Brucie? No thanks. I just wondered . . . Ted really loves that workshop, doesn't he?'

'Seems to. Why?'

'Well, it's pretty big. I thought with a bit of effort it could be turned into a proper self-contained flat.'

'A dream home for Ted and Brucie?'

'Exactly. Do you think we could persuade him? It'd make things a lot easier when the cottage is finished.'

'Dunno. And neither will you unless you ask him.'

Claire rehearsed what she was going to say as she walked towards the workshop at the bottom of the garden. 'Nobody's saying you have to, Ted, nobody's trying to force you into anything. It's just an idea. But I wouldn't charge you rent, and you'd be much more independent.'

Would he like the idea? She hoped so. After all, what she was saying was true. Ted was not the sort of man who would ever be happy with Shaker-style kitchen units and Ikea clothes storage systems.

But was this a good moment to broach the subject? She took a preliminary peek through the workshop window. Sure enough, Brucie was there with his snout pressed up against Anne Robinson. But Ted's armchair was empty. Where on earth was he?

As she strained to see into the corners of the room, she saw him. Not watching the television but sitting on the carpet, with a big black metal box lying open on his knees. A box? *The* box. That was the strongbox she had watched Aidan take down from the chimney, and which Ted had claimed as his own. And it must surely be his, since he had procured a key from somewhere and unlocked it. Now Ted was sitting on the floor with a sheaf of papers in his hands, head bowed, shoulders shaking.

Weeping.

Shocked, Claire hesitated; then took a step back from the window. The clatter as she knocked over a pile of rusted iron drainpipes was enough to rouse the dead, let alone an elderly man whose hearing was only impaired when it was his turn to buy a round.

The workshop door opened and Ted appeared, his face wiped dry but his eyes rimmed with pink. 'What's goin' on? Oh it's you, I thought it were that Geoffrey Willenhall.'

Claire opened her mouth to ask him what the matter was, to ask if there was anything she could do that would make things better. But it was no use.

The moment was gone.

Anonymity was just too much to hope for. As Claire walked into the Spanky-Panky Club, Phil Flowers greeted her like a long-lost wifelet.

'Claire! Doll! Great to see ya!' She sidestepped the full, cologne-drenched mauling, but he managed to get in a decent-sized grope of her bum. 'Don't tell me, you've had time to think and you want to take me up on that job, right?'

'Wrong,' said Claire, but she had the feeling he wasn't listening.

His summoning yell drowned out the House remix of 'Goody Two-Shoes'. 'Trixie, more pink champagne.'

Trixie? Claire blinked at the pink T-shirt and the blonde bunches. The boobs looked noticeably more inflated, but the overall effect was the same. 'Tracey, surely?'

The club owner took the champagne and sent the girl on her way with a couple of twenties in her stocking-top. 'Tracey? Nah, bit too narrow-minded if ya get my drift. All I did was ask her to . . .' He whispered in Claire's ear. 'Not too much to ask, is it?'

Good God, thought Claire. I think I'm going to be sick. 'Mr Flowers.'

'Don't tell me, you're checking out the scene, right?' Flowers' gaze swept over the majestic herds of clubbers. 'Shoe fetish night, it's the next big thing you know.'

'You don't say.'

Well, the Spanky-Panky Club was certainly big on it, anyway, noted Claire. There were shoes everywhere: pink ballet pumps hanging on the walls, thigh-high black boots dangling from the ceiling; oversized yellow DMs supporting the stairs; even little glass slippers on the bar, filled with dry-roasted peanuts.

Then there were the punters. Some of them looked quite normal until you noticed their shoes. One or two appeared not to be wearing anything *except* shoes. And out of the corner of her eye Claire had just spotted a man in a three-piece suit and slingbacks, licking the ankles of a woman in purple kitten-heeled mules. Lorna, she said silently; this had better produce results, because believe me, I wouldn't be doing this for anybody but you.

Phil Flowers was rattling on about projected profit margins at the Pink Playbox, and it took Claire three attempts to butt in. 'Mr Flowers . . . Phil.'

The too-perfect teeth glowed fluorescent violet in the strobe lights. 'What is it, doll?'

'I'm looking for someone. She's called Murf.'

'Who?'

'Jo Murphy?'

'Oh, *Jo*. Nice little mover is Jo, didn't know you two knew each other.'

'We don't, not that well. But I need to see her, it's important.'

Flowers beckoned Trixie over and she scampered to heel. 'What is it, Pooky?'

He coughed. 'Not in the club, Trixie. It's Mr Flowers here, remember? Take the lady out back to see Jo. Then go and put a tighter top on, I didn't pay out three grand for you to hide 'em away.'

The DJ was cranking up 'These Boots were Made for

Walking' as Claire followed Trixie's bobbing bunches in and out of the milling throng and through a door marked 'Private'. The door closed behind her on silent sprung hinges, the din from the club suddenly shut out.

Trixie produced a stick of gum which she fed between her fat red lips. 'Down there, third on the right.'

'Thanks.'

'You're not his type you know.'

'Pardon?'

'Just 'cause you're blonde it don't mean nuffink. You're not his type, you're too old and your boobs are too small. So just keep your thievin' hands off my Pooky, you got that?'

She wiggled away, peeling her T-shirt off over her head.

Well, that told me, thought Claire as she headed for the third door on the right. Instead of a star, a pair of silver stilettos glittered on the door. She knocked.

'Hang on a mo. OK, come in.'

She walked into a dressing room that was twice as big and several times as nice as anything the Jasper had had to offer. If Lorna ever set eyes on this, she'd reconsider that career in topless go-go dancing.

Perched on a pink velour pouffe sat Murf, no longer in Debbie Harry guise or even looking like herself, but dressed up as Dorothy from *The Wizard of Oz*. She barely registered surprise as Claire came in.

'Oh Claire, hi. Take a seat and don't breathe, one sneeze and this stuff goes everywhere.'

'What are you doing?'

'Putting more red glitter on these shoes. I only did them last Thursday, but the punters keep licking it off. There.' She sat back to examine her handiwork. 'What d'you reckon?'

'Very Judy Garland. Murf, we need to talk.'

'Do we?' Murf looked blank. 'Oh God, I don't owe you money do I?'

'No, it's nothing like that. I'm looking for Worm.'

Murf looked somewhere between relieved and disappointed.

'Oh, Martin you mean,' she said unenthusiastically. 'What about him?'

'I need him.'

'Really?' Murf stood up, wriggled her toes into the shoes and admired them in the mirror. 'I'd have thought Phil Flowers was more your type.' She winked. 'He's got a real thing about natural blondes.'

'Murf, be serious will you? I need Worm's help. Or at least, Lorna does.'

'Why – what's wrong with her?'

Claire flopped on to the black leather sofa, felt something knobbly underneath her and pulled out a rubber chicken. 'What's *right* with her? Please Murf, I need to see him right now, he's the only one she'll talk to.'

Murf hesitated for a moment, then rummaged in her handbag and pulled out a key. 'Here y'are then, you'll need this.'

She threw it to land smack in Claire's lap. 'What's this for?'

'To be honest, Claire,' Murf admitted as she touched up her lipstick in the mirror, 'Martin's really been getting on my nerves lately. Oh, it was OK to start with, just a bit of fun, and he was good in the new act. Then he goes all intense on me. And when I knock him back it's "Lorna this" and "Lorna that". I'm not kidding, Claire, it's twenty-four-hour earache.' Her gaze switched to the key in Claire's hand. 'And tonight it got so bad I had to ... er ... take measures.'

'Measures? What measures? You don't mean you've locked him in somewhere?'

Murf gave her heels a jaunty click. 'Try the broom cupboard at the end of the corridor. He's the one dressed as Toto.'

The atmosphere at Low Common Farm was so thick you could cut it into slices and build a cowshed.

Geoffrey Willenhall was not happy. And when Geoffrey was unhappy, somebody had to get the rough end of his tongue. Unfortunately for Emmy, she was the one sitting opposite him at breakfast.

'This toast's burned.'

'It's just the same as you always have.'

'I'm telling you it's burned!' He buttered it so violently that the whole slice fractured into a dozen different pieces, sending shards scudding across the table top and on to the floor. 'Darned stupid woman, always knew I should've married your sister.'

'Why didn't you then?' retorted Emmy, scooping up the bits and dumping them back on to his plate. 'You bedded her often enough.'

Veronica nibbled on a few grains of muesli, one eye on Geoffrey and his bullying, the other on the clock. He wasn't a brave man, she'd decided, just loud and unpleasant. All the same, best be careful how she handled this. She took a deep breath.

'Geoffrey?'

The reply came back as a low bear-growl. 'What?'

'Stop picking on Emmy. You know it's me you're angry with.'

Geoffrey's fat face adopted a sneer, liked it and decided to make it a permanent fixture. 'Oh, so you noticed then?'

'I could hardly fail to, could I? The way you've been going on ever since I started helping Claire with the cottage repairs.'

'Right little Mother Teresa you're turnin' into,' snorted Geoffrey. 'One minute it's "Oh, Cousin Geoffrey, please take me in off the street and help me con my own daughter," the next it's "Oh, Claire darling, why don't you let me help you fix up your cottage for you?" And after all I've done for you, Veronica . . .'

'Well I'm terribly sorry,' said Veronica airily, monitoring the effect of her words. 'But you'll understand it may take a while for me to pay you back all the money.'

Geoffrey's mouth hung open in mid-chew. 'Uh?'

'That's right, Geoffrey, *I'll* be paying you back, you lent *me* the money, remember? Claire doesn't owe you a penny, you've got no claim on that cottage.'

Emmy looked startled. Geoffrey's face was approaching scarlet. 'You cheatin' bitch! I'll have you up in court.'

327

'Please do,' replied Veronica. 'I'm sure they'll be fascinated to hear how you've been fiddling your milk quota forms.'

Scarlet verged on purple. 'You ... you ... I'll throw you out on the street! Back in the gutter where I found you, you ...'

'Cow,' interjected Eric, helpfully.

A massive paw knocked him sideways. 'Shut it, you little runt.'

Veronica was already standing up, dabbing the corners of her mouth with a napkin. 'Actually I'm already leaving. I moved in with Neville yesterday.' She was delighted to note that Geoffrey's entire head had acquired the appearance of an electric beetroot. 'I just wanted to thank you for your complete lack of hospitality. I might say it's been fun.' She dotted a kiss on the end of his nose. 'But why lie?'

Sweeping out of the door, she turned back to face three open mouths. 'You're completely horrible, Geoffrey, and I hope you drown in your own bile.' She gave him a cheery parting wave. 'Ta-ta.'

Once safely outside, Veronica took a deep breath and legged it across the four-acre field to Lilcombe Lane with all the panache her trembling legs could muster.

Neville was standing by the gate, chatting to Ted. 'And you do know I'm thinking of turning that bit of car park into extra nets for the cricket club?'

'So I've heard.'

'Well, the application's coming before the parish council next month. I wondered if Brucie ...'

Ted shook his head obstinately. 'That pig votes the way 'e wants, Mr Shute.' He turned, distracted by the sudden arrival of Veronica. 'Mornin' missus. Something wrong is there?'

Veronica positively beamed at him. 'Nothing at all, Mr Merriman.'

'You did it then?' enquired Neville as he drove Veronica back to the Saxon Cross.

'Uh-huh.'

'How did it go?'

'I'm not sure. But maybe Geoffrey hates me enough now to take his mind off Weed.'

They drove along a little further.

'Veronica?'

'Hmm?'

'Why do you call Claire that? I mean, it's not as if she's tall and weedy or anything, is it?'

Veronica stifled a giggle. 'No, you've got the wrong end of the stick. It was when she was little, she had this really weak bladder. And then one day—'

'I don't think I want to know the rest,' interrupted Neville, parking outside the pub. 'Come on, let's get you settled in.'

'I could murder a cup of tea,' said Veronica, practically dancing up the front path. 'There's this really horrible taste I want to get rid of.'

What with the collection of fireplaces in the hall and the Victorian bath marooned halfway up the stairs, number sixteen Jardine Crescent was looking more and more like an architectural salvage yard.

'I'm sick of this,' moaned Candy, half-heartedly flicking through colour charts as Kieran banged Rawlplugs into the wall above the bay window.

'Sick of what?'

'All this.' She waved her arms distractedly. 'You go out in the morning, and you come back and the bath's disappeared. That kind of thing.'

'Oh, that. That won't be forever. Pass me that curtain pole, will you?'

Candy just went on flicking through the colour charts. 'I think you ought to go for terracotta and shades of citrus,' she announced. 'They did it in a conservatory on *Changing Rooms* and it looked really cool.'

'Oh did it? Well this isn't a TV programme, it's a business venture.' Kieran climbed down off the step-stool and fetched the pole himself. 'Don't suppose you could hold the other end of this?'

'You're the landlord.' Candy flashed him a brief, unhelpful smile. 'By the way, there's fungus under my bed and the gas boiler's making that funny noise again. You will get it fixed, won't you?'

Kieran grimaced. This landlord business wasn't quite as easy as he'd imagined. For a start, the way things were going, it was going to cost him more in routine maintenance than he was getting back in rent, and on top of that, his bloody tenants never stopped whingeing.

'Hello Kieran,' said Claire, so unexpectedly that he nearly drilled his own finger off. 'Having fun?'

He turned round and jumped down. 'Claire ... Worm!'

Worm looked, if anything, even paler and thinner and stringier than ever. 'Hi Kieran. Candy.'

Candy blew him a kiss. 'What do you think – citrus and terracotta, or sky blue and lime green?'

'Take no notice,' counselled Kieran, wiping his sweaty fore-head on his sleeve. 'She's in love with Laurence Llewellyn-Bowen.'

'Laurence who?' said Worm.

'Worm was wondering,' said Claire, nudging him forward. 'Could he have his old room back?'

'Sorry, I let it out last week. Didn't think you were coming back.'

Worm's face fell. 'Oh well. Can't be helped.'

But Kieran slapped him on the back. 'No problem mate, Davey's room's still vacant, and the rent's five quid less 'cause I haven't got round to putting the window back in yet.'

'You can't rent out a room with no window!' exclaimed Claire.

'It's got plastic nailed over it.'

'OK,' shrugged Worm.

'Shut up Worm. Ten quid less and you put the window back in, or he doesn't take it,' said Claire. 'And don't argue because you won't get anybody else and I know you need the money.'

Kieran did not argue.

'It's good to have Worm back,' admitted Kieran as they climbed the stairs. 'But I don't see how this is going to help with Lorna.'

'Just wait and see,' Claire advised him. 'You don't know them like I do.'

Kieran shrugged. 'Well I hope you're right. I need to get in there and fit a new skirting board.'

'Don't you ever think about anybody but yourself?'

Kieran squirmed slightly. 'I'd better go downstairs, I've got a ton of sharp sand arriving at half past.'

Claire held her breath and waited. She deliberately hadn't told Worm about the state Lorna was in; she hadn't had the heart. Was this going to work or turn into yet another abject failure?

He walked up to Lorna's door, knocked, and tried the handle. 'It's me,' he called out. Then he sat down on the lino with his back to the door.

After a little while the key turned in the lock and the door opened cautiously.

'Worm?'

Lorna emerged, and ran a caressing hand over his bedraggled ginger mop. ''S'all right,' she slurred. 'I'll make us some porridge.'

Then she took three halting steps forward. And keeled over.

Chapter 27

'Kieran!' Candy's voice came screeching up the stairs at a hundred miles an hour. 'Kieran, I've just snagged my last pair of tights on that poxy sanding machine.'

'All right, all right.' Kieran's answering growl sounded far from sanguine. 'I'll move it later, OK?'

'Now.'

'Later. I'm going out.'

'Now, and I want the money for a new pair of tights. Oh – and Mr Veidt says you dented his best trombone. And . . .'

A door slammed shut in the distance.

Behind the locked door of Lorna's room Worm, Lorna and Claire were all huddled up together on the squishy drop-end settee, working their way through every video in Worm's collection. They had done a *Bagpuss* omnibus and *The Clangers*, and were now wading painfully through the entire back catalogue of *Star Trek: The Next Generation*. It wasn't Claire's idea of entertainment, but it was all in a good cause: distracting Lorna from the booze.

'What's going on out there?' demanded Lorna, hugging the travelling rug round her shaking shoulders. 'What's all that shouting?'

'Nothing to worry about,' said Claire soothingly. The last thing Lorna needed right now was a load of hassle about the house. The house could wait.

'I'm cold.'

Worm paused the video and bounded to his feet, eager to please. 'I'll switch on the fire. Oh.' He turned apologetic eyes on Claire. 'Don't suppose you've got fifty p?'

Claire dug in her pocket and threw him a couple of coins. 'There you go.'

'I'll pay you back.'

'Whenever. Well,' Claire went on, settling herself back on the settee. 'This is nice, isn't it?'

'Is it?'

'Lovely,' she lied. 'You, me and Worm. Just like the old days.'

'The *good* old days?' snorted Lorna. 'Yeah, they were fab – no money, no job, no prospects. Just like now.' Lorna's abnormally pale face had a sullen droop to it, and it wasn't just her shoulders that were shaking now. She was trembling all over; little beads of sweat were standing out all over her clammy white forehead. This was scary and painful, and Claire would have given anything not to put Lorna through it.

'One bar or two?' demanded Worm, plugging in the electric fire.

Claire threw caution to the winds. 'All three.'

Lorna was sitting with her arms wrapped round her legs, and her knees drawn up to her chin, muttering to herself. 'Shit, shit, it's all shit. Don't know why I don't just give up now.'

'Why? I'll tell you why.' Worm flung himself back on to the settee, sending the whole shebang scudding back several inches, retrieved the remote and pressed 'play'. 'Because we're not going to let you, are we, Auntie Claire?'

'Tell Auntie Claire to mind her own fucking business.'

'Sorry,' said Claire, with genuine regret. 'No can do.'

Lorna huddled between them despondently, like an angry child wedged between two deeply uncool parents. With her hair hanging in greasy rats' tails and her unwashed jogging bottoms, she looked exactly what she was: a mess.

'I'm thirsty.'

333

Worm cracked open yet another litre bottle of Malvern and presented it to her like a bottle of vintage champagne. 'There you go milady, lots of lovely mineral water. That'll flush out your toxins.'

She pushed it aside with a look of disgust. 'I want a proper drink.'

'It is a proper drink.'

'What have you done with my Stolly?'

Worm exchanged looks with Claire. 'Worm poured it down the sink, don't you remember?' she said. 'You told him to.'

'I bloody never.' Lorna's tongue flicked over her parched lips, defying the blurred memory. 'Give me the brandy then.'

'I can't, I put it down the loo,' replied Worm proudly. 'With the advocaat and the beer. Oh, and the Malibu. And don't bother looking behind the hi-fi, because I found those liqueur chocolates as well.'

Lorna rewarded him with a look of pure hatred. 'Bastard.' She threw off the blanket and stuck out a shaking hand. 'Sub me some dosh Claire, I'm going down the offie.'

'Oh no you're not. You're staying right here till you're better. You know it's for the best,' pleaded Claire, who wasn't at all sure that Lorna did. When she was like this, in the aftermath of one of her binges, there was just no reaching her. 'We're only trying to help you.'

'Well don't bother. OK? I don't need anybody.' But Claire noticed how very close Lorna was sitting to Worm, and how whenever he asked her to do something, she swore her head off at him – then did it. There was something between the two of them that Claire might have been envious of, if she hadn't cared so much about getting Lorna well.

'I don't give a toss if you need me or not,' declared Worm. 'You're stuck with me.'

'Until little Miss Perky Boobs comes in wiggling her assets, and then you'll be off like a randy ferret.'

'Lorna, I'm not going anywhere. The Murf thing was all a big mistake, OK?'

'If you say so.'

'We're mates, Lorna. Good mates. I'm not throwing that away for some stupid girl.'

'Huh.' Lorna looked unimpressed. 'Anyway, I don't give a stuff who you're screwing. OK?'

Oh but you do Lorna, thought Claire. You give the biggest stuff in the whole wide world. And Worm's probably too dim to have realised.

An uneasy truce established, the three of them settled down to endure yet another episode of *The Next Generation*.

'Haven't we already seen this one?' ventured Claire with a jaw-cracking yawn.

Worm studied the back of the box. 'Don't think so. No, you're thinking of the one where Picard has a crisis of conscience over a cheap special effect that's disrupting the space-time continuum.'

'Doesn't that happen in *every* episode?'

'Well . . . yeah,' he admitted.

The crew of the *USS Enterprise* were gaping in unconvincing horror at a white thing wafting wispily across deep space. 'I'm sure that cloud thingy was in that other episode,' said Claire sceptically. 'The one where Troi got her kit off.'

'No, that was a cloud of antimatter that looked like a life form, this is a life form that looks like a cloud of antimatter.'

'That's not antimatter, it's cotton wool!'

'What does it matter?' snarled Lorna. 'It's all rubbish. I hate sci-fi. I hate everything.'

'When we were kids you used to be in the *Blake's Seven* fan club,' pointed out Claire.

Worm looked impressed. 'Did she?'

'You betcha. And there was hell to pay if she missed *Doctor Who*.'

Lorna took a grudging swig from the bottle of water Worm was waving enticingly under her nose. 'That was before.'

'Before what?' enquired Worm.

'I was up for the part of the new assistant, you know? Short-list of six and a screen test in the Tardis. Then what happens? The BBC cancels the whole fucking series.' She cackled humourlessly, took aim with the water bottle and crashed it into a shelf-full of china ducks. 'Lorna kiss-of-death Walsh, that's me. Everything I touch turns to shite.'

'Don't be silly,' said Claire. 'You've got plenty to look forward to.'

'Yeah? Like what? Death? Cirrhosis of the liver?'

Hell, thought Claire, I don't know what to say. She floundered. 'Like . . . like . . . all those kids' parties you're going to do with Worm.'

'Playing Auntie effing Banana?' Lorna pushed her comforting arm away. 'Oh fuck off and die.'

'Claire's only trying to help.'

'Help? Give me a break, Worm. We all know I'm never going to work again.'

'Oh yes you are,' Worm insisted, picking fragments of duck out of the fruit bowl. '*We* are. Soon as you're up to it, we're going to get the old act out of mothballs, start to advertise for bookings again.'

The sudden roar of falling masonry, somewhere at the side of the house, ended Captain Picard's attempts to bore the Borg into submission.

'What the hell was that?' demanded Lorna, visibly shaken.

'Kieran!' Stuart's voice roared down from the landing above. 'Kieran, what the hell have you done to the electrics? My PC's just crashed.'

Candy's voice replied from below. 'Save your breath. He's gone out.'

'Wanker.'

Doors slammed. There was another enormous crash of falling rubble. By now Lorna was on her feet, swaying unsteadily. 'Is somebody going to tell me what's going on out there? Or do I have to go and find out for myself?'

Worm sprang to the door and spreadeagled himself across it like a knife-thrower's assistant. Somewhere in the distance, an electric drill whined into life. 'It's just a bit of DIY Kieran's doing.'

'A *bit*? That doesn't sound like a bit. That sounds like half the house coming down.' The TV screen went dark and the lights flickered out. 'Let me out, Worm.'

'No! You're not well enough yet.'

'Well enough for what?'

Claire sighed. 'I think Kieran mentioned something about having the conservatory demolished.'

Lorna was getting better. She knew she must be, because Worm had unlocked her bedroom door and stopped following her into the lavatory to check for contraband booze. He and Claire were only doing this to her because they cared; Lorna knew all that deep down. But it still hurt.

She was sitting in the garden of number sixteen, eating her breakfast at the picnic bench. It was one of those chilly mid-September mornings and her porridge kept filling up with dead leaves; but this was the only place she could get away from the madness that was number sixteen, Jardine Crescent.

Was she going mad? Hallucinating? Or just plain drunk? The last option was hardly feasible, since she hadn't touched alcohol for well over a week. But things in the house weren't the right colour any more, or even the right shape, and discovering that had upset her more than she had thought it ever could. She had always been so happy in this house, so comfortable. It had always felt like home. But now, when she actually owned a share of it, it felt as though it had turned its back on her.

She picked an oak leaf out of her porridge.

'Goot mornink, Mizz Walsh!' honked the bald, long-faced Belgian woman who had mysteriously taken over Worm's old room. 'It is lovely, yes? Most bracink.'

'Oh. Hi.'

Lorna watched her jog past like a particularly ugly foal. That was another thing. You turned your back on a place for five minutes, to have a little bit of a personal crisis; and the next

337

thing, everything had moved round without so much as a by-your-leave. Musical chairs? It was ten times worse than that. Doors had inexplicably switched places, so had half the furniture, the conservatory had disappeared completely. Now people had started doing the same thing. The Belgian woman was in Worm's room, and Worm was in Davey's, and Davey was gone altogether because of something Kieran had said or done.

And everybody, absolutely everybody, seemed terribly unhappy.

I'm unhappy too, thought Lorna glumly. It's all very well Claire and Worm trying to cheer me up; they don't understand. I'm only happy if I'm very, very successful or very, very drunk. And since success just isn't ever going to happen . . .

A shadow crossed her eyeline, almost out of sight. Her prey spotted her a split second before she noticed him, but this time he was too slow to get away.

'Kieran!' she yelled down the garden.

He froze, half in and half out of the french windows, a rolled-up rug balanced on his shoulder. Slowly he slung it down to the ground. 'Lorna. Hi.'

Abandoning the bowl of porridge, she clomped up the garden to the house in her bathrobe and slippers. 'You've been avoiding me.'

He smiled weakly. 'No.'

'Liar.'

'I haven't!'

He had retreated until she had him up against the remains of Mr Papajian's greenhouse. 'I want to know what you've been up to, Kieran. I want to know why Davey's gone and half the house has gone with him.'

'Davey? Oh, he just got pissed off because I wouldn't let him keep his bikes in the TV room.'

Lorna folded her arms. 'Oh? And why wouldn't you?'

Kieran stared at her, then burst out laughing. 'Joke, right?'

'Kieran, we bought this house to make it nicer for us all to live in, not to fuck it up so much everybody walks out!'

338

This did not seem to strike a chord with Kieran. 'Hang on, Lorna, let's get this straight. I ... we ... bought this place to do it up, yes?'

'Yes, a bit, but ...'

'And then flog it at an obscene profit. Right?'

'Wrong! I mean, we never actually said that.'

'Oh come on Lorna, what do you think I am, a charity for penniless no-hopers? We're never going to make a decent living from the rent this lot pay, are we? The only reason they're here now is to help offset the cost of the redecoration.'

'Right. Demolishing a conservatory – you call that redecoration, do you?'

'Well it was hardly decorative, was it?'

'And ripping out the upstairs kitchen while people are still trying to use it?'

'It had to go Lorna, you know that.'

'That's not the point! We agreed to discuss anything major before we went ahead with it – or have you conveniently forgotten that?'

Kieran's exasperated smile mutated into a mocking sneer. 'Oh, so I was supposed to discuss all this with you, was I? And how exactly was I supposed to manage that?'

'What are you saying?'

'I'm saying you've been pissed out of your brain for God knows how long, Lorna. How the hell am I supposed to discuss anything with a roaring drunk?' To her surprise he advanced on her; she stepped back, putting a foot right through Mr Papajian's cold frame. 'Go on, tell me.'

Lorna felt a surge of anger, and then a swift rush of self-pitying tears. She blinked them back. 'You git.'

'I'm just a realist, Lorna. Somebody had to take this place by the balls and you were in no state to do it, were you? You should be thanking me.'

'Thanking you! For setting everybody at each other's throats?'

'For making this house look better than it's ever been. You're going to get a nice fat return on your investment, and none of it's down to you. Remember that.' He smiled at her discomfiture. 'Face it, Lorna. You've been no help at all. In fact, you're bloody useless.'

Later that day Claire dropped by bearing cheesecake.

'It's morello cherry,' she said, wafting a slice under Lorna's nose. 'With lots and lots of double cream.'

'Oh.'

'The chef made it for that big twenty-first do, then we found out they were all vegans. Go on, have some.'

'I'm not hungry.'

'I'll have another slice,' volunteered Worm, holding out his plate. 'If you're stuck for somebody to eat it.'

'Not if you're going to feed it all to the dog.'

'As if.'

A soulful whine drifted up from under the TV room table, and Claire cut an extra slice for Dog. 'Lorna?'

'What?' Lorna was still gazing out through the french windows. In the garden, Kieran was struggling to wedge a length of dado rail into his Workmate, while the odd boy from the attic berated him about dead pigeons in the water tank.

'Aren't you going to drink your coffee? It's going cold.'

'Yes, all right. There's no need to go on about it.'

Claire followed Lorna's line of sight. The argument in the garden was turning into quite a community event, with Stuart, Candy and even Mr Veidt joining in the heated debate. 'Just look at that,' she commented. 'He's going to get himself lynched.'

'With any luck,' agreed Worm. 'That bloke seems to think he can get away with anything he likes now he owns the place.'

Lorna stayed slumped over her coffee. 'I expect it's all for the best,' she said dully.

Claire had never heard her so apathetic before. 'You were tearing lumps out of Kieran yesterday.'

'That was yesterday.'

An uncomfortable silence fell, broken only by the sound of

340

Dog's teeth scraping his empty plate as he tried to chew the pattern off.

'How's work?' asked Worm. 'Is it fun being Assistant General Manager?'

'*Acting* Assistant General Manager,' Claire corrected him. Somehow the 'acting' bit seemed terribly important, like an emergency safety valve she was reluctant to close.

'But I thought you'd agreed . . .'

Claire shook her head. 'Oh, I'm doing the job. But I haven't signed on the dotted line yet. Actually, I think people are starting to get a bit cheesed off with me, Michael's been dropping some really heavy hints about commitment.'

'Don't you want the job?' asked Lorna.

Claire hesitated. 'I don't know,' she admitted. 'I sort of do . . . and I sort of don't.'

Worm chuckled. 'Sounds like you're perfect management material to me.'

'It's funny,' she mused. 'I never used to mind the long hours.'

'But that was before you got yourself a life?'

'Yeah. Yeah, I guess.' She smiled. 'Did I tell you I've started going to proper DIY classes?'

Lorna stopped picking at her cheesecake and showed a flicker of interest. 'No. Where?'

'At the adult ed centre. The thing is, it's twice a week and I really want to keep going, but long-term there's no way I could fit it in with the new job.'

Lorna put down her spoon. 'DIY classes.'

'That's right.'

'Doing what?'

'A bit of everything. You know – how to plumb in a sink, how to tile a bathroom, a bit of electrics, all sorts.'

'DIY,' murmured Lorna, fingers tapping lightly on the table-top.

It was the first thing Lorna had shown any interest in for weeks. Claire pounced. 'You can come with me on Monday if you like.'

341

Lorna drew back. 'I don't know.'

'You don't have to come again if you don't want.'

'No. I don't know. Maybe.'

Worm picked up the cheesecake box, peered mournfully into it and extracted a single squashed cherry. 'Empty,' he sighed. Dog slunk out from under the table, gazing up with large and hopeful eyes, and shoved his muzzle into the empty box. 'Sorry mate, all gone. Play your cards right and I'll buy us a takeaway chilli later on.'

'Gutbucket,' laughed Claire. 'Why don't you ever get fat?'

'Oh, I expect I've got veins of solid lard or something.' Worm got up and walked over to the wastepaper bin in the corner. 'What's this?'

'What's what?'

He bent down and extracted an envelope from the bin. 'This. Looks like a letter from the BBC. Lorna?'

Lorna pushed her plate away. 'Just another rejection, what's it to you?'

'Lorna,' protested Worm, 'how can you know what's in it? You haven't even opened it.'

'I don't need to. Just tear it up and throw it away, it's none of your business.'

Worm slit open the envelope. 'Let's see.' A smile split his face in two. 'Hey Lorna, this is great! You've got an audition at Cotswold Radio next Wednesday!'

'Sit.'

As graciously as a Rottweiler with piles, Lorna sat.

'Open.'

Lorna's mouth remained resolutely shut.

'C'mon Lorna,' pleaded Claire, scarlet lipstick at the ready.

Worm tried to slide a finger into the corner of her mouth but she clamped her teeth shut on it. 'Ow! Lorna, if you won't do this yourself we'll have to do it for you.'

'Why can't you just leave me alone?'

Worm sat down on the edge of the dressing table, facing her. 'Because you've got an audition in an hour's time and we are going to get you through it if it kills us. Are you going to get that into your thick head?'

'Fascist.' Lorna scowled but opened her mouth and submitted to Claire's amateur makeover skills. 'It's going all over the place,' she protested.

'Fine,' replied Claire, presenting Lorna with the lipstick. 'So do it yourself.'

Getting Lorna ready for her audition was like something off *The Generation Game*. For one thing, Claire had never put lipstick on anybody else before, if you didn't count her baby brother, and getting Lorna into her audition gear was like dressing an uncooperative octopus.

'Which one – the green or the brown?' she asked, holding up both outfits.

'Purple,' said Worm, without bothering to look. 'She likes the purple one best.'

Lorna grabbed the purple dress bad-temperedly and started pouring herself into it. 'If you know so much about me, why don't *you* do the stupid audition? It's pointless anyway,' she added, struggling to do up the buttons at the back. 'I'm not going to get any work out of this.'

She was still protesting as they slung her handbag over her shoulder, thrust the script into her hands and frogmarched her down the path to Claire's car. At the gate she swung round, and Claire saw the terror behind the petulant veneer. 'Can't I have just one little drink?'

'No. Have an extra-strong mint.'

'I don't want one, they give me wind.' She tried a different tack. 'Look – do I really have to go?'

'Get in the car, Lorna.'

The waiting area at BBC Radio Cotswold was so new the whole place stank of glue and underlay. A crescent of orange plastic chairs curved round the reception desk, where a thirtysomething woman in ski pants was signing in a man with two tarantulas in a plastic box.

Worm nudged Claire. 'Wonder what they're auditioning for.'

Claire glanced round the room. You could tell who was here for an audition by the way they kept glancing at sheets of paper and mouthing things to themselves.

'You'll be great,' said Claire to Lorna.

Lorna stared sullenly at her script. 'This is bilge.'

'That's never bothered you before,' said Worm. 'I mean, if you can play a talking saucepan in Wolverhampton . . .'

'It's educational bilge,' added Claire encouragingly. 'You'll be doing a public service.'

'Yes, well, sorry if I'm not wetting myself with excitement,' Lorna replied tartly, 'but it's not quite Chekhov, is it?'

Claire had to admit that it was not. What it was, was a five-minute sketch about chip-pan fires. But it was a start.

A door marked 'Rehearsal 1' opened and a young man in an unfashionable pullover emerged. He wasn't bad-looking, thought Claire; if you were into Liberal Democrats. 'Mr Glover, Miss Rayes, Miss Walsh please.'

Claire gave Lorna a quick hug. Worm squeezed her hand. 'Go get 'em, tiger.'

'I'm never going to forgive you for this,' said Lorna. 'Just you remember that.'

Then she stalked off through the door, behind the man with the box of spiders, and disappeared.

Lorna gazed at her feet. Things were not going well. Then again, she hadn't expected them to.

'Is something wrong, Lorna?' enquired Jon, the producer.

She forced herself to at least sound normal. She was an actress after all. 'No. Nothing at all. You want me to do it again?'

'If Vic and Bob are putting you off,' cut in Tom Glover, 'I could put them under the desk where you can't see them.'

'I don't know why you had to bring those horrible spiders anyway,' snapped Verity Raynes. 'It's highly unprofessional.'

'They're my son's,' Tom explained sheepishly. 'Vic's got a

344

swollen leg, I promised Rupert I wouldn't let him out of my sight.'

Lorna's jaw ached with the effort of trying to be pleasant. 'Can we just get this over with?'

The producer tugged thoughtfully at his earlobe. 'Tell you what, why don't you two girls swap parts this time? Verity, you read the daughter . . .'

Verity looked pleased as punch. 'Yes of course, Jon. Whatever you say.'

'. . . and Lorna, you read Mrs Fortune. Tom, you stick with the firefighter. Let's just see if it works any better that way round.'

Verity preened her greying locks. Oh terrific, thought Lorna. Now I'm playing a total imbecile twenty years older than me.

'Ready, everybody? From the top. And remember, you've just been traumatised.'

Tell me about it, thought Lorna. 'Oh dear, Officer Stevens,' she read between clenched teeth. 'I'm afraid this was all my fault.'

'Read that again will you? And this time, can you sound a bit more . . . repentant?'

'*I'm afraid it was all my fault,*' she repeated. Oh knickers, this time it sounded psychopathic.

'Your fault, Mrs Fortune?' intoned Tom Glover. 'You mean to say, *you* were responsible for starting the fire?'

'Yes,' lisped Verity, relishing this belated opportunity to portray simpering adolescence. 'You see, silly Mummy left the chip pan on the heat while she popped out for a chat with her friend Sandra from down the road.'

'Oh dear Mrs Fortune, that wasn't very wise, was it?' scolded the amiable fire officer.

'No it wasn't,' agreed Lorna, by now hating brain-dead Mrs Fortune more than she had ever hated anything in the history of hate. 'And when the pan caught fire, I hadn't the faintest idea what to do, and I thought . . .' Lorna dried up, the words finally sticking in her throat. 'I'm sorry Jon,' she said, standing up. 'I'm afraid I'm wasting your time here. I can't do this.'

The producer looked stunned. 'I beg your pardon?'

She slung down the script. 'I may be desperate for work, but believe me, I'm not *this* desperate.'

Tom cradled his tank of spiders. Verity crossed and uncrossed her legs with middle-class disapproval. 'Excuse me Jon, but are we going to continue the reading or not? I have another audition in an hour's time, and I do pride myself on my timekeeping.'

'Just a minute, Verity. Lorna, you're not happy with the script, right?'

'It stinks.'

'Well!' sniffed Verity.

A smile twitched the corners of the producer's mouth. 'I know it does. I wrote it.'

'Well if I were you, I'd stick to producing.' Lorna snatched up her handbag and swept the rehearsal room with a withering gaze. 'Goodbye, I hope you're all very happy together.'

'Wait a minute,' said Jon, disinterring a bundle of papers from underneath the mess on his desk. 'Before you go, there's one other thing I wanted us to read through. You wouldn't mind, would you? Only I think you might be just right for the female lead.'

Lorna was so taken aback at not being thrown out on her ear, that she nodded. 'OK, whatever.' She took a copy of the script. 'What is it?'

'It's called *Max Turbot, Fish Detective* – a children's mystery musical, I think I'd call it. Unique. You did say you could sing, didn't you?'

Lorna didn't reply. She was staring at the script in her hands.

'What's wrong with her now?' demanded Verity. 'Printed on the wrong sort of paper is it?'

'*Max Turbot*,' murmured Lorna. 'You're really thinking of broadcasting this?'

'Absolutely. If I can ever manage to track down the bloke

who wrote it. Somebody called . . . hang on . . . '

'Steve,' said Lorna quietly. 'Steve Winters.'

'You know him?'

'Know him?' she replied. 'I *am* Steve Winters.'

Chapter 28

'Lorna! Lorna, come back!' The six month-old copy of *Media Week* slipped from Claire's fingers as Lorna strode through reception, punched open the door and vanished from sight.

'Uh-oh,' said Worm. 'I think we've got another crisis on our hands.'

The receptionist took off her glasses. 'Is your friend ill?' she enquired.

Claire smiled awkwardly. 'Not exactly. Excuse us a mo, will you?'

She cursed her own lack of judgement as they headed through the front door and into the street. Forcing Lorna into doing things had always had a tendency to end in disaster, like the time Claire had railroaded her into asking the head boy out on a date, and he'd turned up at the Odeon with his mother in tow.

They found Lorna standing on the corner by the pay and display, hugging a lamp-post. Her eyes were closed and she was white-faced and shaking.

'Beer,' she said. 'I want a beer.'

'Lorna, you can't have one.'

'No, hold the beer, that's not what I want – I need chips!'

'Chips?' said Claire, taken aback.

Lorna's grip on the lamp-post tightened. Her eyes shot open. 'Claire, darling, for God's sake tell me where the nearest chip shop is. It's an emergency. I *have* to eat the biggest bag of chips in the world. Now!'

'I haven't a clue,' admitted Claire, turning to Worm. 'Have you?'

Worm gently detached Lorna from the lamp-post, like a koala from a eucalyptus tree. 'It's all right kid, we know you had a bad time in there, but it's over now.' His voice was soothing and calm. 'And we promise we won't make you go back in there if you don't want to. Will we Claire?'

'No, of course we won't,' agreed Claire, experiencing terrible pangs of remorse, even though it had been Worm's mad idea to go through with this whole sorry charade. 'I'm sorry Lorna, honestly I am.' She stroked the curly black hair. 'Was it really horrible?'

Lorna screwed up her face and Claire was convinced she was about to collapse, sobbing, on to Worm's shoulder. Instead she suddenly grabbed hold of the lamp-post with one hand and spun round it so fast that her skirt billowed up over her purple lace thong.

'Don't you understand?' She whirled to a breathless, swaying halt. 'Everything's all right now, everything in the whole world's wonderful!'

'It is?' Claire advanced on Lorna and took a sniff of her breath. Toothpaste and BBC coffee, nothing else. Besides, she'd never known the BBC to serve up vodka at auditions.

'Yes, yes, *yes*!' Lorna seized Claire by the shoulders, so hard it brought tears to her eyes. 'It was that wacky idea of yours. We were in the Cantina and I was moaning that nobody'd ever give me a chance because they never saw past my charlies. And you said, "If you don't like who you are, be somebody else"' She gave Claire's shoulders a frustrated shake. 'Don't you remember?'

Claire wiped spittle out of her eye. 'Vaguely,' she hedged.

Worm clicked his fingers. 'You'd just finished writing one of your stories. *Max* thingy.'

'Turbot. *Max Turbot*. And it's a musical, not a story, but that doesn't matter. What matters is, I took your advice. I decided to be somebody else, lots of different people in fact. And do you know what I've just been doing in there?' She pointed wildly to the front door of Radio Cotswold, and a row of interested spectators.

'Auditioning for a fire safety sketch.'

'Wrong! I'll tell you what I've been doing, Fraulein Tippy-Toes.' She did a tap dance along the gutter. 'I've been reading from my own script!'

'Sorry?' Claire and Worm blinked in incomprehension as Lorna danced off along the pavement.

Claire set off after her. 'Hang on, just run that by me again.'

Lorna whirled round, caught between ecstasy and exasperation. 'Steve Winters' script – *my* script, don't you get it?'

Claire struggled to follow Lorna's express-train delivery. 'Steve Winters . . . that's one of your pseudonyms?'

'Claire, you are so *slow*! Of course it is. Anyhow, I sent them *Max Turbot* and they loved it, only I forgot to put my address in with the script and they've been all over Gloucestershire looking for me, trying to send me a contract! *Now* do you see?'

Worm's eyes widened. 'You mean they're . . . ?'

'Going to put it on? Yes! Live from the kiddies' ward at Christmas.' She wiggled his ears and engulfed his entire nose in a huge, lipsticky kiss. 'And don't worry kiddo, 'cause there's a part in it for you, too!'

Lorna was springing about the first floor of Paradise Cottage like a manic impala, vaulting the gaps in the floorboards and knocking tubs of nails into Pete's lap.

She slapped the tool into Claire's palm with a triumphal flourish. 'There, that's the one you wanted, isn't it?'

'Lorna,' said Claire with exhausted patience. 'That's not a screwdriver, it's a chisel.'

'But it's blue. You said it had a blue handle.'

Claire hadn't the heart to tell Lorna that most of the tools in the box had blue handles, seeing as she'd bought them as a job lot from the bargain bin at B&Q. 'Never mind, it'll come in handy for scraping all that old brown paint off the window-panes.'

Lorna's ears pricked up. 'I could do that.'

Visions of Lorna putting the chisel straight through the window and showering Ted with broken glass raced instantly into Claire's mind. 'Why don't you just have a nice rest?'

'But I'm not tired! Oops.' In trying to scoop up a handful of spilled nails she dropped several into an open pot of aluminium primer, and tried to fish them out with the chisel. 'I've got all this creative energy, I want to *help*!'

Claire offered up a silent prayer. If there was one thing more alarming than Lorna on the booze, it was Lorna on a natural high. Whatever it was that had plunged her into the slough of despond had suddenly relaxed its grip, catapulting her to the opposite extreme like a mad-haired gonk on a bungee rope. It was pretty exhausting trying to handle her, like being left in charge of a whole classroom full of hyperactive four year-olds. And yet, thought Claire, the one thing I mustn't do is upset her.

Gently but firmly, Claire prised the chisel from Lorna's fingers and wiped it on the leg of her bib and brace. 'Just leave it be, eh? I'll sort this out later. I know you want to help, but screwing the bathroom taps on back to front wasn't really helping, was it? Nor was dropping that bucket of bleach on Brucie.'

'I suppose. I'll just sit here and watch you then.' Lorna promptly plonked her backside right on top of a pile of brand-new radiators, which let out a collective screech of protest.

'Not on there!' Pete slapped a hand to his forehead. 'You'll buckle them.'

'Oh. Sorry.' Lorna got up and skipped around the room, playing football with the first thing that caught her eye. 'What's this round orange thing?' she asked after a couple of minutes.

Claire went on meticulously sanding down a length of new skirting board. 'It's the new ballcock for the loo. Why?'

'I just stood on it and it's gone a bit flat. Does it matter?'

Claire didn't trust herself to answer. She just banged her forehead softly against the windowsill. 'Oh Lorna . . .'

'Oh Lorna what?'

'Hello workers!' trilled Veronica, coming along the landing and into the room. She was carrying an old-fashioned tray with a jug and several glasses; with her hair scraped back and that unglamorous pinny over her trousers, she looked disturbingly like Ma Walton. 'Who's for homemade lemonade?'

Claire sat back on her haunches. 'What – homemade as in, you made it yourself?'

Veronica beamed. 'I'm not *completely* useless, you know. Pete? Lemonade?'

Pete stuck out an arm, took his drink without looking up, and went on feeding electrical wires under the floorboards.

'This is great, Mrs S,' said Lorna, downing her drink. 'Can I have some more?'

'Help yourself.' Veronica winked. 'I know you'd probably prefer a drop of the hard stuff, but it's a bit early in the day, isn't it?'

'Mum,' warned Claire, cringing at her mother's tactlessness. But Veronica was too thick-skinned to notice she'd said anything amiss, and right now Lorna was too hyper to mind anything much. Or so Claire thought.

'Shouldn't you be at home, writing?' enquired Claire when Veronica had gone downstairs to refill the jug.

Lorna's mood instantly darkened. 'Look. I know. OK?'

'You've got another three plays to write, remember.'

'I can hardly forget, can I? With you reminding me every five minutes.'

The BBC commission for three more plays, all to be broadcast from the children's hospital over Christmas, was undoubtedly Lorna's biggest-ever break. There was no question that she was excited about it. But when it actually came down to doing the work, Lorna had never been the most self-disciplined of people.

Claire tucked a stray wisp of hair under her improvised duster turban. 'All I'm saying is, they won't write themselves. Wouldn't you be better off at home, rather than kicking your heels here?'

'That's just it.' Lorna leaned her elbows on the windowsill, stuck her head out of the window and knocked a pot of putty into the rhubarb patch. 'It's *not* home.'

'How come?' enquired Pete, crawling on hands and knees to the door, tracking a length of cable under the floorboards. 'You own the place.'

'Only a little bit of it. And everything's changed. Even the people have changed. It's just not right any more.'

Claire threw down her sanding block, hauled herself to her feet and joined Lorna at the window. 'Is this all about Kieran?'

'Who else would it be about? The snake's only gone and changed another tenant on me, you know. And Stuart's threatening to leave if things don't get any better.'

'Not all bad news then,' commented Pete.

Lorna didn't crack a smile. 'I know Stuart's a pain in the arse, they all are. But that's what makes them *them*.' Head resting on her folded arms, she gazed glumly down at Ted, opening the door of his snug little workshop to beckon Brucie in. 'Kieran's not a human being, Claire.' She shivered theatrically. 'He's . . . he's an accountant!'

'Hmm,' nodded Claire. 'And this is the guy you wanted to fix me up with?'

'Don't rub it in. How was I to know he'd turn out like this? He seemed like a regular bloke when he first moved in.' She turned her back on the window. 'I can't work in that place, Claire. I mean, could *you* write the greatest kids' musical in showbiz history with Kieran banging around in your basement?'

Claire slipped an arm round Lorna's shoulders. 'We'll sort him out somehow.'

'You reckon?'

'For sure.'

Lorna perked up, her face brightening again. 'I do want to help here, you know. I *like* helping.'

'Well, all right.' Claire caught the look of panic on Pete's face. 'But only on one condition.'

'What's that?'

'You come to DIY class with me and learn how to do things properly.'

Lorna gave a double thumbs-up sign. 'Right. You're on.'

Pete was at death's door.

Sitting on the bottom tread of the rickety staircase, he was turning in a performance that would have done credit to Lorna.

'That's right,' he wheezed into his mobile, squeezing out another consumptive cough. 'I'm really sorry, Dr French, but I won't be able to make the start of term.'

The voice on the other end of the line rose half an octave.

'I know, I know,' he agreed. 'But how can I? The doctor says I'm going to need at least another week's bed rest.'

The deed done, he switched off his mobile and whistled merrily as he bounded back up the stairs to tackle the cistern.

Veronica was waiting for him on the landing. And she didn't look pleased. 'Pete,' she said. 'You do realise you're being incredibly stupid?'

He scowled. 'Hasn't anybody ever told you it's bad manners to listen in to people's conversations?'

He pushed past her but she followed him into the bathroom. 'Look son, I admire you for what you're doing. But you're messing about with your future. What about your education?'

Pete grabbed a plumber's wrench and started unscrewing the old ballcock. 'I've finished off the electrics and I'm going to sort out the rest of the plumbing before I go back to college. It's the least I can do, Claire's my sister.'

Veronica sighed. 'Why can't somebody else do it?'

'Because it needs specialist knowledge.'

'Oh, and you're the only specialist she knows are you?' Pete was grimly silent. 'What about her friend Aidan? She could ask him to help, couldn't she? I know you're only being loyal to Claire, but really.'

That was just too much to take. He turned on her, thunder-faced. 'And what the hell would you know about loyalty?'

She swallowed. 'I know you're still angry with me, Peter.'

'Too damn right I am.'

'But I'm your mother, I've a right to worry about what you're doing with your future.'

'You? Have rights? Don't flatter yourself. Any rights you had, you threw out the window the day you walked out on us.' He brandished the spanner in her face and for a moment she wondered if he was going to hit her with it.

'Pete, I . . .'

'Why did you come back, Veronica?' he snarled. 'What the hell are you doing here? And more to the point – what's in it for you?'

'Right everybody,' said Shona the course instructor, securing her long brown hair in a turban. 'Let's just run through all those steps again, then you can do some plastering exercises on your own.' She gave the wet plaster a stir. 'First, we scrape a manageable amount of browning plaster on to the hawk, using the trowel.'

'Which one's the hawk?' hissed Ros, a middle-aged mother of eight with the saggy look of a worn-out Friesian.

Claire pointed at the mortar board. 'That one there. In her left hand.'

'Don't take too much on the face of the trowel,' Shona counselled. 'Now, hold the loaded trowel horizontally and tilt it at an angle to the face of the wall . . .'

It glided on like frosting on a chocolate brownie.

'Shona makes it all look so easy,' sighed Ros wistfully. 'Do you think she'd come and do my back bedroom?'

'It *is* easy,' retorted Lorna. 'Just like icing a cake.'

'Oh you think so, do you?' laughed Ros. 'Well I bet you make a dog's breakfast of it.'

Lorna tossed her head confidently. 'Bet you don't.'

'. . . and don't forget to apply the plaster firmly, with a vertical upward stroke, or it may not stick to the wall.'

Claire and Lorna gathered around their instructor with the eight other women who had signed up for Intermediate Home

Maintenance. They were a mixed bunch: from seventy-two year-old widow Iris, who wanted to build a garage for her new quad bike, to eighteen year-old twins and an assistant bank manager who was sick of her husband's unfinished DIY projects.

In the three weeks she'd been coming to the classes, Claire had already been through several rites of passage: Aligning Floors, Laying Ceramic Tiles, and Papering a Stairwell. She felt she was finally getting into her stride. Suddenly all this DIY nonsense was beginning to make sense.

Then there was the momentum it had brought to her life. Little by little, Claire had begun to wonder what she would do with herself when it was all over, when Paradise Cottage was finally finished and there was nothing left to put right. When there were no more excuses.

'OK,' said Shona, wiping her hands on a damp rag. 'That's all there is to it. Fancy having a go on the practice wall?'

Claire couldn't help but be impressed by any woman who could plaster a brick wall without so much as chipping her nail varnish. And there couldn't be many women of thirty-five who could build you a brick wall, plaster it *and* look good in Prada.

'Come on then,' said Lorna, pouncing on a trowel and a sack of plaster. 'Let's get started.'

'Wrong plaster,' Claire pointed out. 'That's the finish coat, you want browning.'

'Do I?'

'You've not been listening, have you? Let me give you a hand.'

Lorna pouted. 'No way! I can manage. Go and do your own bit of wall.'

Claire went off with Ros and attacked a mocked-up chimney breast with her trowel. It was messy, but even more fun than it looked.

'You've done this before, haven't you?' moaned Ros, comparing her own undulating efforts to Claire's nicely squared-off section of brickwork.

'Never.' Claire scraped up another glob of plaster. 'Why?'

'Because I don't want to believe that anyone can get that good without practice. *You* don't fancy doing my back room do you?'

'No fear. I've got enough plastering at the cottage to keep me going till Christmas.' She went back for another dollop of plaster and took a peek at Lorna's wall. Her own was far from perfect, and Ros's was a bit on the irregular side; but Lorna's looked like a freeform sculpture in chocolate spread. Claire waved her trowel as Lorna approached, trowel in hand. 'Everything OK?'

'Can't stop, it's going off.' Lorna raced past and flung another trowelful of plaster at the wall. It hung there for a moment, then peeled away in slow motion, leaving bare bricks behind. 'Oh sod!' she shrieked. 'Why's it doing this to me?'

'Did you wet the brickwork first?'

'Of course.'

'Show me how you put the plaster on.'

Lorna grudgingly slammed the trowel into the wall.

'Oh well, there you are then. You're not supposed to let the whole face of the trowel come into contact with the plaster,' Claire explained.

'Why not?'

'The suction pulls it off.' She picked up Lorna's trowel and demonstrated. 'But if you do it *this* way . . . see? Stays stuck like glue.'

'Well bugger me.' Lorna wiped a plastery hand across her brow.

'Can you finish the rest yourself? Only I've got to go and level off before it hardens.'

Claire was levelling off her wall with a wooden ruler when Shona came by to offer advice. 'That's good, Claire. Excellent for a beginner. You've done this before I take it?'

Claire laughed. 'No.'

'Hmm, I'm impressed. Last week tiling, this week plastering. If you go on like this I'll be out of a job.'

She moved on to the next group and Claire took a breather.

Ros grinned. 'Teacher's pet.' Claire stuck her tongue out.

357

'Claire!' wailed Lorna as the entire sheet of wet plaster began peeling off her wall, like skin off a ripe banana.

'Told you she'd make a mess of it!' declared Ros merrily, putting the final touches to her stretch of wall. 'Mine may look crap, but at least it's got plaster on.'

Claire stood, hands on hips, and surveyed Lorna's very own disaster zone. 'Maybe if we scrape this lot off and start again.'

'Er, no thanks. Between you and me, darling,' confided Lorna, teasing a great big gobbet of plaster out of her hair, 'I don't think I'm quite cut out for this plastering lark.'

'It's electrics next week. Maybe that's more your thing,' suggested Claire.

'Hmm,' said Lorna non-committally.

'Or interior design?' Yes, it was a lot easier envisaging Lorna devising artful arrangements of terracotta pots and twisted willow than clambering about in plaster-covered DMs.

'Feng Shui, that's more me,' said Lorna dreamily. 'I could go round Paradise Cottage with a compass and some fabric swatches. And tell you off whenever you left the toilet seat up.'

'Yes, well, don't get too carried away, we haven't even got plaster on the walls yet.'

Plaster dripped wetly on to the workshop floor. On the other side of the room, a girl was trying to chip her trowel out of a mound of quick-drying cement.

'You know something,' said Ros to Lorna. 'Your mate's bloody good at this DIY lark. Makes you sick.'

'Tell me about it.'

'I'm not!' protested Claire.

'Shut up, yes you are. Shona's only got to show you something once and you've got it, just like that.' She laughed. 'If I had a talent like that, I'd make money out of it.'

It was only a throwaway remark, a parting shot with no particular weight to it. But for some reason Claire couldn't quite banish the thought from her mind.

Make money out of DIY? But how? And in any case, why would she want to?

Chapter 29

When it came to method acting, Robert de Niro had nothing on Worm.

He paced the kitchen of number sixteen, hands on hips. 'So I'm playing this fish, right?'

Lorna offered up another prayer for patience. 'A turbot, Worm. You're Max Turbot, Fish Detective, I don't know how many times I've told you.'

'Hmm,' said Worm, rubbing his chin.

'Never mind "hmm",' scolded Lorna, scribbling changes on her rough copy of the script. 'We've only got till Christmas to get this right. I thought you wanted this part.'

'I do! What colour are my scales?'

'*What?*'

'What colour am I? Silver? Blue? Purple with green spots? It's a reasonable enough question.'

Lorna lowered the script with barely-contained irritation. 'Worm, *darling*, what the hell does it matter what colour you are?'

'It matters to me. You want me to do justice to the character, don't you?'

Sigh. 'You're brown.'

'Not silver?'

'All right then, you're silver.'

A shadow of suspicion crossed Worm's face. 'You're just saying that to shut me up.'

'Worm.'

'What?'

'Just get on with it, will you?' She raked a hand through her uncombed hair. 'Oh God, all this stress. I'm gasping for a—'

'—nother can of dandelion and burdock?' Worm promptly thrust one into her hand. 'Third AA meeting tonight, remember? Can't have you falling off the wagon when you're doing so well.'

'Fall off it?' she replied darkly. 'I'm that full of gas I'll probably blow it up.'

The kitchen was definitely not the ideal place to walk through Lorna's play, but the only other room empty enough was the upstairs bathroom, and that was no-go since the incident with the wasps' nest in the water heater. These days it was almost impossible to get any peace and quiet at number sixteen; and with gangs of sniggering workmen traipsing through with bits of fitted wall unit it was worse than busking on Cheltenham High Street.

Worm tried out a few facial expressions. 'How's this?'

'Not fishy enough.'

'What about this then?' He sucked in his cheeks and made a sound like a blocked vacuum cleaner.

'Fish don't slurp. And can you play it, you know,' Lorna waved the script for extra emphasis, 'fatter?'

Worm frowned. The glass door of the microwave reflected back the physique of a consumptive string bean. 'Lorna, are you *sure* you wrote this part specially for me?'

A carpenter came in, tracking mud across Kieran's brand-new cushioned vinyl remnant (fifty quid cash from Mister Carpet, no VAT, buyer collects).

'Gawd, you want to get that squint seen to, my son,' he remarked with a glance at Worm's face. 'They can do wonders, them surgeons.' Then he dumped a load of cupboard doors in the corner and sauntered out again.

Worm glared after him. Lorna trudged across to the back door and closed it for the umpteenth time. 'Right. Let's try and work through this dialogue again. And this time I want it shorter and fatter, OK?'

'You're a tyrant.'

Lorna bobbed a curtsey. 'Thank you.'

Worm retaliated with the ultimate threat. 'You're starting to sound just like Petronella.'

'Good.'

'Hang on, don't move.' Worm left the room for a moment and returned with a scatter cushion, which he stuffed up his jumper. Then he splayed his feet out at right angles to his legs, and let his knees sag to make himself a foot shorter. 'Better?'

'That's not fat, that's pregnant!'

'Lorna . . .'

'Oh all right, I suppose it'll do. Till we get the fish costumes.'

'How about I do this next bit in a kind of gargly voice?'

Worm had just opened his mouth to deliver the next line when the carpenter returned with a man in a boiler suit and a six-foot length of MDF. 'Don't mind us darlin', we'll work round you.'

The man in the boiler suit shook his head as Worm waddled out of the way. 'Terrible thing is yer irritable bowel,' he tutted, plugging his drill into an extension cable. 'Wife's sister's a martyr to it. Blows her up like a zeppelin.'

'Excuse *me*,' said Lorna tartly. 'But we're trying to work in here. Can't you do that later?'

The carpenter sucked in breath through his badly-fitting dentures. 'Ooh, dunno if we can do that, missus. That Mr Hart told us to get this done quick as poss.'

'Well I'm the co-owner of this house, and I'm telling you to bog off and come back later.'

The carpenter wiped his nose on his sleeve. 'What you reckon Marty?'

'There's a little caff round the corner. If somebody was to sub us ten quid . . .'

'Don't push it,' said Lorna, jerking a thumb towards the door. 'Just go.' As it clattered shut, she threw down her pencil.

'This is a total waste of time.'

'No it isn't.' Worm picked up the pencil and wrapped her fingers back round it. 'Come on, I'm really in character now. I *am* Max Turbot. Remind me what happens next, it's ages since we looked over this bit.'

Lorna consulted her much-amended script. 'OK, so Max is on the trail of the evil Crayfish Twins, who've kidnapped the beautiful princess – that's me . . .'

'Naturally.'

'. . . and are holding her to ransom. Only I've just escaped and now I'm running away.'

'Swimming away.'

'Are you going to let me finish?'

'Sorry.'

'Anyhow, I'm being chased.' She galumphed across the room, dodged round the table, and vaulted the vacuum cleaner. Dog barked with excitement and tried to join in. 'Down Dog, you're an enchanted undersea forest. Now, round the ruined castle . . .'

'And so on and so on,' nodded Worm, flipping through the pages. 'And absolutely everybody gets arrested. And then?'

Panting, she staggered to a halt, took Worm's hands and placed them on her waist. 'The same as happens in all the fairy-tales. Max kisses the princess.'

'Do fish kiss?'

'He *kisses* her, and they live happily ever after. Till Max Turbot's next case.'

'Which you haven't written yet.'

'I will!'

'It's got to be done by Christmas.'

'Shut up and play the part.'

Worm frowned. 'And they live happily ever after? That's not very PC.'

Lorna stifled an urge to scream. 'PC's old hat, haven't you heard? These days everyone's into romance.' She gave him her winsomest smile. 'Pucker up and get on with it.'

Worm's lips were hovering half an inch above hers, and she was sure he was going to take the hint at long last. Then the hall door burst open and the bottom half of a Welsh dresser rolled in.

'Where shall I shove this then?' enquired the man in the flat cap.

Lorna told him exactly where.

'Morning, Claire.' Michael Tang was all smiles as he accompanied her into Naomi's office. Then again, he'd been like that ever since the Board officially confirmed his appointment as General Manager. 'So you've finally seen sense about the job then?' He stuck out a hand. 'Congratulations, welcome to the team.'

'Actually,' began Claire.

Naomi sat back in her chair and gave Claire a long, hard look. 'You're not going to take the job, are you?'

'Of course she is,' retorted Michael.

Claire shook her head. 'Sorry.'

Michael looked like a man who'd just stuck his hand up a transvestite's frock. 'If this is a joke I don't find it very amusing.'

'It's no joke, I've made up my mind. I thought about it, and I realised I don't actually *want* to be Assistant General Manager.'

'But Claire, you can't just say no.'

'Yes I can.'

'What – and stay in the same dead-end job for the next thirty years?' Michael wasn't just shocked, he was angry; angry with himself for betting on a racing certainty that had promptly refused at the first. 'This is your big career break, you have to take it!'

'I'm sorry, really I am,' said Claire. 'Especially for keeping everybody up in the air for so long. But I had to be sure I was making the right decision.'

Naomi gave her a searching look. 'And you are?'

Claire nodded. 'Oh yes. Thanks for offering me the job, though. It's very flattering that you think I'm capable of it.'

'You're insane.' With a backward glance of utter contempt

363

Michael turned and stalked out of the office, leaving the door quivering in its frame. And Claire was more certain than ever that she was doing the right thing. Be Michael Tang's stooge, she thought. I should coco.

Naomi stood up and shook Claire by the hand. 'Thank you.'

'What for?'

'Without you, this place would never have survived the past couple of years. Half the time you've been carrying me as well as doing your own job, and that's not right. I even heard you've been unblocking the drains.'

'I'm a troubleshooter, it comes with the job.' She didn't add that it was a fantastic way of getting free lessons in DIY. If Naomi wanted to think she was some kind of saint, that was OK by her.

'Try telling that to Michael. He's a talented boy but he could use a touch of humility.' She shuffled the papers on her desk and turned up a half-eaten sardine sandwich. 'Oh *that's* where it got to, I was wondering where the smell was coming from.' She picked it up, looked around unsuccessfully for a bin, and dropped it into the out tray. 'So what happens now?'

Claire clipped her pager on to her belt. 'I go and sort out the arrangements for Brent Lovelace's light show.'

'And after that? What then?'

'Who knows? But don't plan any leaving dos, I'm not going anywhere just yet.'

Back in the general office, Claire stood and stared down at her desk. It was a nice desk, cosily situated in a quiet corner of the office where you could lurk behind the acoustic screen and watch the world go by. Own spider plant, half-share of cuddly badger, easy access to the photocopier, it was what you might call the des res of workstations. When the time came, she was going to miss it.

She picked up the autographed doodle Rolf Harris had done for her at the last charity gala. They'd had all the problems in the world that day: collapsing marquees, belligerent drunks, stolen goods in the car boot sale; and while everyone else was running around like headless chickens, she and Mattie and Mel had sorted the whole lot out. No fuss, no sweat. Almost too easy really.

I need a cup of coffee, she told herself, putting down the doodle. A strong one.

Eyes followed her across the office to the kitchen. She could feel them boring into her back, wondering how anyone could be so stupid, or cowardly, or just plain inadequate, to turn down *that* job. Maybe they were right. Or maybe she was imagining it, and it was just the product of her own doubts, stubbornly resurfacing after a few hours of crystal-clear certainty.

As she was waiting for the kettle to boil there was a knock on the doorframe. It was Mattie. 'Mind if I come in?'

'Help yourself.'

'I just heard the news.'

'Ah.' Inevitable, thought Claire. It's going to be like this all day. 'I suppose you're about to tell me I'm mad too?'

'I wouldn't dare. You'd flatten me.'

'Everybody else seems to think I am.'

'Nah, they're just curious.' Mattie helped herself to biscuits out of the Tupperware box by the sink. 'Actually,' she admitted, 'so am I. Why did you turn the job down – or aren't I supposed to ask?'

'It's no big secret.' Claire dashed milk into her coffee. On impulse she added, 'Come with me, I've got something to show you.'

Intrigued, Mattie followed her back across the office to Claire's desk. 'There you are, see?'

'I can't see anything. There's nothing there.'

'Exactly!' Claire swept her arm across the polished surface. 'It's empty. Nothing but a few bits and bobs in the in-tray.'

'So what are you saying?' puzzled Mattie.

'Just that it's all become so predictable.'

'Predictable! Your job? You're joking. No two days are ever the same.'

365

'No. But they're never that different, either.' She perched her bottom on the corner of the desk, one foot resting on the seat of the swivel chair. 'When I first came here it was exciting . . . well actually it was a bit terrifying, you never knew what was going to hit you next, or what you were going to do to sort it out. It was all improvisation, thinking on your feet. But little by little I guess it just got boring and, well, easy.' A thought struck her. 'Does that sound arrogant to you?'

Mattie shook her head. 'I just wish I had your confidence. So you're saying there's nothing new any more?'

'Yeah. Yeah, I guess I am. Oh, there are still problems, of course there are, but I know I can solve them. The challenge has gone. Even my contingency plans have got failsafe backups, there's nothing left to have the heebie-jeebies about.'

'So why not take the AGM's job?' reasoned Mattie. 'Surely that would be a challenge, something new?'

Claire slipped her foot in and out of her shoe. 'That's what I thought at first. Something new, something to get the juices running again. But no. It's even further away from rolling up my sleeves and getting stuck in, and Mattie, that's what I'm *good* at.

'I know what that job entails. It's three months a year drawing up strategic plans, another three justifying them, three more adapting them so as not to get up anybody's nose, and then three months taking a load of shit because the plans didn't work out. It's not me, Mattie.' She paused. 'But you'd love it.'

Mattie laughed. 'And what's that supposed to say about me?'

'It says you're a bloody good manager, and that job's right up your street.'

'Thanks,' said Mattie quietly. 'I know you recommended me to Naomi. I appreciate it.'

Claire downed the last of her coffee. 'Well just remember me when I'm standing outside Woolworths selling the *Big Issue*.'

Mattie's eyes widened. 'You're leaving Brockbourne Hall?'

'Well, not immediately. But sometime.' She hopped off the desk. 'Sooner or later I'll have to move on.'

366

'What will you do?'

'I haven't a clue. The only thing I'm sure of is, I don't want more of the same.'

The first Claire knew about Pete's little scam was the breakfast-time telephone call she got from Derby.

'Hi, this is Kelly, from Derbyshire Uni. You must be Pete's sister.'

'Hi Kelly. Shall I get him for you?'

Kelly sounded taken aback. 'Well, only if he's up to talking.'

Claire switched ears to pull on her other shoe. 'Why shouldn't he be?'

'Because of the swine fever of course. We'd have come up to see him, only he told us he was still infectious.'

That phone call was the reason why Claire had to spend her precious afternoon off frogmarching Pete through the peeling portals of Cheltenham Spa station.

'Sis!' he protested as she slung his rucksack on to his back and jammed his woolly hat on his head. It was just like the day, ten years ago, when she'd had to forcibly throw him on to the school bus because he didn't want to go to Big School.

'Don't you sis me, you scheming adolescent! I've got better things to do than check you're not skipping class.'

'I was only trying to—'

'Shush. No more arguments, I'm not listening.' Claire clamped a hand over his mouth. 'Railcard.'

Reluctantly he produced it from an inside pocket; and she pushed him towards the ticket window. 'Go on.'

'One to Derby please.'

'Return?' enquired the booking clerk.

Pete caught the warning glint in his big sister's eye. 'Single.'

He moaned all the way across the bridge and down the steps on to platform two. 'She shopped me, didn't she?'

'Who?' Claire cocked half an ear to the tannoy. Ten minutes late, cows on the line at Newark.

'Veronica. Who else?'

367

Claire regarded her baby brother with puzzlement. 'What are you on about?'

'I don't know why you're defending her. She told you I was skiving off college, didn't she?'

'She never said a word.' Claire folded her arms across her chest. 'Are you telling me she *knew* about this all along?'

Pete sniffed. 'Nosey bitch. Listening at doors, pretending she's nice as pie. I know it's all a front.'

'Pete . . .'

'You've got to see through it, sis, she's up to something.'

The northbound train was chugging into the station, brakes screeching, wet leaves plastered to its grimy sides. 'Pete, I know you don't get on with her, and I can't say she's my favourite person in the world, but when all's said and done she's still our mother.'

He grabbed her by the wrists. 'I'm telling you that woman's poison. She's trying to worm her way in, get between us, I don't know why, but there's something she wants and she'll do anything to get it.'

'Something? What, Pete?'

'I don't know yet,' he admitted sulkily. 'But I'll find out.'

'The train's going in a minute, Pete.' Claire bundled him on with his baggage and shut the door. He promptly pushed down the window and stuck his head out.

'Don't take any notice of what she says, Claire. She doesn't give a damn about us.'

And then the train was steaming out of the station and Pete was receding to a tiny, waving arm in the far distance. Not waving but drowning, thought Claire. Poor Pete. They'd always been so close, and this business with Veronica had brought out all the old insecurities. But you couldn't go on blindly hating somebody for ever, just because your brother wanted you to. Could you?

Friction, that was what this all boiled down to. Friction between people who couldn't come to terms with what really was, and hankered after what had never really been; Veronica, who wanted to play the perfect mother; Pete, with his child's-eye view of the world; even Dad, playing his game of Fantasy Families.

And what about me, wondered Claire. Giving up a perfectly great job to run after . . . what? Will I even recognise it when I find it?

Claire turned her coat collar up and trudged back towards the car park, wondering what it was like to be normal.

'There.' Claire skimmed the last of the top coat on to the freshly-plastered wall, and stepped back to admire the effect. 'What do you reckon?'

Hands in pockets, Aidan walked the length of the sitting room, picked up the inspection lamp and shone it across the wall. 'Oh dear, oh dear.'

She frowned. 'What's wrong with it?'

'Look at that there.' He tutted as he pointed to a minute irregularity in the surface.

'That's tiny!'

'And just look at that gap under the window frame!' He shook his head disapprovingly. 'You could drive a truck through that.'

She looked. Oh bugger, he was right. It had seemed all right at the time, but now she looked at it more closely it was huge. Then she saw the corners of Aidan's mouth twitch. 'You're having me on!'

He roared with laughter. 'Had you going there, didn't I?' She lobbed the empty bucket at him, but he ducked and it bounced off the wall. 'Hey, careful – you'll dent it!'

'You rotten bastard.' She smoothed over the slight mark on the wall. 'I slogged my guts out over this plastering.'

He nodded. 'I know you did. And you've made a good job of it.'

This time, she could tell he wasn't joking. 'You really think so?'

He clapped a hand on her shoulder. 'You remember that bet

we had? Well I was a prat. I knew first time I set eyes on you you could do any damn thing you wanted.' He thrust a hand into his pocket and slapped fifty quid into her palm. 'There you go.'

'What's this?'

'Winnings.'

She gazed around the empty room. 'But the cottage is nowhere near finished!'

'Oh yes it is. Look at it, Claire. All the important things have been done – the roof, the walls, the electrics, all the bits you needed help to do. It's all interior design and stuff from now on. Your arty mate Lorna can help you with that.'

'You mean . . . ?'

'I mean, from here on in you don't need me any more. Do you?'

She opened her mouth to protest, but no; he was right. No more trading insults with Aidan as she lay on the bathroom floor with her arm stuck round the U-bend. No more weekends spent hanging off a chimney stack while he yelled instructions from the yard. No more trips to A&E because she'd stuck her finger to her nose with superglue.

At the sudden realisation, something in her heart quietly died. 'No,' she said softly. 'I suppose not.'

There was a significantly long silence. Then Aidan lowered himself, very carefully, on to the floor next to her, accompanied by a series of loud crackles. 'Ouch.'

'Back playing you up again?'

'I think I'm getting old. Claire . . . '

He edged a little closer. Brucie promptly waddled over, lay down in the gap between them and laid his head in Claire's lap.

'Hmm?' murmured Claire, scratching Brucie's ear as she gazed through the putty-smeared window at the dusk sky.

Aidan tried to ignore the triumphant smirk on Brucie's face as he tried – and failed – to sneak an arm round Claire's shoulders. 'I've been thinking. With all the projects I've got on the go, and my dodgy back, I really ought to take on an assistant.'

'Sounds like a sensible idea.'

'Glad you think so.' He attempted to shuffle a bit closer, but Brucie raised his snout and gave him the evil eye. 'How would you fancy working for me?'

Claire's head jerked round. 'I'm sorry, I thought you just said: how would I like to work for you.'

'I did. How'd you fancy it?'

'*Me?*'

'You did say you were looking for something different. You'd have a chance to learn the trade, get qualifications if you wanted them. And we could negotiate a share of the profits—'

Claire put up a hand, halting him in mid-flow. 'Just hold it right there. You're offering me a job? As a builder?'

'A builder's apprentice anyhow.'

'Aidan, a few months ago you told me I was an incompetent girlie who couldn't change a tap washer.'

He shrugged unconcernedly. 'You were. But you're not now.'

She laughed her socks off. 'So the great Aidan Ross is actually telling me I'm *competent*?'

Aidan pursed his lips. 'Well, your plumbing's a bit ropey, and I wouldn't let you loose on my wiring . . . but your plastering. Mwah!' He kissed the tips of his fingers. '*Magnifique!*'

Claire scratched under Brucie's chin; the pig's mouth lolled open, emitting a foul reek of stale Brussels sprouts. 'Aidan,' she said. 'Why do you want to take me on?'

'I just told you. I need an assistant.'

'Gloucestershire is teeming with sixteen year-old would-be apprentices. Why me?'

He took a deep breath. 'All right,' he admitted. 'I need an excuse.'

'An excuse? To do what?'

'To go on seeing you.'

Chapter 30

Geoffrey stormed in from the five-acre field like a man with murder on his mind.

'You sorted out that drainage ditch then?' Emmy poured boiling water on to a Pot Noodle and gave it a vigorous stir. 'You get them muddy boots out of my kitchen,' she added, dropping the spoon back into the tin of cat food. ''T'ain't hygienic.'

'Never mind the damn drainage, woman,' snarled Geoffrey, slinging himself on to the nearest chair and hurling a mire-encrusted boot across the room. 'I've just seen *her*.'

Emmy plonked the Pot Noodles down in front of him. 'Who – Veronica?'

'Not her. *Her*. The girl.'

'Oh, Cousin Claire.'

'Cousin my arse. Cousins don't steal your inheritance. There she is, bold as brass, unloadin' trestle tables with that fancy-pants Aidan Ross. And you know what that means.'

Emmy cut herself a slice of homemade fruit cake and sat down at the table. 'No,' she said, with less than fierce enthusiasm. 'But I expect you're goin' to tell me.'

'It means she's finished the plasterin'! She's done all the structural work, and now it's all frills an' fripperies.' He thumped his wind-reddened fist against the authentic reproduction antique pine table, and a bottle of Cooper's Patent

Calf Drench fell over. 'Soon the whole place'll be finished, and *she'll* be moving in!'

Emmy picked a sliced almond out of her cake, realised it was a toenail clipping and laid it carefully in her saucer. 'Still,' she said philosophically, 'you've got to hand it to the girl, she's made that tatty old cottage look real nice.'

'Nice!' Worms of chicken-flavoured noodle hung, wriggling, from the corners of Geoffrey's mouth. 'She's movin' in and taking what's rightfully mine, and all you can say is, it looks *nice*? How am I going to get my hands on my inheritance with her livin' there?'

Emmy shrugged. 'Just let it lie, that's what I say.'

'How can I?' Geoffrey stabbed his fork into the slimy, steaming mass. 'What about the letter? What about that, eh?'

'She were half doolally when she wrote that letter,' retorted Emmy.

That lit Geoffrey's fuse good and proper. 'I won't have you talkin' about my poor dead mother like that!'

'What, the way everybody in the village talked about her? The woman who knitted balaclava helmets for chickens? Face it, Geoffrey, she were just plain barmy.'

He chewed venomously. '"When you read this,"' he intoned, as though reciting from Holy Scripture, '"I'll be six foot under and so will Mary Willenhall. So you'll know the gospel truth of it. In that cottage is all that's owing to you. Don't think bad of me, son, I were the best mother I could have been."' 'There, you see? *In that cottage.*'

'Like I said.' Emmy's teeth made contact with something gritty; she washed it down with a mouthful of PG Tips. 'Doolally.'

Geoffrey got up from the table and started pacing the kitchen, his fat little body radiating frustration. 'In the cottage, in the cottage.'

'Yes Geoffrey, you said.'

'But *where* in the cottage? And what is it? Money? Jewellery? Deeds?'

'If it's in the cottage,' pointed out Emmy, 'the girl's probably found it already. She's turned that place upside down.'

Geoffrey's troubled countenance turned thunderous. 'She can't have, I'd have heard. No.' He gripped the edge of the sink. 'It's still there for the taking, I know it is. But if I don't do somethin' about it quick, it's going to be too late.'

'Claire?' Aidan waved a hand in front of her face. 'Claire, say something. Even if it's only "piss off".'

She swallowed hard. Brucie got up, shook himself and backed off several paces.

'Me? And you?'

'Why not? You do like me, don't you?'

'Er . . .' She was too shocked to come up with a coherent answer.

Aidan's confident smile took a denting. 'Ah. You *don't* like me. Knew I should've kept my big mouth shut.'

She laughed at his embarrassment. 'Oh Aidan.'

'It's OK, let's just forget I ever said any of that, shall we?'

'Aidan, come *here*!'

'Why?'

'Because.'

He turned towards her and she made her move, so forcefully that the two of them toppled backwards in a heap. Kneeling over him, she pressed her lips against his, and was pleased to find that kissing him was every bit as nice as she'd thought it would be. OK, so he tasted of plaster, but it was still worth waiting for.

Somewhere at the back of her mind she could hear her own voice, telling Lorna that never, never, never in a million years would she fancy an arrogant, sarcastic pig like Aidan Ross; a man who liked to parade round the village with a selection of painted bimbos. A man who'd practically laughed in her face when she said she was going to renovate Paradise Cottage.

Ah well, to hell with it.

When she pulled away, she noticed he was gasping. 'Took

your breath away did I?' she giggled.

Aidan smiled weakly. 'Oh God, this is becoming a habit. I think I've done my back in again.'

'Pain is instructional, Mr Ross,' scolded Dr Milner, taking off his shoes and socks. 'It tells us when we've been stupid.'

Aidan gritted his teeth and moaned into the hearthrug as the doctor started jiggling his vertebrae back into place. Claire hovered in the background, not sure what to do but reluctant to leave. It felt like there was unfinished business between her and Aidan.

He moved his head to one side and squinted up at her with one slightly distorted eye. 'Claire? Are you still there?'

She came forward and crouched down. 'I'm here.'

'Sorry I wimped out like that.'

'It's not your fault you've got a dodgy back.' She suppressed a smile at the sight of him lying there, shirt up round his armpits and his nose squashed sideways.

'Go on, mock the afflicted.'

'Sorry.'

'Anyhow, you can see I was right, can't you? I *do* need an assistant.'

'Maybe,' she conceded.

'Claire, I know it's early days between us,' he said, reaching out for her hand. 'But I really think it's going to work.'

Dr Milner went on bone-crunching. Claire felt her cheeks burn. The geriatric GP might be weird, but there was nothing wrong with his hearing. 'Aidan, can we talk about this some-where . . . you know . . . more private?'

But Aidan was on a high. 'This house – what do you reckon to it?'

Claire gazed about her. Gorgeous high ceilings, sumptuous bay windows, classically elegant proportions. What was there not to like about the Old Rectory? 'It's stunning,' she said.

'Oh good. I'm glad you like it.'

'Now hold still, this may hurt just a tad.' Dr Milner dug his big toe into Aidan's sacrum and the patient howled like a rabid coyote. 'Good, excellent, I thought that was the seat of the trouble.'

Aidan let out a tortured gurgle. 'Claire ... like I said, it's early days, but we've been working together for ages and I really feel I know you.' His squashed face manoeuvred itself into a rather grotesque smile. 'I know I don't always show it, but I really like you, you know.'

The embarrassment factor was sky-high and climbing. 'Aidan, please.'

'And like my mother's always saying this house is way too big for one. It's a family house. So I was thinking: how about it?'

'How about what?'

'Moving in with me.'

She stood up and stepped back. It was an instinctive, reflexive thing. 'Aidan, we haven't even been out on a date yet!'

'Turn over,' commanded the doctor; and Aidan flopped on to his back like an arthritic sealion. 'Right, brace yourself young man. We're going to do a bit of stretching now.'

'Oh no,' groaned Aidan. 'Not that. Not ... owww!'

'Lie still and do as you're told. Or it's six weeks on your back in the orthopaedic ward.'

'Claire,' Aidan panted as his right arm twanged back into its socket, 'I know we've not been seeing each other for long ...'

'We haven't been seeing each other at all!' Claire reminded him, increasingly uncomfortable with the scope of Aidan's assumptions. 'Besides, aren't you forgetting something?'

'What?'

'You're married!'

'No I'm not.' he objected. 'Well, not really.'

An hour ago, she'd been on cloud nine. Now Claire was starting to lose patience. 'How can somebody be "not really" married? Either you are or you aren't. So which is it?'

'All right, I am, but—'

'Look Aidan, there's something you should know. I don't make a habit of going out with married men.'

By now, Dr Milner was walking up and down Aidan's left arm. 'Relax, man!'

Aidan yelped. 'But ... ow, you sadist ... but I'm getting *divorced*.'

'Hmm, yes, well, that's what they all say.'

'I am! Uncontested, five years' separation. I haven't seen her in ages. Ask Nev if you don't believe me.'

All of a sudden, it didn't really matter any more. Claire felt curiously detached. Here she was, standing in a room with a wizened old fakir of a doctor, and a man who seemed to think one impetuous snog was a prelude to waltzing her up the aisle and straight down the maternity hospital for one of each. And all that before he'd even bothered to unhitch himself from his current wife. The future rose up before her, grinning sadistically. Complications, she thought to herself. Ex-wives, tangled relationships, excess baggage. Mum and Dad. Me and Aidan. I'm not sure I want any of this.

'I think I'd better go,' she said, picking up her handbag from the satinwood library table.

'But Claire ...' He tried to sit up, but was thrown back on to the carpet by a hefty jerk to the pelvis. 'Claire, if there's something wrong we can ... aaah! ... talk about it.'

She headed for the door. 'Some other time.'

'Frankly Mr Ross,' commented Dr Milner when the door had closed behind her, 'I think you could have handled that better.'

'My friend Lara says this is a great place to shop,' enthused Ros as the people carrier pulled into the car park at the outlet village. 'She got a variable-speed hammer drill for under thirty quid.'

'Never mind hammer drills, I'm heading straight for the designer gear.' Jacqui rubbed her nicely-manicured hands together. The youngest of Claire's evening class crowd, her idea of DIY was making tea while her boyfriend put together a flat-pack wardrobe.

Shona, the course instructor, leaned across and gave Veronica

377

a friendly nudge. 'How about you, Mrs S?'

Veronica yawned and rubbed her eyes. 'Sorry? Did you say something?'

'I was just wondering what you're after buying. Ros says there's some great bargains.'

'Me? Oh, nothing.'

Claire glanced at her mother in the rearview mirror. Window shopping was one of Veronica's favourite occupations; yet she had been unnaturally quiet all the way from Lilcombe Magna. For weeks now she'd been wittering on about window treatments and paint effects, and now, when they were actually here to get some ideas and Claire was worried sick she'd try to take things over, Veronica's mind seemed to have drifted miles away.

'You lot all right back there?' called out Claire.

'Just let me at those Jasper Conran originals,' sang back Jacqui.

'I thought you were all here to help me choose things for the house,' Claire remarked, painstakingly reversing the massive car into the only empty space she could find. It was good of Mattie to lend it to her, but it was brand new and she was terrified of returning it covered in dents.

'Well *I* am, anyway.' Lorna scooped her duffel bag from under the seat. 'Look. I've got *Practical Feng Shui*, a compass, some astrological colour charts . . .'

'Come on,' said Ros, dragging her out of the car. 'And leave that rubbish behind.'

They walked across the massive car park to the huddle of disused railway sheds which had been transformed into a massive discount shopping complex.

'So what's your colour scheme going to be?' asked Jacqui.

'Well, I was thinking maybe blue and . . . Jacqui?'

Jacqui's eye had been caught by a window display of Karen Millen separates. 'Oooh, look at those. Tell you what, you lot go on, I'll just nip in and see if they do the pink one in a twelve.'

She vanished into the shop. One down, thought Claire. Still, she wasn't entirely sure why she'd asked Jacqui along in the first place, since a weakness for pink Lurex clam-diggers did not necessarily translate into a talent for choosing nice furnishing fabrics.

'You can't go too deep if you have blue,' cut in Shona. 'It won't work with the stonework, you need something softer.'

'You want to choose good-quality paint,' added Ros. 'The cheap stuff flakes off in no time. And don't forget, you have to leave the plaster to dry out before you paper it.'

'Yes, yes, I know.'

'Are you going to sand down the floorboards, or get a carpet?' asked Shona.

'If that pig's going to be hanging around,' counselled Lorna, 'you'd be better off with a tarpaulin and wellies.'

Claire half expected Veronica to chime in with some comment about pigs and their disgusting lavatorial habits, but she just kept on walking, head down, scarcely looking in the shop windows.

They lost Ros in a shop that sold nothing but lawnmowers. Veronica held on gamely till the third home furnishings store, but Claire could tell her heart wasn't in it. She vanished without trace after a man tried to interest her in a range of foam rubber stencils.

By two o'clock Claire, Lorna and Shona had found their way to the luxury wallcoverings section of HomeGiant.

'Ugh,' said Claire, running her hand over a sheet of anaglypta. 'East Cheam, circa 1961.'

'They're all pretty horrible if you ask me,' mused Lorna. 'Mind you, nobody uses wallpaper any more, do they?'

'Don't they?'

'Only grannies and people with no taste.'

'Can't say I'm surprised, if this is the best you can get.' Claire eyed up the range on offer. Luxury was not the first word that sprang to mind. 'If it's not moons and stars, it's stripes.'

'Or big pink roses.' Lorna pointed to a particularly nauseating design that reminded Claire of a boarding house she'd once stayed in in Belgium.

'Or giant zigzags,' added Ros.

'Ah well, it's the *Zeitgeist*, isn't it?' sighed Shona, with a flick of her bobbed brown hair.

'If you say so,' said Claire dubiously, not entirely sure what Shona was getting at.

'What I mean is, it's all so extreme, so ... end-of-the-Millennium. There's no middle ground any more, and there's *definitely* nothing new.'

'Postmodern,' said Lorna.

'Exactly.' Shona leafed through a book of samples. 'Even the pop music's recycled.'

'All the old bands re-forming,' agreed Lorna.

'Yes, what's that one?' Shona tapped her forehead as though she expected the answer to come flying out of her nose. 'Lead singer thinks he's a wizard or something. They're doing a big open-air concert on New Year's Eve.'

'Facade?' ventured Claire, with half a smile.

'That's right, Facade. Absolute rubbish. Why anybody'd pay fifty quid to sit in a wet field listening to that lot is completely beyond me.'

It wasn't like Veronica to duck out of a shopping expedition. Nor was it like her not to give advice, whether you wanted it or not. And it definitely wasn't like her to be first into the food court.

Claire found her sitting alone at a table by the big plate glass window, overlooking the windblown car park where children swarmed over a defunct steam engine, its wheels embedded in concrete. A cup of coffee sat in front of her, untouched. One single, solitary carrier bag lay crumpled on the table.

'Bought yourself something nice?' asked Claire.

Veronica looked up. 'Just a pair of tights.' She stuck her leg out. 'I laddered these.'

In the cruel autumn light from the north-facing window, Claire noticed how much her mother's gingerbread tan had faded. She was almost a normal colour now; even her lipstick had been toned down several degrees, to a subtle beigey-pink. She'd always seemed quite youthful to Claire; but maybe that was because she'd always been smiling. Now her face looked much older.

Claire sat down. 'Where did you get to? We missed you.'

Veronica smiled but did not look up. She pushed a couple of ten-pence pieces around the table-top. 'Did you? That's hard to believe.'

'Veronica, is something the matter?'

'No.'

'You don't seem your usual self.'

'I told you, it's nothing. I'm just a bit tired.'

'But you're never tired,' protested Claire, more certain than ever that something was seriously wrong.

'Aren't I? How the hell would you know?' The sudden burst of annoyance faded from Veronica's voice. 'I've been meaning to tell you, sweetheart,' she said. 'About me and Ronnie. I should've told you ages ago really. We're getting a divorce.'

'Ah,' said Claire, hardly bowled over by the revelation. 'I did wonder ... I mean, with you and Neville ... Is that why you're sad?'

'Sad?' Veronica laughed grimly. 'Darling, how could anyone be sad about a man who wears nylon Y-fronts?' She sniffed, but not with disdain. 'I tried to phone Peter just now,' she said quietly.

'And he wasn't in?'

'Oh, he was in all right. He just wouldn't speak to me.' Veronica raised her eyes and Claire saw that they were bright with unshed tears. 'He won't speak to me, Claire, my own son won't speak to me. I try and I try and I just get nowhere.' She seized Claire's hand. 'Tell me honestly, I want to know. Was I really such a bad mother?'

Claire hesitated. She wasn't a vindictive person. But if her mother wanted the truth, she would have it. 'Not really,' she said slowly. 'Not until you left.'

She saw the pain spread across Veronica's face, and felt a surge of remorse, mixed with just a tinge of satisfaction. I'm not so very different from you, Pete, thought Claire. She hurt us and you want to hurt her back, I can understand that.

'I know I caused you a lot of pain Claire, you and Peter and Daddy,' stammered Veronica. 'But all I'm asking for is some kind of relationship with my son. Is that so wrong?'

'He's still hurting, Mum. We both are. You can't wipe out half a lifetime's hurt with a bit of polite conversation.'

'No. No, you're right.'

'If you're ever going to get close to Pete, you're going to have to make him believe you're really sorry. And make him understand that he has to grow up.'

Veronica nodded. She took out a tissue and blew her nose. 'Thanks.'

'For what?'

'For helping me to make up my mind. Claire, you know I promised I'd be here to help you with decorating the cottage?'

Here we go again, thought Claire. Empty promises. 'Yes. Why?'

'I'm sorry, but I won't be. Neville knows somebody with a little place in Derbyshire, I'm going to stay there for a while. Maybe if I'm closer to Pete, maybe if I try really hard, he'll start believing . . . ' She dabbed her eyes, stuffed the tissue into her handbag and drew herself up, straight-backed and determined. 'And if it doesn't work out, then at least I'll have tried.'

Owen Pendle was not particularly surprised to see Veronica. After all, she had been besieging his office with visits and telephone calls every week since she arrived back in England. The subject was always the same: Mary Willenhall's bequest.

'Hi Veronica, take a seat.' He indicated a chair. 'I'm afraid I can only spare you a few minutes.'

'That's OK, this won't take long. It's about the inheritance.'

'I thought it might be.' Pendle extracted the Willenhall probate file from the teetering pile marked 'pending'. It was starting to look depressingly well thumbed. 'So – you've come to tell me you've fulfilled the conditions of the bequest?'

'Well, no,' admitted Veronica. 'Things are a lot better with my daughter, but Peter still won't have anything to do with me.'

The solicitor promptly tied up the folder and slung it back on the pile. 'In that case I'm afraid we're both wasting each other's time. You know I can't release the bequest until you've satisfied me that you've achieved a full reconciliation with both Claire and Peter.'

'Yes, yes, I know all that,' interjected Veronica impatiently. 'I came to tell you I'm going up to Derby for a while, to be near Peter. This is my temporary address.' She took out a slip of paper and handed it to Pendle. 'I *will* do this, you know,' she added. 'I'm not giving up.'

'Oh, I don't doubt it,' he replied with a smile.

'No, you've got me wrong, Owen. I'm not doing this for the money, not any more. That's the other thing I came to sort out. When things are right again, and it's mine, I want it to go to my kids.'

Pendle could not have been more stunned if a singing giraffe had just can-canned across the parquet. 'You want Mary's seaside villa to go to Claire and Peter? Are you absolutely sure about that?'

She nodded. 'They deserve it Owen, I don't.' Picking up her bag, she headed for the door.

'But what about you, Veronica?' objected Owen. 'Surely you need it for yourself?'

'Oh, don't you worry about me.' There was a twinkle in her eye as she delivered her parting shot. 'The world's full of wealthy men, and there's life in the old girl yet.'

Owen gazed after her as her heels clip-clopped away down the stairs. 'Mary Willenhall, you sly old bird,' he murmured. 'I bet this was what you wanted all along.'

383

Chapter 31

'*Et voilà*!' With reckless abandon, Lorna swished magenta emulsion across the living-room wall, spraying droplets in all directions. 'What do you reckon to that?'

'I reckon the pig looked better without the polka dots.' Claire pointed to Brucie, who had had the misfortune to stroll into the room at exactly the wrong moment and now looked as if he had a nasty dose of acne. 'Come here boy, let's get that paint wiped off your nose.'

Brucie submitted placidly to Claire's damp rag, but Lorna was impatient. 'Never mind beautifying the pig, what about the *colours*?'

Claire stood back to consider the twelve different shades of pink they had tried out on the bare wall. 'Well you can forget that one,' she said, indicating something the colour of fairground candyfloss. 'And that one, it reminds me of Barbara Cartland's poodle.'

Lorna looked put out. 'That's my favourite.'

'Which just goes to show what a sad individual you are.' Claire cocked her head on one side. 'Maybe the peachy one, I quite like that.'

'I had a bedspread that colour when I was in hospital,' reminisced Lorna. 'There was this really big stain . . .'

'All right, all right, maybe not the peachy one. How about,' Claire eeny-meeny-miny-moed and pointed her brush at a muted terracotta, 'that one?'

'Ugh. Vomit orange.'

'The one next to it?'

'Uh-oh.'

'What's wrong with it?'

'You might as well paint your walls with taramosalata.'

They tried out another couple of colours on the wall. 'If I don't find the right one soon, I'll have to go back and try all the blues,' sighed Claire. 'And you know what Shona said about blue.'

'What you need is an unbiased opinion,' declared Lorna, helping herself to a sandwich from the plastic box on the windowsill. 'Why don't you ask Aidan?'

Claire prised the lid off a tester pot of Mellow Puce. 'No thanks.'

Lorna's sandwich vanished into her mouth like waste into an industrial shredder. 'You're not *still* angry with him are you?'

'I'm not angry.'

'So why have you been avoiding him all week?'

Claire winced. It was a fair cop. 'I haven't.'

'Liar, liar, your bum's on fire.'

A stripe of Mellow Puce appeared on the wall. 'Don't be so juvenile.'

'Me, juvenile! Hark who's talking. It's no good pretending Claire, I know bad acting when I see it.' Claire didn't answer. 'He really is getting a divorce you know, I asked Neville.'

She swung round. 'You did what!'

'Well somebody's got to save you from dying a lonely spinster.'

In the circumstances, Claire decided, the only possible option was to ignore Lorna's constant nagging. 'What do you think of this?' She dabbed on a blob of Rambling Rose. 'I think it's rather nice, don't you?'

'*I* think you should go and make it up with Aidan.'

'Will you shut up about Aidan! And since when were you an expert on relationships anyway?' She dropped her brush into the bucket of cold water, determined not to take any advice from

385

Lorna. This was, after all, the girl who had once unwittingly gone out with an armed robber for three months. 'Shouldn't you be somewhere else?'

'Like where?'

'Like at home. Writing.'

Lorna pouted. 'Oh I see, trying to get rid of me, are you?'

'Of course I'm not! But you've got a deadline to meet, remember? And all those kiddies in the children's ward won't be very happy if there's no play for them to watch on Boxing Day.'

'There will be.' Lorna's chin jutted. 'It's just not easy, OK? Trying to be creative in a madhouse.'

Claire took a sandwich and sat down cross-legged on the floor. 'Kieran's no better then? Still turning the place upside down?'

'It's like one of those package holidays where you get there and the hotel's not finished. Only worse, because you can't get the next plane home.'

'Can't you put your foot down? Tell him you want more of a say?'

'Telling him's one thing, actually getting him to listen is another.' Lorna groaned. 'And then there's the tenants.'

'I thought you liked them!'

'I do. But Kieran's hardly there most of the time, so all day long it's "Lorna, Kieran's had my floorboards up again," "Lorna, my radiator's not working," "Lorna I've got bedbugs, what are you going to do about it?" Is it any wonder I can't write?'

'Oh I dunno, sounds like great material to me.'

'For Jimmy McGovern maybe, not for a kids' musical!'

Claire lay back on the bare boards and surveyed the patchwork of colour on the wall in front of her. Maybe she was on completely the wrong track and yellow would be better. 'So what you're saying is, you need a bit of peace and quiet?'

'Correction, a *lot*. I've tried working down the reference library, but I keep being chatted up by old men.'

'Hmm,' mused Claire. 'What about here?'

Lorna stopped in mid-munch. 'What about it?'

'It's quiet here. And it'll be fit to live in in a week or two. I know Ted and Brucie are moving back in then, but—'

'Hang on a minute.' Lorna stopped her. 'Why don't *I* move in here?'

'That's what I said. It's not that crazy an idea is it? I mean, you're not actually allergic to pigs or anything. And Ted needs somebody to keep an eye on him.'

'Crazy?' Lorna's face lit up. 'It'd be wonderful! You really mean it? I could move in here until I've finished the play?'

'For as long as you like.' Claire got up and wiped her hands on her trousers. 'Bring Worm too if you want.'

Worm. A sly smile crept across Lorna's face and she engulfed her best mate in a paint-spattered hug. 'Claire Snow,' she declared, dancing her round the room in a frantic polka, 'you are a *genius*.'

It was getting late, and Paradise Cottage lay swathed in darkness as Geoffrey trudged across the garden towards the light burning in the workshop. He'd waited a long time for this, too damn long; and he wasn't prepared to wait any longer.

The old man took an eternity to come to the door; when he did, he barely opened it two inches. 'What you want?'

'Just a word Ted,' wheedled Geoffrey, for the moment on his best behaviour.

'What about?'

'Let's talk about this inside, eh?'

'Why?'

'Come on Ted, I don't mean you no harm. It's chilly out here.'

Reluctantly Ted stood aside and Geoffrey stepped into the warmth. As ever, the television set was blaring out and Brucie was lying on the rug in front of it, apparently absorbed in *The X Files*.

'What's this about then?'

Geoffrey closed the door behind him with a soft click. The pig looked up, gave him a hard stare, then went back to watching Gillian Anderson. 'I want what's mine, Ted.'

'Well there's nothing of yours here, so you might as well go back home.'

'Oh yes there is.' Ted stood his ground as Geoffrey advanced a couple of steps. '"In the cottage", that's what the letter said.'

'What letter? What you on about?'

'What letter do you think?' The farmer strove to conceal his impatience. 'The letter what my ma's solicitor sent me after old Mary died. "You'll find it in the cottage," she said. "Everything that's owing to you." Well that's what I've come for, Ted. My due.'

'I told you Geoffrey, I don't know 'bout no letter, an' there's nothin' of yours here. Why don't you just leave me alone?'

Maybe it was because Ted was such a bad liar, or because Geoffrey was such a good one; but Geoffrey spotted straight away that the old man wasn't levelling with him.

'It's in here, isn't it?'

'No!' Ted backed away, and would have collapsed into his armchair if Geoffrey hadn't seized him by the shoulders and hauled him back to his feet.

'It's here, I can see it written all over your face. You found it, didn't you? You sly old beggar. You found it an' you thought, why don't I keep it for myself?'

'You're mad, you. You don't know what you're sayin'.'

Brucie was on his feet, long yellow teeth bared, but Geoffrey was too carried away by his own flash of inspiration to notice. 'I want it Ted, it's rightfully mine.'

'I ain't got it.'

Geoffrey shook the old man like a terrier shaking a rat. 'I said *give it to me!*'

It was too much for Brucie. With a high-pitched squeal of fury he launched himself at the hated man who was attacking his beloved master. Head down, a full hundred and eighty pounds of prime pork thudded into Geoffrey's legs, knocking him sideways and forcing him to let go of Ted. The farmer would probably have fallen full-length on Ted's blue carpet if he hadn't reached out and clutched at the table, sending a plate of bread and cheese crashing to the floor.

It was pure luck that his other hand happened to land on the shaft of Ted's coal shovel.

'Brucie!' roared Ted, hurling himself forward as Geoffrey swung the shovel back behind his head. But he was too late.

The pig didn't stand a chance.

'You know something,' mused Neville, 'it's really quiet without Veronica around the place. And the customers miss her.'

It was funny how Veronica had stamped her personality on the Saxon Cross in such a short space of time. OK, so she served over-generous measures and tended to flirt with any man under seventy who still had his own teeth, but she had the makings of a fine pub landlady.

'Old John certainly misses her,' agreed Aidan, acknowledging the familiar blue-overalled figure at the other end of the bar. 'She used to give him free drinks.' He drained the last drop from his own pint. 'When's she coming back?'

'Dunno,' replied Neville wistfully. 'Maybe when she's sorted things out with her son, however long that takes.' He picked up Aidan's empty glass. 'Another one in there?'

'Go on then. I'm not driving.' He hauled himself up on to a bar stool and scooped a handful of peanuts out of the dish on the counter. 'How many different traces of urine did that survey find on pub peanuts? Twenty-four wasn't it?' He chewed morosely. 'Oh well, I suppose it adds to the flavour.'

Neville delivered the promised pint. 'You're not yourself tonight.'

Aidan shook his head. 'Nope.'

'Woman trouble is it?'

'What am I going to do, Nev? Claire's still avoiding me.'

Neville helped himself to a small brandy. 'Is that any wonder? You did make a prat of yourself,' he reminded Aidan, none too gently.

'Tell me about it.' Aidan folded his arms on the bar top and rested his chin on them. 'Women. Why can't I get the hang of women?'

'They're a mystery, that's why,' Neville grunted. 'Mind you, if anyone can you should, you've had enough practice.'

'I don't want practice, I want . . . ' Aidan lowered his voice as the entire public bar tuned in to his lament. 'I want Claire. What should I do, Nev? I tried ringing her but she didn't return my call.'

'Don't ask me.' Neville loosened his tie and unbuttoned his shirt collar. 'The only sexual healing I'm getting right now is sniffing a pair of Veronica's old knickers.'

The door to the street opened. At that moment all conversation ceased, as the regulars concentrated on staring at the new arrival, a very young, very sweaty man with teeth so huge and regular they could have doubled as fridge doors.

'I'm sorry to butt in,' he panted, 'but I'm hopelessly lost. This *is* Lilcombe isn't it?'

'Lilcombe Magna,' said Old John. 'You want Regis, you have to turn back at the fork an' head off up the hill.'

'Magna, yes, yes, that's it. Lilcombe Magna. I don't suppose any of you happen to know where Paradise Cottage is, do you?'

'Why?' enquired Aidan, curious.

'I'm a locum vet, there's been some kind of serious accident.'

Aidan banged down his glass. 'Come on Mr . . . '

'Digby, Joe Digby.'

'Come on then Joe, I'll take you there myself.'

'Please Mr Merriman,' urged the vet. 'If you could just let go of the pig for a moment, so I can examine him.'

Ted was on his knees on the workshop floor, tears pouring silently down his cheeks, cradling Brucie's head in his lap. The pig lay very still, a trickle of dried blood running down one bristly cheek.

'Brucie! Brucie boy, wake up.'

'Mr Merriman, please.'

'You did the right thing Ted, phoning the vet.' Aidan eased

Ted away from the pig. 'Now let go, let the man do his job. Have you called the police yet?'

A look of absolute horror jolted Ted out of his shock. 'No police.'

Aidan reached into his pocket for his mobile. 'Don't be silly Ted. Whoever did this to Brucie—'

Ted knocked the phone out of Aidan's hand. 'I said no police, don't you listen to nothin' I say?'

Aidan bent down and retrieved the phone from the coal scuttle. 'I don't understand.'

'Just leave me be. Make my Brucie better an' leave me be.'

The vet touched Aidan on the arm and drew him aside. 'I'm going to have to admit the pig for X-rays. Is the old chap going to be all right here on his own?'

No way, thought Aidan. He took out his phone and dialled up Brockbourne Hall. Maybe Claire could talk some sense into Ted.

Chapter 32

'Please Ted,' coaxed Claire, nudging a mug of hot, sweet tea towards the old man. 'It'll do you good.'

Ted sat huddled in his armchair, arms hugging his own shoulders, rocking gently back and forth. 'Brucie,' he murmured. 'My Brucie . . . '

Aidan patted him on the knee. 'He's in the best place Ted, the vet's only taken him to the surgery to do a few X-rays, just to be on the safe side. He's sure it's only concussion.'

'I'll take you there in the morning,' promised Claire. 'Come on, have some of that tea.'

With great reluctance, Ted took a sip. 'That Geoffrey,' he said flatly. 'That Geoffrey, how could he turn out so bad?'

'Geoffrey!' exclaimed Claire. 'He did this?'

'Ted, you have to let us call the police,' urged Aidan. 'You can't let him get away with this.'

'No!' snapped Ted, with sudden energy.

Claire shushed Aidan. 'It's all right Ted, you don't have to do anything you don't want to.' The old man looked fractionally reassured. 'But can't you tell us what this is all about?'

'Are you afraid of Geoffrey?' asked Aidan. 'Is that it?'

At this, Ted looked extremely put out. 'I've never been afraid of no man in my life!'

'Then why, Ted?' Claire squeezed his hand. It felt frail and cold, barely more than skin and bone. 'You can trust us, you do see that don't you? We only want to help.'

Ted's watery eyes moved from Claire to Aidan and back again. 'You ever loved anythin' in your life?'

Aidan looked at Claire. 'Yes.'

'I loved her, you know. My Mary. Never loved no other woman, an' she loved me too, though it weren't right she should.'

'Not right?' puzzled Claire. 'Why wasn't it right?'

'She were a married woman. An' things were different in them days, folks talked a lot about duty an' such like. You got a husband with no legs and half his brain blown away, you don't go fallin' in love with no farmhand, like you was some slip of a girl. You stays home an' you does your duty.'

'I don't understand,' said Aidan. 'Has this got something to do with Geoffrey?'

'Everything.' Ted got up from his chair, crossed the room to the cooker and opened the oven door. Inside sat the black cashbox. 'This is what he come lookin' for. His inheritance, he calls it. His mother told him there was somethin' of his hidden somewhere in Paradise Cottage.'

'So that's why he was so keen to buy it!' exclaimed Claire. 'It wasn't just for the land.'

Aidan peered at the box. 'So what's in there?'

Ted shook his head. 'Not what he thinks.' He carried it back, put it on the table and unlocked the lid. Inside lay a pile of old photographs. 'That were her husband,' he said, handing Claire a faded print. 'Mary's Rodney.'

A tall, dark-haired man in tennis whites smiled out from a sepia-tinted landscape. 'He's very good-looking.'

'That he were. Not so pretty after the Jerries blew him up at Arnhem though. Couldn't hardly remember his own name. She needed a lot of help lookin' after him, that's where I came in, see. Only ...' Claire saw that his eyes were filling with tears again. 'Only Mary were a lovely woman, in the prime of her life, she still had ... feelings.' He handed over a sheaf of photographs. 'That's her, see, when she were young? Her an' me.'

Aidan gasped. 'Claire – she really does look just like you.'

393

It was true. Claire had never quite understood the villagers' comments before, but now she saw her great-aunt as a young woman it was exactly like looking at a photograph of herself, dressed up in Forties clothes. Mary Willenhall was standing next to a young man you couldn't call handsome, but who had a friendly, open face. The man in the bath chair between them didn't have much of a face at all.

'And this is Geoffrey's inheritance?' murmured Claire. 'Why would he want a box full of old photographs?'

'He don't,' replied Ted. 'He thinks there's a load of jewels or money or some such nonsense.'

'Then why not give him the box so he'll leave you alone?'

''Cause he'd not believe it was what he was lookin' for. An' 'cause of this.' There was one more thing left in the box, a single sheet of creamy-white paper, folded in four. Ted took it out, unfolded it and spread it out on the table.

'A birth certificate?' Claire scanned the details. January 1948, in the parish of somewhere she'd never heard of, way up north. A boy, Geoffrey Eric. Mother, Mary Emilia, Father . . . Her jaw dropped open. Slowly she raised her eyes to meet Ted's. 'You and Great-Aunt Mary? You mean to say you're . . ?'

He answered her with infinite sadness. 'Yes. I'm Geoffrey Willenhall's father.'

'Rodney died in '47,' explained Ted. 'Came in one mornin' an' there he were, stone dead in his bed. An' where had I been all night? With Mary.' He shook his head. 'Nobody knew, nobody never knew. But we knew. An' then, when Mary found out she were carryin' Geoffrey . . . '

'But I thought Geoffrey's mother was Mary's sister,' protested Aidan.

'So did the whole village. Bess had been married five year an' no sign of any child. She an' Mary were close in them days, they put their heads together an' arranged that when the child were born Mary'd give it up to Bess and she'd make out it were her own.'

394

'But what about you?' asked Claire. 'It was your baby too.'

Ted hung his head. 'It were my shame. An' Mary's. That's why I went away from Lilcombe for so long. An' it broke my Mary's heart to see how Geoffrey grew up after she an' Bess fell out. Each year he got meaner an' nastier, like our shame had got inside him an' turned him bad. Towards the end she couldn't stand the sight of him.'

'And he never knew who his real parents were?'

'Never.' Ted snatched back the birth certificate. 'Nor will he, nor anybody else.'

'Whatever have you got in that box?' asked Claire for the umpteenth time, as Aidan's 4×4 bumped up the track to Low Common Farm. Behind her, on the back seat, lay an oblong wooden case about four feet long and a foot wide.

'I told you, something special.'

'What are you up to, Aidan?'

'Trying to sort things out. Look.' He turned into the yard and braked. 'Geoffrey's expecting something a bit out of the ordinary, right? Something that'll satisfy him that he's found his inheritance? Well, I think what's inside that box might just do the trick.' He jumped down and fetched the heavy box off the back seat. 'Coming?'

'Just try and stop me.'

They walked across the muddy yard, past an assembly of battered milk churns, to the back door. Usually wide open to let out the steam from Emmy's cooking, today it was very firmly locked. Aidan put down the box and hammered on the Regency-style panels.

'Geoffrey? Geoffrey, it's Aidan Ross.'

Keys turned and the door opened just wide enough to reveal Emmy Willenhall's head. Her tone was hostile, but she looked scared. 'Go away, he's not in.'

'Please Emmy,' said Claire. 'We need to talk to him, it's important.'

A voice drifted out of the kitchen. 'Who is it?'

'That Ross man an' your cousin Claire. I told them to go away.'

There was a pause.

'Let 'em in, they've got business with me. I'll have to tackle it sooner or later.'

Emmy stepped reluctantly aside and they squeezed past into the kitchen. Geoffrey was sitting at the table in his shirt sleeves, his normally ruddy face distinctly haggard and peppered with clumps of inexpertly-shaved stubble. A plate of congealing bacon and eggs lay before him, untouched save for the fork speared right through the egg yolk.

'Been expecting us, Geoffrey?' enquired Aidan coolly. 'Or did you think it was the police?'

Geoffrey swallowed and half rose from his seat. 'How is he?'

'Ted? Pretty shaken up. Brucie's got severe concussion but he's going to be OK, no thanks to you.'

'We told the vet to send you the bill,' added Claire.

Geoffrey did not argue the toss. He sank back on to his chair, rubbing his hands over his thinning scalp. 'I swear, I never meant to hurt him.'

'Save your breath, Geoffrey, that's not why we're here.' Aidan pushed aside Geoffrey's breakfast and laid the wooden box on the table. 'I understand you've been looking for this.'

The farmer's beady eyes took on a sudden glint of avarice. 'What you on about?' he demanded warily.

'Don't give me that, we know all about your little "inheritance".'

'Oh,' said Geoffrey, eyes firmly fixed on the box. 'An' you mean to say that's it?'

'We found it when we were opening up one of the old fireplaces, didn't we Claire?' He gave her a light kick on the ankle.

'What? Oh, yes. Bricked up in the grate.'

'Somebody'd obviously hidden it in there, and when Ted told us about the letter, well, we figured out this must be what you've been looking for all along.' With the utmost care, Aidan opened the box. Inside lay what looked like a bundle of oily linen.

396

'Old rags?' grunted Geoffrey, his face falling.

'Wait.' Aidan painstakingly unwrapped the folds of grubby fabric, gradually revealing a tarnished old sword, a sheet of yellowed parchment covered in indecipherable brown writing and a creased transcript, typed on flimsy paper. 'Listen.' He cleared his throat. '"To my sons, and their sons to come, I bequeath the only wealth that remains to me: my honour and this sword. For I have with right cheerful heart given up my lands and title to the Parliamentary cause, and may God bless my penitent soul and the Lord Protector of all England. In the year of our Lord sixteen hundred and fifty-one."'

'Wot?' Geoffrey wrinkled his nose.

'There's no name, but seeing as you're the eldest son I suppose this must belong to you.' Aidan picked up the sword and held it out to Geoffrey, whose knees promptly buckled under its weight.

'A sword?' He looked at it as though it had just stabbed him in the back. 'That's all my inheritance is? A poxy sword?'

'A nobleman's sword,' Aidan corrected him. 'And he must've been quite a wealthy landowner by the looks of it. Or at least he was until he gave it all up for Cromwell.' He snapped the box shut with a sly wink at Claire. 'Congratulations Geoffrey, you're a Roundhead.'

Geoffrey was less than bowled over. In fact he looked down-right disgusted. 'You're tellin' me there was nothin' else there?'

'Not a thing.'

'No jewels? Nor money, nor nothin' valuable?'

'Nothing but the sword.'

The farmer's face distorted into a suspicious scowl. 'An' I'm supposed to believe that, am I?'

'You'll have to, won't you?' Aidan leaned over the table until his face was a couple of inches from Geoffrey's. 'Or would you prefer to have a little chat with the police?'

Geoffrey's scowl deepened, but he said nothing.

'You might get a few hundred for the sword at auction,' Aidan continued. 'Mind you, I don't suppose you'd want to part with a family heirloom.' Aidan glanced at the clock above Emmy Willenhall's head. Her mouth was gaping so wide Claire half expected a cuckoo to shoot out of it. 'Hmm, ten o'clock already. We'd better make tracks.'

'I'm taking Ted to the vet's to see Brucie,' explained Claire with calculated malice. 'Don't suppose you'd like to come too?'

'He can't,' said Aidan as they headed for the door. 'He might miss his visitors.'

'What visitors?' demanded Geoffrey.

'Oh, just a couple of men from the Ministry. Something about fraudulent milk quota forms, I think.' He patted Geoffrey on the arm. 'Don't worry, I'm sure they'll explain all about it when they get here.'

'Aidan Ross,' exclaimed Claire as they drove back down the lane, 'you missed your vocation. You should've been a con man!'

Aidan winked. 'I'll take that as a compliment.'

She folded her arms across her chest. 'Where ever did you get that sword?'

He avoided her gaze. 'Does it matter?'

It does to me, thought Claire, thoroughly intrigued by his evasiveness. 'Did you buy it?'

'No.'

'So where did it come from?' She stuck her face in front of his. 'Was it a present?'

'Don't do that! I can't see where I'm driving.'

'Then tell me!'

Aidan capitulated with a sigh. 'If you really want to know, it was sort of a family thing I had in the attic.'

'A family thing! What – as in, totally irreplaceable, and your mother'll kill you if she finds out you've given it away?'

'Hardly. Anyhow, it's never really meant anything to me, it's just a worthless old sword.'

'I don't believe you,' declared Claire. 'I think that sword meant a lot to you.'

'Don't be silly.'

'And you gave it up just so you could get Geoffrey to leave Ted alone.'

He shrugged dismissively. 'Somebody had to do something, you know what Geoffrey's like. He wouldn't have stopped hassling you and Ted until he got what he thought he was looking for.'

Claire flung herself back into her seat with a little laugh. 'So now Geoffrey thinks he's a Roundhead. You do realise he'll probably join the Sealed Knot or something?'

Aidan chuckled. 'Oh I do hope so, we could all do with a good laugh.'

'You're full of shit, Mr Ross. Did you know that?'

'So I'm told.'

Suddenly, and quite without thinking, she leaned over and planted a kiss on his cheek.

'What's that for?'

'For being nicer than I thought you were.'

They were just approaching the end of the farm track when Aidan suddenly brought the car to a halt and switched off the engine. 'I think we'd better stop right here, don't you?'

'Why?'

'Because if I kiss you while I'm driving I'll probably crash into Geoffrey's muck-spreader.' He took her face between his hands and moved in for the big romantic clinch; but at the last minute she drew away. 'Something wrong?'

'Just take it easy this time, OK? Don't expect so much so soon.'

'Whatever you say.'

Then he kissed her, and she thought, oh what the hell. And kissed him back.

Chapter 33

Lorna was sitting at the breakfast bar in the brand-new fitted kitchen that Kieran had conjured up at a knockdown price. It was clean, it was modern, it was trendy, and it wasn't a patch on the old one.

'That's right,' Candy purred, tucking the telephone under her chin as she ironed her size eight winceyette pyjamas. 'I'm a forty-six double-D cup, and I'm wearing a black leather open-crotch catsuit, with zippers all over my . . .'

Lorna cast an eye over Candy's pink towelling bathrobe and shower cap, and marvelled at the power of the human imagination. 'You should be on the stage,' she commented, pouring herself another slug of Diet Sprite. 'You're wasted working on that sex line.'

Candy put her hand over the mouthpiece and gave Lorna a reproachful look. 'Shush, I've got to keep the punters on the line as long as possible, or I don't get my bonus.' Turning back to her client, she switched back to the seductive purr. 'That's right, I'm a *very* bad girl, would you like me to spank myself now?' Putting down the iron, she grabbed a wooden spoon from the drainer and started hitting the ironing board with it.

'My God,' said Alethea. 'How on earth do you put up with living in this place?'

'Oh, you don't want to worry about Candy, she's fine.' Lorna offered Alethea a biscuit. 'But if you take the room, you might

400

want to invest in some earplugs, when she fakes an orgasm it sounds like Mariah Carey being run over by a steamroller.'

'Hmm,' said Alethea, 'I can see why you're moving out. You're a writer aren't you?'

'Trying to be. But I could use some peace and quiet.'

Right on cue, Candy started accompanying each whack of the wooden spoon with an ear-piercing squeak. 'Ooh master, master! Ooh! Do it to me, big boy! Ooooooh!'

The back door swung open, almost knocking over the ironing board. 'Forty thousand bloody damns,' cursed Kieran, tramping in from the yard with a black binliner. It vanished swiftly behind his back as he caught sight of the lovely Alethea. 'Oh. Hi.' He stuck out his hand. 'Kieran Hart. And you're?'

'This is Alethea,' said Lorna. 'She was thinking about taking the room.'

Alethea got up hastily. 'But I don't think it's quite for me.'

Kieran was visibly disappointed. 'You're sure you wouldn't like me to show you round?'

'No thanks, must be going. See you Lorna.'

''Bye.' The door closed behind her. 'Nice girl,' commented Lorna.

Kieran gazed wistfully after her. 'Yeah. Very. Don't suppose you got her phone number?'

Lorna picked casually at her nail varnish. 'Alethea's an Environmental Health Officer, you know. We're meeting up for a drink tomorrow night, fancy coming?'

Kieran's face fell several storeys. 'Environmental Health? Christ, you didn't let her see the basement did you?'

Lorna smiled sweetly. 'Only trying to help you find some new tenants, darling.'

'Shit.'

'Oh, did I tell you? My producer's coming round tomorrow. His partner's a Rent Officer. By the way, what's in that bag?'

Kieran froze. 'What bag?'

'The one you're trying to hide behind your back.'

Kieran reluctantly revealed the binliner, knotted at the top

401

and dangling heavily from his fist. 'A dead rat.'

'Oh dear, another one? You'll never sell the house at this rate.' Lorna finished off her drink. 'By the way, Worm and I are moving into Paradise Cottage tomorrow.'

'What!'

'When can I have my money back?'

Les Lynch flipped a tortilla on to a plastic plate and squirted it with guacamole. 'So he's really going to pay you back then?'

'Yes!'

'When?'

'Within a month, he promised. *And* I got it in writing.' Lorna threw her arms round Les's neck and kissed his unshaven cheek. 'You were right, I called his bluff and it worked! You're a genius.'

Les looked inordinately pleased with himself. 'Yeah, well, you don't get to be Carlisle and District Hack of the Year for nothing, you know.' He gazed reflectively into his pan of bubbling chilli. 'If it hadn't been for that nastiness over the lady mayoress and the lobster thermidor, I could've been editor of the *Penrith Advertiser* by now.'

'Ah, but think of all the actors who'd have starved to death without your economy chilli, darling.' Lorna collected up a pile of empty cups and went into the kitchen, where Worm was weeping copiously. 'Something wrong?'

He hawked mucus back up his nostrils. 'I flipping hate chopping onions. You couldn't blow my nose for me, could you? There's a tissue in my pocket.'

'Worm, guess what!' She wrapped the tissue round his nose. 'OK, blow.' He did, and half a gallon of liquid snot blasted out round the edges. 'Ugh yuk, did you have to do that all over my fingers?'

'Sorry. What am I supposed to guess?'

'Kieran's paying me back *and* Claire says we can use Ted's workshop as a rehearsal studio! Isn't that great?'

'Where's Ted going?' asked Worm doubtfully, chopping away at his onions.

'He's moving back into the cottage with Brucie.' Worm's mouth opened but Lorna silenced him. 'Don't worry sweetie, they can't be any more bother than Kieran and his industrial sanding machine.' Lorna did a little dance round the kitchen, inadvertently knocking the best part of a jar of chilli powder into the salsa dip. 'It's all happening at last, Worm! We've got money, somewhere nice and quiet to live ...'

'A pig crapping in the living room.'

'It's got a big litter tray thing, you'll hardly notice. Worm, it's going to be brilliant!' Forgetting about her snotty fingers, Lorna seized him by the ears and dotted kisses all over his face. 'Oh, there is just one thing though,' she added.

'What?' spluttered Worm, unable to retaliate without covering Lorna in more onion-flavoured snot.

'Well, with Ted in the little bedroom, that means there's only one bed left for us. It's ... er ... a double,' she added slyly.

Worm did not react in quite the way she'd expected. In fact he looked positively glum. 'It's OK, don't worry,' he said, gentlemanly to the last. 'I'll kip down on the floor.'

'Worm,' groaned Lorna, 'were you born thick or do you just practise a lot?'

Les Lynch stood in the kitchen doorway and watched Lorna pour an entire bowl of economy chilli over Worm's head. He smiled. Head over heels, he thought to himself. Ah well, never mind. I can always dock the chilli out of Lorna's wages.

It was the winter solstice, 1999, and Claire's tiny flat at Brockbourne Hall was bursting at the seams. If she wondered occasionally what her mum and dad were doing, she didn't dwell on the thought. Lorna, Worm, Candy, Aidan, Pete: all the people she cared most about were here.

'Look,' said Worm, his arm round Lorna's waist, 'Facade are coming back for another encore.'

'Bunch of old hippies,' scoffed Pete. 'Got any more of that trifle?'

Music boomed out across the lawns of the Hall, almost

invisible beneath the vast tide of humanity. Lasers sliced across the night sky, blotting out the stars. TV cameras trained their lenses on the gig of the Millennium. From the window of her sitting room Claire couldn't quite make out the stage, but the giant video screens relayed massive images of a capering pixie in silver trousers, rubbing himself up against a big lump of granite.

Candy pressed her nose up against the window. 'Is he having sex with that standing stone?'

'I heard he prefers goats.'

Claire deliberately turned her back on the shenanigans and cut herself a large slice of cake. At least that way she didn't have to look at the state of Brent Lovelace. She could pretend it was 1986 again, and he was performing the live version of 'Turn Your Second Face' that had landed him in court.

'Penny for 'em.' Aidan helped himself to a bite of Claire's cake.

'Oh, just thinking.'

'About me, naturally.'

She tweaked his nose. 'Don't flatter yourself, sunbeam.'

'All right, I'll flatter you instead.' He took her hand and kissed it. 'My lady, you are the most beautiful creature in the whole of Brockbourne.'

'Except me,' cut in Lorna, with a playful toss of her black curls. 'But that's OK, I won't sue you.'

The door to the stairs opened, and Mel shoehorned her way through the chattering mob. 'Claire!' she boomed, easily drowning out Brent's guitar solo.

'Uh-oh.' Lorna nudged her friend. 'Looks like trouble.'

'Mel,' pleaded Claire, 'I'm supposed to be off duty.'

'Yeah, well, tell that to those cretins in the band! Bunch of bleedin' morons.'

Claire surrendered to the inevitable. 'Just tell me what's happened.'

'You know the bass guitarist's little boy? The one with the ears?'

I've got a feeling I know what's coming, thought Claire. 'Go on. What's he up to this time?'

'Only gone and done a bunk again. I wouldn't ask,' wheedled Mel, with unusual diplomacy, 'only nobody knows those ventilation shafts like you do. You couldn't just . . ?'

On stage, Brent Lovelace was exhorting the fans to 'Give your Love to the Mother . . . One More Time!'

'Sorry folks, duty calls.' Claire stuffed the last of the cake into Aidan's mouth and headed for the door. 'Come on, show me where you last saw the little monster.'

'Thanks Claire, I appreciate this.'

'You know Mel,' remarked Claire as they descended the stairs, 'you're going to make a great Operations Manager.'

Mel halted on the landing, puzzled. 'Me? But you're Ops Manager.'

Claire smiled and carried on walking. 'Maybe not for too much longer.'

Epilogue

SIX MONTHS LATER

A seafront villa, Weston-super-Mare

Claire stood and watched Pete prising planks off the window with a crowbar. She shook her head.

'I still can't quite believe it.'

Pete half turned, revealing the painted placard propped up against the front wall of the house. It read: SNOW & SNOW, QUALITY RESTORATIONS.

'Inheriting this old place you mean?' He surveyed the salt-damaged brickwork, the warping window frames, the air of genteel neglect that did not quite detract from the house's Victorian elegance. 'It's in pretty bad shape.'

'Not half as bad as Paradise Cottage was. And it'll be really beautiful when we've done it up.' She stroked her hand over the sun-warmed wall, feeling the rich life stored up within it, just waiting to be released. 'I keep wondering . . . why didn't Owen Pendle tell us Great Aunt Mary had another house? And why has it taken so long for it to come to us?'

Pete shrugged. 'The letter said the original beneficiary didn't want it, and we were next in line.'

'But he didn't tell you who it was?'

'Nope. He said he wasn't allowed to.' He chuckled. 'If you

ask me, they took one look at the state of the place and thought, no way!'

'Good job we like a challenge then, isn't it?' Claire spat on her hands and started throwing rubbish into the skip. 'Come on, if we get this cleared by twelve I'll buy you a bacon sandwich.'

Claire hadn't seen many huge white limos since she gave up her job at Brockbourne Hall; and she certainly didn't expect her mother to step out of one on to the front at Weston-super-Mare.

'Mum!' She was so startled she dropped half a brick on her foot and hopped around the front garden like a one-legged cricket.

'Wee—' Veronica corrected herself just in time. 'Claire, darling!' They embraced. She patted a coiffure of positively Nordic curls. 'How do you like my new look?'

Claire struggled to find the right words. 'It's very . . . er . . . blonde.'

'Just like yours, eh?' Veronica held out her arms. 'And Pete's here too! How are you, sweetheart?'

Pete put down his crowbar and submitted good-naturedly to a hug. 'Hello Mum, what are you doing here?'

'Oh, I just thought I'd pop over and see this old house of Aunt Mary's.' She looked it up and down. 'Well well, what a lovely surprise for you both.'

Claire felt a twinge of irrational guilt. As far as she could see, they'd come out of this with two houses and a building business, and Veronica with nothing. 'I wonder why she didn't leave it to you, Mum.'

Veronica smiled. 'Oh, I expect she had her reasons. Besides, what ever would I do with a house? I'm never in one place long enough to enjoy it.' Her cheeks dimpled. 'Actually, while I'm here, I wanted to introduce you to somebody.'

'Oh?' Pete raised an eyebrow. 'Who?'

'A new friend. Coo-ee, Phil darling.' Veronica waved to the limo and a tinted window rolled down. 'Come and say hello.'

To say that you could have knocked Claire down with a Dulux colour-card was an understatement. Her jaw hit the deck, bounced back up again and almost knocked her teeth out. 'Phil? Phil *Flowers*?'

'Claire, doll, how ya doin'?' His thirty-thousand-pound teeth dazzled in the summer sunshine. 'Why didn't you tell me you had such a gorgeous mother?' He gave Veronica's bottom a generous goose, sending her into paroxysms of girlish giggling.

'Not here Pooky, you naughty boy,' she scolded him, tugging down her tight white skirt.

Pete gawped. Claire blinked. 'Er, how's Trixie?' she ventured, more out of curiosity than spite.

'Trixie?' Phil scratched his streaked blond mane. 'Oh, you mean *Trixie*. Bit on the immature side, you get my meaning. Now Veronica here, she's a *real* woman, ain't you doll? Soon as I set eyes on her in the Spanky-Panky I said to myself, that doll's up for anything.'

'The Spanky-Panky!'

Veronica winked. 'You know me, sweetheart, I like to keep up with all the latest trends.'

'Mr Flowers owns a lot of nightclubs,' Claire explained to the shellshocked Pete, who looked like a man weighing up the frightening possibility of gaining Phil Flowers as a stepfather. 'He offered me a job once. In Stockton-on-Tees.'

'Did he, darling?' Veronica looked at Phil. 'That wasn't very nice.'

Phil laughed it off. 'Anybody can run a club in Rio, doll. It takes class to do it in Stockton-on-Tees.'

'Now you *will* look after yourselves, won't you?' urged Veronica, hooking herself on to Phil's arm. 'Till I get back.'

'Back from where?' asked Pete.

'Acapulco, didn't I tell you? Pooky's got a lovely new club there and he wants me to host the grand opening. I expect we'll stay on for a month or two, but we should be back by Christmas.'

'Christmas!'

Veronica put her arms round Claire and gave her a hug. For the first time, it really did feel like being hugged by a proper mother, not some stranger who was playing the part from a badly-written script. It felt like she really meant it.

'Mum . . . be careful,' Claire blurted out.

'Don't worry,' whispered Veronica. 'It's just a bit of fun. I'll be back soon – and that's a promise.'

ONE YEAR LATER

Paradise Cottage

Crisp winter sunlight had turned the hills around Lilcombe Magna into a chiaroscuro of dark dips and snow-dusted hummocks. Claire sat up in bed with a cup of tea and a pile of invoices, watching birds flutter past the window and listening to Ted and Brucie snoring in harmony through the bedroom wall. It was a perfect Sunday morning.

'That pig's got indigestion again,' remarked Aidan, cocking an ear as he leafed through the business papers he had spread out on the duvet.

'Well, if you will feed him Black Forest gâteau.'

'He likes it.' Aidan's foot sneaked over to her side of the bed and tickled her leg affectionately. 'And I bet I know what you like . . .'

'Aidan!' she giggled, swatting him with an invoice. 'Not now, I've still got these accounts to do.'

He nibbled her earlobe. 'Have you and Pete finished that job over Winchcombe way?'

'Almost. How about you?'

'Oh, we're just about to start on that barn conversion.' He chuckled as he picked up the *Lilcombe Argus*. 'Snatched that one from under your nose, didn't I?'

'Only because you found out what my quote was and under-cut it!'

'Ah well, you know what they say. All's fair in love and the building trade. Oh look.'

She leaned her head on his shoulder. 'What at?'

He jabbed his finger at a couple of column inches on page three. 'Looks like the vicar's got a grant to restore that ornamental ironwork.'

'Really? Hmm, could be quite lucrative.'

A slow smile spread across Aidan's face. 'Fancy a little bet?'

'What kind of bet?'

'Fifty quid says I land the contract.'

Claire put out her tongue and licked the end of his nose. 'Make it a hundred, darling, and you're on.'